SHADOWBORNE

Book One

MATTHEW CALLAHAN

Roguish Creations

First edition

ISBN: 978-1-7329222-0-4

Cover art by Patrick Knowles

Editing by Meredith Tennant

❀ Created with Vellum

CONTENTS

GET A FREE COPY OF VALMONT'S DESCENT

Get a FREE copy of Valmont's Descent: A Tale of the Relics of Antiquity.

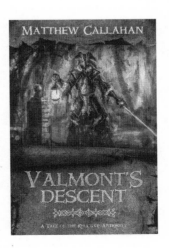

Pre-dating the events of Shadowborne by over five-hundred years, this tale is a look at Dorian Valmont through the eyes of Fen Kuang, a warlord from beyond the Daurhi Wastes. Filled with magic, suspense, and history, follow this powerful pair as they enter a realm of death and decay in search of an artifact that can turn the tide in Valmont's battle against the Hesperawn - the Codex of Ahn'Quor.

Claim your FREE book now!

❦ I ❧

SHADOWS GATHER

William Davis was four years old when the shadows first embraced him.

On a crisp Halloween night his family was walking through Old Town, en route to meet his grandfather for the first time. Will, laughing delightedly as his brother raced to the street corner and back, latched on to his mother with one hand while the other firmly gripped the wooden sword she had helped him make. He was dressed as a pirate, a dashing rogue with both a mustache and eyepatch drawn on with his mother's eyeliner. His older brother, Madigan, had chosen to go as Babe Ruth, a Louisville Slugger clutched in his hands and an old Yankees cap atop his head. Halloween was magical, and this one promised the most excitement yet.

Will jumped and pulled on his mom in delight as he imagined meeting his grandfather, finally. Excited by both the promise of candy and the meeting, the trio had set out trick-or-treating while the evening was still new. But by the time they had each filled their small baskets and boarded the train that would take them downtown, night had fallen. When they got off the train, Will knew it was almost past his bedtime, but Mom was letting him stay up extra late. He was big, now, and tonight was special.

Both Will's and his mom's eyes were fixed on Madigan as the boy whooped and hollered, waving his cap and baseball bat in the air. He was running at full tilt, hollering "Bambino!" and had just reached the corner when their mom suddenly staggered. Will screamed when he saw the tall man in the big coat hit her again, knocking her head against a brick wall. She slumped to the ground before stumbling to her knees. The tall man snatched at her purse, which she limply offered. Will saw a flash of metal glisten in the streetlights, clutched in the man's other hand. Will's mom froze.

Will stabbed the man in the leg with his sword. It didn't stop him. He stabbed again and kicked the leg as hard as he could. The man spun and backhanded the boy across the face with his mom's purse, sending him to the ground. Will saw his mom lunge toward him, crying out, and the man thrust his blade into her chest to the hilt. Will watched as she gasped and fell back against the wall, the knife jutting from her body.

Her attacker, momentarily stunned by the sudden change in the situation, did not see the return of the bat-wielding Madigan. Sprinting, roaring, the large boy struck the man below the ear with the Slugger. The man crumpled to the ground, his eyes wide, torn jaw no longer where it should be. Will watched, horrified, as his raging brother smashed the bat onto the man's skull again and again.

Will, crying and determined, grabbed for his mom. He began prying at the knife protruding from her chest, his small hands unable to grip the slick handle. She grimaced and turned her eyes from Madigan to Will. Through his tears, Will saw that the night was getting darker, that even the streetlights seemed to be going out.

Madigan was still roaring; the sounds of the bat splintering as it came crashing down seemed distant and muted. Will sobbed and the darkness grew. He felt a sudden surge of strength as he worked and worried at the blade in his mom's chest. She no longer grimaced. She kept blinking and trying to swallow something over and over. She never stopped looking at Will.

The knife came free, loosed by Will's small hands. The dark shadows converged upon him, twisting and wrapping him while warm blood pooled about him.

And there, wrapped in swirling darkness on a cold Halloween night in Old Town, Will watched his mother die.

THE BOYS' GRANDFATHER, JERVIN DAVIS, TOOK THEM IN. Although far removed from the years when he had raised his own child, Jervin proved to be everything the boys could have wished for in a surrogate parent. His patience with the two knew no bounds. He had once been a teacher, he told them, and his pension from those years provided for a comfortable, if humble, life. While the relationship between the three of them may have started under awful circumstances, the Davis brothers discovered their grandfather to be a loving, creative man. Together, the three found the means to overcome their grief and loss. Eventually, their home was filled with imagined adventures and laughter each day.

Still, the boys knew enough to realize that their lives were different from the other kids in their new neighborhood. Jervin schooled them at home, a rigorous education of science and history and physical prowess. He explained that he was modeling them after the Ancient Greeks, who strived for balance between mind and body. Jervin didn't want them to fall prey to other people's whims and desires; he wanted to ensure that their minds would be their own. The family explored both Eastern and Western myths, reading everything they could in every language they were able. They passed their youth a world apart from the modern age.

In addition to all the stories of the ancient world, Jervin told his own to entertain the boys. He created fantastical tales, tales of magic and impossibility—yet when set against the scope of existing myth, "Are they really so impossible?" he would ask the young minds. Olympus, Heaven, Asgaard, nearly every faith had their kingdom, their mythical dominion of the gods that seemed to be fantasy. But as they traced back the threads of mankind's history, the lines between myth and reality blurred in every culture.

Jervin spun a continuous story, set in a world he called Aeril. From his imagination he designed a forgotten realm of immortality and adventure, connected to their own world by the mysterious Ways. The Ways, he said, served as a passage between worlds that transcended the scope of human thought. If reality was like a human body, he said, and the known worlds were the organs, the Ways were the blood vessels, connecting and fueling all worlds. Jervin spoke of them as the gateways to endless eternities, conduits that fueled energy into the worlds and the paths through which they were accessed.

With a smile on his face, he crafted tales of Aeril for the wide-eyed youngsters. He told them of the heroes from *The Veleriat*, an epic clash of good and evil that spanned the first world and shattered it into many. The titular Velier became for them what Achilles had been for the Greeks and Aeneas had been for the Romans: a model of excellence and human ingenuity.

To the boys' delight, over time Jervin developed darker stories. Stories of the Theros, the cruel afterlife where those damned by the Hesperawn—the Aerillian gods—were cast in disgrace. Seeing the look of thrilled fear on their faces, he created its sister realm, the Nether. Within the Nether, magic flowed pure and unadulterated, an Aerillian heaven. It was the heart of reality, the source of all magic that flowed through the Ways. Only the most devout, the most faithful met their glorious end within its gates. With shining eyes, the boys would laugh and cheer and beg for more.

Jervin obliged, and their new favorite stories became those of the Wars of Dawning. He wound a tale of the Aerillian forces of Shadow and Radiance tearing at the fabric of reality in their pursuits of power. Within those stories he created Dorian Valmont, the Bloodbane, a tragic sorcerer who led the Halls of Shadow into battle. To the brothers' thrilled horror, the magnificent man succumbed to his own anger and fell in battle against the Hesperawn. As seemingly both man and god in one, Valmont was simultaneously filled with rage and piety, and within each, wildly misdirected.

Combining their love of the tales from *The Veleriat* with the Wars of Dawning, the Davis brothers took over the fantasy as they grew, telling each other their own stories. Playing during the day, the children would imagine themselves within the Wars of Dawning and defeating the maddened legions of Radiance. Fashioning themselves as both Velier and Dorian Valmont, they would champion the Halls of Shadow to pursue their dreams of power and build their own legends.

Every evening before bed was a new adventure, a tale of deception or bravery. Mystical stories filled their head during the day and set the stage for their dreams at night. But throughout all, Jervin would remind them that every hero was flawed, and

5

that even one of their favorite heroes became the villain of his own story. "A measure in patience and humility," Jervin would say, raising his eyebrows in conspiratorial knowing. "Everyone is gifted, not only those who seek power."

And every night, when the boys were safely wrapped in their blankets and dreaming of worlds beyond their own, Jervin would return to the living room and light his pipe. Stoking the dying coals of the evening's fire, he would seek his own answers to the questions he asked the boys. *What is right? What is good? What is justice?* Questions that mankind had asked for thousands of years. Questions that he, himself, had asked for more years than his boys could ever imagine. But the question that had been in his mind every night since he brought the boys home was the one that haunted him always—*Am I doing the right thing?*

That was the dangerous question, the one he found himself most hesitant to turn his attention to. Often, he had thought he was doing the right thing. Often, he had been wrong. He thought he was doing the right thing by taking the boys in. He thought he was doing the right thing when, against his better judgment, he trained his first pupil. He thought he was doing right when he confronted his daughter, Diane, so many years ago before the boys' birth. He'd been wrong so many times; would this be any different?

His thoughts drifted back to Diane as he puffed at his pipe and watched the coals. He had not seen his daughter since they had had a disagreement when she first became pregnant. He said some harsh words, mainly directed toward the absentee father of the unborn child, and in the pride that only an educated twenty-something can fully understand, Diane cut off contact.

Jervin knew he had overstepped, even if he had been right about "the donor" as Diane later called the father of her children. The man disappeared when she told him she was pregnant. And when he returned one cold winter night nearly three years later, he stayed just long enough to put another baby in her womb. That was the last she ever saw of him, and to Jervin, that was just fine.

Following that initial fight, Jervin made regular attempts to reconnect with his daughter but always let her bear the ultimate decision. Every birthday and every major holiday he sent a card, always signed with his love and regards. He knew she threw the cards away, being too proud and too busy to pay any mind to anyone as old-fashioned as her father. But she was his daughter, with the same stubbornness but also the same dedication to her family. Eventually, she wrote him back. After a smattering of letters and a multitude of phone calls, the burned bridge had been rebuilt.

That was before. He never got to hold her again, to tell her all the things he hadn't known how to tell her in her youth. To explain. Instead he got a broken heart and two small boys to help put the pieces of it back together. He'd first met them on the night when the world swam with ghost stories and the promise of magic. As the ghosts of his past faded, the boys became his future—his own promise of magic.

Yes, he had often been wrong, but not this time. This time everything was right. The boys were special; he knew that and they knew that. But there was something more. He could see the potential in William, and though he had never seen it manifest, he knew that some things were only a matter of time. There was nothing wrong with his boys, though. They were everything that was good and right in his world and, if everything went according to plan, they would become the same to countless others.

THE SECOND TIME THE DARKNESS CAME TO WILLIAM DAVIS, HE was twelve. Despite the years of training and guidance Jervin had given the boys, there were still some things that he could not control, and the misplaced rage of preteen males was one of them.

Things had been difficult of late for the young boy, for that is what he certainly remained. While William remained but a youth, his brother had moved into manhood. That had not stalled his grandfather's training, nor had there been any reprieve for Will when he was paired against Mad, who now towered above his brother. Will's own movements had grown awkward and imbalanced as his feet grew faster than the rest of him, giving him a clownish gait when he walked and tripping him whenever he tried to do more than that. As such, the days had grown hard for Will.

In response, Will had taken to embracing the solitude of night. He had always been most comfortable in the darkness. It wasn't that he didn't love the feeling of the sun on his skin, but he found something refreshing about withdrawing from the brightened glare of the world and relaxing in the shade. He could remember times when, as a young child, in the evenings and even the middle of the night he would venture into the yard on his own to play. Eventually games in the yard extended to the nearby streets, where he avoided the streetlights and darted from one shadow to the next, always in search of whichever space happened to be the darkest. Something about the darkness was comforting, like the first rains of autumn after a summer drought.

While during the daytime Will begrudgingly trained with his brother and grandfather, during the night he was left to his own devices. When Madigan's growth spurt seemed at its peak, Will used the nights to sneak out and wander the city.

It was harmless at first. He spent his time chasing after cats and avoiding the headlights of passing cars. Eventually, however, he grew bored and progressed to less noble pursuits. He discovered the daring, perverse thrill of shadowing people without their knowledge. He began to test his limits by getting as close to them as he could while remaining out of sight, sometimes barely a breath away. A misstep or a scattered pebble might cause them to whip their head around, but Will found he could sink and fade into the shadows. Freezing, the followed would see nothing, just the shadows of the night playing tricks on their mind. Will felt at one with the darkness, a natural, that's how good he was—or so he thought.

At twelve, without truly meaning to, he flirted with adding pickpocketing to his skill set. Whether the decision stemmed from frustration or simply a natural progression from stalking, he justified it to himself as something potentially useful. He justified it by promising himself that whatever he might snatch, he would be certain to return. He justified it to himself for all the wrong reasons.

The day of the shadow's coming had been more rigorous than expected and Will was exhausted, both mentally and physically. For hours, Jervin had drilled him in combatives and Ancient Greek philosophy until Will was boiling with frustration, that anger of youth that has seemingly no cause and no outlet. He snuck out into the night and hit the streets for a distraction.

He wandered without purpose for a time, brow furrowed in frustration. It was late, nearing two in the morning, when he saw a well-dressed man walk out of a 7-Eleven. The man slid his wallet into his back pocket before opening a fresh pack of cigarettes. Will momentarily struggled with an internal ethical debate before hotheaded youth overtook reason. He moved toward the man.

After lighting his cigarette, Will's quarry began to jaywalk across the street. Will followed, silently closing the distance. As he neared, he prepared to make his move (though he was far from certain how to go about such things), but he wasn't being attentive to his surroundings. A tinny sound on the blacktop shattered the silence as his foot caught some bit of trash. Will flinched, only inches behind the man, as the metal clattered through the street. The adult whirled to stare at the boy. His brow furrowed and the corners of his mouth turned in a snarl.

Yet, as Will watched, the blood drained from the man's face. His jaw went slack and his eyes widened. Will stood in shock as the man's head darted from side to side searching for something. Staring in disbelief, Will realized it was him that the man's eyes couldn't locate. Will took a careful step back and looked around as shadows swept the area. Shadows in the night that moved and swirled. Shadows impossibly darkening the street lamps. Coiling and ghosting, tendrils of darkness danced across the blacktop and into the night sky.

What happened next was a perfect storm. As the man stood stupefied, his cigarette turning to ash in his hand, a flash of light split the darkness and Will heard a screech of tires, rousing him from his own shock. A truck, previously unnoticed, was barreling toward them. The wheels locked up as the driver slammed on the brakes. The man, mouth still agape, stood stock-still as his body became illuminated against the night by the headlights.

Adrenaline surged through Will. He lunged forward into the path of the truck, toward the frozen man, and yelled. To his amazement, the shadows moved with him, enveloping the man as Will dove to reach him. The truck was already upon them though. As Will latched on to the man's arm and pulled him away he felt the shocking tremor of an impact behind him. He heard the crunch of metal colliding.

Will turned around, steeling himself for the horrific vision he was sure to see. Yet he found the man on the ground alive, completely unscathed. The truck was stopped, the front quarter panel ruined by the force of impact. Will's mind raced. Impact upon what? He crept back toward the sidewalk as the man emerged from his shock, frantically looking around.

"Hey, buddy! Are you okay? You alive over there?" Shouting, the driver of the truck had emerged and was running toward them. "Sweet Jesus, buddy, please be alive!"

The driver reached the man as he was struggling to his feet, thumbing his broken cigarette and glancing about. "The kid, where is he? Where's the kid?"

The driver was staring in disbelief at the unharmed man. "There was a kid? Jesus, I never saw a kid, oh Jesus."

"He just vanished, right in front of me." The man was babbling now. "Where is the kid?"

"There was only you, man, only you and you flew!" The driver was shaking his head, still staring. "You flew and my truck stopped! I thought for sure I'd hit you and you'd be dead! How did you do that, man?"

But the man wasn't listening. He just shuffled a few steps and kept on looking around, more than once staring straight at Will. "The kid . . . where's the kid . . . he just disappeared . . . "

The darkness continued to envelop Will as he backed away step by step, abandoning the pair to the night. He was stricken, terrified. The swirling shadows were a twisting cloud. He felt faint and cold as the world spun around him. He stumbled aimlessly, one street at a time, until he suddenly realized that the darkness surrounding him had vanished. He spun, searching for any trace of whatever it had been, but it was gone.

Will trekked home in a daze. The crisp night sky was just starting to lighten as he arrived. The house was still dark, but he could see the flicker of firelight from the windows and smoke rising from the chimney. He made his way to his window but stopped before climbing through. His trembling hand rested on the windowsill. His knees bent and he dropped to the ground, shivering as he rested his head against the house. He stared at the ground. Something had happened, something he couldn't explain. Something terrifying and something shocking. Something he desperately needed to uncover the truth of.

His grandfather was awake already, the smoke told him that much. Grandda with his fantastical stories. Grandda with his exhausting lessons. Grandda with his ceaseless knowledge. Will glowered in the darkness. His grandfather knew something about this, he was sure of it. Steeling himself with the self-assured confidence that only a twelve-year-old can muster, William stood up and marched straight in the front door.

❧ 2 ❧

A WORLD REVEALED

Jervin sat in his chair in front of a small fire, reading. He was sore, the bruises on his arms from carrying too much wood visible beneath the tattered plaid shirt he wore. It was unbuttoned and against his chest were the small, corded keys he was never without. He ran a hand through his short grey hair as he sensed Will approaching. He checked the time and shook his head slightly, a tired smile tugging at his cheeks in sharp contrast against his strong jawline. He didn't look up as Will entered the house, only turned a page in his book.

"You've awakened earlier than I expected," he said.

He could feel cool anger bubbling within Will, that frustration and overconfidence. "I've been awake all night, actually," the boy said. "I never even went to sleep. I went out."

Jervin finally looked up from his book, face seemingly absent of emotion in the way parents always manage just before a lecture. "I know. You've been sneaking out for some time now,

Will. You're not as quiet as you think." He paused and smiled. "But that's not what I meant."

"Oh yeah?" Will said. "Well just what do you mean, Grandda? If you're so smart about me sneaking out, what else do you think you know about me?" As he spoke, he stormed over to Jervin and stood in front of his chair, the flames of the dying fire flickering with the movement.

Jervin closed the book and set it aside. He leaned forward in his chair and met Will's glare with a patient smile. "What should I know, Will? Why don't you tell me what you think I should know."

And then William did what any angry, confused, frustrated twelve-year-old would do: He burst into tears. He started screaming at Jervin. Through his shouts, Jervin learned everything about his night out, minus Will's natural embellishments. All the while, the child's voice was shaking and tears streamed down his face.

Jervin's heart ached for the boy. He could see he was absolutely terrified. Sitting patiently and listening, Jervin's gentle smile never wavered as William yelled. He didn't react to any of the harsh names Will called him, never interrupted him as he ran through the whole story. As it reached its end, the boy collapsed onto the fireplace ledge and began sobbing into his hands.

Jervin moved from the chair and sat next to Will, wrapping him in his arms and letting him cry. He whispered all the sentiments that parents do to calm their children down until Will's body was finally exhausted. Tears having run dry, he broke into small, scared quakes. Finally, even those subsided and the two of them sat together in silence for a time.

While the fire smoldered behind them, Will asked the question that was burning in his mind.

"What's wrong with me, Grandda?"

Jervin couldn't stop the sad, heartbroken breath that escaped his body. "Nothing, Will, nothing. You're as perfect as you've always been." He held the boy closer, his own eyes welling with tears. "This is my fault. I'm sorry."

"What's your fault?"

Will's head shot up from where it had been buried in his grandfather's chest and saw his brother leaning against the doorframe. Madigan's hair was tousled from blankets and his sharp eyes were still puffy from sleep. Will squirmed to get free of his grandfather and compose himself.

"Mad, come sit," Jervin said. "It's time the three of us had a long-overdue talk."

The morning sun was peering through the window and casting light beams on the wall. Madigan sighed and grabbed a blanket from the back of a chair and, wrapping it around himself, flopped onto the couch across from them. The two boys watched their grandfather, Will's wide eyes begging for an explanation and Mad's, drowsy with sleep, struggling to stay open.

Finally, Jervin spoke. "Where to begin? This is going to be difficult. I keep wondering if it would have been wiser to start this conversation years ago but . . . actually . . . William, what do you recall of Dorian Valmont?"

Caught off guard by the bizarre question, Will opened his mouth to speak but paused. He gave an uncertain glance at Madigan, but the older boy had only burrowed deeper into his blankets. He looked back at Jervin with a confused expectation as he struggled to answer.

"Just ghost stories, really," Will said. "Campfire games that Mad and I played. Battles between good and evil, dark magic and light magic, legendary wizards and dragons, that kind of stuff."

Jervin nodded. "That's good, Will, but what about the stories themselves? Do you remember them?"

"Well"—doubt clouded the boy's features—"Valmont was a sorcerer who went crazy and battled the Gods."

"Close enough," Jervin said as he chuckled under his breath. "Keep going."

"He was trained by a warrior, the greatest swordsman who ever lived," Will continued. His voice grew more confident as the memories began to return. "He studied Shadow magic in the Vale of Shadows. He challenged the Gods of his world but was defeated and then disappeared after killing those who judged him, never to be heard from again. Supposedly he haunts children's dreams and appears to—"

"That's fine, we don't need to go into the superstitions," Jervin interrupted, "and it was the Halls of Shadow, not the Vale. Madigan, anything to add?"

"He was a genius and then turned to evil." Madigan shrugged and burrowed deeper into his blanket. "He was always fun to play because he raised an army of followers and he could cheat death. That was his ultimate secret."

"Good," Jervin said with a sigh. "Good." His eyes hardened and his voice became serious. "Before getting too ahead of myself with what's going on with you, William, will you allow me to tell one of my stories?"

Will bit his lip, glanced at his brother, then nodded.

"Thank you," Jervin said. "I know you have a lot of questions but maybe this will help." He looked at each of the boys and smiled. "Very well," he said as he turned and began stoking the last dying embers of the fire. "Let's begin."

He reached for a small bundle of kindling and added more fuel to the few remaining coals. "Magic exists," he said simply. "It is not as prevalent in this world as it once was, nor as easily accessed as stories would have us believe, but in one form or another it exists."

He prodded the glowing coals as the kindling began to catch fire. "There is an energy that permeates all things in all worlds, an energy that weaves its way into everything and flows within it, timeless. Everyone senses its effects, though the majority of humanity is not even aware of what they're feeling. It is found in cold shivers on a cloudless summer's day, in a sense of dread in a darkened room, when you pass through a doorway and have no memory of why you did so, or when you catch something out of the corner of your eye, only to look and find nothing. All such things are signs that the magics of the universe are speaking to you. For some, it is possible to read these magical flows, to sense them always, and even to manipulate them for one's own use.

"Since time began, for ages beyond remembrance, there have been stories of other worlds and mystical, magical creatures. Countless beings have devoted their entire existence to studying the universe into which they were born in an effort to gain greater understanding of it. They explored their curiosity, their wonder, and along the way discovered the magics that make up reality.

"The magics, however, were not the illusionary parlor tricks of the modern age. They were forces of their own, primal and raw, and the manipulation of them did not stem from mastery but from symbiotic link. While the races of the universe found power and knowledge in the magics, it is unknown what the magics found in them. The mortal races linked with the forces, were carried by them—were Borne, as it came to be known.

"The Hesperawn sent down mighty Guardians to educate the mortals, to guide them and find harmony. Orders were adopted. Paths were forged. And, ultimately, wars were fought. On the prime of the mortal worlds, Aeril, great men such as Velier of the *Crimson Twilight* sought order amongst the chaos. Dorian Valmont, the Bloodbane, and Jero din'Dael of the Maddened

Flame undid millennia of that peace in a clash that resulted from the pursuit of their own ends. The golden age passed, and the Paths fell into decay.

"Of the primordial magics, only Shadow maintained its strength and found power in the new age. Valmont had won renown in the wars but it twisted his mind. He believed too much in his own power while doubting the might of the Hesperawn. He fought them and lost, and in losing, he destroyed countless lives and left Aeril broken.

"Valmont's lesson is a lesson in humility. All the knowledge and training in the world cannot prepare one for a taste of true power, no matter who you are. It is up to you to determine what kind of person each of you will be and how you will handle the power you will acquire. It is my hope and belief that each of you will grow into wonderful, just men."

Will, bristling with questions, shifted in his seat as his grandfather's story ended. The cresting morning sun began pouring in, illuminating the quiet room. The cadence of his grandfather's voice always created vivid imagery in Will's mind, the gaps filling in gradually from countless stories over the years.

"And here I thought we were going to hear something new." Madigan yawned extravagantly. "Don't get me wrong, Grandda, your stories are still fun but what, exactly, merited this retelling so early in the morning?"

Jervin gestured to Will. "Ask your brother."

"What?" Will said as Mad gave him an expectant look. His words jumbled together. "Um, what do you want me to say?" Jervin didn't offer any help and Madigan continued to stare at him, giving slow, measured blinks, his mouth twisted in a smirk. "Okay. Well, Mad," Will said, sitting up straight and giving his brother the most level, serious look possible. "I can become invisible."

Madigan's face broke and he burst out laughing. Will turned his eyes to the floor and huddled into himself.

"Enough, Mad," Jervin said. "And Will, that's not exactly it."

Mad's brow furrowed. "Wait, what?"

"You don't become invisible, William. More that the dark energy just allows the eye to move past you."

"Hang on a second, what?" Madigan sat up from the couch, suddenly more attentive. "What are you talking about?"

"And, truth be told, that is only scratching the surface of possibility."

"Grandda! What is going on?" Mad was leaning forward and staring at Will with the look of a five-year-old who just found a squished slug on the sidewalk.

"Humor me for a moment, Madigan," Jervin said, his hand held up for a pause. "Just for a moment, imagine that everything I told you was true. Imagine that you, me, and your brother were all a part of that story."

Mad's eyes darted between his grandfather and his brother before he shrugged and muttered, "Fine, whatever."

"In that story, Mad, in our story, William can do fantastical things."

Mad slumped back into the couch and rolled his eyes. "Fantastically annoying, maybe."

Jervin gestured toward Will and gave an expectant look. "Show him, Will."

Will bit his lip and looked at his grandfather. Jervin always excelled at pushing his limits, but in this case he genuinely had no idea where to begin. He rose to his feet, grit his teeth, and clenched his fists. He tried his hardest to produce something but only succeeded in feeling exceedingly self-conscious. Jervin, seeing his frustration, stood and moved behind him, placing one hand at the base of the boy's skull and the other between his shoulder blades.

"Now, just breathe."

And, just like that, the sun pouring into the room faded away and darkness flooded through. For a moment, black tendrils coiled at Will's feet like snakes ready to strike. The darkened cords surrounded his clenched fists and ran up his arms. They were the most terrible and beautiful things he had ever seen.

Madigan flew to his feet, cursing, and scrambled backward on the couch before tumbling over the back of it. When Jervin released his hands and stepped away from Will, the darkness remained. And yet, it wasn't truly darkness. The sensation was cool yet temperate, a breeze passing through shade on a hot summer's day. While Madigan was cowering in fear, Will's own senses were relieved and alive and exhilarated all at once.

"Shade, Will," Jervin said. "It's commonly referred to as a Shade. Or, more appropriately, your Shade."

"What the hell is going on?" Madigan called from behind the couch.

"Come on out," Jervin said gently. "Everything is fine."

"What the hell?" Mad repeated as his head popped up. "What the hell was that?"

"Like I said, Mad," Jervin said. "In that story, Will can do fantastical things."

Will's brother stood and stared at him while his own head was swimming at the rapid changes to his world. Easing himself to the floor, Will put his head between his knees and focused on breathing. He looked at the darkness of the Shade and reached out a trembling hand to touch it. A thin tendril wound its way around his finger on contact, somehow both solid and immaterial, pliable but sturdy.

"Grandda, are you saying that the stories are true?" Will asked.

Jervin smiled. "I am."

Will pushed at the Shade with his mind, trying to imagine it into some sense of logical density. To his surprise, the more he focused, the more stable his control seemed. The changes were subtle changes, yes, but changes nonetheless. He couldn't see where it attached to him, not like a normal shadow that has a clear line of sight. Instead, any connection seemed to disappear just before he looked at it.

"All these years, all these lessons in swordplay and fighting and"—Madigan's voice was shaky—"it was because it's real? It's really real?"

Will raised his eyes. His grandfather nodded.

"And Will, he's one of those shadow people?" Mad's voice lost its tremor, becoming cool and considered once more.

"Your brother is Borne by Shadow, yes," Jervin said.

Will stared at the two of them and reached out with the Shade, his heart racing as he saw the coiled tendrils begin to slink across the floor. When he was ten, he had gotten stitches for the first time. As his Grandda skillfully sutured the wound, Will couldn't help but laugh at the sensation of the thread tickling him with each pull. Stretching the Shade outward, the sensation came again. Giggling, he focused harder and stretched it out nearly eight feet before that same light tug turned into a wretched ache, like he had been smacked hard between the legs. The Shade recoiled and vanished as Will doubled over, gasping.

"Careful, Will," Jervin said. "Don't overdo it."

Will had tears in his eyes. For a moment it felt as though his insides had been ripped apart from within, his body threatening to retch their shredded remains onto the floor.

Jervin walked over and rubbed the young boy's back. "I

should have warned you. I'm sorry. You're untrained and you don't know your limitations yet. Don't overextend."

Recovering, Will blinked back tears and nodded. Madigan was shaking his head, staring at their grandfather with his brow furrowed.

"How did you keep this from us? How do you know about this stuff?" His eyes narrowed. "You're from there, aren't you? Aeril?"

Jervin nodded slowly.

"It's real then? How did you get here? I mean, what did you even do when you first got here?"

"I learned how to fit in," Jervin responded, ignoring the first two questions. "There was a world to explore and ships in which to do it. I traveled for years before I met your grandmother and allowed myself an attempt at normal life." He gave a quick laugh and shook his head. "She always knew I was older, she just could never put an exact difference to it. After she died giving birth to your mother, I worked on learning to be a father. Considering my background, I'd say I did better with your mom than I expected."

"And Valmont, he was real?" Will asked. "Did you know him?"

"Unfortunately, I did," Jervin said. His eyes were downcast. "No one knew what he would become, how could we have? Still, I can't help but feel like I should have seen it coming earlier and found a way to stop him before it was too late."

"But he died, right?" Mad said. "I mean, he has to be dead by now."

Jervin shook his head. "Vengeance and madness consumed him in the end. Whether he managed to survive or not, no one really knows. Most of Aeril believed him dead by the time I left. There were still those who were hunting him, though."

Madigan sat back down on the couch and leaned forward. "So, what then?"

Will glanced at him. "What do you mean?"

Madigan gestured to Will as he addressed his grandfather. "I mean, don't get me wrong, Grandda, Will being some shadow dude is really cool and all, but what's the point?"

Will began to protest but Jervin raised a hand to quiet him. "It's a valid question, Will, it's okay." Jervin stood and moved his way to the fire and stoked the coals. "The point is that you both deserve the truth, simple as that."

Madigan rolled his eyes. "Things are never that simple with you, Grandda."

Jervin chuckled. "True, true," he said. "But now that you know the truth, perhaps we—"

"But what about Valmont?" Mad interrupted.

"And Aeril!" Will said, nearly overlapping his brother. "And more of the Shadowborne!"

"Boys, just give me a moment to—"

"It sounds fantastic," Mad said. "Like, it's actually fantastic. It doesn't sound real."

"But it really is, isn't it?" Will chimed in.

"Boys, calm down for one second," Jervin said, a small smile tugging at his cheek. After a moment, the brothers quieted, though they continued to fidget. "Allow me to ask one question: What would you think about going to Aeril?"

Will's face lit up. *Going to Aeril?* He glanced over at Madigan and saw his brother's eyes widen before he leaned back onto the couch. Except he wasn't relaxed, Will could tell. He could see the ready tension in Mad's neck, the way he sat with his legs under him, ready to spring. Madigan was nervous, despite his efforts to hide it. Why would Madigan be so nervous?

Because everything just changed.

It occurred to Will that he may be taking everything a little too well. Years of his overactive imagination encouraging him to believe in a world of the impossible made the impossible seem, well, possible. Magic was real, it was a part of him. It was like waking from a vivid dream and realizing that the best parts were all true. For his brother, though, it was just another day. It was supposed to be normal. *He's terrified,* Will realized.

"I think," Will said, his voice cautious, "I think we have a lot of questions."

"I would imagine so," Jervin said. "What would you—"

"When do we leave?" Madigan interrupted, catching both Will and Jervin off guard. Will stared at his brother, mouth agape.

"It would take some time," Jervin said. "Quite a bit, actually."

"But you've been planning for this, right?" Madigan said, leveling his gaze at Jervin. "That's why you homeschooled us, pushed us constantly." Madigan waved his hand, gesturing at the house. "That's why all of this has always felt so temporary."

The hint of a smile appeared at the corner of Jervin's mouth again. "Yes," he said finally, "although this is not exactly how I'd planned on broaching the subject."

"But why not tell us sooner?" Will burst out. "Why did you wait?"

Jervin's eyebrows narrowed. "Because I'm human. I've been uncertain if it really is for the best. The Aeril I left was suffering, it was in pain. I don't know what the situation there is anymore, but here at least, here I know.

"But the truth is, I think you two both belong in Aeril, Will's ability notwithstanding. This realm has changed more than I ever imagined it would. The magic that once thrived here, it's as if it has died, only hints of it remain. There's less in this world than there once was."

"How so?" Will asked, interrupting.

Jervin winked at the boy. "Traces linger. You yourself are rather subject to forgetfulness where doorways are concerned." He grinned as he saw Will's jaw drop. "Regardless, that's a story for another time. The truth is, I want you both to live a long, happy life in a place where you can do some good. And while I know you could both do amazing things here, I believe in my heart that you could do even more in Aeril."

Will and Madigan were both quiet. Their grandfather turned his head to the brightening sky and sighed. "I think," he finally said, "that I'll go put the kettle on. We've got a lot of work to do."

❧ 3 ❧

THE ADVENTURE BEGINS

F rom that day onward, the games of their childhood became a regimen in reality for Will and Madigan. For seven years, the family prepared. Seven years of rigorous training and the basics of Aerillian history. Seven years of pushing themselves to learn faster, train harder, respond quicker. Jervin continued his teaching of combat and strategy, logic and philosophy, rhetoric and anthropology—yet everything became a fantastical case study into the imaginative.

For Will, his newfound ability filled him with excitement and disbelief and fear. He was too young to have any sense of control over it, only able to harness its power under the direct instruction of his grandfather, but the older man did what he could to guide him. As the years passed, Will never quite mastered the ability to draw on his power consciously, but he did learn how to keep it hidden under any circumstance. The physical and mental strain of it all stopped Will's nighttime adventures and instead replaced them with strange dreams.

They were dark and twisted and he would often wake up freezing, his body drenched in sweat and his mouth dried and cracked. Often, he would see the deaths of his family. Sometimes, he would lose control of his Shade, seeing it whip and surge and injure the people closest to him. Sometimes the Shade was gone, and he stood bound and helpless to save them as they died. In the end, though, the dreams always ended with his own death as flames consumed his body, every sensation more vivid than reality. Jervin would wake him from his screams, voice calm and strong, and remind the boy to breathe.

On the day the family's life changed forever, Jervin found Will in exactly that way.

***

"WILL," JERVIN SAID. HIS VOICE WAS STRONG AND SECURE AS HE placed a hand upon Will's shoulder to steady him. "Wake up and breathe, kiddo."

Will's eyes shot open. His breath came fast and heavy and he shied away from the morning sunlight that flooded the room. Jervin removed his hand while Will sat up and wiped the sleep from his eyes.

"Sorry, Grandda," the young man said, running a hand through his hair. "I'm okay."

His grandfather looked worn and tired but smiled at Will nonetheless. "Another dream?"

"Yeah, the same one as before." Will's parched throat made his voice crack as he spoke. His muscles were aching and his head was pounding. He rolled over and looked at the clock, seeing that it was barely past 6:00 a.m. Muttering, Will kicked his legs over the edge of the bed and again ran his hands through his eternally unkempt hair. Despite the early hour, he was awake and sleep would not return to him.

"Sorry to wake you, Grandda. I'm fine. Go ahead and go back to bed."

Jervin chuckled and shook his head. "Kid, I was up way before you started thrashing about."

"Yeah, I'd say it's your brother you should be more concerned with," came a cocky voice from the doorway. Will groaned and looked past Jervin to where his big brother stood.

For Madigan had indeed grown big, becoming a solid wall of muscle over the past few years. Strong and deceptively quick, all six-foot-three of him was fast and flexible as a cat. The years spent in books and libraries had crafted a clever, if impatient, mind to match.

And though the two boys were less than three years apart, where Madigan had grown muscular, Will had remained lean and wiry. It was good for moving silently, especially when he managed to control his Shade. But the majority of the time, he struggled to keep up with his brother's power. He had long since outgrown letting it get to him. Being quick was enough for him and he still knew how to give his brother a run for his money, Shade or no Shade.

Madigan was leaning against the doorframe, barefoot and dressed only in faded sweatpants that had once been black. Flipping the switch for the light, he walked casually into the room. After three strides he quickened his pace and leapt at Will.

Jervin stepped out of the way and, before Will could rise and defend himself, Madigan crashed into him. Falling backward onto the bed, the two boys grappled and struggled. Will, sensing a weakness in Madigan's defenses, rolled hard and threw himself at the bigger brother. It was only after he had committed that he realized it had been a feint. Instead of overpowering his brother, the younger man crashed onto the floorboards. Leaping from the bed, Madigan was on top of him, pinning him to the ground.

"Someone's a bit slow this morning," Madigan said as he pushed himself to his feet. "Did you sneak out for nips of Grandda's cooking sherry again, Will?"

Will pushed himself to his knees, head throbbing substantially more than it had been moments before. Sighing, he reached for a nearby t-shirt while trying to come up with a witty comeback for his brother.

"Downstairs," Jervin said. "Breakfast should be finished in about fifteen minutes."

Will glanced up. "Breakfast this early?"

Jervin smiled and nodded. "Trust me, you two will be needing it today." Turning, he disappeared from sight down to the lower level of the house.

"Fifteen minutes?" Madigan said. "Plenty of time for you to come up with something clever." Madigan grinned and tossed a pillow at his brother's head, then made to follow their grandfather out the door. "Come on, Will, you're even slower than usual this morning."

As Madigan walked away, Will pivoted and, bracing himself on an arm, kicked out. He caught his brother's trailing leg, snapping it out from under him mid-stride. Eyes widening, Madigan let out a quick "Oh!" before stumbling toward the stairs. Will leapt to his feet and darted forward, grabbing hold of the doorframe and catching his brother with his free hand as Mad flailed, nearly tumbling down the stairs.

"I'm sorry," Will said. "You were saying something about being slow?"

Mad grinned and gave Will a playful punch in the arm. "I just enjoy keeping you off balance."

Breakfast was a hearty scramble of vegetables and spiced

sausage tossed with fresh herbs and bacon on the side. Will hadn't even finished his first serving by the time Madigan was already helping himself to a third. Will knew that if he didn't finish it quickly then his brother would swoop in and do it for him, so he wolfed down the last few bites of veggies and grabbed the last three strips of bacon. Madigan pretended to pout then gave a quick grin and took one of the pieces of bacon from Will's plate. Will didn't protest. Madigan's appetite was a force to be reckoned with and it was never good to stand in its way.

Will stood and cleared the table of the plates while Madigan went and refilled the water before moving it to the fridge. He opened the door and scoffed before giving Will a puzzled look. "So, either I raided the kitchen in my sleep or we desperately need to go grocery shopping."

Will raised his eyes from where he had begun rinsing the dishes and glanced inside the fridge. Where usually it was filled to bursting with meats and vegetables and an assortment of quick snacks that would easily maintain two active young men and their grandfather, today it stood empty.

"Maybe this is one of Grandda's tasks for the day," Will said. "A remarkably lame scavenger hunt to find lunch."

Madigan laughed and closed the fridge. "Well, he did say to eat up but somehow I doubt that's it. I'm sure we'll just end up hitting the store after training. He probably wants to exhaust us and then make us carry groceries just for the hell of it."

Will grinned and the two of them made their way outside to the yard. The sun was shining, somehow breaking through the usual morning cloud cover, but there was a chill in the air. Summer had finally come to a close and the first days of autumn were upon them. Will always felt like the changing of seasons in Oregon was something Mother Nature took very seriously; he could taste the change in the air almost immediately.

The morning was peaceful and pristine with a light dew on the grass. A soft breeze rustled through leaves that were beginning to dry and crackle. The air tasted clear and fresh, like newly fallen rain. Though they were not far from the city and freeways, the sounds of them were nearly inaudible, drowned out by the croak of frogs from the nearby stream and the wind in the air. Despite his headache, Will smiled at the beauty of the morning.

The boys crossed the lawn and joined Jervin who was stretching on the dry, compacted ground beneath their large cedar tree. Wordlessly, they began to stretch as well, gradually easing out the kinks of sleep and warming up their muscles. Will's breathing slowed and matched the rhythm of his grandfather's. With eyes closed, the three of them remained silent, calming their minds and letting their awareness of the surrounding world grow.

Fifteen minutes passed before Will detected the change in his grandfather's breathing. He opened his eyes as Jervin slowly rose and exhaled deeply. Will glanced over at Madigan, still in deep meditation to his left. He rose, then crouched and rubbed his knees to get the feeling back into them before stretching his right leg back into a deep lunge.

Madigan stirred and opened his eyes, pausing a moment before rising. Grinning, he shifted forward onto his left foot and pivoted hard, spinning and kicking out his foot to sweep Will's legs out from under him. At the last second, Will pushed into the air and leapt away from him, landing in a roll and rising to his feet with a smile.

"A bit lighter on your feet now you've had some breakfast, eh?" Mad said. Will laughed and walked over to help him to his feet. The two looked over at Jervin who was smiling and watching them. He straightened and walked over, placing a hand on each of their shoulders and drawing them in.

31

"It's nice to see you both in good spirits. Hopefully, I'll not have broken them too badly by the end of the day."

"Oh yeah?" Madigan said. "Have something special in mind?"

Jervin smiled as he winked. "You could say that."

⚜ 4 ⚜

TRAINING'S END

Without warning, Jervin suddenly took off at a full sprint. Their property was situated well away from the road amongst many trees. It bordered a nearby grass-covered levee, one which their grandfather often used in their runs, and Jervin headed in that direction. Madigan and Will followed, breathing rhythmically and keeping stride with their grandfather. Yet instead of stopping when he arrived at the grass, Jervin surged onward and upward with a speed they had not seen him exhibit before.

Without hesitation, Mad raced after him, his surprise at the older man's speed lending him the determination to match it. He lost speed though as he split his concentration, focusing on safely navigating the waist-high grass. Will moved ahead of him, maintaining his speed, seemingly fearless of ankle-turning rocks or the uneven ground. Mad began to fall behind.

He tried to clear his mind and let his feet fly over the ground, his eyes watching Jervin disappear from sight as he crested the hill.

"Come on!" Will shouted from ahead and Mad's adrenaline kicked in. Seconds later he reached the crest of the hill and scanned the levee for his grandfather. He was down near the stream, running smoothly as if the marshy ground near the bank gave him no pause. Mad stared, unable to believe how much ground the man was covering without breaking pace.

Will, too, had paused to watch their grandfather. Madigan grinned and shot past him and half running, half sliding, proceeded down the slope to reach the water's bank. Will didn't follow. Madigan heard him whipping past tree branches atop the ridge, angling himself as he watched their grandfather's path. He cursed as he realized that Will had had the right idea. Crashing through the reeds, he threw caution to the wind in an effort to regain lost time.

Jervin reached a turn in the stream and Madigan picked up speed, making sure to keep his grandfather in his field of vision. Will was racing through the trees above but fell behind, having lost his own line of sight and needing to use Mad as a guide. They rounded the bend and Mad cursed again, seeing Jervin sprint up the hillside right into Will's path. Mad ran up the slope at an angle while Will again picked up speed as Jervin passed from Mad's view back into Will's.

Will's lead was brief, however. He turned and raised a quick, mocking thumbs up to his brother. In doing so, he managed to throw himself off balance and suddenly stumbled before crashing to the ground. While he scrambled to his feet, Madigan, lungs burning, closed the gap and darted past him.

"On your left," he said without breaking stride.

Mad reached the path along the hillside where it curved into the clearing the family used for combat training. He was hoping for a quick respite but realized immediately that the hope was in vain. Jervin set upon him as soon as he rounded the bend and drove him back, away from the path. As the two figures locked in a dance of martial combat, Will rounded the corner, gasping for air. Mad ducked and tumbled, bewildered when he saw that, while he and his brother were both struggling for breath, somehow Jervin barely even had any color to his cheeks.

He didn't let himself become distracted. Each of the older man's steps was sure and controlled, every blow calculated and powerful. Mad countered each successfully but was gradually losing ground against him, unable to strike out with any offense of his own. The hairs on the back of his neck rose and a wave of excitement swept over him as he heard Will's racing footfalls. Shade or no, anytime the two of them went toe-to-toe with Jervin, Will always had a few tricks up his sleeve. The tables were about to turn on their grandfather.

Will closed the distance in a manner of seconds and rushed to his brother's aid. Madigan, gaining a brief respite from Jervin's focus, rolled backward to catch his breath. Will darted in and out, up and down, strikes less powerful than Mad's but coming in such a flurry that Jervin was momentarily driven back, a small smile of satisfaction upon his face.

Recovered, Madigan kicked forward to sweep Jervin's legs out from under him. He was narrowly dodged and came down into a hard lunge as Will briefly withdrew. Mad pushed forward and swung his back leg around, unsuccessfully attempting to catch Jervin off balance. He grit his teeth in frustration, planting his outstretched leg on the ground and lunging forward with an uppercut from his right elbow. Again, Jervin avoided it and Madigan realized he had just lost his advantage and his back was now exposed. Jervin planted a leg behind Mad's and grabbed his extended elbow. Before Mad could recover, Jervin twisted and pulled, sending Madigan crashing onto his back. Jervin dropped to a knee and prepared to deliver a victorious strike.

At that moment, Will rejoined the fray. Jervin, normally so aware of his surroundings, had somehow missed that Will had slipped behind him while he was engaged with Madigan. When his brother was thrown down, Will lunged forward, wrapping one arm around his grandfather's neck. He held two fingers from his left hand to Jervin's throat while the thumb on his right pointed inward toward his grandfather's chest.

"Dead," Will said in a voice barely above a whisper.

Madigan rolled out from his grandfather's control and pushed himself to his feet. Jervin chuckled as Will let his hands fall away.

"Good," Jervin said with a smile. "Very well fought. The first point of the day goes to Will."

Struggling to catch their breath, the boys' eyes grew wide as they looked first to their grandfather and then to each other.

"First?" Madigan said.

"The day is won by the first person to reach seven," Jervin said. "There will be no breaks until a victor is declared." And with that, he took off running back in the direction they had come. Madigan groaned and doggedly picked up his feet, beginning the pursuit. Reluctantly, Will followed.

THE REST OF THE MORNING PASSED IN THE SAME MANNER. AFTER the initial round, the resulting challenge had been a three-man free-for-all with Madigan gaining the point after he used Will to distract Jervin and overpowered him.

Without pausing, Jervin took off running once more.

Next, weapons were incorporated, each combative interlude introducing the various styles they had learned over the years. Long swords, short weapons, dual wielding, staves, Jervin mixed it up by throwing each style in at different times. Whatever he set, Madigan or Will always found themselves at a disadvantage in reach or pairing. He pitted them against each other, with Jervin himself lending aid to whoever held the situational advantage instead of the one who was struggling. Each time a victor was declared and a point made, he set off running again. By the time they had reached the thirteenth circuit, both boys were shaking and exhausted, but the score was tied.

On the final circuit, they ran to the combat circle only to find Jervin had continued past it, making his way to the nearby rock face at the edge of the clearing. He grabbed hold of a rope on the right side of the cliff and kicked his feet against the rock, scaling it with ease. Once at the top, he pulled the rope up after him, leaving the boys to their own devices. Panting heavily, Will put his head between his knees. Madigan looked at him, trying to hide his own exhaustion, and flashed an unreciprocated smile as he clapped his brother on the back.

"Come on Will," he said, jogging toward the rocks, "let's finish strong."

Madigan's smile faded as they closed the distance. Jervin was taking exceptional liberties with the day's training, if you could even call it that. For reasons unknown, he seemed to be taking every bit of knowledge and skill garnered over the years and throwing it back at them all at once. Normally Jervin would set a focus for the day, be it speed, endurance, or knowledge, and that was all. Sometimes, if he really wanted to push them, he would give them an 'exam' of sorts, but in the past there had always been notice given. He wanted them mentally prepared, sharp and aware so no accidents would occur. For whatever reason, today Jervin had thrown all caution and moderation to the wind.

Madigan surveyed the rock face before them and groaned. It was not the first time they had scaled it. In fact, they had climbed it so many times that each knew a path up the rocky slope that was most suited to their own particular strengths. Under ordinary circumstances, it would be an easily overcome obstacle. Unfortunately, the day was proving to be something quite outside of the usual.

"Definitely not ordinary," Mad muttered as he studied the changes Jervin had made since their last climb. The long-established trails of handholds up the wall were gone, the rock patched and smoothed. The wall was foreign, all familiarity erased by their grandfather's hands. New chisel marks and holds were visible, but how and when Jervin had managed such a feat was beyond him.

He scanned the cliffside as Will removed his dirty, sweat-drenched shirt and reached down for a rock. Draping the shirt over one of the low boulders, Will scored two lines across the cloth and then tossed the rock aside. Gripping it tightly, he tore at it, shredding the t-shirt into three long pieces.

"It was relatively ruined anyway," he said when Madigan raised an eyebrow. "Hell, it had enough rips in it that I probably could have done without the rock." Will began wrapping his hands in the cloth and bracing his wrists, tying the third around his forehead as a makeshift sweatband. "Gods know I could use the extra wrist support right now."

Madigan nodded. He considered doing the same to his own shirt, which was in just as bad shape after the morning's activities, but he wasn't about to give his little brother the satisfaction of copying him. Instead, Mad looked for the nearest handhold and began to climb. Pushing himself to his feet, Will gripped the nearest crevice and followed suit.

Mad grit his teeth against the trembling in his limbs. His muscles, long since exhausted, struggled through each movement. He tried to control his breathing, tried to stay focused on the task at hand, but fear was starting to set in.

At just past halfway up the climb, he heard a cry from his brother. He glanced over quickly and saw that Will's grip had failed on one of the handholds and he was hanging on by his left hand only. As he fell back against the cliff, the resulting impact twisted his left shoulder. Madigan winced as his brother grimaced, his eyes watering. Mad paused, battling the urge to rush to his brother's aid, and was relieved to see Will rotate himself back to face the wall, finding a foothold to support him. After a moment, his fingers found security and he clung to the wall.

Will's face grew briefly calm before contorting in rage. A thin darkness swept over the cliffside, encompassing both of them. The surrounding air grew cool and Mad's skin began to prickle from the chill. Will suddenly began climbing again, every motion smooth and precise. The climb became steady, his hands finding their placements with ease, each previously daunting leg extension now gracefully balanced. He flew past Madigan.

Madigan, too, felt strangely renewed. His motions were nowhere near as graceful as his brother's, but his climb became more assured all the same. When the summit came, he saw Will slide himself over without hesitation. Madigan pulled hard at the top, kicking his legs over the edge and rolling away from it before coming to rest in a crouch.

Will was kneeling not far off, breathing steadily, face calm once more. The trailing darkness that had moved with him dissipated as Mad watched. When it faded, Mad saw their grandfather stirring a pot over a fire near a small wooden footlocker some twenty yards away. Jervin stood and approached, gazing at the pair of boys exhausted on the ground before him.

"Point, William," he said. "With an impressive display at the end of the thirteenth round. Well done, you two. Will, the day is yours."

5

GIFTS OF DARKNESS

Jervin helped the boys to their feet and they walked to the simmering pot of food. To Will, it smelled better than anything he had ever eaten, but somehow he didn't feel hungry. To his surprise, he found that the various scrapes and scratches along his torso seemed less prevalent as well. In fact, he didn't even feel tired or fatigued anymore. He felt renewed.

"Grandda," he said as Jervin passed him a bowl of steaming stew. "The Shade, it was different this time."

Jervin raised an eyebrow. "Oh? Different how?"

Will shook his head. "I can't explain it, but I feel fine. Better, even, than earlier today."

"Me too," Mad said as he took a bowl from Jervin. "When the cliffside went dark I felt cold, but, I know it sounds odd, but I felt restored. That's never happened before."

Jervin pursed his lips. "Interesting," he said. He was quiet for a moment and stirred their lunch before looking at Will. "Was anything else different this time?"

Will shook his head and took a bite of stew. Jervin raised an eyebrow at Madigan who also shook his head.

"Very interesting," Jervin said. "I'll have to think on that."

The three of them ate in silence for a time. Will ate two helpings, despite not feeling tired or hungry. His mind was hazy, akin to a brain fog from not eating for too long, but food didn't seem to help. Madigan finished and began to stretch the fatigue from his muscles while Jervin gathered up the food supplies and set them aside. After a short time, however, Will's patience deserted him.

"Grandda, I've gotta know," he said. "What was this today?"

Jervin looked at Will and raised his eyebrows. "This was lunch."

Madigan snorted and Will twisted his lips. "I mean the training," he said. "Why was it so different today?"

"Well, the training wasn't really that different, Will," Madigan said. "There was just more of it. Lots more."

Jervin laughed and Will rolled his eyes. He started to respond but Jervin held up a hand to quiet him.

"Today was different," Jervin said, "because I wanted to know if you were ready for more."

Madigan cracked his neck and rolled his shoulders. "We're always up for another round, Grandda. Let's go."

Jervin smiled and shook his head. "That's not quite what I meant. Years ago, you asked me to teach you what it would take to venture to Aeril."

A chill went down Will's spine. *This is it,* he thought.

"And, for better or worse, I have done what I can to prepare you," Jervin said. "So, it is time."

"We're finally going after Valmont?" Madigan said, nearly shouting.

Jervin's eyes narrowed as he studied the boys. Will felt

exposed under the intensity of the gaze. His grandfather seemed to have disappeared and in his place was the cold, ancient warrior from the stories. As quickly as the transformation occurred, however, it was gone and Jervin was smiling and shaking his head.

"No, my boy," Jervin said, "but you two are ready for the next step. You're ready to venture to Aeril and truly begin your training."

Will and Madigan exchanged excited grins.

"Not that I don't have a few tricks up my sleeve still," Jervin said with a smile. He gestured to the box at his side. "You have both excelled over the years. It is time you were outfitted accordingly."

Will looked down at the footlocker while Jervin began removing its contents. He watched his grandfather lift a bundle of leather from within and trace its lacing with his finger. Setting it atop the box, he began to unwrap it.

Within were four small objects along with an ancient, weathered note. The first was a simple black ring, adorned with foreign symbols along the band. The second appeared to be the tattered remnants of a leather glove. It was missing each of the fingers and had a strand of looped leather where the middle finger should have been.

The remaining items were a pair of strange knives with worn, dark brown leather wrapped around the hilt. Within the pommel of each was a dark red stone riddled with black imperfections. The blades were nearly identical, the only difference being that one was slightly longer than the other. Each lay atop a sheath of the same leather, simple and unadorned. The blade of each knife was slightly curved along the underside and was a darkened, matte grey. Despite their simplicity, Will was fascinated, knowing that each of the four objects was from Aeril.

"The weapons of a Blade of Shadow," Jervin said, "ancient and beautiful. These are the remnants of an old life. Remnants I now pass on to each of you."

He reached down and fit the glove over his right hand and slid the strange ring onto the middle finger of his left hand. He clasped his hands together and then carefully drew them away from one another. A void of darkness appeared between his hands. Taking shape, the void narrowed and solidified, angling itself and gently twisting into a weapon. Will and Madigan were both transfixed, watching wide-eyed as Jervin stood and dropped his left hand to clasp the hilt of the blackened bastard sword he now held.

"One of the noctori, a shadowblade," he said, gazing at the weapon. "Pure Shadow energy condensed into whatever dimensions your mind desires. Unbreakable, it will never lose an edge. Should you ever lose your grip in battle"—he flung the sword from his hands and it disintegrated into nothing—"the blade will not fail you." He clasped his hands together quickly and another blade appeared as soon as the other had disappeared. "No matter the length, no matter the weight your mind wishes, the blade is perfectly balanced." The sword vanished from his hand and he gently removed the ring and glove from his hands, placing them on top of the box before him. "Madigan, take them."

"What?" Madigan said, his incredulity interrupting the trancelike state Will had fallen into as he had stared at the blade.

It was like my Shade, Will thought. *As if my Shade was solid.*

"The noctori is yours, Mad," Jervin said, gesturing. "Please."

Madigan stretched out a hand toward the glove and then stopped, giving Will a tentative glance. Will nodded, his eyes wide and excited. "Hey, if you don't take them I will."

Madigan grinned, stood, and reached forward. With wonder in his eyes, he touched the glove as if it were fragile crystal.

Upon making contact with the leather, his eyes lost focus, growing distant. After a moment, they returned with a new clarity.

He took the glove and slid it over his right hand. It fit perfectly. He picked up the ring and mirrored his grandfather's action of sliding it over the middle finger of his left hand. He stepped to the side with a sudden grin of confidence and then clasped his hands together, mirroring Jervin's previous actions.

A momentary grimace crossed Madigan's face. His arms seemed to pulse, threatening to surge away from each other. With difficulty, he managed to keep his hands together, his brow furrowed in concentration. With even and measured breaths, he drew his hands apart.

A darkened glow hovered between them. As the darkness began to stretch, Mad suddenly broke the bond and dropped his arms to his sides, falling to one knee and breathing hard. Within his gloved hand was a dark grey-brown blade. Sucking in deep breaths, Mad stared at the creation with a mixture of joy and terror plain upon his face.

"Not bad," Jervin said, his face stretching into a wide grin, "not bad. Most novices' first experience with a noctori ends immediately after the initial burst courses through their veins. I'm surprised you held out as long as you did."

"That was incredible," Madigan said. He regained his composure and rose to his feet, staring at the small dark blade.

"Once you get some practice, it'll grow," Jervin said. "And once you master it, it will grow to whatever dimensions you desire."

"Incredible," Mad said again, his voice filled with wonder.

Jervin continued assisting Madigan with the nuances of the noctori, demonstrating the most basic of steps to get it to function properly. Will watched as Madigan's skill progressed and the reality of the situation began to sink in. No more what-ifs, no more wishful dreams, it was all happening right in front of him. Curiosity and excitement overtook his initial trepidation as he considered the possibilities of everything to come.

While Jervin worked with Madigan, Will's eyes fell to the two remaining objects atop the wooden box: the knives. They were elegant in their simplicity, the dull grey marked by imperfections and frequent notches in the blades. The scars added to his curiosity, evidence of past adventures, stories of the blades' use over the years. Surely, if the noctori was for Madigan, the knives were for him, yes? Surely so. He couldn't help himself; a closer examination while he waited for his grandfather couldn't hurt.

He picked up the smaller of the two and grasped the hilt, raising the strange weapon to his eyes for closer inspection. The leather was soft and warm to the touch. His hand gripped it snug and comfortable, as if he had been the one to wear the leather in over the years. Touching the blade of the knife, Will was surprised to be met with not the cool feel of metal but something akin to smooth stone. His curiosity building, he ran a fingertip along the edge, his fascination for the weapon overcoming any caution. Warmth poured into his finger and extended through his hand and forearm. Upon reaching the tip of the blade, he caressed the curve and jerked his hand back as the fine point pierced his skin.

Will's world became fire and ash. His stomach clenched. His hand burned as if it had been thrust into the heart of a volcanic flame. He struggled to catch his breath, falling to the ground in agony as the scorching sensation spread throughout his limbs, consuming every fiber of his body. He writhed and the world ceased to exist—no time, no memory, only the blazing agony. A distant shout registered against the cacophony of heartbeats and sobs as the world twisted and he felt his body bursting into flame. *Dying, I'm dying.* His blood boiled in his veins, his own life force murdering him from the inside out.

And then it was over. Gasping and sputtering, the cool normalcy of the world shocked Will. He tried to sit up and felt a hand braced against his chest, steadying him.

"Slow down there, tiger," Jervin said, reaching for the water jug by the footlocker. "Looks like someone got a bit overzealous, eh?"

Will gulped down the water. "What the hell happened?" Warily taking stock of his body, he realized that he was totally fine. His skin was covered with a light sheen of sweat but there was no residue of the fire. He was unburnt, completely unchanged with only a bit of dirt still clinging to his sweaty body from the day's activities.

Looking at Madigan for reassurance, Will found his brother with arms crossed, smirking in his direction. Next to him was a three-foot shadowblade thrust into the ground. Madigan was leaning against the pommel as if it was the most natural thing he'd ever done.

"Wow, Will," he said with a chuckle. "I haven't heard you scream like that since you were a baby."

"What?" Will said, confusion crossing his features.

Madigan laughed. "Squirming around on the ground and staring at your hands with your mouth open, wailing. Did the firewood give you a sliver there, kiddo?"

"A sliver? I was dying, you ass!"

"No, you weren't," Jervin said. His voice was smooth and calming but Madigan laughed aloud. "You were just a bit over-whelmed. The fang releases a toxin into the body to incapacitate its victim. Thought you were burning alive, didn't you?"

Will nodded while Madigan kept chuckling and picked up the

noctori, stepping away and guiding himself through various martial forms. Sighing, Will looked at the knife still clutched in his hand. "That was terrifying."

His grandfather was suddenly ruffling his hair like he was six again. Jervin smiled and helped Will to his feet. "You will find that dragon fangs are unique in many ways, William," he said. "Fire was the dragon's weapon in more ways than one."

"Dragon fangs?" Will stared at the object in his hand. Realization dawned on him. The knife wasn't metal. It wasn't stone. It was the tooth of a dragon. "But, dragons? Real dragons? They exist?"

"They did long ago," Jervin answered, "in a better time. No longer, unfortunately. The last of them was murdered by Valmont in the destruction he wrought when he escaped." He raised the companion blade to the one Will still clutched and for a moment he became that same terrifying warrior as before. Only this time, it seemed to Will, this time there was something hollow about the man. Some part of his strength had vanished.

"A Disciple of Shadow was trained to wield dragon fangs most effectively," Jervin said, "able to manipulate the primordial flows of life and death equally. The root of the tooth is wrapped in dragon hide to protect the wielder, as is the sheath in which they are held. Of all the weapons and tools found in the realms, dragon fangs were both the most feared and most desired. Unfortunately, their proper use is now lost to the ages, thanks to Valmont."

"What was their proper use?" Will said as he accepted the second weapon from Jervin, extra mindful of the blade's edge. They each felt like extensions of his own arms, natural and comfortable, and the leather continued to warm his skin. With reluctance, he replaced them in their belted sheaths and looked at Jervin. The old man smiled and nodded, gesturing at the belt.

An excited grin spread across Will's face as he lifted the belt and fastened the weapons around his waist.

"Life, as well as death." Jervin's eyes were sharp as Will drew and tested out the maneuverability of his new gifts. "But that ability is, unfortunately, gone. The blades still maintain their lethality despite the diminishment of their other powers. Just as strong and deadly as Madigan's noctori but with surprises of their own."

He paused and beckoned for Madigan to come listen. Madigan stopped the motion of his blade and paused, closing his eyes for a moment, and then allowed the weapon to flicker into nothingness. He stretched his arms above his head as he made his way over, looking remarkably at ease.

"A Blade from Umbriferum, the Halls of Shadow, was trained equally in both of these weapons, with Adepts of Shadow wielding the noctori and Disciples of Shadow learning the art of the blood fang. Blades were chosen from the most worthy of each order separately and then trained to mastery with both, along with other, now forgotten, skills.

"Unfortunately, I don't have time to teach you the intricacies of these weapons right now, but trust me on this," Jervin said as he put a hand on each boy's shoulder. "You two need each other. Madigan, you have mastered the sword all these years for this purpose, to act as an Adept, to wield a noctori. William, dexterity and speed were always more your allies than any sword, and so you were focused on short weapons, blades similar to the blood fang, so that you would be aided along the path of Disciple. Together, the two of you have the weapon proficiency of a Blade of Shadow. It is not enough but it is a start."

"Hell, Grandda, this is plenty," Mad said as Will nodded in agreement.

"I appreciate that, boys," Jervin said. "Nonetheless, there is one more thing."

Will glanced back at the final item that remained: the note. Yet, rather than reaching for it, Jervin lowered his head and removed the long leather necklace he always wore. On it were the two intricate keys, dark with silvered hues. Will had seen them countless times in his life, yet now he eyed them with a new curiosity, speculating what secret of his grandfather's they held. Jervin held the leather tightly in his grip and looked at the boys. To Will, it seemed like his eyes were filled with hope and reverence.

"What are they?" Madigan asked, taking a step forward. "What do they open?"

"Just your minds, boys," Jervin said. "Your minds and your spirits." As he spoke, he pulled and broke the leather cord into two pieces and wove one key into each. He took a deep breath and drew himself to his full height, extending his hands forward with a key in each palm. "William, you won the day. Here is your prize." He smiled. "First choice."

Will smirked and nudged Madigan, goading him in the way that only siblings can. Approaching Jervin, he made a show of gazing intently at the keys as Madigan groaned behind him. After a moment though, Will's gaze changed from whimsical intent to serious. The keys both appeared identical and yet he could sense something unique and different in each. He could feel it. Something in the keys made the back of his mind tingle. He noticed small differences in color, an ever-present shifting of patterns amongst the darkness. Each key seemed to exude a magnetic pull directly upon him.

He ran his fingers along the first one, feeling its cool temperature and smooth surface. A sense of peace came over his mind as he caressed it. The key called to him, as inviting as a swim in a warm pool on a cloudless night. His mind relaxed, the tingling subsided. Smiling, he was about to voice his decision but paused and reminded himself to look at its partner to be certain.

Reaching forward to touch it, he felt a burning shock against his fingertips before it instantly changed to a calm and soothing balm. The darkness revealed hues of purple and silver and orange that seemed to appear and disappear, a reflection of the night sky stretching outward to embrace dusk. Forked patterns of darkness and light danced hypnotically across its surface. Will was enraptured by its beauty and magnificence, like the eye of an eternal hurricane. On and on the delicate dance played across his senses.

"This one."

The sound of his own voice broke Will's reverie and he glanced around him, blinking against the day's sun. He hadn't even meant to speak but withdrew his hand and nodded to Jervin. His grandfather smiled, but his eyes looked different, pained somehow. Nonetheless, he gestured for Madigan to step forward.

Madigan grasped the unchosen key and touched its surface. Will could imagine the cool metal lightly numbing his fingertips the same way it had his own. Mad's face betrayed nothing, however. *Perhaps it affects different people in different ways?*

Mad glanced at Will before turning back to Jervin. "And I shall take this one with much gratitude, Grandda," he said, embellishing his speech as he teased Will, "unlike some people who appear to have forgotten their manners."

A hearty laugh broke from Jervin. Will sputtered and blinked, lost again in his own thoughts. "Oh, right," he said. "Sorry, Grandda. Thank you very much."

"Of course, boys, of course," Jervin said. He smiled and placed the keys into his pockets. "They'll be yours before the sun goes down. Now, have a seat again, we have much to discuss and I'm not certain how much time in which to do it."

"Grandda, what about that?" Will said as he pointed down to the note.

Jervin's soft sigh was almost imperceptible but his face melted into weary fatigue. Gone was the energetic man and in his place was a stricken shell. When he spoke, his voice was harsh and forced. "That," he said, "that is the last known message from Valmont. That is . . . " He bent and, as though it caused him pain, lifted the note. He did not open it but extended it to Will.

The hairs on the back of Will's neck prickled as he reached out to accept it. Unfolding it, the flowing script of the writing took his eyes a moment to adjust to. There was something jarring about it, something repulsive.

I AM NEAR THE END. I'VE LEFT A LEGACY OF NOTHING. NO MORE. I will endure, even if I must rip the very fabric of nature and watch the heavens bleed from the sky. Mortals know too little. There is no time. If knowledge is power, then I shall become a walking god. This is the first, you will not find the rest.

I am the first, there shall be no others. Cthonaex terraq'uillian Cthonguinos.

WILL HANDED THE NOTE TO MADIGAN, THANKFUL TO RELEASE IT from his fingers. While Mad scanned it, Will glanced back at their grandfather who still looked shaken. Madigan's voice broke the silence.

"Arrogant man, wasn't he?"

Jervin barked a laugh and the weathered expression faded. "Yes, my boy, that he was."

❧ 6 ❧

THE KEEPER'S PLANS

A t a gesture from Jervin, the three of them took their seats again. Madigan began testing out smaller blades on his noctori while Will thumbed the gems on the dragon fangs. But he was distracted. The note had shaken him for reasons he couldn't explain.

"All things aside, Grandda, you never answered Will's question," Madigan said. "What exactly was this all about today? I mean, we're taking everything as it comes, and I'll admit the noctori and the keys are amazing, but a bit of actual explanation beyond the basics would be much appreciated."

"And so we come to it," Jervin said before sipping his water. "Fair enough. I'd planned to wait longer but the truth is, you've both far exceeded my expectations. What I propose is this: We reopen the Cascanian path to the Ways and enter Aeril. From there we make our way to Undermyre. It is, for all intents and purposes, the capital of Aeril."

Will clapped his brother on the back and laughed in excitement as Madigan broke out into a wide grin. *I was right,* Will mused, *it's finally time.*

"I appreciate your enthusiasm," Jervin said, raising a hand to quiet them, "but you must understand that we'll be trekking into a world far different than this one. There are elements of similarity, yes, but it is more dangerous than this. There is no true governing force. Laws are brutal, unforgiving. In the old days, people who traveled to Aeril from the Ways needed to present themselves to the council of Undermyre, a check-in of sorts. I don't know how much has changed but that will be our first point of business. From there, the journey will only become more perilous."

He paused and drank from his cup. Will fidgeted, his mind still distracted. If there were dangers, surely the three of them could handle them. He was more concerned with the note. And then there was the key and its intricate designs and the hypnotic effect it had on him. All in all, he was finding it quite difficult to focus on what Jervin was saying.

Looking at Madigan, he saw that his brother's attention was fixed firmly on their grandfather. Mad seemed to hardly blink, drinking in every word the old man uttered. Will had rarely seen his brother so focused on anything outside of the sparring ring, while to him the conversation felt rather anticlimactic. That troubled him. *Probably nerves, that's all. I don't think there's a written guide on how to take this kind of thing in.*

Jervin set his cup down and wiped the moisture from his lips with the back of his hand before continuing. "Originally, I'd hoped to spring this on you and then have more time to teach you the great history of Aeril, but we can do that there. We'll have the right books, the right tools. The education you've received so far has been a warrior's education, you have to remember that. My skills were in sword and strategy in my home, but the intricacies between Radiance and Shadow and the subtle maneuvering of politics have never been my strength."

"We'll manage, Grandda," Mad said. "You've trained us well."

"Thank you," Jervin said, shaking his head. "But for us to truly find our home in Aeril, you'll need more than just your wits and physical strength. Politics are unavoidable and always slow things down. As I said, there are similarities with this realm, but you must always remember that it is vastly different from what you've known up till now. It will take time to adjust."

"Wait," said Madigan. "What do you mean when you say politics?"

"We need the ruling council to guide us to any remnants of the Halls of Shadow to elevate Will's training," Jervin responded. "I taught the Blades of Shadow how to fight, but only a true Blade will be able to teach you to control your ability to any real extent, William."

Will had been absentmindedly caressing the gem in his knives again and musing about the key but finally looked up. "Control? I have control, Grandda. I know how to hide it."

"Ah, but hiding it is the last thing you'll ever want to do with it again, my boy," Jervin said with a smile. "Did you think this power was only a passive part of you? No, Will, a Blade of Shadow is far more than that. And as Shadowborne, well, when I left Aeril it had been quite some time since the Halls of Shadow had seen any Borne with the raw power you possess."

Will cocked his head to the side. "So, I'm something special then?"

Jervin laughed. "Well of course you're something special, Will. You both are," he said, giving Madigan a wink. "But on this topic, I'd say it's more akin to having a head start. You'll see once you reach Umbriferum."

55

"Wait, are you saying we're going to split up?" Madigan asked, interrupting his grandfather. "As soon as we arrive, Will will be leaving us?"

Jervin shook his head. "No, not if all goes according to plan. Like I said, these things take time and we should be able to get established well before Will leaves for training. And even then, it won't be for long."

"How long?" Will said, growing nervous at the prospect of being separated from his family in an unknown land.

"The isolation period as one initiated into the Halls of Shadow is generally no more than five to ten years," Jervin said. "Although it may be a bit longer now, depending on the state of the Order. We'll just have to see when we get there."

"Five to ten years?" Will said, his eyes growing wide. "But that's a lifetime!"

Jervin chuckled and leveled his eyes at his grandson. "It's a far cry from a lifetime, William. It's a blink of an eye. Time in Aeril does not exist in the same sense that it does here. You'll be fine."

"But, Grandda." It felt to Will that his lip had a slight tremble to it as he spoke. "I couldn't go. I just couldn't."

Jervin laid a hand on the young man's shoulder. "Trust me, Will," he said. "You're far more capable than you know. You'll see when we get there."

"And what about us, Grandda?" Madigan said as Will gaped. "Do we simply wait this whole time?"

"No, Mad." Jervin's eyes still shone in the dimming afternoon light as he spoke. "We shall integrate you into Undermyrian society. We'll continue your own education and build alliances with my former contacts. We shall build a life."

Madigan shifted in his seat. "It sounds like you're grooming me for politics, Grandda."

"If I was, could you blame me?" Jervin said with a shrug. "Madigan, you have the makings of a brilliant commander, and you're the finest student I've ever trained to use a sword. But more than that, you care. You want the best for all people, you bring out the good in them. The Aeril I left was broken and hurting. It needs someone like you."

"I don't know," Madigan said as he ran a hand through his hair. "I think I'm more suited to swordplay. Can't you teach me to train and be a Blademaster, like you?"

Jervin chuckled and shook his head. "Oh, Madigan, if only it were that easy. We'll talk. Once we've arrived and you've seen Undermyre, we'll talk. We've got time."

Will looked at the aged man before him, conversing with his brother about leadership and making connections, and felt a pang of jealousy. *They're planning a life without me,* he realized. *They're already talking about leaving me and moving on.* Something inside him began to ache, but he fought against the urge to interrupt.

"Regardless, there's still much to learn for both of you," Jervin said. "We'll have more time for details while we're on the road. One thing is absolutely paramount, Will. Do not discuss your Shade with anyone."

"What? But I thought the whole point of Aeril was that they understand."

"It wouldn't do for the wrong people to be made aware of it. Yes, people are aware of the power, but it's a different culture there, a different world entirely, and one filled with superstition. Protect yourself until you reach Umbriferum."

"Why does it need to be secret?" Will asked. "It makes sense here, I know, but all the stories you've told make it sound like it's a perfectly normal thing in Aeril."

"It's dangerous, Will," Jervin insisted. "The wrong type of

person could try to do you harm simply because of what you are. We can protect each other well enough but I'd rather not risk it."

Sighing, Will relented. "Okay, you've got my word."

"Really, Grandda," Madigan chimed in, "you've trained us well. We know how to fight. If it comes to that we can handle it. Hopefully, however, it won't."

"Indeed," Jervin said with a smile. "But I've tried to prepare you more than just training you to fight. As it stands, I've put together supplies to get us into Aeril safely, assuming all goes well. They're in our old storage unit, a few miles down near the river. Madigan, you remember the one?"

"Where we used to keep the canoe before it sank?"

"That's the one. We're about to wrap up here. When we get back to the house I want you two to go get them. It's not a lot to carry but it'll go quicker with two."

"We can do that, sure," Madigan said.

"What will you be doing?" Will asked.

Jervin leveled a stern gaze in Will's direction. "I shall be doing the most important thing that can be done before we leave. I shall be cooking dinner." His face broke into a grin and all three laughed.

"The entrance is nearby, then?" Madigan said. "I mean, if what we need to travel with is light enough for Will and me to carry, it's got to be nearby."

"Yeah," Will said as he thumbed the knives again. "Plus, something tells me you would've wanted to stay close and keep an eye on it, just in case."

"Very good," Jervin said, nodding in approval.

"Mount Hood?" Will said as he raised an eyebrow at his grandfather. "Or hidden somewhere in the forests nearby?"

Jervin shook his head. "Not quite."

"It would be hidden, though," Madigan mused. "But hidden

nearby. Something closer than the mountain. Something hidden in plain sight."

Jervin smiled and nodded. "Keep going."

"The Ways are like tunnels, right?" Will piped up. "So it has to be underground."

Jervin stayed silent as the two boys racked their brains. After a moment, both looked up at him and shrugged.

"Need a hint?" he asked them. They nodded. "Well, in that case you'll have to *press* me more."

Will eyed his grandfather. Have to press more? Press Grandda? He knew he didn't mean it in the sense of pushing him harder for a hint; that was the hint. *When you press someone, you're trying to get something out of them. You're pressing them for service.*

"Ha!" Madigan said as he clapped his hands together. "I've got it!"

Jervin held up a hand to Madigan and looked at Will. *Pressing him for service.* His mind rolled it over and over. *Pressed for service and hidden in plain sight nearby. Nearby Portland.* Then it dawned on him.

"The Shanghai Tunnels," he said. Madigan shot him a confused look as Jervin smiled. "The entrance is in the Shanghai Tunnels."

Will thought of everything he'd heard of them, a sprawling set of dilapidated and decrepit tunnels that spanned the city beneath its streets. Back in Portland's early days, when it had been a major port for the west coast, the tunnels served as a means of transport for unloading ships that docked in the river. But urban legends told of a different purpose, a dark purpose. They fueled the underworld with a haven of opium dens, prostitution, and slave labor. Sailors could be drinking in a bar when a trapdoor would spring open under them and the next thing they knew they'd been press-ganged into slave labor aboard ships. A web of dangerous corridors and traps awaited any prisoner who attempted escape.

"Impressive again, Will," Jervin said. "Beneath the tunnels, though, not in them."

"Damn," Madigan said. "I'd gotten the press-ganging part so I was thinking of the river. How'd you get to the tunnels from that?"

"Another name for getting press-ganged is being Shang-haied," Jervin said. "Rumor has it, that's where the tunnels got their name."

"But how did Will get there?" Madigan asked, raising an eyebrow at his brother.

"I read it in a book, back when I was reading all those pirate histories," he said.

Madigan just kept staring at Will. Finally, he shook his head and looked away. "You and your damn pirates." Will just grinned and shrugged so Madigan went on.

"Alright, Grandda, if the entrance is just in the tunnels, how come no one has found it?"

"Well, it's been over a century since the tunnels fell into disuse. The majority have either been flooded by the river, collapsed, or purposefully filled in to create stronger foundations for new buildings. There are no maps, no lights, and they're falling apart at every turn. They're practically death traps now, even more than they used to be."

"Sounds like fun," Mad said, his voice laconic. Will eyed him warily.

"But even before that, the entrance was protected," Jervin continued as if Madigan hadn't spoken. "It had its own perils in addition to wards to guard it from prying eyes. No one who didn't know what they were looking for would have been able to find it."

"Couldn't you have just said it was hidden?" Will said, his nerves rattled by the notion of underground passages scattered with ancient booby traps and magical protection. "That would have made it sound mysterious and kept the appeal."

Jervin laughed. "A bit less excited now, are you? We'll be fine, kiddo. I know the way."

"And I'll even bring a flashlight to protect you from the dark," Mad said with a grin. Will gave him a light shove and cracked a smile. *As long as we know where we're going, we'll be fine.*

"Regardless," Jervin said as he rose to his feet, "let's get home. We'll rest and relax tonight then be on our way before first light."

Will and Madigan grinned and stood. Around Will's waist, the belt and the blades it housed moved silently with his motion. His thumb absentmindedly started rubbing one of the gems again. *Today is awesome.*

"Ah, yes, one small point of official ceremony before we go," Jervin said. He reached into his pockets and removed the keys from where he had stored them. Will's head swam as he looked at them again, their colors seeming suddenly more vivid. How had he ever thought they were identical?

Jervin held a key in each of his hands and held them to his chest, closing his eyes and whispering something that neither of the boys could hear. When he opened his eyes, he extended his hands outward. "As Keeper, my body forsakes the protections of the one, but my blood embraces it. Once protection of three, now broken to two, may their guidance and luck extend unto you. *C'thak n'eran sangueras.*" He opened his palms. "These are

61

yours now, yours alone. Keep them secret. Never let anyone else possess them."

"Nice speech, Grandda, very poetic." Mad grinned as he fastened his key about his wrist.

The remaining bit of cord on Will's was slightly longer than his brother's and he was able to tie it around his neck. It was heavier than he expected. The key settled against his skin at the base of his neck and stayed there, seemingly sending faint waves of electricity coursing through his body. He was taken by a brief twitch between his shoulder blades and a few involuntary blinks, but then the sensation passed and all was normal.

Will shook his head a few times and moved around a bit to familiarize himself with the feel of the necklace, but it was unnoticeable, not in the least bit foreign. It settled and rested against his skin in the same way the dragon fang had settled into his hand, the same way the belt had along his waist.

Jervin, who had seemed to be holding his breath, visibly relaxed. He leaned down and picked up the remnants of their meal and the footlocker. "Alright, well, let's be off then so you two get home before the sun really begins to set. I want to make sure that—"

He was cut off by a loud explosion, close enough that the ground shook beneath them. The sky darkened rapidly as plumes of darkness shot into the air. Not only the sky, it was the air, the earth, everything was growing darker. Yet off in the distance Will could still see the sun shining brightly.

He glanced around as clouds of smoke began to rise into the air, their blackness offset against the greying world. Smoke that seemed to be coming from a direction that housed only one thing: home.

The color drained from Jervin's face. His eyes grew wide as they beheld the rising plume of smoke. "It's impossible, how could . . . " His voice was hoarse and broken and tired, the voice of a very old man.

"Grandda," Madigan said, his voice barely audible over the distant rumbling. "What's happening?"

The air became frigid. Will felt the hairs on the back of his neck rise. He had never seen his grandfather scared, let alone terrified. That whatever was capable of evoking that emotion from such a powerful man was near their home made his mouth grow dry. A thunderous, distant collision reverberated through the air and his eyes snapped back to his grandfather.

"Gods be damned," Jervin said, throwing down the foot-locker. "Run!"

Will's knees trembled.

They ran.

7

KEEPER'S FALL

They rounded the curve in the levee and Will saw the thickening smoke billowing and furling upon itself. It rolled and cascaded, a smoking snow globe of ash and fire. At his side, Madigan cursed. Jervin remained silent, only increasing his speed. A terrible sense of foreboding twisted Will's insides—there was no doubt, the smoke was obviously coming from their home.

They pressed onward and Will eased the knives in their sheaths. He again became aware of the key resting against his chest as it seemed to begin pulsing, rhythmically fluctuating between warm and cold. As its pulses grew in intensity, a tingling sensation gripped his limbs. Despite the circumstances he couldn't help but grin at the sensation, so alive and foreign.

They crested the final slope of the levee and halted, the grin slipping from Will's face. A short distance away stood a horrific caricature of their home. It was as if the house had been obliterated from within, the yard covered with the scattered remnants of the house's exterior. The scorching wooden timbers of its framework were the pyre upon which Will's entire life was burning. The grand cedar tree, engulfed in flames, was broken at the base and sagging against the ruined house.

And the fire, Will realized, there was something about the fire. Something unnatural in the scorch marks and burns. He studied the flames, which were dark purple and red and gave off no blinding light. The smoke was a terrifying shade of black that seemed to wrap in on itself. Within the globe, the very world seemed to have plunged into a mystical darkness, all sources of illumination winked out. Despite the roaring carnage, no heat came from the flames and, as the family drew closer, no smoke filled their lungs.

"I'm too late." Jervin's voice was nearly inaudible. The quiet terror in it sent ice through Will's veins. Automatically, his knives found their way to his hands. Madigan clasped his arms together and formed a massive shadowblade. The two brothers looked at Jervin for direction. There were tears in his eyes.

"No," the old man whispered, the quivering order sounding hollow.

The word was as much of a shock to Will as the horrific scene. "What?"

"This is the work of Valmont," Jervin said, shaking his head. "You need to get to the supplies. Now."

"Grandda, you can't expect us to go." Madigan's voice trembled with rage as he pointed the noctori toward the inferno. "That's our home!"

"Don't be a fool, Madigan!" Jervin shouted over the roar. "You don't understand, there is so much you still don't know. Neither of you are experienced enough to contend with—"

Whatever their grandfather was going to say was suddenly

cut off mid-sentence. The air grew still, the crackling of the fire disappearing into silence as a guttural hiss crossed the air.

"Keeeeperrrr . . . "

Will froze. A shape was forming in the haze. The air grew stagnant and wretched, a heavy, putrid smell of iron and bile. The shape, the size of a man at first, grew and seemed to solidify as it began to pull itself forth from the midst of the wreckage. Around it, the unnatural fire silently consumed all in its path. The devastation of his home was forgotten as fear gripped Will's mind.

By the time Will could fathom what was happening, the creature was gargantuan, something more terrifying than any nightmare. Its slick, oily red skin was so dark that at first he thought it jet black. The monstrous creature slavered, its gaping maw of jagged fangs nearly half the creature's size, each drop of drool sizzling and steaming upon the charred ground. Ridges along the folds of its back, jagged and broken, projected at least five feet into the air. And as it moved, the shadowy darkness moved with it.

Two massive forelimbs dragged its torso as tentacles at the base of its back gripped the ground and propelled it forward. It pulled itself through the flames, smoky tendrils of shadow swirling around its base as it lurched in their direction with unnatural speed.

"Light's fall," Jervin swore, his voice regaining its strength as he whirled on the brothers. "I told you to run!"

He left no room for response as he hurled himself down the embankment and into the smoky field to meet the creature. The darkness surrounding the brothers began to withdraw, light again breaking through as Jervin raced forward.

"It controls it," Mad said, his voice shaking. "That thing controls the darkness."

"Is that a Shade?" The words fell from Will in a gasp. "Gods,

Mad, it has a Shade." Never, not even in his dreams, had he imagined a creature such as this. A sickening crunch shattered the eerie silence as the remains of the house crumbled in the distance.

"We have to do something, Mad," Will said, his eyes stinging from the smoke. "We can't just let him do this alone!"

Madigan spun to face his brother, his face suddenly calm and collected. "We won't. Come on."

He turned and ran toward the flames, the noctori angled behind him as he closed the distance. Will hesitated only briefly before following, looking at their grandfather. Jervin had reached the creature and paused. He was weaponless, defenseless, and anything that might have aided him was engulfed in the fallen structure. He would be obliterated in a heartbeat.

And then Jervin rushed in, faster than Will had ever seen him move. He shot past the creature and toward the crushed remains of the fire pit. As the creature spun to follow, Jervin thrust his hands into the rubble-strewn, sandy ground of the pit and withdrew a massive claymore in one swift motion.

Will stared in amazement. Darting this way and that, Jervin maneuvered the magnificent, shining claymore in his hands, light as a feather, nimble as a fencing foil. For the first time, Will truly saw the Master of Blades at work.

He was sprinting before he even recognized the will to move, knives downturned in each fist as he chased after Madigan. He had no plan, nothing in the years of training having even remotely prepared him for this situation. All he knew was that he needed to be there. *I need to help.*

Despite its size, the creature's speed seemed matched with his grandfather's. Wherever Jervin moved, the creature was there, lashing out, snapping its terrible jaws. The Shade surrounding it was moving in ways Will had never considered, stabbing, slashing, bludgeoning, doing everything it could to pierce Jervin's rapid defense—for Will quickly realized that that was all Jervin could manage, pure defense. No matter how fast he moved or where he positioned himself, the creature was always a step ahead of him.

Madigan was doing his best to stay at the creature's back, opposite his grandfather. He was slashing wildly at the tentacles whenever the noctori came within reach, but his speed paled in comparison to the creature. Not only that, but Will realized that speed was not the only force acting against them. As he drew nearer, the darkness grew thick and heavy again, the air even more vile. He could scarcely breathe, let alone keep his eyes open for any extended period of time. Madigan at least had the reach of his noctori to aid him, something Will's knives severely lacked.

In the haze he tried to gauge the positions of his family. The air was so thick he could scarcely hear his brother's battle cries and the only sounds from Jervin's direction were the wet hisses and snarls from the beast. The sound was sickening. Will could only hope they were in frustration at its elusive quarry. He spaced himself equally between the two and stalked forward into the darkness, pressing himself low, blades at the ready.

A sickening thud to his left spun him around and he leapt forward through the darkness. He could just make out the outline of one of the slick tentacles. He thrust his knife forward and down, throwing all of his weight into the blow. The tentacle whipped away before the blade hit home but he felt it jar and rattle in his hand and he knew that at least he had grazed the beast.

An ear-splitting roar confirmed it. But the cry didn't sound injured in the least bit; it sounded angry. Will remembered the immense pain of the blade scratching his skin and imagined some sliver of it wrestling into whatever consciousness the creature possessed. He fought against a tremble of fear at the roar, but still he reveled in the knowledge that the monster could feel pain.

The volume of the creature's roar was overwhelming. Will tried to shrink back as he realized that the beast had turned its focus to him. Then he was on his back staring into utter darkness as something batted his feet out from under him. Slick, red tentacles encircled his legs, their grip squeezing and crushing. He couldn't get away.

Reacting out of instinct, he drew himself forward to his knees and plunged both knives downward to the tentacle that encircled his immobilized legs. The blades sank in, the left sliding into the slick hide nearly to the hilt as it bit into the flesh. The creature roared again, threatening to burst Will's eardrums once more, but his legs were free.

Will scrambled backward in the cloud of darkness as another tentacle lashed out and slashed across his chest before disappearing back into the darkness. He cried out and covered the wound with his hand as he pushed himself away. Barely finding his balance, he made his way to aching legs and fled back in an effort to disengage and regroup. He heard Madigan's furious cries somewhere to his left and he ran toward them.

Another red-black tendril shot from the darkness toward his face, faster than he could dodge, but it was deflected in an instant. Stricken, he glanced around and saw his own Shade surrounding him, its darkened wisps shifting and flexing in the gloom. *Instinct,* he realized, *thank the gods for that.*

Emboldened by its presence, he abandoned all sense of stealth or tactics. He shouted for Madigan, for Jervin, for anyone near. Muted sounds rushed toward his back in the darkness and he spun, knives braced defensively as his Shade whirled about him.

"Dammit, Will, get back!" Madigan shrieked as he appeared from the haze. Blood covered his face and torso. The noctori in his hands was a fraction of the size it had been when he engaged minutes earlier, no larger than a dagger. "Get the hell back!"

Will needed no more prompting. He took off with all the speed his battered legs could muster and darted past his brother. Mad turned and followed, favoring one leg more than the other as he ran. The screams of the beast behind them were seemingly staying put. The crashing of its limbs amongst the smoldering rubble of the house confirmed it.

"Grandda?" Will said between gasps for breath upon reaching the outskirts of the darkness. His chest burned where the beast had cut him, but the wound seemed only to have been glancing. "Did you see him?"

Madigan shook his head. "No, I couldn't see a damn thing in there." He collapsed to a knee and looked back in the direction they came. "I could barely hurt it. Whenever my blade connected it was always a glancing blow. It had me on the defensive almost the entire time and it kept battering the noctori from my hands. The force of that bastard was so intense . . . " He shook his head, trying to return his breathing to normal. "When it turned its focus I had to fall back. That's when I saw you."

"Then Grandda is still in there with it," Will said, gazing back at the cloud of destruction. Around him, his Shade disappeared involuntarily. He paled and stared at the darkness before him, then pulled himself upright. "I'm going back for him."

Madigan's face was grim but he nodded. Wincing, he stood and extended the noctori back to its full length. "I'm with you. We stay together."

Without another word they made their way back into the

70

darkness. Will knew their grandfather was still alive by the creature's thrashing and refusal to chase them when they retreated;
there could be no other conclusion. Before, separated, they
hadn't been able to affect the course of the battle. But together
the three of them could fight it—they just needed to get to their
grandfather. Or if he and Mad could distract the beast, then
perhaps Jervin could strike a killing blow. They just needed to
find him, to fight as a family.

Darkness descended around them once again. Bracing themselves, they raised their weapons and charged in. The creature's
limbs shot out from the shadows and both brothers yelled and
raised their weapons. Before they could strike, the fury of the
thrashing suddenly subsided, the limbs drawing backward into
darkness.

"Issss that all, Keeperrrrr? Your whelpssss are a
letdownnnn."

"You will not engage them, filth," Jervin said. "You will
drown in your own blood first."

The voices were distant, perhaps twenty yards away. Will
turned and made straight for it as Madigan broke into a limping
run.

"Your wordssss are ash on the windssss, ancient. You are as
brokennnn as your blade." The beast's voice gave a rough
shudder and Will realized it was laughing. As the volume
increased, the surrounding darkness suddenly swept up and away
from them and the soft light of dusk burst through in its absence.

The brothers halted as their field of vision cleared. Will
stifled a cry at the sight of their grandfather.

Jervin stood facing the immense creature. His left hand was
gripping his shoulder, but the arm had been twisted, bent in the
wrong direction so that it was pinned against his shoulder blade.
Even from so far away, Will could see the white bone of the shat-

tered elbow jutting from the skin. A broken piece of Jervin's claymore impaled the mangled limb, holding it in place. His right leg had been torn off roughly below the knee and shredded muscle hung around the splintered remains of his shin.

Jervin leaned on the remainder of the claymore as a crutch, swaying lightly, his face gaunt and ghostly white. From his stomach jutted a charred branch of the shattered magnificent cedar tree, still smoldering where it emerged from his back. Within the grotesque ruin of his face, his remaining eye focused on the creature before him.

"Ash is all you shall receive, Senraks Bloodbane," Jervin said through bubbles of blood. "The strength of my line shall be your demise."

Harsh laughter again erupted from the beast, but Will couldn't take his eyes off his grandfather. Tears streamed down his face as he stared at the great man's broken body. Jervin tore his stare from the creature and met Will's gaze, sorrow upon his face.

"Keep them safe," he called out quickly, blood dribbling down his chin. "Get to the tunne—"

His words were overpowered by the shrieking roar of the beast as it surged forward, mouth wide and dripping to devour the remains of their grandfather. With a cry matched in equal fury, Jervin freed himself from the cedar stake and flung himself backward, supporting himself upon the broken claymore.

Blood pouring from his body, Jervin crouched and leapt into the air with a battle cry and met the beast head on. Darkness shattered the light as the creature unleashed its Shade when the two collided. A crash of thunderous fury burst from their joining, driving the brothers to the ground. Darkness swept the area.

There was a tug at Will's sleeve.

"We have to go, Will," Madigan's cracking voice sounded far away. "We have to run."

Will pushed himself away from the battle raging before him and met his brother's wide-eyed stare. The edges of Mad's face blurred and Will found himself nodding, his own voice sounding frail and broken as he spoke.

"We run."

8

FINDING A PATH

The final wet drops of Madigan's lunch splattered from his mouth to the ground, the balance long since lost during the flight from home. Tremors gripped his body, sore from retching. *An involuntary purge due to emotional necessity,* a rational voice said in his head. He pushed the thought down into his empty insides.

He had driven them forward, shouting encouragement to Will whenever his brother began to lag. They made it to a small dock by the river before darkness forced them to stop. Mad attempted to put on a brave face, to remain collected and focused on escaping while all that they knew burnt to ash behind them. Will's face was ghost white and distant as he held the scraps of his shirt against the wound on his chest. Mad shook his head—perhaps the strong front hadn't been as effective as he hoped.

His jaw clenched in anger at his trembling stomach, at the ineptitude he felt. He could feel the fury building inside. He tried to remain calm, tried to fight it back. In the face of despair and

74

brutality, he had to keep Will going. Yet, still, the fire inside his empty body roared in anger. He wanted to scream.

And Grandda thought I would have the fortitude to lead men in battle, in death.

He shook his head again and took a deep breath.

Death.

His grandfather's broken and bloodied form appeared in his mind and his body heaved violently forward again. The battered body. The blood. The exposed bone. That was what death looked like.

Thanks for the final lesson, Grandda.

His diaphragm ached but the next spasm stopped before he pitched forward. He nodded to himself slowly. That was good. Either he was regaining some sense of control or his body was giving up. He wasn't sure which option he preferred.

Will had dropped to his knees in the sand and was sobbing silently.

Fatigue gripped Mad's body. His injured ankle throbbed and he was covered in bruises that spiraled along his torso where the creature had coiled around him. He'd thought he was done for, alone and trapped in the darkness, but the thing had screamed and released him. *That must have been when Will stabbed it. He saved my life and doesn't even know it.*

The chill of the night sent a shiver down his back and he realized that he was cold. Cold was good. Cold meant he was starting to process things properly again. Cold meant he was coming down off the adrenaline. His body began to hurt. Whatever that blasted monster was, it had done some damage to him.

Not as much as it did to Grandda.

The fury that had been building erupted. He picked up a rock from the base of the pier and hurled it into the river as his core screamed in protest from the sudden movement. As it struck the water he whirled and ran toward the stone of the dry seawall. His noctori became a bastard sword and with a scream he brought it crashing down on the wall.

Stone chips began to fly in the air. Tears streamed down his face as he smashed the blade against the wall, the shock of each stroke numbing his hands. Screaming, he brought the blade down again and again, the night's deceptive silence shattered by his rage.

"Christ, Mad." Will's voice was strained, like those nights he awoke from the nightmares. "We have to keep quiet."

Mad had obliterated a large section of the wall. His eyes were filled with rage, the dried blood caking his body giving him the look of a madman. He was panting, his nostrils flared from the deep gasps. His eyes bore into his brother and he opened his mouth to unleash an onslaught of anger. Instead, the noctori fell from his grasp, vanishing from sight as he sank to his knees, sobbing.

He felt like a fool, breaking down in front of his brother. He was supposed to be the strong one, the titan of the family, always sure in everything. He was supposed to be a model for Will. *Guess I've failed there, too.*

The tears running down his cheeks were saturating the dried blood and bringing it down his face in red-flecked streams. He tried to wipe it away, to hide the evidence of his pain and shame, but the grime of his clothes only made it worse. He couldn't stand the sight of his trembling, bloody hands. He buried them in the sand and closed his eyes.

They stayed that way for a time, Madigan with his hands in the gravelly sand and Will kneeling there, supporting himself against a beam. Night had long since fallen and the hour was impossible to determine. Mad stared up at the moonless sky and let his mind go.

A gurgling sound brought him back to reality, half choking sob, half guttural groan. He realized he had been the one who made it. His body had run out of tears and all that was left was pain. He climbed to his feet and again attempted to brush the blood-caked dirt from his hands.

"I'm sorry, Mad," Will said, his voice barely a whisper.

Madigan looked up, forced determination on his face. "For what?"

"I should have . . . " Will said, his voice stuttering. "I mean, you just—"

"Shut up, Will," Mad said, not unkindly. Will looked up, his attempt at a smile nearly breaking Mad's heart. He nodded in return and walked to the water's edge, the calm lapping of the water a stark contrast to the earlier horrors.

"Do we keep going?" Will asked.

"Of course." Madigan didn't hesitate. He looked in the direction they had come, nausea again threatening to overwhelm him. There was no sign of pursuit, no smoke, no sign of fire, no sign of anything amiss whatsoever. But it was there, even if all traces had been extinguished from existence. The images were burned into his mind, his grandfather's kind, smiling face forever matched in memory alongside that final image of him broken and bloodied from battle. There was nothing left behind them.

He turned around and found Will rising to his feet, brushing the tears from his own face. "Right," Will said as he looked at his older brother. "Lead the way."

MADIGAN TOOK THEM TO THE ONLY PLACE HE COULD THINK OF, and a short while later, the pair arrived at their grandfather's storage unit. They'd visited a few times, years ago, before venturing out on the occasional camping trip. But now, he knew,

Jervin had outfitted it for a different purpose. He'd been preparing for this venture and whatever was in there would give them a clue to the next step.

The facility was quiet in the night but not unaccustomed to activity at odd hours. Usually used by hunters and boat owners in the off season, it was easily accessible from both the river and the highway while also being off the main roads. Thanks to early morning fishermen and the occasional outdoorsman preparing for a long day out in the nearby woods, the facility was used to accommodating its patrons coming and going at all hours.

The parking lot was vacant, and the darkened windows of the warehouse signaled that the brothers were thankfully alone. No matter how easygoing the facility was, Mad knew that two young men stumbling in with torn clothes would raise suspicions. Especially when one was wearing a set of blades like a gun belt while the other was covered in blood. They had no key for the padlock, but the chain link fence was easily scaled and the rusty barbed wire along the top was clipped by a quick flick of Will's blade.

"Do you remember the unit number?" Will asked when he dropped to the ground inside the complex.

"Thirteen," Madigan said, his feet hitting the ground beside his brother. "Remember how Grandda always joked that it was lucky and I told him he had his facts mixed up?"

"It seems like you might have been right," Will said under his breath.

Mad's lips pursed but he ignored the comment and set off through the small complex. He was doing his best to stay focused and didn't want to get locked up in grief again. He had to stay strong for his brother. He had to keep them going.

The unit was only a short distance away, near the outer fence with the river to its rear. It was smaller than a garage, with a single entry door as well as a rolling one for larger objects.

Madigan stepped forward and punched in the code for the lock. Will looked at him and raised an eyebrow.

"Like Grandda said," Madigan said, "he was going to cook dinner and we were coming here. He gave me the code."

"Too bad the gate to this place wasn't coded as well," Will said in reply.

Madigan nodded and pushed the door open. Stepping forward into the darkness, Mad felt the air warm against his bare arms. It was surprisingly fresh, too, and he felt some tension release from his shoulders. He flipped a light switch and illuminated the room, revealing something more akin to a dormitory than the cluttered, stacked boxes he remembered.

The walls were orderly and lined with shelves, each categorized and summarized on a clipboard that hung at the end of each shelf. He opened a rough-cut armoire that revealed simple outerwear meant for travel. Against the far wall were three cots draped in various satchels and knapsacks, their number a harsh reminder. He pushed the thought from his head as Will made for the nearest one, leaving Mad to sort through the room in silence.

WILL CLEARED THE COT OF ITS CONTENTS AND COLLAPSED ONTO it, grimacing as the movement aggravated the gash on his chest. He drew his legs onto the small bed and lay back. He ached all over. He knew he should probably have Madigan take a look at the wound on his chest, but he was too distracted to focus on things like that. The cut wasn't bad, he'd live—something Grandda couldn't say.

His eyes welled with tears as he thought of his grandfather and the terrifying creature. Senraks, Jervin had called it, Bloodbane. Where had he heard that name before?

He withdrew his grandfather's key from his pocket. He had torn it off when they were at the riverside and Madigan was raging. Its electric, tingling sensation had been too much to handle and he had needed a release, an escape. Now, it was all tangled in its cording. Untwisting the strands, he focused on the key and tried to block out all other thoughts, thinking of his grandfather's words when he handed them over—purposefully vague, as always.

Just your minds, boys. Your minds and your spirits.

Sighing, blinking tears away, Will wrapped the cord around his knuckles and held the key in his palm. *How the hell are we going to do this?*

"So, the Shanghai Tunnels," Mad said, his thoughts echoing Will's. His voice was forced, but steady. "They're supposed to be huge, right?"

"I don't know. Maybe there's a guide or a map or something filed with the city?"

Madigan barked a laugh. "Yeah, a map that shows an entrance to some goddam mystical other world. Asking for that'll go over great." He shook his head. "I don't know, Will. I just don't know."

"You'll figure it out," Will said softly. "You always do."

"Thanks," Mad said, looking over at him. "We've just gotta make sure that—Jesus, Will, you're bleeding all over your cot!"

Will raised his head and looked down. Mad was right; the gash on his chest had reopened and there were a dozen smaller cuts all over his body that were making a mess of his bedding. "I'm okay. Yours is gonna look just as bad whenever you lie down, I imagine," Will said and gave a weak smile.

"Let me find a first aid kit," Mad said as he began combing through the storage unit. "I'm going to fix you up."

Will protested but his brother quieted him, so he settled back on the cot and closed his eyes. His mind immediately drifted to his grandfather, his kind, laughing grandfather. The image was almost immediately replaced by an image of the man in his last moments and Will's stomach twisted. *Gods, what have we gotten ourselves into?*

He curled into a ball and drew the key close to his chest, his grandfather's final gift to him. His closed eyes burned with the tears he fought against, doing everything in his power not to cry. Clutching the key, a cool, ephemeral blanket swept over him and he snapped his eyes open. It was his Shade. He smiled, wiped away the tears, and looked down at the key in his hand.

It was still captivating. Its surface glistened through the mess of blood and tears, the hues of purple darkening from their presence. Hypnotic colors and the streams of light that dance along the back of eyelids pulled Will in. Distantly, he realized that his Shade was growing darker, intensifying, concentrating around his hand and the key within.

The world began to spin and he tried to sit up but a burning pain tore through his body. His eyes felt dry and cold, ancient charcoal within his skull, and all sound left the world. Panic gripped him as he tried to stand, only to fall to the ground as his knees gave out. His head slammed against the metal bed frame as fiery twilight burst into his field of vision. Images raced through his mind too fast and frantic to distinguish. Nothing made sense. Sound returned in a roar, a cacophony of deafening screams and cries.

Water. He was wading through oily water in an immense cavern. Decayed wooden structures led to a hole in the high ceiling. Something gripped his legs, dragging him below the surface, filth entering his mouth as he sank. His fingers scraped desperately against the rocks as he descended, finally finding purchase on something cold and metallic. Wrenching with all his strength, he pulled himself up till his head broke the surface and he spit out the disgusting water.

A rusted, circular handle had been his savior, the handle itself secured on a door out of a storybook. Symbols were carved into the ancient black wood while black iron made up its frame. Crude filigree was inlaid along the metalwork and where the door met the rock wall it was covered in scores of deep gouges. Awe replaced fear as Will looked at the rents in the door's beauty, his eyes finding the light that pushed through from the other side—light like the glow of the full moon. A beautiful voice filled his mind.

Come, it said.

"Shit, Will! Come on, man, don't do this! Shit, shit, come on, man! Come on!"

Madigan was shouting only inches from his face. Will realized that he was cradled in his brother's arms. Coughing and sputtering, his eyes focused. They were on the floor. He tried to push himself up. "Mad?" His voice was hoarse, barely a whisper, and the taste of the brackish water still clung to his tongue.

"Shut up, just shut up and breathe, dammit!"

Mad's arms held fast and Will took his advice, inhaling deeply and finding it a challenge. For nearly a minute the two of them sat there in silence, Will trying to breathe while Madigan kept him immobilized. Finally, the older boy's grip slackened and Will pushed himself onto his hands.

"I'm okay, really," Will said, feeling unsteady as he tried to climb back onto the cot. "I must have passed out or something. Don't worry about it."

"Passed out?" Madigan said, staring at his brother. The terror on his face turned to anger as he rose to his feet and stared down at Will. "Passed out? The hell you did! Jesus, Will, you scare the shit out of me by screaming bloody murder out of nowhere and then I look up and suddenly you're spasming out! Then your goddam Shade started ripping the goddam room to shreds! Look at what happened to the goddam bunk!" His hand shot up and pointed to the ceiling.

If Will hadn't known it had been a cot, he would have had no idea what he was looking at. The metal framework was peeled apart and embedded into the ceiling, the surrounding walls all scratched and impaled with bits of debris. It had been crushed and crumpled and completely wrapped in on itself. Will was struck by images of the devastation wrought by tornados and the twisted remains they leave in their wake.

"Then you just up and collapse to the ground and everything stopped." Madigan's face was white and he was shaking. "Gods, Will, that was more terrifying than anything else. You're tearing this place to shreds and then all of a sudden you're limp as a goddam rag doll on the floor, Shade gone, not one goddam peep out of you. No more spasms and by the time I get to you you're not even breathing and I can't do a goddam thing about it. And you try to pass this off by saying you passed out?"

Will stared at his brother, aghast. He broke off eye contact and scanned the room. He stretched out his bruised legs in front of him and shook his head. He ached everywhere. The spasms wracking his already battered body placed his comfort level somewhere between burning alive and having every inch of his body pummeled by a sledgehammer.

"You can't do that, Will," Mad said, his voice quaking. "I can't lose . . . you can't scare me like that."

"Grandda isn't around to explain this one, Mad," Will said quietly. The words hung in the air, sounding harsher than Will intended. He was overly conscious of the throbbing of his head and quite desperately wanted his brother to keep his voice down. "I don't have a good explanation for you. I'm sorry."

Madigan's temper had deflated, his face pale and concerned. "You can't do that to me. I won't allow it."

"You won't allow it?" Will said, coughing lightly as he chuckled. His head and heart were both pounding. Madigan was terrified, he knew, but what he'd seen had been so clear—the door, the voice—he had to tell him.

"Nope." Madigan shook his head. "Nope, not one bit. You need to get your act together."

"I'll do what I can," Will said with a wry smile. There was a moment of silence as each of them stared at their hands, the day's events vivid in each of their minds. Will's eyes began to brim with tears again but he pushed them back. "Listen, Mad. Can I say something that sounds a bit crazy?"

Madigan stared at him for a moment and then put his head in his hands. "You mean crazier than whatever that shit was?" He sighed. "Sure, Will, go for it."

"I think there's a door in a pool of water that will get us where we're trying to go."

His brother raised his head, blinked at him, and then slowly lowered it back into his hands. "Alright, fine, I'll bite. *Why*, Will? Why do you think that?"

Will hesitated for another moment before responding. "Um, well . . ."

"Gods above, Will," Madigan said. "Did you have a vision or something? Is that what that whole thing was?" Will shrugged and gave a silent, uncomfortable nod. "Did you hear voices too?" Mad went on, still shaking his head. "Did a mystical voice from the heavens set you on the path to your destiny?"

"Um, actually . . ."

Madigan dropped his hands and looked at his brother incredulously. "You're joking."

Will shook his head then winced at the throbbing pain. *The rest of me feels numb, why can't my head too?* He looked at his brother and searched for answers. None came. "What can I say, Mad?" he said in as lighthearted a tone as he could manage. "I guess I've got the whole magic package here—visions and voices included."

Madigan couldn't help but give a good-humored snort; he leaned back against the nearby bunk. "Alright, tell me what you saw."

Will did. As he spoke, Madigan nodded but didn't interrupt, letting him tell the whole thing from start to finish to the best of his ability.

"It's possible," Mad said when Will had finished. "Grandda said the entrance was in the Shanghai Tunnels and those go all over by the river. It wouldn't surprise me one bit if there was some sort of underground cavern somewhere. It'll just be a pain to find it."

Will looked at him sidelong. *He's really trying to believe me here.* "So, we try the tunnels, then?"

"We try the tunnels," Mad said resolutely. "After all, we don't have anywhere else to go. Whatever happens, though, one thing is clear." Will stared as his brother's face grew hard and angry. "Valmont must pay."

Will nodded, not trusting himself to speak. It felt like a long shot but at the same time . . . *maybe not.* He moved over to the spare bed and sat down to rest, to try and recuperate his strength from the terrible day. Yet the moment he closed his eyes, Mad's voice brought him right back.

"You're still a mess, kid," he said, walking over with the first aid kit and sitting himself next to his little brother. "Come on, let me get you patched up."

❧ 9 ❧

THE SHANGHAI TUNNELS

They spent the next three days in a daze. They washed their blood off in the river while it was still night, the frigid water soothing as it numbed their bodies. During the daytime, they remained in the unit, trying to heal their bodies and spirits. Jervin had filled the place with food, water, and clothing and they used what time they had to recuperate.

Will rarely slept. Whenever he closed his eyes, his grandfather's grim countenance appeared behind his eyelids. The blood-drained flesh, the gaping hole of his eye, the broken stance from the absent leg, all of it was too gruesome for him to face yet.

He began to meticulously pack everything away into a corner of his mind, forcing himself to think of something else, anything else, whenever his thoughts began to drift back toward the evening Jervin died. He convinced himself it wasn't denial. After all, he wasn't denying what happened, he was simply forcing himself to block it all out. He thought it to be completely logical, a far better method of grieving than having to actually acknowledge the facts, but deep down he knew he was only pushing away the inevitable.

Madigan spent the majority of each day somewhere between calmly meditating on the floor and organizing supplies. It was unlike him to be so quiet, but Will appreciated his focus on preparing for the journey to come. As such, it was easy for Will to ignore his brother's nightly disappearances and subsequent return hours later in tattered clothes, covered in dirt and sweat. Will had checked the supply of clothing; they were fine. Mad could ruin as much as he liked for at least a week before he'd have to start being more careful.

On the fourth day, Will went to the library to do as much research into the tunnels as possible. Most of what he found wasn't much more than what he already knew from growing up in Portland, but he did find articles about a local enthusiast who made a career of excavating a portion of the tunnels and offering tours. His website even had an online calendar with tour dates and times. Will made a few notes before returning to the unit to fill in Mad.

The news brought little more than a nod, but over the next few days Mad's mood changed drastically. He stopped going out at night and taking his frustrations out in whatever fashion he had been. Occasionally a bit of humor began to seep into their halting conversations. Will could feel that something had changed and, while nothing was truly better, it felt good to smile again. The morning of the planned tunnel tour, as they were putting the final touches on their gear, they finally began to talk again in earnest.

"Having a goal helps," Madigan said quietly, "a mission of sorts. Something to work toward, I suppose. But with what happened to Grandda and knowing that that thing is out there somewhere, I just haven't known what to think or do this past week."

"I know, Mad, I know," Will said. "Just, do me a favor—try and be an ass, okay? That usually comes as naturally to you as breathing."

Madigan punched his brother in the arm and smiled. The pair shouldered their packs, locked the storeroom, and set out across the city with no idea of when they might return.

THE BROTHERS RODE THE BUS IN SILENCE ACROSS THE RIVER AND into downtown Portland. Will watched the city as they passed through. Districts that had always been industrial were alive with new construction, the signs of future growth sprouting up around them. It was strange to see. While he had never been one for venturing downtown often, the changes to his normally quiet town were striking. He couldn't help but wonder what the future would hold and, if he and his brother were successful, what he would make of the city when they returned.

If we return.

They reached the meeting point for the tour group an hour before it was set to begin. The evening was cool, the day's warmth having rapidly dissipated, and Will was thankful for the scarf wrapped around his neck. His coat was cut close at the waist and not long enough to hide the dragon fangs, so he had secured them within his pack. He felt strangely naked without them, exposed. He had taken to wearing them as often as possible in order to grow accustomed to moving with them, and already they felt like a natural part of him. He had adjusted to his other gift, the key, in much the same way, its rhythmic pulsing something akin to a second heartbeat.

"We've got some time," Mad said as he shifted his pack and adjusted the noctori's ring on his finger. "What do you say we grab some coffee and warm up a bit?"

The pair found a nearby cafe and began their watch. Shortly after they sat down, the first few people arrived to wait for the tour. During the next forty-five minutes more arrived until there were a dozen people waiting. Laughing and chatting, they displayed a levity that Will couldn't match. *They have no idea what they're walking into,* he thought as he watched them. *They don't know that they walk the fringes of reality.*

He was just draining the last bit of coffee when the group's guide arrived. The animated man spoke to the tour for a few minutes before leading them down the street. Without a word, Madigan and Will shouldered their packs and exited the cafe, observing from afar.

The tour soon stopped outside a small bar. Gesturing for the group to wait, the guide went inside briefly before emerging alongside two new men. Rejoining the group, the guide beckoned for them to make way as one of the newcomers walked past them. He unlocked a metal trapdoor in the sidewalk and lifted it high before descending into the dark hole. Laughter followed as a loud, overly embellished "Watch your step!" from the tour guide carried down the street. Once all members were within, the remaining man from the bar closed the trapdoor behind them and disappeared back into the building.

"So that's it then," Mad said. "We just pick that lock and go down tonight after the group comes out."

"Seems straightforward enough," Will said in agreement. "Although it won't be as easy getting down there without being seen. This street isn't exactly off the beaten path."

"True," Mad said, glancing around. The street was one of the main throughways of downtown and would be active at all hours. "Something will pan out. Maybe we'll get lucky."

Twenty minutes later, the man from the bar exited again. He spoke into a walkie-talkie and lifted the trapdoor. A moment later, four of the tourists and the guide emerged from below. The group appeared to be shaken yet were also apologizing profusely to the guide who was making an effort to calm them down.

"Will, come on," Mad said. He was already crossing the street. Glancing quickly at the open trapdoor, Will drew his scarf a bit tighter and followed, keeping his head down.

The shaken group had walked toward the entrance to the bar, seeming to be in a hurry to put as much distance between themselves and the tunnel's entrance as possible. The guide and the man with the walkie-talkie ushered them into the bar, laughing and reassuring the tourists. The entrance to the tunnels were momentarily unguarded. Madigan made his move and raced down into the darkness. Will hurriedly followed his brother into the entrance, expecting a shout of alarm. None came.

At the base of the ladder was a dimly lit room. Pipes ran along the cement walls and a small rope path marked the way forward. Madigan stood a few paces in front of him but there was no one else in sight. Murmurs echoed from farther down the corridor, where the tour had obviously made it a short distance before the interruption and were waiting for their guide to return. Out of earshot, Madigan and Will still kept their voices to a whisper.

"We have to move quick," Madigan said as he began to move toward the waiting group. "That guide is probably right behind us."

As if on cue, Will heard voices above and saw someone stepping down onto the ladder. Madigan beckoned quickly and darted into the shadows behind the steps. Will followed, heart pounding, and did his best to shrink into the darkness. He dropped to a crouch and leaned back into the shadows, letting his body fill the space as much as he was able. A moment later, the guide appeared from above, chuckling and saying something about jumpy tourists. He paused briefly, glancing around, and then moved forward to rejoin the group.

Will waited until he was well out of earshot before speaking. "So, do we stay put and wait until everyone leaves, or do we move forward and hope for the best?"

"Come now, Will." Will could hear the grin in his voice as Mad nudged his brother forward out of the darkness. "We've hardly begun. Where'd be the fun in hiding?"

Feeling the hairs on the back of his neck bristle, Will followed his brother and crept forward into the Shanghai Tunnels.

The path was well lit and surprisingly dry, despite the subterranean setting. They moved slowly, expecting to stumble upon a straggler from the group at any time. There were no hiding places if things didn't go their way; the area had been excavated well enough that the only remaining debris was left with intent. Fortunately, the people ahead were loud enough that the brothers were able to tell when someone was near.

Mad led from room to room, passing small cells with ancient sleeping quarters that were smaller than a closet. Will shivered as they passed piles of rotted shoes and rusted, rectangular bars enclosing tiny cells. These terrifying spaces had housed men once; they had seen violence and tears and atrocities, he could feel it in the air.

"This place is twisted," Mad whispered. "I'm getting the creeps."

Will didn't answer. He realized that the voices ahead of them had stopped, all save one who was speaking above the rest—the guide. He couldn't make out what he was saying exactly but the general sense of his tone said enough.

"They're at the end of the tour," he said, laying a hand on his brother's arm. "We've got to hide."

Mad whirled and gestured for him to backtrack. Will nodded and began winding back through the passages. He paused as they entered the room with the cells. *Maybe it's dark enough here.* The voices behind them had grown louder; they were moving faster than he and his brother. He jerked his head in the direction of the far corner and flattened himself on the floor, shoving his pack behind him in the shadowed corner.

"You've got to be kidding," Mad said under his breath. "They'll see us."

"We don't have time for anything else," Will said urgently. The ground pushed his grandfather's key, cool and tingling, against his skin. *Please let this work,* he thought as he tucked his face into the crook of his arm.

Madigan shook his head but followed Will's lead, shuffling off his pack and pressing himself into the darkness. No sooner had they settled into their positions than the tour came into eyesight. They were walking quickly, talking amongst themselves and laughing. They barely even glanced around as they passed through. When they exited the room, both Madigan and Will breathed quiet sighs of relief.

"That was all luck," Madigan said after a moment, rising to his feet. "There's no way that should have worked."

"But it did," Will said with a smile. He dusted himself off and picked up his pack. "Let's get moving, just in case."

Madigan nodded and led the way once more. They moved more quickly, covering the ground they had already explored. They had just made it back past the cells when the lights suddenly went out. Will jumped and threw himself against a wall. The instantaneous darkness was oppressive, claustrophobic. His heart raced and leapt in his chest as a flash of light suddenly shone from his side.

"Looks like they were responsible enough to turn off the

lights when they left," Madigan said. He shone the light at Will whose eyes were wide with surprise. "What, you didn't have yours ready? We're underground, Will, what did you expect?"

"I expected they'd leave the lights on," he said, peeling himself away from the wall and retrieving his own flashlight from his pack. "I don't know why."

"It's Portland, green living is a must," Mad said. He gave his brother a friendly shove with his elbow. "A bit jumpy, aren't you?"

"Like you said," Will replied as he fought to calm his pounding heart, "this place is creepy."

"An ancient, derelict network of tunnels, rumored to have once been devoted to drugs, press-ganging, and prostitution?" Mad clapped Will on the shoulder. "Yeah, it's lovely."

They made their way into the next room, where the tour had ended, and discovered that the way forward was blocked off by yellow caution tape. Ducking underneath, they passed from tourist-approved areas into ones still under excavation. The surrounding debris and rubble had been pushed aside, allowing a narrow path forward. Ropes hung from the walls like handrails, guiding the way.

The difference between the zones was startling. They found more of the small cells, these caved-in and filled with rubble. Each one sent a shudder down Will's spine as he imagined their former inhabitants, years of their lives lost in the blink of an eye. *And all around my age, most likely,* he thought as he pushed past them.

After a few minutes they came to another room that had been largely cleared out. More caution tape, older and covered with dirt and grime, barred the far side of the room. A modern door had been poorly fitted over a gaping hole in the wall.

"I think they may have more of this place excavated than they let on," Will said with a grin.

"Maybe," Mad said, "but look how old that tape is. This place has been blocked off for a while."

Will stepped closer and carefully crossed the barrier, shining his light along the doorframe.

"You're right," he said. "This door looks like it hasn't opened in years. Even the padlock is rusty."

"Be my guest." Madigan shone his light on the padlock. "You were always handier with locks than me."

Will slipped off his gloves, removed the lock-picking kit from his pack, and set to work. The exterior of the lock wasn't in good shape, but the tumblers fell easily enough after a few moments' work. He felt the satisfying click of everything falling into place and he yanked the rusted bolt open. Pocketing his tools, he pulled the door on its unsteady hinges. Before them was a steep downward ramp cut into the ground with a wide hole at the bottom. Another rope, covered in wet grime, was strung along the ramp's edge to act as a handrail.

"Well," said Madigan, shining his light into the gloom, "going down?" He stepped forward and edged his way down the slope to the bottom and looked over the hole. "There's a ladder. Or what used to be one."

Will eased the door shut behind them and slid down the rope till he met his brother at the bottom. Shining his light into the hole, he could see that the floor of the hole was just over seven feet below. Sure enough, there was a rotted wooden ladder that looked ready to crumble at any moment.

"Oh yeah. This looks just great," he said as he shone his light around the darkness. "Be my guest, Mad."

"Works for me," his brother said, clipping the flashlight to his belt. "Don't worry, I'll catch you if you fall, kid."

Madigan crouched and grabbed the ropes on either side of the pit, gradually lowering himself into the darkness. The ladder creaked and groaned beneath his weight. Will tensed as he waited for the crash of his brother falling amidst a pile of rotten wood, but it never came. Instead, Madigan shone his light up and gave a thumbs-up.

Will braced himself against the ropes and lowered his feet onto the first rungs of the ladder. It shuddered and creaked as he descended. The wood was soft in his hands and he could feel it giving way under his weight. Just over halfway, his foot stepped through a rung and the entire thing came apart in his hands. Yelling, he pushed himself backward and leapt off. He managed to land on his feet, but the sticky mud sent him stumbling into Madigan.

"Oh, well done, Will," Madigan said as he steadied his brother. "Well done, indeed."

Will readjusted his pack. "I like to keep things interesting."

"Right, of course," Mad stepped away from the broken ladder and shone his flashlight into the darkened passage. His eyes narrowed as the beam barely cut the gloom. "No reason to wait. Let's go."

Will nodded and followed behind. He lost his balance as the suction of the mud gripped his foot. He freed it with a sharp pull that sent him stumbling against the slime-encrusted wall. Pulling himself away, he wiped his grimy hands on his pants and shook his head. *Oh yes, this is just great.*

"I'm sorry," Madigan said as he flooded Will's face with a beam of light, "did you need a moment to stop and enjoy the scenery? By all means, take a seat and relax."

"What can I say?" Will said as he pushed away from the grime with a grunt. "This place has a nice, low-stress vibe to it. Maybe we should just set up camp here and settle down."

Both grinned and Will wrapped his scarf around his face. He was trying to keep the mood light, trying to distract himself and block out his dank surroundings. He failed.

The air was stale with age and smelled of decay. Their flashlights barely illuminated the space, as if the darkness itself was battling against the light. Each footstep was a struggle for balance and both lost their footing on more than one occasion. Before they reached any kind of bend in the tunnel, the brothers were covered in the slick, stinking mud.

Finally, they approached a curve that angled down. Will's feet slid as he trailed in Mad's wake. The path evened out into murky standing water that rose past his ankles, the mud underneath even more precarious than before. Still, the ground under the water felt different. It was jagged, not quite rocky, but definitely as if there was more than a fair scattering of gravel hidden in its surface.

"What the hell," Madigan said. "There's glass in the mud."

Will aimed his light down, toeing some of the ground above the water's surface. Glass and rusted bits of metal were interspersed throughout the mud. Every step they took, Will could feel crunching and grinding beneath his feet.

"I always heard that when sailors got Shanghaied the first thing their captors did was take their shoes," he said as a shudder went down his spine. He imagined terrified men with bare feet trying to make their way through the darkened tunnels, every footfall sending the debris tearing through their flesh. "Now we know why."

10

HAZARDS AND DOORS

Mad shook his head in disgust and pressed forward, his pack shifting on his back with each step. The brothers walked slowly and carefully, following the twists and turns of the strange labyrinth beneath the city. Will pulled the fangs from his pack and used one to mark arrows on beams, hoping they would be sufficient to follow back if needed. They came upon doors that led deeper into the earth, the wood long since rotted so that only the metal framework remained. Some tunnels were completely filled from collapsed roofs. More than once, they found more rusted bars and cages at dead ends, forcing them to backtrack until they could find another fork.

Hours passed with no conversation, their focus only on putting one step in front of the other and navigating the darkness. Will imagined his old storybook heroes slogging through trenches and wondered if they ever experienced the absolute boredom that was overtaking him. Everything had been all fun and adventure when they first entered the tunnels. Now it was just mind-numbingly dull and dreary. He wanted something different, to run from a giant boulder or swing over bottomless pits. Instead there was only glass-ridden mud in the darkness.

"This is ridiculous," Mad said, his voice edged with frustration. "We've doubled back again and again. This entire section of the city is one big dead end from the cave-ins."

"I'm open to any ideas, Mad. I don't really know what you were expecting." Will was surprised at the sharpness of his own tone. How long had they been wandering? How long since they had had anything to eat or drink?

Madigan barked a laugh at that. "Expecting? I was expecting a bit more help here, not just to be dragging along a silent pack mule."

"You said you'd lead the way," Will said, ignoring his brother's comment. "So, I'm letting you lead. I don't know what you think I can do."

"It isn't like there's a map, is it?" Madigan said as he shone his flashlight into Will's face. "Be useful, whip out your Shade and point it like a compass or something."

"What? That's not how it works." Will swatted the lamp away from his face.

"Have you even tried? How do you know?" Madigan raised the flashlight to his face again. "You're the magical one here, do something magical!"

"You're an idiot," Will batted the light away again. Madigan kicked mud at him. Will kicked mud back. They stood in silence, both daring the other to escalate the situation, until Madigan started laughing.

"This is ridiculous," he said. "I'm sorry. Truce?"

"Truce," Will agreed, smiling at the absurdity of it all. "I'm guessing we're both a bit thirsty."

"And hungry." Madigan frowned and glanced around the

tunnel. "Though the thought of eating anything while we're down here is really unappealing."

Regardless, the pair took a moment for a snack and a drink. While he ate, Will eyed their surroundings again. There were no discernible markings or indications of direction. Whoever had used these tunnels years before had either erased all traces or knew instinctively where to go. Still, there had to be some way they could figure out where to go, or at least where they were.

"Your dream, or vision, or whatever it was," Madigan said, interrupting Will's train of thought. "You said you were in a cavern?"

Will nodded. "Yeah, some cavern with a big deep pool and broken beams and the like." He tried to remember all of the details. Few came. "All the debris made it look as though there was some kind of big structure at one point. Or, at least, the skeleton of a structure. The start of something, maybe? It was old though, old and broken."

Despite the darkness, Will could see Madigan thumbing his key. His description of the room wasn't much to go on, but still his brother was trying to envision it, trying to find any potential clues to guide them. Suddenly, Mad started.

"A scaffolding," he said, voice brimming with excitement. "It was a scaffolding. You said there was a hole in the ceiling, right? The debris from the structure was its access!" His eyes were bright with enthusiasm at the revelation.

It made sense. Will didn't remember any other kind of entrance that could have led to the pool. "That's actually a really solid idea, Mad."

"We've got to double check every path we've crossed," his brother said, continuing as if Will hadn't even spoken. "We'll search for any hint of an exit by our feet that's been blocked or sealed or obscured, anything."

The pair set off, backtracking and scanning. Over the next hour they searched tunnel after tunnel, scoured rooms and cells, but found nothing. Throughout, Madigan kept twisting the key in his hands, making Will more aware of his own where it lay against his chest. He'd been distracted and hadn't noticed that its distinctive hum seemed to have increased. It seemed to nearly be throbbing. As they turned down a particularly dark corridor, the key suddenly sent a pang of electricity against his body and he yelped.

"Find something?" Madigan asked, turning back to him.

"No," Will shook his head. The key was dormant again. "I just felt something weird, like static electricity. It's nothing."

Madigan traced his steps back to Will. "With you, nothing is ever nothing. Let's look around a bit closer."

The blackened tunnel was damp, but the ground at their feet seemed dryer than the surrounding area. Will glanced around but couldn't find any cause of drainage; the walls seemed solid enough, no breaks to be seen.

Madigan began making his way along the opposite wall, shining his flashlight up and down as he scanned. Will felt the key jolt again as he turned to walk farther down the corridor. He paused and turned back. As he looked at the wall, he was inescapably drawn to a smoother portion near knee height that he hadn't noticed before. It was dirty, but something about it felt out of place. He crouched and traced his fingers along the wall. An outline seemed to form in the darkness, invisible to the naked eye but as though it was just on the edges of his vision.

"Will?" his brother called. "What is it?"

"There's something here," he said. "Something we didn't see before." He closed his eyes and imagined his vision, picturing the cavern. He thought of his grandfather and his years of gentle guidance. He thought of himself, Shadowborne, and imagined his Shade stretching through the cavern. Nothing came.

Frowning, he opened his eyes. Still, something seemed to have changed. It was as if he could see hair-thin cracks in the wall that formed an outline. Will leaned his body against the wall and pushed. It felt immense, immovable, but still he pushed. Madigan crouched beside him and, without asking why, joined him. The pair of them grunted and groaned, straining their bodies, when a sudden hiss of air escaped. Gradually the stone within the wall began to give way, pushing inward. Then it fell before them with a solid thud, revealing a small, dry crawlspace.

"Now this looks promising," said Mad. "How did you know?"

My key zapped me, Will mused, feeling foolish. Thinking that his brother would scoff at such a silly idea, instead he said, "Like you said, I'm the magical one."

Madigan eyed him speculatively. "Well, if you get any more magic feelings, let me know."

Will nodded then leaned forward and entered the small, low-ceilinged tunnel. As soon as he entered, his flashlight flickered and died. He stopped, thumbing the switch, and Madigan bumped into him.

"The light isn't working," Will said.

"Mine neither. It died just a second ago."

"Can you reach the batteries?" Will asked. His pack began to rustle as Mad rifled through it in the utter darkness. Will suppressed a foreboding sense of claustrophobia and forced himself to be patient. After a moment, he heard Mad unscrewing his flashlight before flicking the switch a few times.

"Nothing," Madigan said after a brief curse. "They're not working at all."

"Do you have a lighter?"

"Yeah, but we can't use it very well while crawling."

"Great," Will said. He closed his eyes and opened them rapidly as his head spun in the darkness. "We'll just move forward slowly, then."

They crept forward at a snail's pace on hands and knees. Will was thankful that this area had apparently been outside of the slavers' knowledge and, as such, the passage was free of any sharp debris. The path twisted after a few dozen feet and descended sharply before leveling out and twisting again. After what felt like hours, the passage finally began to grow in height. Overwhelming relief flooded into Will as he could finally move more freely. He shifted to a crouch and tried his light once more, to no avail.

"Mad, can you pass up the lighter?" he asked. After a moment's fumbling, he felt his brother press it into his hand. He wiped his hands on his pants and flicked the wheel, the sparks sending stars dancing across his eyes. The flame caught and Will held out the small light source in front of him.

Inches ahead was a rotten wooden beam embedded with rusted sawtooth blades. Sharpened railroad spikes and nails protruded from wherever a blade wasn't present, some straight and some curved to look like barbed fish hooks. Will shivered. Without the light of the small flame he would have collided with the trap.

"That looks . . . unpleasant," Madigan said, having reached the edge of the tunnel.

Will nodded and raised the flame to scan the passage. The walls were riddled with the harsh beams, protruding from all different angles. The ground grew slick again, the mud littered with the impaled beams and embedded with rounded stones. The passage sloped down at a frighteningly steep angle. The slightest slip would send them crashing down into the rusted blades.

"Whoever did this certainly didn't want anyone else passing through here," Will said as he eyed the trap-laden passage.

"I believe," Madigan said in a humorless tone, "that that was our grandfather."

"Right. So, we watch our step and we don't fall."

"Brilliant plan, Will, top of the class. Just be careful."

Will took a deep breath of the stale air. They weren't about to turn back, not when they had come so far, not when things were getting so interesting. He stepped forward, holding his breath as each step threatened to roll his ankles and tip his balance. The rocks squished in the mud and ground against one another as he moved, every stone treacherous. More than once, he wavered and barely caught himself when a stone sank too far or he misjudged a step.

Casual curses from behind let him know that Madigan was following his lead, stepping wherever Will had and testing his footing. Will crouched and maneuvered under the twisted wet beams and their bladed occupants, wishing for a handhold to brace himself against. Instead, he was met with spiderwebs that filled the spaces between the beams and laced his arms and face. The path twisted and turned, winding deeper and deeper into the earth. Will's heart raced, his teeth only unclenching whenever he needed to spit the tacky spiderwebs from his lips. His legs were cramping from having to constantly crouch. His body was screaming for him to straighten them and let them rest, but there was nothing for it.

Mad's curses increased as the sloped path became steeper and steeper, the stones more slick and the beams more prevalent. Will began to search for safe places to support his weight on the beams themselves, the minuscule spaces between the blades where there weren't hooks and spikes. He found few. More than once it seemed that there was no way to continue; the steeper the path became, the less safety there was.

And then, suddenly, the path began to level out. The stones beneath their feet flattened and the lethal beams lessened. To Will's relief, the mud became firmer and the rocks disappeared. After a few minutes, he finally began to lower his guard, breathing easier.

The dull hum of his key spiked again and he froze, shining the flame around the passage. He saw nothing. He stepped forward cautiously as the tunnel took a sharp, hairpin turn. The path ended abruptly at a hole in the ground. A faint glow was emanating from its depths. Will crept forward and flattened himself before peering over the edge.

A pale green light filled an immense cavern below, the glow coming from a murky pool in the center of the space, illuminating it. Decayed beams, broken and discarded, lay strewn throughout the cavern. The room itself was round and deep. Will's mouth went dry. He scanned the water's edge, searching for the intricate door that he knew was there. And then he saw it, half hidden by the pool, ten feet in from the bank against a small rock outcropping.

The cavern was exactly like his vision. They had found the entrance to the Ways.

Will turned back to his brother. "It's real, Mad. It's just like I saw it."

"Seriously?"

"Seriously. Bigger, but it's there."

"Good thing too," Madigan said with a grin as he pushed past his brother to look into the cavern. "Maneuvering backward out of this tunnel would have been more of a struggle than I'd care to admit."

Will gave a nervous laugh then squirmed next to his brother.

Both stared at the water below, at the wooden beams, at the door. As he looked, Will realized there was one key element of the equation missing. He nudged his brother. "Any brilliant ideas on how we get down?"

Madigan paused for a moment before responding. "We aim for the water."

Will sighed and shook his head. "That was the exact same thought I had. I just hoped you'd come up with something better."

He didn't like how far down the drop appeared. While in the vision the water seemed deep, they had no way of knowing for sure. Plus, there was a ghost of a memory of something else within the water, something he wasn't keen on encountering. He did his best to gauge the distance.

"Well"—Will rose to his knees—"I suppose there's no reason to delay." He took a breath and cast off, flinging himself down toward the pool. He had a brief moment to pray that his pack would keep him afloat should he lose consciousness upon impact.

Luck was on his side, it seemed, and he hit the water without losing his breath. It cascaded over his head as he went under, plunging downward. He fought the urge to open his eyes and look for anything sinister in the dark depths. The water had an oily tinge to it, slick against his face as he rose to the surface. Finally, his head was above the water and he was able to open his eyes. Gasping for air, he saw nothing and quickly began to paddle his way to the shore.

"Quite the splash, kid!" Mad called down, his voice echoing through the cavern as Will rolled onto the bank. "I'm right behind you."

From where Will lay, the fall didn't seem nearly as high as it had from above. But watching his brother descend and plunge beneath the surface of the pool was terrifying. He breathed a sigh of relief when Madigan's head broke the surface. Still, it was only a minor consolation as his imagination ran wild with what else could be lurking in the water.

"This water is disgusting," Madigan said after he spat.

"Then get over here and analyze its flavor when you're out," Will called back to him. The key thrummed against his chest and he could feel his hackles rising. Something didn't feel right. He looked around. There was no way to get back up to the hole in the ceiling. The door was their only exit.

Madigan paddled over to the bank easily. "Let's hope these packs are as waterproof as Grandda always said."

"I'm sure they're fine," Will replied quickly. "We need to go."

"Bit jumpy, aren't you?"

It suddenly occurred to Will that he may have missed a few key points in his initial description of his vision. He opened his mouth to fill in the details but stopped as a deep rumble filled the cavern. The waters of the pool began to churn. Will stepped away from the bank, frantically pulling Madigan back with him.

Madigan, however, hadn't hesitated for even a moment. In a heartbeat, the noctori took on the form of a bastard sword and Madigan was at the ready, knees bent, eyes intent on the water before him.

"Get to the door," he said as he raised the sword. "I'm right behind you."

Will took off at a run. He was racing for the opposite end of the pool, the one closest to the ancient door, when the creature broke the surface in a spray of putrid water. His path was blocked.

Will froze, paling before the creature. *Senraks* . . . But no, it was not Senraks. There was nothing magical about this being. It stank like long-dead ocean life, so potent that Will momentarily gagged. It was covered with massive tentacles, seemingly made up of them entirely. Smaller tentacles and beady eyes surrounded its surprisingly small body. The body itself appeared to be almost entirely taken up by its jagged, beak-like maw. It clacked open and he could see sharp, pointed ridges jutting up from within.

It moved as if by instinct. Its tentacles shot out, wrapping around anything they could touch as if their grip was reactionary. Will jumped aside as one flew toward him. He landed and rolled out of its reach as Madigan's noctori slashed down in an arc that severed the limb.

A gurgling, wet howl erupted from the creature as it turned its attention in their direction. Gripping the walls with its tentacles, it propelled itself forward, limbs flowing like an octopus. Madigan slashed again and again as the creature pressed forward. Will withdrew the fangs from his belt and distanced himself a few yards from his brother, dodging the creature's flailing limbs and stabbing at anything that moved as he raced toward the door.

Suddenly, the creature launched itself toward them, moving faster than Will had imagined possible. He cried out as he tripped and fell to the ground. A massive tentacle came crashing down toward him. He closed his eyes, preparing for the brutal collision, and electricity shot through his body. His chest went numb.

His mind felt somehow split, as though a dormant part of him was awake and battling. He opened his eyes and saw his Shade had deflected the blow and was surrounding him. More tentacles, smaller ones, kept crashing down but the Shade was shielding him, deflecting attacks. Will scrambled to regain his footing. Dimly, he realized that some part of him was controlling it, was aware and conscious of each block. Behind Will, Madigan roared as he parried one blow only to attacked immediately from the other side, sending the noctori flying from his hands.

The creature had managed to push them between itself and the pool, gradually forcing them backward. Mad had created another noctori but the weapon was a fraction of the size it had before. While his Shade was deflecting blows, Will's blades weren't long enough to sever through the tentacles and, surprisingly, the pain they inflicted only seemed to drive the beast into further rage. He thought of the door behind him, tantalizingly near but still too far to offer them escape.

Then, just like in the dream, he was in the water. He had backpedaled directly into the fiend's lair with his brother right alongside him. The farther back they were pressed, the slower their responses became as every action became heavy and sluggish in the water.

Madigan howled in pain as the beast gripped his legs and pulled them out from under him. Will leapt toward him, momentarily propelling himself out of the water. He stabbed down into the tentacle as hard as he could and Mad was able to squirm his way out of its grasp. When Will landed, however, he realized that they had reached the shore's drop-off point and the ground gave out beneath them. Will had no choice but to shove the fangs back into their sheathes and tread to stay afloat.

"The door, Will, get to the door!" Mad was struggling to reach the shoreline in an attempt to block the creature's path, but it was no use. Again, the creature hurled itself forward and slammed into Mad, tearing at his clothes and surrounding his body with its limbs. Will shouted as he looked to his brother, limbs outstretched like a crucifixion. He watched helplessly as the creature drew Madigan away and enfolded him in its tentacles.

"No!" The defiance roared from within Will, a blazing fury of heat that propelled him forward onto the land. Will's Shade disappeared in an instant as the cavern became charged, static heavy upon the air. The hair on his arms raised, the wetness of the pool evaporating from his clothes in an instant. Lightning appeared in brief spurts throughout the room, booming and crackling. The creature became frantic, its tentacles thrashing wildly. Lightning was crashing against it, burning it more with every movement it made.

Madigan appeared from within its grasp and scrambled backward, gasping for air, eyes wide. Coughing, he regained his feet and drew his noctori once more to full size and pressed forward, shrieking in his battle rage. The air crackled and the lightning stabbed, drawn to the beast like a metal rod in a storm.

Will stepped forward slowly and deliberately, his arm thrust toward the creature like an accusation of guilt. Its attack had stopped, and it was in a panic now as it tried to flee. Yet every movement called more and more electricity toward it. It shrieked, beak clacking over and over as it writhed in the cavern.

Madigan retreated; the beast was recoiling faster than he could catch it. Will heard his voice, suddenly frantic. "Will! Will, get the hell out of there! Will!"

"Go." Will's own voice was foreign to his ears, yet the creature's screams were sweet music.

"Will," his brother screamed. "The roof! It's collapsing."

As if in a dream, Will's eyes looked toward the ceiling. Great fissures ran throughout the cavern and stones were beginning to fall from it. He glared and stepped toward the retreating beast. The lightning intensified upon the terrified creature, corralling it back toward the falling stones.

"Go," Will said again.

A massive boulder fell directly upon the creature's body, immobilizing it. The torrent of lightning and stone continued while it screamed in agony, trapped within its own sanctum. To Will, the melodic beauty of its death throes seemed like a choreographed dance, each motion perfectly in time with the next. He found himself laughing.

Something crashed into Will from the side and he tumbled to the ground, gasping. A falling stone had shattered right next to him, exploding as it collided with the ground and knocking him off his feet. His head swam. Blinking, he looked around and took in the scene before him.

The creature's movements ceased. Its formerly grey-white skin was charred and blackened, cracked and split to reveal the reddened flesh beneath. The lightning, too, had ceased. Dizzily, Will turned toward his brother.

"Mad?"

He seemed so far away, standing within an opened door. The light from behind him was soft and brilliant, cool and inviting like a summer's night. Will stumbled toward him on unsteady legs, the pool hissing and sizzling as he passed through it once more. He heard rumbling and looked up to see more stones falling from the roof of the cavern. Falling backward, he floated on his back and stared at them—raindrops falling on a stormy night.

Hands gripped his pack and he was moving through the water. Passing through an arch, he saw the intricate filigree of the door from his vision for a brief moment before it closed behind him. He lay down on the ground and stared into the darkness of another tunnel, his cheek against the ridged stone floor.

Except the ridges didn't appear natural. They looked like cart tracks, etched deep within the stone and overlaid with a black metal. The stone was foreign, something outside of Earth's elemental plane, unnatural to every fiber of Will's being. But there were cart tracks. Like Jervin had always said.

The stories were true, all of them.

11

WITHIN THE WAYS

Madigan didn't know how long he sat there savoring the stale, acrid air. The ground felt cool but dry. He leaned his back against the door, resting his head against his palms, and stared down the passageway and the crudely etched tracks in the floor of it. Everything about his surroundings reminded him of a lost memory, like a distant déjà vu from his youth, something he couldn't place. Everything, that was, except for the blackened beams of the ancient door at his back, the evidence of the shattered and scarred room sealed behind it.

Will was sprawled before him on the ground, immobile. They were alive because of Will, alive because he had manifested his strange powers in yet another unknown way. His eyes were open, Mad could see, but staring at the ceiling without focus. His clothes were still steaming. Madigan remained silent, glancing between his brother and the dark passageway before them.

Eventually, Will blinked and his eyes began to flutter. He groaned and rolled to his side. As Madigan looked on, Will tried to sit up. He managed to get his arms underneath and nearly raised himself halfway before his trembling limbs gave out and he collapsed back to the floor.

"Ow," Will said.

Madigan didn't move to help his brother to his feet.

"Enjoying the view from up there?" Will said, the levity in his voice a poor mask for the strain.

"You scare the hell out of me sometimes, you know that?" Madigan said. His voice was a whisper against the darkness, a soft echo oppressed by the air.

"I know, I know." Will succeeded in pushing himself to a seated position and collapsing against the wall. "I'm an idiot and I should have just run when—"

"It's not that," Mad said, eyes dropping to the ground as he spoke. "You've gotten yourself in and out of plenty of tricky situations, Will, but that's not what this is. I'm not scared for you. I'm scared of you. You terrify me."

He heard Will's breath catch, the silence between them a physical force. Finally, Mad glanced back at him only to see that Will wasn't even looking in his direction. His eyes were far away, lost in thought, his voice only hinting at what was going on within his mind.

"We're fine, Mad, that's all that matters," he said, his voice a hushed monotone that didn't even echo within the tunnel. "I'm just still getting the hang of this. It's nothing to stress over."

Madigan gaped at his brother. "Lightning?" he said. Will snapped out of his pseudo-trance and looked at Madigan with a shrug.

"Apparently." His voice regained its usual levity as he raised his arms above his head in a stretch. "Trust me, it was just as surprising to me as it was to you. I've never had anything like that that I can remember." His face scowled in a grimace as he stretched and twisted. "And from the way my body is feeling, I think I'd remember pretty well."

"Your back is still steaming."

"Still . . . what?" Will's voice dropped again.

"You don't understand," Madigan said as he shook his head. How could he explain it to Will? How could he explain what had happened? "You were in the middle of it, Will, a whirlwind of lightning so bright I could barely look at it. But there you were. And you destroyed everything around you. Whatever the hell that thing in the water was, it was screaming—pain, terror, all of it. I've never heard a scream like that."

Will opened his mouth to speak but then paused. "I don't know what to tell you, Mad."

"Yeah, I figured that."

With nothing else that he could think of to say, Madigan stood and walked over to his brother, helping him to some very unsteady legs. For the first time, he realized that the wall they had been leaning on was actually a monument of sorts, some kind of inscription. On either side of them was a sheer chasm that stretched out toward the cavern's distant walls.

This was nothing like the tunnels they had come through previously. The narrow path was a single track of rock jutting forth, the doorway through which they had come set upon a lone, crude pillar of stone. He craned his neck and saw that beyond the pillar was only empty space and vast darkness. He turned back and saw that the rock ran for a short distance and then stopped; the path beyond was a bridge over the chasm. At the far edge of the bridge appeared to be a tunnel of some sort. The tracks led toward the passage.

Despite the emptiness, there was something grand about the cavern. It was no ancient river, long since dried, nor was it the result of shifting tectonic plates. This place had been shaped with purpose, with intent. The small wall of the monument was inlaid with intricate filigree carvings and strange designs, runes and ancient writings that Madigan could not comprehend in the least.

"So, is now the time we're supposed to lose our minds in excitement?" he said, trying to alleviate the tension between them. "I mean, we're actually in one of Grandda's stories now. If we were younger, we'd be bouncing off the walls." He paused and nodded his head toward the far side of the abyss. "Well, not that one at least."

Will chuckled then grimaced. "Yeah, I hear you. I just hurt too much to be excited right now."

"I'd believe that," Madigan said. He walked back to Will and traced the etchings in the wall with his fingers. "We've arrived. We're here. But where, exactly, is here?"

"Not Portland," Will said, shaking his head.

"No, definitely not Portland."

Will slid back down the wall to a crouch and put his head between his knees. Looking at the door they had come through, Madigan saw that the entrance was far bigger on this side. A large stone arch covered the column, inlaid with tree roots that bound and held them all together. It stretched upward and the tree formed the head of the arch, standing majestically and towering over the entire cavern, its branches stretching along the ceiling. Yet, like so much of the cavern, it was marred by a great crack that spanned the length of the tree and down along each root.

He turned and dropped to a knee next to Will, laying a hand on his brother's shoulder. He reached for his brother's water bottle only to discover the metal had melted within the blackened straps of his pack. Giving Will a small shake, he pulled the pack off as his brother groaned and shrugged out of it. The groan turned to a wince and a small laugh as the pack came free.

"You okay?" Mad asked.

Will nodded. "Some kind of static in the air or something. That key from Grandda keeps zapping me." Madigan shrugged, his own key cool and silent against his skin, and returned to inspecting his brother's pack.

It wasn't ruined, not entirely. The outer layer was charred and shredded while the small outer pockets had burnt off entirely. The emergency rations and first aid kit were gone, but for the most part the outer layer held the worst of the damage. The sleeping roll at the base of the pack was gone, one lone strap dangling from where it had been secured. The main inner pocket was mostly intact once he scraped past the ashen remains of Will's heavy jacket at the top, and beneath it the contents had survived. All in all, it would suffice for the time being.

Will managed to stand up and move around, wandering a short distance down the path, tracing the wall and staring at the roof. "Where do you think the light comes from?"

Mad hadn't noticed before but Will was right—there was no visible light source but the entire cavern was lit with a dusky glow. No shadows were visible, as if the pale light filled every crevice. "Is it crazy if I said it looks like it's coming from the rock?"

"Crazy? Yeah," Will said. "But also accurate." He abandoned the wall and walked back toward Madigan. "What do you think?"

"I think," Mad said, glancing back toward the carving of the tree and the strange light that surrounded them, "that we better get moving. This place doesn't feel right."

Will shouldered his pack and followed him forward. As Madigan moved, his key suddenly began throbbing, sending a cool little jolt along his skin, a shiver down his spine, the sensation like the first touch of the frigid waters of the Oregon coast.

He turned and glanced at Will to find that his brother had paused and, with burnt gloves, was fumbling at the zipper along his outer jacket, pressing against his chest. Madigan pressed his key against his own skin. The feeling stayed the same.

"Yours too?"

His question obviously caught Will by surprise but his brother nodded. "Yeah, constantly."

"Hmm. Mine just started," he said. The icy chill was slow and steady, a strange hum. "Do you sense anything?"

"Sense anything, what?" Will said, his face a blend of confusion and trepidation. "What do you mean?"

"You know," Madigan said, dropping his voice to a whisper and giving his brother a surreptitious glance, "sense anything. Your version of spidey-sense, shade-y-sense, or something? Super powers are always like that."

Will's expression flattened.

"I mean come on, 'Super Will,' you've got to be sensing something."

"Shut up."

Madigan laughed and turned, dragging his hand along the monument again as he began moving. He hoped that Will couldn't hear the effort behind the laughter, the force of the joke. While it may not have been genuine, he felt that the attempt at banter was probably for the best. It had been a long week, an especially long evening, and somehow he knew that things weren't going to get any easier. Between indoor lightning storms and magical keys and gateways into other worlds, the last thing either of them needed was to get lost in their own imagination.

They moved on, treading carefully along the bridge to move away from the door within the stone tree. The stone bridge neither veered nor curved, the tracks set within impossibly straight and level. The filigree extending from the stonework of the arch was mirrored on the cavern walls as they drew toward the mouth of the tunnel, the designs growing in size and detail. The lighting never wavered nor dimmed and cast no shadows. Even when they raised their feet for each step there was no shadow beneath it, the ground itself glowing.

They breathed a sigh of relief as the bridge ended and they had walls to either side once again, the vast chasm now behind them. Moving forward into the tunnel, the great stone tree passed completely from their sight. They followed the etched tracks along the passage until they arrived at a large junction where the tunnel opened into another massive cavern. This one, fortunately, contained no sheer drops whatsoever.

The walls were slick but far from smooth, like molten rock that had been molded as clay upon a crafter's wheel. Carvings jutted from the stone like friezes on ancient Greek temples, yet something about them felt older than Madigan could even imagine. The friezes were grand and detailed with figures from the depths of his imagination: dragons with flames surrounding them, warriors with weapons fending off demons and creatures he couldn't name, centaur and minotaur and every being from all the fantastical stories he dreamt of as a child. All were depicted before him like an enormous panorama of a horrific battle from his nightmares.

Will paused and his breath caught as he spun around slow and took in the spectacle. Madigan, knowing that his brother could very easily get caught here for hours by so many carvings, pressed forward. Will made a noise of protestation as he realized that his brother wasn't going to let him explore.

"Mad, come on," he said as he ran to catch up. "Look at it all! Have you ever seen anything like it? We should camp here and regroup."

"No, I've never seen anything like it and no, we're not going to camp here to regroup," Madigan answered his brother without stopping.

"But Mad—"

"This place is ancient, Will," Madigan cut him off. "Which means it isn't going anywhere. We can come back once we have some idea of where we are."

"Forward then, I take it?" Will said, his voice a mixture of resignation and petulance.

"Unless you've got a better idea. Grandda didn't explain much about this part. He just said that we'd get through the Ways and from there set out to Undermyre."

"But he had a plan for after that, right?" Will said hopefully. "One he shared?"

Mad paused and considered before answering. "He had a plan. We're just going to have to improvise."

"Wait," Will said, catching his arm. "Back on top of the mountain, the two of you were talking, planning!"

Mad nodded and shrugged out of his brother's grasp. "A bit, yeah. But it was for while you were supposed to be away training. Somehow I think lots of that got put on hold. "

Madigan didn't know how to tell Will that he was completely in the dark, that Grandda hadn't filled him in in the slightest about what this was or where they were supposed to be going. All he could do was keep moving forward and hope for the best, trusting their luck to guide them.

Luck. They'd been lucky, whether he wanted to admit it or not. In spite of the misfortunes they'd experienced they had still managed to come out alright. Most of the time, it seemed to have nothing to do with any of the training either of them had received. It was all just plain dumb luck.

As if the universe had the same thought at the same moment, everything changed. A distant sound echoed faintly down the corridor they'd moved into. At first, Madigan thought he was imagining things. A moment passed before he heard it again.

They weren't alone anymore.

Something was coming.

Madigan raised a hand. Will stopped in his tracks and dropped to a crouch, removing the tattered remnants of his gloves and placing a hand upon the metal tracks in the ground. He closed his eyes and cocked his head to the side. There was silence again as the pair waited, bodies tense in the faint luminance of the passage. Then the sound came again.

"Something's coming," Will said. "The vibrations are faint but they're there."

Madigan glanced at his brother askew. "You could feel something that faint in the tracks?"

Will gave a quick nod. "Barely."

Madigan cursed under his breath. There was nowhere to hide. Behind them lay only the cavern with its sprawling expanse of carved artwork, and behind that was only the way they had come. To backtrack at this point and stay far enough ahead of whatever was coming would require speed, and in their condition, there was no way they could do so quietly. Whatever was coming would be alerted to their presence immediately.

"Any chance you can whip out that Shade of yours?" he asked Will.

"Tried already," Will said, shaking his head. "Plus, with all this light coming from the stone, a shadow would draw attention like a flare."

"Of course," Mad said, his voice a hushed hiss. "Nothing can ever just be easy."

The sounds were increasing in volume and Madigan was able to make out that they were footsteps. Not loud and thundering, not another gargantuan creature, but small and in near unison.

Multiple things then, not just one. Maybe people? Their grandfather had come from here, so there was no reason to expect that whatever was coming would be anything other than human. *Unless it's multiple shadow monsters or tentacled water beasts.*

He shook the thought away and looked back at the cavern—there was nothing there to give them any kind of advantage. Glancing at Will, he saw that his brother had loosened the blades at his sides, clasping and unclasping the hilts repeatedly.

"People, if we're lucky," Mad said, his voice a whisper. "Hold back unless absolutely necessary. We don't know anything about this place. Not really."

Will didn't meet his brother's eye, instead keeping his gaze focused on the corridor. "Play things close to the chest, got it."

"And whatever happens, keep yourself under control," Mad went on, feeling the hairs on the back of his neck rise. Was it nerves? Or was Will about to break out in another lightning storm? "Don't let them know about your Shade, otherwise we may not be able to let them leave here alive."

"What?" Will said as he met Madigan's gaze with a glare. "What if things get out of hand? Are you really suggesting that just because someone finds out that—"

Madigan grabbed his jacket and pulled him close. "Grandda warned us about the dangers and we have no idea what we're in for here. You're Shadowborne. I don't know much about that but I do know that it can be pretty goddam divisive down here. If they're hostile and you make a move, I'm keeping you safe."

After a moment, Will nodded and Madigan released him. The footsteps were closer, only moments away from rounding the bend in the tunnel. Once more he scanned the walls looking for a crevice, a nook to hide in, anything—but they were unnaturally without blemish. Even if they were somehow able to reach the friezes high above, they were shallow at the base and offered little in the way of cover. There was no way around it: He and Will were exposed.

"We got lost," he said, his voice barely a whisper. "You're injured. We were exploring the tunnels for fun and got into trouble. We don't know where we are. Nothing about Shades. Nothing about Valmont."

It was the best kind of lie he could muster, staying close enough to the truth to be convincing. Plus, with Will's ravaged clothes, he certainly looked the part. It wasn't much to go on, but it was the best he could do.

Will, though, was never one to just let things go. Moving quickly, he unclasped the belt that held his knives and stuffed it into his tattered pack but not before he slipped one of the fangs from its sheath. Before Madigan could stop him, he had tucked it under the arm of his shirt, clutching it against his side and hugging the arm as if it were injured.

Madigan opened his mouth to protest but halted as the footsteps rounded the bend. In the distance, a group of armed soldiers appeared. There was the briefest pause before they erupted in a flurry of shouting and drawn weapons. Fighting every instinct to draw his own weapon, Madigan put on a mask of nerve-wracked fear and raised his hands in a gesture of submission.

The group charged and both brothers tensed. This was not the elegant band of soldiers depicted in Grandda's stories, bedecked in plumed helms and shining plate. This ragtag assembly before them wore intricately cut, blackened leather armor that bore no resemblance to any armor Madigan had ever seen. On each of their left shoulders was an epaulette in the shape of a giant raven with a silver beak. Each of them carried an elaborately adorned halberd. As they moved to surround the brothers, Mad saw the weapons' edges shimmering in the dim light.

Still, Madigan could tell that there was something strange about the band of soldiers, something he had not expected. There was an air of sadness about them, something tired. Their bodies seemed rough and harsh, as if hewn from salt and rock. The leather of their armor was cracked in places and poorly kept. They looked old, ancient even, despite the youth of their faces.

Three of them barked out orders at once and turned to look at each other sharply. Something was amiss. Madigan realized that they were out of their comfort zone. That could be bad. It occurred to him that the troops were patrolling the Ways, a destination that his grandfather had basically called a dead-end after it had been closed. So, either these soldiers never expected to find anything and Grandda had been correct, or something had drastically changed since the last time he'd been here.

"Sorry to startle you." Mad shifted slightly and spoke in a calm, even voice as he opened the conversation. "We seem to have gotten a bit turned around here."

He was met by cold stares. Whoever they were, they didn't look surprised to see them. Instead, determination and cool fury were building within them. After a brief pause, Madigan continued speaking.

"My brother here took a rather nasty tumble, as you can see from how banged up he is," he said. "We were simply trying to—"

"Silence, filth," said a voice he couldn't locate.

"Really now," Mad said, balking at the comment, "there's no cause to—" He was cut off by the butt of one of the halberds ramming into his stomach. He wheezed harshly and sank to the floor, gasping for air.

Will gave a shout and whirled to help him to his feet but was struck across the face by another of the weapons. Madigan saw Will glare up toward the group with as much defiance as he could muster. He was about to speak to his brother but was cut off.

"Either one of you speaks another word, I'll slit the other's throat," the same voice spoke again, closer this time. Will spat blood as Madigan, clutching his abdomen, laid a quieting hand on his shoulder. Mad looked up to see a gap form in the surrounding troops as another soldier, taller than the rest, stepped forward. A halberd was strapped to his back and in his right hand he carried a cruel-looking dagger. Madigan bit his tongue and swallowed the rage rising in his throat.

"Good, you're learning," the man said, glaring at the boys and gesturing to the soldiers at his sides. "Take them."

There was a rush of movement as rough hands and biting ropes overtook the brothers. Their packs were torn from their bodies and thrown to the stone ground. They were thrown to the ground and searched and, to Madigan's shock, they somehow missed the knife Will had hidden. The corners of Madigan's mouth grated as a large knot of rope was shoved between his teeth. His eyes bulged in pain as the gag was forcefully tied around the back of his head.

The leader of the band had ice in his eyes as he gestured for another from the guard to confiscate their packs. Madigan gave a cursory struggle, knowing beforehand that there was no way of fighting now. Will flinched as the rope enveloping his torso was tightened. Madigan imagined the concealed blade pressing against his brother's flesh and hoped that it didn't break the skin. Will's flinch apparently didn't go unnoticed, and the man gave a cruel smile at his discomfort.

Thoroughly bound, the brothers stooped in pain and discomfort. The leader withdrew a stiletto from a sheath at his side and approached, placing the point of the thin blade to Will's neck. Madigan shifted and shouted through his gag but was silenced by a strike from the guards. His eyes darted back to Will as he continued to struggle, forcing himself to suppress the building fear and rage as guards began kicking and beating him.

His eyes never left Will as the man pulled his immobilized brother close and whispered something in his ear that Madigan couldn't hear. He drew back and Will's eyes were wide with terror. A drop of blood appeared as the stiletto pierced Will's skin and Madigan watched as his brother screamed through the gag and collapsed to the ground, suddenly silent.

Enraged, Madigan shot to his feet and, though bound, managed to pull himself away from the soldiers. He ran toward the man. With a slight flick of his wrist, the stiletto flew through the air and bit into Madigan's shoulder. His world exploded as a maddening white sheet of pain overtook his mind before the world went black.

12

SENESCHAL OF THE COURT

W ill's body was rigid, a useless block of flesh and bone, but his mind raced. His limbs felt weak, his body sensitive to every touch. His senses were muddy; the only part of him that was alive and vivid was the overwhelming sense of pain. It was a crushing weight, locking every limb in pre-death rigor mortis.

Rigor mortis, a distant part of his brain mused. *Mortis, from the Latin word mors, meaning death. Feminine, third declension noun, genitive form.* He latched on to the memory of the lesson like a drowning man grabbing a piece of flotsam, something to remind him of a world outside of his wrenched body's agony.

Still, he was alive.

He stayed in that state for some time, unable to comprehend anything other than that he needed to keep breathing. He couldn't even will his eyes to open. *Breathe. Breathe.* Periodic spasms of pain wracked his brain and jolted his entire body, but he repeated that one word to himself over and over.

Eventually, the pain finally began to lessen. His heart was

still racing from the adrenaline and his mind began to work enough that he was on the verge of a complete fit. He forced himself not to panic. He had no idea where he was or where his brother was or if Mad was even alive.

Gods, please let him be alive.

Another spasm of pain jolted through his body. It subsided much faster, however, and the stiffness in his limbs lessened. The reprieve gave him a chance to organize his thoughts, muddled though they were. A significant amount of time had obviously passed although he had no idea how much. He managed to open his eyelids and was met with darkness. For the briefest of moments, he was convinced he had suffered a head injury that had cost him his eyesight and very nearly panicked again but quickly realized that a hood had been placed over his head. Cursing himself for his own foolishness, he decided his best bet to keep the panic at bay was to try and take stock of whatever he could.

They were moving, that much was easy to determine. His arms were bound tight against his body, but his dragon fang was still pressed against his skin. He feared that every bump and rock in the road might drive the sharp edge into his body. While they never did, they still sent jolts of pain through his aching head. What didn't hurt, surprisingly, was his neck where the soldier's awful blade had pierced it.

The soldier. With little to gauge of his surroundings, Will focused on him and his troops. They had been armed with halberds and blades, which meant they probably didn't have firearms or they would have used them. Their clothing and armor had been weather beaten and tarnished, so they had probably been on the road for some time. So, wherever they were taking him, he probably had some distance to travel still.

Except he and Mad had been in the Ways, the space between

realms. They hadn't gone very far in them and looked far worse than those troops, so perhaps they hadn't come far at all. Maybe the soldiers had just been through the same kind of hell as he and Mad and pressed on before returning to wherever they had set out from.

At any rate, it seemed he would soon find out. Sound was muffled through the hood, but they had come to a stop and Will heard an exchange of unintelligible shouts. The pain in his head was nearly gone but he still couldn't fully focus. Horror stories of concussions and permanent brain damage began to race through his head, but Will pushed them out. He couldn't spare the effort and distraction; there was too much at stake.

A sharp bark from a commanding voice cut off the shouting exchange: the soldier. Will's mouth twisted at his voice but he took a small comfort in his presence—if he was still here, that meant Mad was probably nearby. That was good. Will had his blade still hidden away, safe and secret, but Madigan would even the score substantially. He couldn't recall if Madigan was wearing his noctori ring when they were captured. Though, knowing Madigan, whatever happened, he wouldn't need a blade to defend them. Having one would certainly make things smoother, yes, but his body was its own weapon.

And so is mine, Will reminded himself. Madigan had told him to keep his Shade suppressed, but things had escalated quickly since then. *I'm not going to take any chances.* If he could find a way to get them to safety using his Shade, he was going to take it. *Even if that means zapping every soldier I see.*

A nearby groan confirmed his suspicion that Madigan was close. Will couldn't help but smile a bit. When his brother came to, he would be like a raging bear. As soon as the opportunity arose, the poor bastards wouldn't know what hit them.

They started moving again. Will figured that they had to be in some kind of old-time horse cart as there were no sounds of engines nearby. In truth, now that he paid close attention, there were no sounds of the sort anywhere. There were noises of people and commotion, to be sure, but it reminded him more of a large mob, like a crowd at a stadium. The dull roar of people moving about, voices and action, the sounds of movement and life and working. They had reached somewhere populated.

A city perhaps? The road was certainly smoother, and those shouts from before could have been the guards gaining entry. *That has to be it, it would make sense.* A city would be good. He and Mad could get out of this tangle and disappear into the crowds and lose anyone who might try to chase them. They knew how to blend in. They knew how to quite literally disappear, some of the time at least. They knew how to survive.

The cart turned through the streets for some time. Will tried to gauge the speed and distance, memorizing the path and turns, but eventually his skills fell short. All he could really make out was that they were moving slow and had gone farther than he'd like from whatever entrance they had come from.

It hit him, then, that he knew literally nothing about this place. He knew nothing about this world beyond stories and visions, nothing about where to go or where they were or how to get back to the Ways, how to get back home.

Panic again crept into his stomach, the blinding hood suddenly claustrophobic. They were lost, stranded in a foreign world without a map or currency or guide of any sort. He tried to think back to the cliffside and whether he had heard his grandfather tell Madigan where to go. Surely he had. Surely Mad had a plan. Mad always had a plan. It might end in split knuckles and bloody noses but Mad always had a plan. *Mad will get us out of here.*

They stopped again and more shouts were exchanged outside.

After a brief moment, the cart began to lurch forward and upward so steeply that Will nearly began to slide. Up and up the cart climbed, still winding, still weaving its way along. While time was nearly impossible to tell, an hour at least must have passed as they ascended before the path finally leveled out.

A loud, grating creak ripped through the darkness. Something massive was moving in the distance ahead and Will's mind danced with pictures of castles and drawbridges and moats. Childish fancies, he knew, something safe for his brain to latch on to, to keep terror at bay. It helped.

The cart continued to press forward, never stopping or slowing. After a few moments, the loud creak again pierced the blackness inside the hood, but this time it was behind them. They had entered something large, something that had a big gate. And they had reached it only after climbing for a long time. *Alright, maybe escape isn't going to be as easy as I thought.* But it was still doable, they would get it figured out. They could still get through this.

The cart stopped. There was more commotion outside, more shouts and commands barked. Will smirked. Apparently they were generating quite the fanfare.

"They give you any trouble?" the head soldier's voice called from a short distance away.

"None at all," said an unfamiliar voice. "The small 'un has been awake for a few hours but the big guy is still out cold. Little 'un hasn't said a word."

"Get them moving."

Will froze. How had they known he was awake? And if Madigan was still unconscious, well, that wasn't good. Their window of escape was shrinking rapidly. His mind raced. Should he try to get them both out? Should he make an effort to fight? Even if he did try, how could he get Madigan out?

He didn't have a chance to act before rough hands closed around his ankles and yanked without warning. Will left the vehicle unceremoniously and was momentarily airborne. When he crashed to the ground below, the air was forced from his lungs. He desperately tried to fight off that awful feeling of suffocation and panic. Even as they started to fill again, the hood covering his head caught in his mouth and made breathing difficult and forced. A thud next to him signaled that Mad received the same treatment.

"You bastards," Madigan said, gasping as he seized air. "You goddam bastards."

Good. Awake and angry. Will suddenly felt a bit better about their chances.

"Ensure they're bound tight and get them moving," a soldier said. "The seneschal awaits."

Will was pulled to standing, the ropes around his wrists biting sharply into his skin. Still blinded by the hood, he was forced forward, taking tentative steps as he sought any pitfalls that might send him tumbling. The going was rough but he only stumbled a few times and managed to stay on his feet.

Every few moments Madigan uttered a curse at their captors. Each time, Will could hear the sound of something blunt meeting something soft. Will could feel his brother seething. He grit his teeth and moved forward. *This isn't going to be easy.*

They stopped and started multiple times, passing through various checks and points of entry before they finally came indoors. It was cooler there and the smell of smoke touched Will's nostrils. He could hear the crackling and snapping of wood in a fire, reminiscent of so many summer nights with his grandfather around the firepit. The same firepit where a great sword had been hidden, where he had died to give them a chance to escape. *And look how far it got us.*

They were drawing nearer to the fire, so near that Will could feel its warmth radiating against his skin—a small comfort stretching toward his ragged wrists and torn clothes. But they didn't stop moving. He was pushed continuously forward. Quickly, his comfort from the flames faded. In its place was plain fear as the temperature increased, the flames growing too close, their warmth intensifying into uncomfortable heat.

Sweat trickled down Will's back. He shortened his steps. Still, he was forced forward. Madigan began to protest more and more as both were corralled toward the roaring fire. The heat continued to rise and Will began to fight against the forward motion, digging his heels into the ground and leaning away from them. Hard shoves from behind propelled him forward and onto the scorching stone floor, the heat from the fire surrounding him.

His bonds were seized and yanked above his head. The dragon fang shifted against his side but somehow stayed put. He was forced to kneel backward against a tall stone pillar. The ropes binding his wrists were secured to it and the flames seemed to lap at his broken skin. Every time he tried to shy away, he was struck and forced back against the pillar.

"Enough." A voice like slime oozed through the darkness. "I believe they are sufficiently secure. Now, Commander, let us see what you have brought me?"

Will flinched as the hood was ripped from his head. He gasped for air but immediately froze in terror. Tall flames surrounded him, leaping and dancing an arm's reach away. He could feel his skin reddening. Every inhale was filled with scorched air. Eyes darting frantically, he scanned the room and saw his brother tied to a pillar just a few feet to his left.

Madigan's face was bruised and bloodied and filled with rage. One eye was swollen almost shut but still he glared out toward a figure beyond the flames. Following his gaze, Will witnessed their captor standing on a raised platform, leaning over to stare down at them, a sick, predatory smile on his face.

"Children?" he said, the repugnant voice creeping its way into Will's ears. "You bring children before me, Commander? How quaint. Might I inquire as to why?"

"They were found trespassing within the Ways, Master Seneschal," said the leader of the band who had captured them. Will twisted away from his brother and saw the man more clearly than before as firelight danced across his armor. "They were attempting to hide near the Ruins of the Breaker. We bear them to the Crow."

The seneschal raised an eyebrow at that and looked toward the brothers, bound and blistering. At a gesture from him, the flames suddenly diminished, the scorching heat blessedly lessening. The respite gave Will a chance to glance around and take stock of his surroundings.

They had been brought to a large, enclosed chamber that was shrouded in an oppressive darkness despite the roaring flames. The roof must have been above, but he could not make it out. A haze hung over all things, grime and smoke staining the nearby colonnades. There were no windows to be seen, no lights other than the flames. Even the entryway was somehow hidden, clouded from sight.

Beyond the border of flames, their captors surrounded them, seemingly at ease. Their leader, the commander, stood ahead just below the seneschal. The seneschal himself was small and mousey with pinched lips and eyes that looked like he'd find joy in plucking the wings off flies and watching them suffer. He stared at Will unblinking, seemingly salivating with pleasure at whatever machinations his mind was turning.

"The Ruins of the Breaker? My, my, my, now doesn't that create quite the conundrum for you, little ones. As you know, passage through the Ways is strictly forbidden, but to enter the Ruins of the Breaker?" He made a sloppy tutting noise. "Well, the punishment for that is more severe, I'm afraid, even for such sweet, delicate babies."

"Cut me loose and I'll demonstrate just how delicate I am," Madigan said in a low growl, his voice iron.

Laughter filled the room. The seneschal's mouth stretched into a wet grin, his weepy eyes gazing at them hungrily. "Oh, I have no doubt that you're quite the warrior, little one. You have all the anger and rage of a mewling kitten, and I'm sure your little claws are no less ferocious."

More laughter sprang forth from the surrounding soldiers. Will's mind was darting this way and that, sizing up the room and the opposition while trying to loosen the bindings at his wrists without notice. All of the room's attention was focused on Madigan who had forced himself to his feet in defiance.

Will used the distraction to shift position to get his feet under him and into a crouch. The cool tingle of the key at his neck was soothing, grounding. He focused on it, allowing him to think beyond the panic of the moment. The heat from the fire was not as bad as he had thought, not really, and the bindings had not rubbed his wrists nearly as raw as he had thought. Yes, they were painful, but not really. Not by half.

The laughter died as the seneschal spoke again. "Commander Shifter, I truly must thank you for this little joy. It has been too long since I last saw such defiance. This is no matter for the Crow. No, no, I shall gladly deal with this myself." He began striding around the dais and down toward a break in the line of flames. There, he halted a moment then walked forward toward Madigan, withdrawing a jagged dirk from the folds of his cloak.

"You see, little ducklings, as I stated before, trespassing at the Ruins of the Breaker carries a rather harsh penalty. Only

Necrothanians dare attempt to enter there. While I am surprised at the brash nature of your passage, by process of elimination you must certainly be Necrothanian. Therefore, the penalty is death."

"What?" The shout erupted before Will could stop it. He had been focused on his slowly loosening bindings, but hearing a sudden death sentence brought him back to reality in an instant. "That's ridiculous!"

"Necro-what-ians?" Mad's brow was furrowed but he maintained eye contact with the seneschal. The man began to needle his fingernail with the tip of the dirk as he walked. "Look, I told the commander, we got lost down there and—"

"Enough lies, little sweetlings, there is no need for them here," the seneschal said, cutting Madigan off. "This is a house of truth and honesty and purity. You have already defiled this place enough by your mere presence." He extended his empty hand and placed it on Madigan's shoulder. "The only remedy is a cleansing from your blood. Don't worry, little one, the blade will go in so much smoother if you relax." The hand on Mad's shoulder gripped it hard and he raised the dirk to strike.

It was the moment Madigan had been waiting for. With a roar he smashed his head down and forward, slamming into the seneschal's nose with a sickening crunch. He leapt up and wrapped his legs around the reeling man and twisted hard, sending him spinning and crashing into the flames as the dirk fell from the stunned man's hand and landed at Will's feet. The commander barked an order and the surrounding soldiers rushed forward as the seneschal screamed in the flames, scrambling to get out.

At last, Will managed to get one hand free and he scrambled for the dirk. As soon as his fingers closed around it, he threw it toward his brother. Madigan caught it in his bound hands, snatching it out of the air. Within a heartbeat, he severed his bonds just as the first of the guards passed through the flames. Madigan barreled into him and sent the man crashing down. He rolled to his feet and flung the dirk across the room to intercept the next soldier who fell with a cry of pain, the small blade embedded in his shoulder.

The guards surrounded Madigan. He clasped his hands together and rapidly produced a brilliant bastard sword from the noctori. The guards drew up, suddenly hesitant. Madigan pressed forward, parrying and deflecting blows as the guards regrouped and attacked with their own weapons. Locked in combat, he battled seven of them at once, constantly spiraling as his feet danced across the rough floor.

Will managed to free his other hand and shot to his feet. He raced forward to his brother but could see no safe entry into the fray. Plus, miraculously, Madigan seemed to have it well in hand —the guards were having no success. Trusting his brother's safety to his own prowess, Will turned and started for the commander, who was standing apart and barking orders to his men.

Will apparently hadn't been forgotten as a soldier suddenly turned and raced toward him. He reached under his shirt and slid the dragon fang from its hiding place. He moved to meet the soldier, shock plain upon the man's face at his suddenly armed opponent. As the pair met, Will leapt and tumbled past the soldier's strike, extending his own blade and feeling it bite into flesh.

The agonized screams divided the soldiers' attention. Madigan struck hard and disarmed two guards before knocking them out cold. The group returned their focus to him and rejoined the fight. Their renewed vigor pressed Madigan back. He held them off with skill but they had rounded on him. The fire, now at his back, was growing ever closer as he lost ground.

Without breaking stride, Will rose to his feet and closed the distance to the commander. The man eyed him with amusement and stepped forward, flourishing his halberd in such a way that a trickle of fear gripped Will. He stopped just out of range of the weapon and spoke as the sounds of battle raged around him.

"Shifter, right?" Will said, meeting the commander's eyes. "This has all been a huge misunderstanding. We just want to leave. We're not whatever you think we are. Please, just let us go."

"You really ought not have wandered so far," Shifter replied. Hearing a cry from Madigan, Will glanced away. His brother was at the edge of the flames, nearly off balance. Will turned back to meet Shifter's glare as the commander continued to speak. "How unfortunate. But here's a little tip for you." In a lightning fast motion, Shifter withdrew and hurled his stiletto. As it pierced the flesh just above his knee, Will cried out and stumbled. Shifter smiled. "Know your place."

He spun forward and swung the halberd down. Will dodged out of the way of the blow, wrenching the stiletto from his leg. The pain was nearly unbearable. The limb began to stiffen. He pushed the pain away; he couldn't afford to lose focus. No sooner had he started to recover, however, than Shifter had rebalanced and re-engaged.

The reach of Will's knife was nothing compared to the commander's weapon and any feint he made was immediately recognized as such. No matter what he tried, Will couldn't get close. Dancing back and forth, Shifter maneuvered and countered him at every turn, smiling all the while.

With every step Will's injured leg grew weaker and weaker. The ground was growing slick with his blood and his feet scrabbled and slipped over the stone. In a desperate effort, he flung the stiletto back at his opponent but the commander easily stepped aside. Shifter pressed the attack and Will lost his footing, landing hard on the knee of his injured leg. The room spun before him. Shifter approached and stood over him.

"Will," Madigan's shout filled the room. "Don't hold back!"

Will risked a glance toward his brother and saw that he had also lost his footing and was struggling to stay upright amidst the flurry of oncoming weapons. Will's heart wrenched at the sight but he couldn't do anything, he was failing in his own fight. Despite it all, still his brother was cheering for him. *How can he think I'm holding back? How could he—*

His Shade, of course. Will had spent so much effort suppressing it since they were captured that once the fighting started, he was too busy trying to survive to stop. Abandoning the disconnect that his grandfather had instilled in him after years of training, he allowed the rage and fear to fill him.

As Shifter's halberd cleaved down to end his life, Will rolled away. His key electric and alive, Will leapt to his feet. Dark tendrils intertwined his legs. Shifter's eyes widened as Will vanished into the hazy darkness of the room. His mouth opened and Will barely heard him whisper, "Shadowborne . . . "

The tinted cloud of smoke within the room became Will's armor as he moved unseen. Shifter closed his eyes and cocked his head to the side, listening. At a distance, Will thrust forward and the darkness collided into the commander, propelling him backward and slamming him against a wall. Will closed in and the halberd was wrenched from Shifter's grasp and crunched, folding into a mass of metal.

Filled with fury, Will hurled the commander across the room again. The battered man pushed himself to his feet, the whites of his wide eyes a stark contrast in the dark haze. Will descended on him and sent him colliding into one of the remaining opponents facing Madigan and they both crashed to the ground.

Drawing his Shade back to surround him, Will ran forward and wrenched the commander up by the hair as the soldiers fighting Mad halted. Will knelt and surrounded Shifter in his Shade, binding him in a vice-like grip. He held the helpless man close, bound tight, and brought the edge of the dragon fang to the captain's neck.

"Now, I've been told my anger can have a bit of an edge"— Will pressed the sharp of the blood fang against Shifter's skin, nearly breaking skin—"but thanks for the tip."

A bark of laughter emerged from the wall of darkness. The remaining troops surrounding Madigan stepped back, not lowering their guard but clearly pacified. Mad struggled to his feet, still holding his noctori at the ready. The scorched seneschal and multiple soldiers lay unconscious at his feet. Shifter stopped struggling against Will's grasp and waited. Silence stretched across the room.

Light poured through the chamber as if a drawn curtain had been lifted. The dark haze vanished and the room seemed to triple in size. Suddenly, the brothers were surrounded by hundreds of guards with weapons raised and directed toward them. Just beyond the guards sat a dozen men and women in elaborate robes, and at their center, the man who had laughed. He had an unnerving smirk on his face and his eyes bore into the brothers. He leaned forward in his seat to stare intently down, his head almost unnaturally pushed forward.

"That's quite enough of that, boys. Lower your weapons, all of you. These two have nothing more to fear here."

The guards around them relaxed immediately. Madigan and Will didn't move. The pain in Will's leg flared again and he grit his teeth. Shifter loosed an audible sigh, as though bored by the situation. The stooped man continued to eye the brothers, unblinking.

"Cautious," he said. "Yes, of course, cautious. That is all very well and good. Be cautious then."

Will refused to blink against the glaring light, nervous of missing the slightest thing. His brother coughed and a smattering of blood hit the stone floor. Will took a deep breath and looked toward the new man. "You will release us, unharmed, fully equipped," he said in hushed tones. "Indeed, you shall send us forth with your blessing and thank us for coming lest you incur my wrath further and I lose patience."

Madigan gaped at his brother through swollen eyes. Will didn't falter, his blade against Shifter's throat. Madigan slowly lowered his noctori but did not release it. Through panting breaths he spoke.

"Who are you?"

"A start," the man said, his smile stretched tight around his teeth. "Yes, a start. A good start. I am your host, young child of Thorne. You may call me the Crow. Welcome to Undermyre."

13

AN AUDIENCE WITH THE CROW

"So, my young guests," the Crow said. "It appears that you deny the sentence of death?"

The man at the heart of the room was dressed in black robes, piled high atop his shoulders. His receding black hair was streaked with silver while wild, bushy eyebrows enhanced his piercing, inquisitive eyes. His stooped back added to the impression that he very much resembled a humanized version of his namesake. He turned his focus from Will to Madigan and finally to Shifter.

"Either kill him or be done with him," the Crow said with an edge. "You've nothing left to fear here, but I grow impatient when people are indecisive."

Will glanced at his brother who gave him a brief nod. Will lowered the blade and released the commander from the dark embrace of his Shade. Grunting a bit, Shifter stretched his neck before giving Will a sidelong glance and a quick smirk.

Is he smiling? There was definitely a turn in his mouth that could only be interpreted as a smile.

Shifter turned his back to the brothers and stepped up the dais and toward the Crow. As the commander approached, the Crow nodded toward the moaning seneschal. "Have your men see him to the infirmary, Commander. I would have words with him later."

The room seemed to grow colder at his words, but Shifter, unfazed, ordered his men toward the seneschal. Madigan stepped back as they dragged the injured man away and saw to their unconscious comrades. Will relaxed his grip on his blade and rolled his wrist out. Then, after the briefest consideration, retreated his Shade to a mere whisper of its former self without releasing it. A murmur went through the crowd before a gesture from the Crow silenced them all.

"I see you have inherited your father's propensity for silence," he said, easing himself back in his seat. He motioned for the boys to step forward. "Tell me, where is the Blademaster and why does he not accompany you?"

"I'm assuming you're referring to Jervin," Madigan said, his tone neutral but, nevertheless, it echoed throughout the bright hall. He glanced at his brother who shook his head, willing Mad to hold back.

"Yes, yes, Jervin Thorne." The Crow leaned forward again. "He is your father, yes? A blood relative, to be certain. But yes, Jervin."

"Davis," said Madigan. "Jervin Davis."

The Crow chuckled and waved a dismissive hand. "Yes," he said. "Jervin Davis, of course."

"He was our grandfather," Madigan said.

"Was?" The Crow raised a bushy eyebrow.

"He's dead."

The Crow's eyes became stone and his brow furrowed as the chamber erupted in whispers. The murmuring grew throughout the hall and Will noticed a few people turn and race through the doors. Shifter rolled his shoulders back and adjusted his grip on his halberd. The whole room was awash in nervous energy.

"So, the Keeper is dead then." The room quieted as the black figure spoke again. "How?"

Mad shook his head at that. "No, Crow. You get nothing else from either of us until you answer our questions."

Again the room erupted into murmurs and nervous laughter. The guards tensed and Will saw more than one ready his weapon. Madigan had done something wrong, that much was obvious. Will spun his blade in his fingers and relaxed his knees though it made his injured leg scream. It didn't matter, he was prepared to strike at whomever approached. Madigan stood square-shoul-dered and tall, maintaining a level gaze at the Crow. Will heard the sound of a blade being drawn somewhere and spun into a low crouch, his Shade erupting forth in an instant.

The crowd hushed again. No weapon emerged from the masses as darkness swirled around Will, purple and black in the harsh light. *Maybe I can find a way to keep it in this half-state all the time?*

Madigan hadn't moved, his noctori still active but lowered by his side. The silence stretched around them, the tension its own tangible presence. The Crow and Madigan both stared, Madigan in defiance, the Crow with seeming amusement. Not a sound was to be heard.

"Very well, young Davis," the Crow said. "Ask your questions."

Will smiled in relief and relaxed a bit at that but realized quickly that, if anything, the tension in the room had increased. Every single eye was on the two brothers. Mouths were agape at Madigan's apparent indiscretion, his impertinence, the impu-dence of daring to defy the Crow. Madigan himself was still cold and featureless, his stance revealing nothing of his intent. Even Will, knowing his brother's mannerisms so well, could glean little from him. Like everyone else, Will waited for him to make his mind known.

After another moment's contemplation, Madigan spoke. "Will your man survive?"

Will was as taken aback by the question as everyone else. The seneschal had been cruel, condescending, and close-minded at every turn, even threatening them with death. Yet, before all else, Madigan inquired after him?

The Crow's bushy eyebrows rose and the hint of a smile tugged at the edges of his face. "The wounds you inflicted upon him will not kill him," he said. "As far as you are concerned, yes. He will survive."

Madigan nodded. His posture relaxed a bit and he let the noctori vanish. "Do you mean any harm to my brother or me?"

The Crow maintained his unblinking stare, the foreign smile sending unused muscles quivering. "No."

"I would have your word on it," Madigan said.

Again, hushed whispers and nervous shifting rippled through the room as the Crow's smile broke into a toothy grin. It was not, however, reflected in his eyes—they were chiseled and cold and altogether unamused. "Young brothers Davis," he said as he rose, "it is the word and will of the Crow that you shall walk safely within the walls of Undermyre, free from harassment by any under my charge, for thirteen months, thirteen days, and thirteen hours from this moment." He paused. "Intentional violation of this oath by any will result in the casting of the culprit. By the Hesperawn, old and new, this is my decree."

Will had no idea what he meant when he said casting but knew the Hesperawn from his grandfather's stories. From the faces surrounding him, he could tell it was a serious oath that none of them would break. Following Madigan's example with the noctori, he allowed his Shade to dissipate completely. He returned his blade to the tattered remnants of his shirt where it sat cool and calm against his skin.

Madigan nodded to the Crow again and clasped his hands behind his back. "Very well, Crow," he said. "I appreciate your hospitality and I swear by the Hesperawn, old and new, that my brother and I will strive to abide by your laws, as we learn them, and to practice safety within the borders of Undermyre for thirteen months, thirteen days, and thirteen hours from this moment."

Will stared at his brother, aghast. *What the hell did he just say?* Madigan had sounded so confident, so proper and formal. *But neither of us have any idea what he just swore by.*

Whatever it was, it seemed to have the desired effect. The crowd nodded in approval and the Crow returned to his seat. Madigan glanced Will's way and gave the briefest of shrugs before turning his gaze back to the dais. Will nearly burst out laughing at the absurdity of it all. Madigan was flying by the seat of his pants when their very lives could be in the balance and was doing it all as brazenly as one could imagine.

"You will need accommodation, of course," the Crow said as he gestured passively toward one of the subordinates at his side. "Will you be staying in Undermyre long, then?"

"As long as it takes, thank you," said Madigan.

The Crow smiled again at that, the dark, eerie, too-long-teeth smile that stretched his face. "Ah, as long as what, pray tell, takes, hmm?"

Madigan remained quiet and glanced in his brother's direction. Will stared back, embarrassed by the blank expression on his face. Madigan turned back to the Crow and spoke. "As long as—"

"Perhaps, Crow," Will found himself interrupting, "we could better discuss these matters in private? It is a matter of some delicacy."

The Crow's sharp eyes darted to Will as soon as the words began to form in his throat, the force of the gaze threatening to drive him to his knees. *Why did I speak up? What the hell was I thinking?* At least the relief on Madigan's face was welcome.

"Wise words from such a young mind," the Crow said. He still hadn't blinked. "I do believe you are correct at that. Come. Follow and we shall discuss these . . . delicate matters."

He stood and turned sharply, retreating from the brightly lit room. Everyone separated to make a path so Will and Madigan could pass through the crowd of onlookers. Shifter smirked and turned on his heel, disappearing from sight into the throng. A moment passed. Finally, Madigan stepped close, giving his brother an appreciative nod. Together, battered and bloodied, the pair followed the Crow into the darkness.

WILL'S EYES STRUGGLED WITH THE ADJUSTMENT OF MOVING from the brilliant light into a dim room. The edges on everything seemed to be all askew, the colors of the room flowing together, twisting and playing tricks on his brain. The Crow stood before a large chest and poured an amber liquid from a decanter into a small glass. He gestured to the brothers and motioned them forward.

"When did you last eat?" the Crow said.

Will suddenly realized how starving he was. "Too long ago."

"As I expected." The man chuckled as he filled two more of the small glasses. Madigan crossed the room slowly while Will took stock of their surroundings. The room was not terribly large but definitely far from small. It was filled with ledgers and leather-bound books. Maps covered the walls and small, scribbled drawings were tacked up at random intervals. A large desk sat in a corner of the room, tidily maintained and angled toward the overly large chair that sat in the middle, its back turned to the door. Near the desk were multiple other, smaller, chairs, and a bench with a cushion placed atop.

Will's eyes were drawn to the far wall where a large grandfather clock stood. It had a face unlike any he had ever seen before, with no hands but rather there was an exposed network of brass and silver gears all spinning rapidly. The scrolling filigree surrounding its face glowed like firelight in the dark room, while just the faintest hints of a vibrant, smoky darkness edged the farthest fringes of the design. On its face, bright sparkles swirled and collided with the smoky darkness, but always the same amount of each remained. The curious piece held his attention as the colors interwove and separated repeatedly.

"I imagine you have not seen such an exquisitely designed Measure before, hmm?" the Crow said. His voice snapped Will back to attention. The man walked forward and handed each of the boys an amber-filled glass. "I do not think that your grandfather would have had such, ah, questionable pieces where you lived, no?"

"No"—Madigan swirled the liquid in the glass as he looked down—"I'm afraid we're unfamiliar with it."

The Crow nodded. "Unfortunate, but understandable. Come, sit." He moved to the corner desk and sat. Passing by the center chair, Mad and Will seated themselves. A small tray between them held warm, damp cloths. The Crow gestured to them and inclined his head. The brothers each took one and methodically started wiping the dried blood and grime from their faces, wincing as they touched the more tender spots.

"Drink," the Crow said as they drew to a finish. "It will help."

The liquid in Will's glass was somehow both warm and cool at the same time, the smell of it combining cardamom and vetiver with a hint of something he couldn't place. *Vanilla, perhaps?* No, it was something subtler, something completely foreign. Catching Madigan's eye, Will halfheartedly smiled and raised the beverage to his lips and took a small sip. It tasted divine.

"Good, is it not?" the Crow said with a smile, one far less pinched than before. "Atlantean, their finest vintage. Shame there will never be another crop."

"Atlantean?" Madigan said, squinting as he stared at the glass in his hands. "As in, Atlantis?"

The Crow nodded to Madigan and inhaled deeply, swirling the liquid. "Yes, that's right. Have you not . . . ah of course, Cascs have built a mythology around it, yes? A fable. Hmm, that means you are the first native Cascs to have tasted Atlantean wine in quite some time." The Crow smiled and raised his glass to the brothers. "I hope you enjoy the experience."

Will raised his glass and nodded appreciatively. Madigan's swollen eyes widened as his lips touched the liquid. Another small sip and Will felt less fatigued, less starving, less empty. "You called us native Cascs," he said. "What do you mean?"

The Crow set down his glass and leaned back in his chair. "Your grandfather certainly did not educate you much on the basics, did he? Fine, fine. You're familiar with the Ways, that much is at least certain. The Ways pass beneath the realms, connecting them, yes? Your realm is known to most as Cascania."

Madigan chuckled and gazed appreciatively at his glass.

"Funny, back where we live it's called Cascadia," he said. "You obviously knew our grandfather, then. How?"

The Crow was quiet for a moment as he studied their faces. Setting down his drink, he steepled his hands and looked to the ceiling. "Jervin Thorne and I had many and varied interactions over the years," he said, finally. "We were not friends, know that, but we were not enemies either. He was the Keeper before he became the Breaker, and for that much he had my gratitude."

"Keeper and Breaker," Will said. Another sip of the liquor had landed him at fully content, as though he had slept hard for an entire night after a filling meal. "I heard him say both of those once. What do they mean?"

The Crow waved his hands dismissively. "Unnecessary details for now," he said. "Another time. You said certain matters were best discussed in private. Here we are. I trust you see I have no intention to harm you, so if you would kindly honor me with your names . . ."

"Madigan Davis," Mad said. "And this is my brother, William."

"Well, brothers Davis," said the Crow, his smile broadening again into the too-tight, toothy grin. "Welcome to Undermyre. Now, why are you here?"

Will shifted in his seat. Their grandfather had told them to get to the ruling council of Undermyre, but he felt uncomfortable with the idea of divulging everything. When they had been sitting atop the cliffside, marveling at the keys and weapons and stories, everything seemed so grand and adventurous. But now, after all that they had gone through since, the horrible tunnels and getting captured and battling in the chamber just outside, now that he had a chance to sit, suddenly he began to question everything. Why, exactly, were they there? What did they really expect to accomplish?

"After the death of our grandfather," Madigan said after a moment, "we realized we had no true home. Growing up, he told us stories about this place. For years we believed them a fantasy. When we learned they were true, well, we wanted to come here and experience the world he spoke of. We set out not really planning on ever actually finding the place, and when we did, well, things just got away from us."

"Yeah," Will said, nodding in agreement. "You could say we got a bit caught up in the moment as everything just happened. We didn't really think things through."

The Crow gave the brothers a measured look and then nodded. "Yes, I'm sure," he said. "The weapons you carry, gifts from your grandfather, then?" Will and Madigan nodded. "Very fine. Did he pass anything else on to you from this realm?"

The key sat against Will's chest, cold and tingling. Something about it burned in his mind. Like his Shade, a part of him was always aware of it, always conscious of its pulses and vibrations. He looked to the Crow and shook his head as Madigan spoke for both of them. "Just stories," he said. "Stories with the proof being these gifts."

"And your gift, William Davis." The Crow gestured to Will and raised his eyebrows, cocking his head to the side ever so slightly.

Startled, Will glanced from Madigan to the Crow, hand absentmindedly reaching to the key at his neck. "My gift?"

"Tell me," the Crow said. Beneath his gaze, Will felt laid bare. "When did you first awake, Shadowborne?"

Of course, Shadowborne. Will's hand dropped from the key. Suddenly, however, he felt even more protective of it. "A few years ago."

"Remarkable," the Crow said, his eyes narrowing. "And Jervin managed to teach you to control it?"

"He did what he could," Will said. He was determined to make things as vague as possible. The Crow and Madigan may have sworn oaths, but Will was dubious. Something still wasn't sitting right, he just didn't know what. "Generally, I just focused on keeping it hidden."

"Fascinating," the Crow said as he leaned back in his chair. He took another drink before looking at Madigan. "And you, Madigan, are you Shadowborne as well?"

Mad shook his head. "No, Crow, I am not Shadowborne," he said. "I'm just a simple older brother who has to deal with a younger brother who doesn't know how to fight fair."

The Crow laughed, loud and jarring. Nodding his head repeatedly he said, "Yes, yes. Well, you never know, Madigan. You are still younger than most. Who knows what your future has in store?"

Silence crept into the conversation and the three sat sipping Atlantean wine, mystical weapons and magic keys hidden under tattered clothes. Will's leg had long since stopped bleeding and the pain had diminished substantially. The Crow had been right, the wine helped. Will thought back to the story Madigan had concocted for the Crow and realized how hollow it sounded. Whether the Crow believed them or not, he didn't know.

But I wouldn't have.

He and Mad were by no means old and tired but neither were they so young and foolish to go running about, trying to enter another world without a plan. Who would do that? Who even would consider it rational? The more he considered it, the more uncertain he became.

Will looked at the dark-clad man sitting across from him. The Crow had made a promise to them, a vow in front of all his retainers, that they would be safe from harm while within Under-myre. For thirteen whole months, they had a safe place where they wouldn't have to be concerned. *That's more than we had back home, more by a long shot.*

He drained the last drops of his wine and thought hard for a moment longer, then withdrew his blade and rubbed his fingers across the worn leather. His grandfather's voice echoed in his head, his words Will's words as the young man rolled the dice, betting everything on luck.

"Tell me, Crow," he said as if making idle conversation, "what do you know of Dorian Valmont?"

Madigan froze, glass halfway to his lips, and stared at his brother. The Crow stiffened in his chair, head bobbing ever so slightly. Folding his hands, he leaned his elbows on the dark wood of the desk and gave Will his measured, unblinking stare.

"Dorian Valmont, is it?" the Crow said. "Oh yes, young Shadowborne, I can tell you much of Dorian Valmont. My question to you in return is, why do you wish to know? What is your true purpose in being here?"

Will's palms grew sweaty under the intensity of the stare. The Crow had promised them safety and, despite his own misgivings a moment before, Will was determined to take him at his word. "We're here to kill him."

The Crow's laugh was nearly a bark, one loud single note that filled the room. His bulbous eyes glistened under the dark, bushy brows and he stood up and stooped his way over to the decanter. Refilling his glass, he turned back to Will and raised it. "The descendants of Jervin Thorne, sent to Undermyre to kill Dorian Valmont? Cheers, boys." He tipped the cup back and quaffed it in a single motion before returning to his seat.

Madigan's temper flared. He never handled embarrassment well and his silence spoke volumes. Will tried his best to think of how to proceed. After all, he had started them down this conversational path. He came up blank. For all the theatrics of his reaction, the Crow had not said one way or the other what his stance on the matter was. So, Will waited and let the silence stretch.

The Crow finally calmed and gestured to the seething Madigan. "Forgive me, Master Davis," he said. "You misunderstand. I do not mock you. Only, it is rare that I am met with such brutal honesty, especially when the end goal is quite so lofty."

Madigan softened in his seat. "We've been training for a long time," he said.

The Crow nodded. "Of course you have been. Years, no doubt. Given your ages, what, ten years at least, training under the most skilled Blademaster that Aeril ever produced as his only pupils? Impressive."

The compliment was not fully genuine, Will could tell. There was an edge in the Crow's voice, something withdrawn and condescending and altogether biting. It was sour, like liquid cream two days off, only noticeable after the third swallow. His smile didn't reach his eyes, but Will could not help but wonder if that was his natural state.

"Fifteen years, give or take," Madigan said, his tone flat. "Jervin started us early."

"Yes, yes, a very intense regime, I imagine?" the Crow said and refilled his glass again. "I've seen your combat styles. They definitely have a taste of the Breaker to them, definitely a combat-heavy regimen. How about politics?"

Mad and Will gave one another a quick glance.

"No?" said the Crow, feigning surprise. "None of the intricate workings of Undermyre, or the surrounding territories, or the greater part of Aeril for that matter? How about religion? I'm going to assume that also is a no, which means that political leanings of the various cults are also unknown. You, Shadowborne, when did you first visit Umbriferum?"

Will flushed. "I—"

"Quite," the Crow said, cutting him off. "At the very least, certainly there was extensive history, yes? Time is a strange thing here, Velier's gift saw to that, but surely you knew that. Did your grandfather at least share how long he trained Dorian Valmont as his apprentice?"

His eyes narrow and his mouth set in a hard line, Madigan shook his head.

The Crow's smile showed too many teeth. "Fifty years, give or take."

Will's jaw dropped. "Fifty years?" he said, unable to stop the waver of incredulity in his voice.

"Give or take," the Crow said with a shrug. "Aerillian combat mastery. Tactics. Strategy. Warfare. Things with which you are familiar, I'm sure. But Thorne was only one of his many tutors."

Madigan cursed and ran his hands through his disheveled hair while Will tried to wrap his head around such a passage of time training, let alone as an apprentice.

The Crow spread his hands and raised his brows. "So you see, boys," he said, "I am interested in your plan. Very interested, in fact. Because if you have a plan to kill Valmont Bloodbane, whose history I'm sure you're aware of, at least, I am deeply intrigued. What is it that you two, young as you are, bring to the fold that years of war and the combined strength of Aeril, of Radiance and Shadow and the very Hesperawn themselves were unable to? What is your great plan?"

Doubt crept through Will's body like a sickness. He suddenly felt very small and insignificant, a minuscule fleck on the backside of a titan. Madigan's face had not changed, the grim line of his jaw unshaken, his flint eyes revealing nothing.

"As I thought," the Crow said. He clasped his hands back

together as he returned to his seat. He paused as if enjoying the uncomfortable silence. "The Keeper died recently, didn't he?"

Madigan was a statue. Will gave a small nod.

"And it was sudden, unexpected."

Will nodded again.

"How?"

There was nothing for it. Surrendering, Will recounted the events of that day to the hunched figure, omitting the details pertaining to the keys. As he recalled the last moments of his grandfather's life, his voice broke slightly.

The Crow remained silent throughout, only showing the briefest flicker of emotion as Will described the sudden emergence of the creature that destroyed their home. With the destruction of the house, he stopped the story, choosing not to go on. He had answered the Crow's question. His throat was uncomfortably dry and kept catching. Growing silent, Will reached for the decanter and drained the last of the wine.

"Senraks, Jervin called it?" the Crow said after he realized that Will wasn't going to say more. "Yes, I've heard of one called by that name." He eyed the empty decanter before setting his glass down. "Senraks was the supposed leader of the Vequian, strange amalgamations known as blood beasts. Terrible creatures, golems of a sort, their origin is not known but Valmont found them to be his most ferocious trackers. For centuries, he used them in battle and assassinations when he wanted to, ah, make a specific point. When he wanted it to be particularly graphic." The Crow's face soured. "How he managed to control them was one of his many secrets."

"Did Grandda kill it?" Mad said, his voice stoic and calculating.

"Kill it? No." The Crow shook his head. "No, I would think not. I am surprised that he was able to elude it for as long as he did. It is most likely that Valmont dispatched the creature soon after Jervin's flight."

"So what happened to Senraks?" Will asked.

"Most likely? It completed its task and returned to its master," the Crow said with a smile. "Or at least tried to."

"Tried to?" Will said. "You mean it couldn't return here? It's still stuck back in our world?"

The Crow pursed his lips and gave Will a disapproving look. "So many questions. Do you ever wait for an answer?"

Will flushed and pushed himself back in his seat.

"The beast failed," the Crow said, "because, gentlemen, Valmont is dead. Congratulations, your quest is complete."

Madigan shot to his feet as Will's jaw dropped in incredulity. His head swam, though whether from the liquor or the sudden news, he didn't know which. *Just like that, Valmont is dead?*

"You're certain?" Madigan said.

The Crow gave him a disapproving gaze. "Valmont has not been seen in nearly a century. And the last sighting—"

Madigan cursed again and interrupted the Crow. "So, the trail is cold then?"

"Interrupt me again, Madigan Davis, and you will learn exactly how binding that sworn oath is," the Crow said coolly. Will thought, not for the last time, that opening up to the Crow may not have been the best move he ever made. "To answer, however, for a trail to be cold there would need to be some semblance of a trail. The last sighting of Valmont was when he plummeted to his death from the peaks of Umbriferum, the blood fang of a Blade embedded in his heart."

Will shuddered. *Not a pleasant death, not at all. Good.* His fuming brother stood and began pacing under the scrutinizing eye of the Crow.

"Then why would Grandda even set us on this path?" Mad's

voice rose in anger. "He wouldn't have just set this into motion without a plan. He was orchestrating this because he had one."

"Ah, and therein lies the rub, Madigan Davis. Your grandfather was working on outdated information. And, even if that were not the case, he obviously did not intend for the two of you to undertake this excursion alone. He was the key element that everything hinged upon. He would have supplied the means to survive in this realm. He was the answer to every single one of your troubles." The Crow steepled his fingers once more and leaned back in his chair. "And he is dead."

Will watched as Madigan's furious face froze as he looked at the Crow. He adopted a neutral mask of indifference as he met the man's gaze. "Yes," he said. "He is."

"So," the Crow said. "Knowing all that you face and aware of all that you do not know, young brothers Davis, I ask you for a third time: What is your purpose in being here?"

To Will, the question seemingly bore the weight of the world and placed it square on their shoulders. His throat ashen, he waited for Madigan to speak. Mad looked at him, eyes iron, and raised an eyebrow. Trusting his brother, Will nodded in return.

"As my brother told you, Crow, we came here to kill Dorian Valmont," Madigan said. "But since we are too late, then we shall settle for justice against the creature that killed our grandfather."

The toothy grin crept its way across the man's face as he leaned back in his seat and eyed the boys appraisingly. "Justice, is it?"

Both brothers glanced at one another again then nodded to the Crow in unison.

"Very well, then. If justice is your aim, then I do believe I can be of assistance."

"You're going to help us?" Will asked cautiously. "Why?"

"Would you rather I not?"

"Well, no," Will said, fumbling for words. "It's just that . . . I thought—"

"What my brother is politely trying to ask, Crow," Madigan cut in, "is, what's in it for you?"

"That is concern enough for myself, I think," the man said with a nod. "Yes, just so. And as you are guests here and new to our way of life, it will serve you well to know that I do not stand for my orders to be questioned, not at all. My position in Undermyre was not earned by answering every child's whimsical curiosity. You are foreign here, and therefore I have allowed for your social transgressions. You have received more answers in an hour than many do in a lifetime. Be grateful for what you receive but do not presume to inquire after my mind."

Madigan had clearly touched on a sensitive topic, something their host kept close to the chest. Valmont was dead, but the Crow was still interested in destroying his minions. Yet, if it were out of a sense of justice, why not just say it? *No. No, no, there's something else at stake here.*

Will suddenly realized that in a land where centuries were spoken of in casual conversation, the duration of thirteen months, thirteen days, and thirteen hours could pass in the blink of an eye. Gracious host or not, he figured it would serve he and Mad best to be wary of this man and his position, whatever that may be.

The Crow clapped his hands. "Come," he said. "If you are to hunt the hunter, you shall need to be outfitted properly. It will take some time to set everything into motion, of course, but such things cannot be avoided if one wishes to do things the proper way. And trust me, this course that you have determined to set yourselves on allows no room for error."

"We have a lead, then?" Madigan said.

Again the Crow showed too many teeth as the skin tightened around his face. "You have only wind, ever-changing and ephemeral. I, however, have my own ways."

He rose to his feet and motioned for the brothers to do the same. Turning, he lurched and stumbled his way to the door, as though the act of walking was foreign to him. Upon reaching it, he raised his dark cloak higher over his shoulders and exited from the room, Mad and Will following just behind him.

The immense, bright room stood nearly empty now. The conversation of those remaining died when the Crow, followed by Madigan and Will, reentered. The Crow made his way back to the grand chair on the dais that overlooked the room and collapsed into it. No sooner had he sat than Will heard footsteps striding with purpose. He turned and saw Shifter approaching the Crow.

"Yes, Commander?" the Crow said, his voice again adopting its weary, detached tenor.

"Reports of a skirmish on the roads west of Letchbrook. Scouts have only just arrived," Shifter said as he extended an unsealed scroll. "The city guard was dispatched under the command of Tyril."

The Crow took the scroll and lowered it to his lap. "Very good. And?"

The commander's eyes flicked to Madigan and Will. "Rumors have already begun circulating regarding your guests."

"Halt them," the Crow said. "No matter the consequence. I want no word of this day leaving the citadel, do you understand?"

Shifter snapped to a rigid salute. "Yes, Crow, it shall be done."

The Crow dismissed him and looked back at Madigan and

Will. "Now, to the two of you. You generated quite a bit of interest with your little display."

Mad opened his mouth to protest but was silenced by the Crow.

"I don't want to hear it," he snapped. "No, certainly not. You are unfamiliar with our ways, a lack of education that must be rectified. That, however, shall take time."

"How much time do we have?" Will asked.

"Less than some, more than others," the Crow said dismissively. "While arrangements are being made, you shall remain here under my roof. Quarters have already been prepared for you. I'm sure you will find them somewhat less commodious than you are used to, but you will make do."

"I don't suppose a change of clothes is out of the question?" Madigan's voice dripped sarcasm.

The Crow's expression showed that it was not well received. "It is being taken care of. You will find your belongings in your room. The maidservant, Ynarra, will see you tended to. Naturally, I require that you remain confined to your quarters until word of your, ah, demonstrative introduction, fades."

The point was obviously not up for debate. Will bristled and Madigan muttered under his breath, but both of them nodded in understanding.

"Good," said the Crow. "Once proper arrangements are in order you will hear from me again."

Dismissed, Mad and Will turned to find a waifish girl, not much older than they, awaiting them at the base of the dais near the fire. Her sandy hair was tied back into two loose braids and a small tattoo was marked underneath her left eye. She dipped her head politely and they began to descend the stairs to join her.

"One last thing, Shadowborne," the Crow said.

Will stopped in his tracks and glanced back.

"Your Shade is impressive, particularly fierce, in fact," the Crow said. "You will maintain control over it while within Undermyre. Do not give cause for additional rumors to spread."

Will stared for a moment in uncertainty. The threat in the man's words was barely masked. He nodded once and turned away.

❄ 14 ❄

WITHIN THE NORDOTH

The room transformed again as the brothers approached their guide, returning to a hazy darkness as they moved from the dais. The girl, Ynarra, was smiling softly, her eyes alight and calm, the color of mocha. The small tattoo was subtle but intricate, the marking itself nothing Will could remember having seen before.

"Welcome to the Nordoth, young masters," she said, giving the smallest of curtsies. "Please, allow me to show you to your quarters."

Mad ran his hands through his tousled hair again and gave the room one last scan before gesturing for Will to go ahead. Will fidgeted a moment before stepping forward. As he closed the distance, Ynarra turned and started to walk away, her steps brisk and quick. Leaving Madigan behind for a brief moment, Will shuffled quickly to catch up, wincing at the jolt of pain through his injured leg. He decided to see what he could glean from the girl in the small window of privacy.

"So" he said, trying to sound nonchalant, "do you live here then?"

"Yes," the girl said without breaking stride.

"For a long time?" Will said as he quickened his pace.

"Yes," she said again.

Will pursed his laps. He wasn't going to gather much information from their monosyllabic guide. He dropped back a few paces to walk with Madigan. His brother's swollen gaze was intent on their surroundings and Will realized he was mapping out their new home. Will cursed silently, chiding himself for failing to have done the same. Already they had made several turns and it was unlikely that, left to his own devices, he could even have made it back to the large chamber unaided. Deciding that conversation could wait, he instead took a note from his brother and surveyed the Nordoth, as Ynarra had called it.

The hallway was tall and wide, allowing at least ten men to walk abreast. The doors they passed, too, were oversized, far larger than they had any right to be. The air was dark and heavy, similar to how it had been in the chamber of the seneschal before the Crow had somehow transformed it. The walls were a smooth stone. At first, Will thought they were marble. As he looked closer, however, the color seemed slightly off and there was something strange about them. After a moment, he realized that he could find no seams, no mortar of any kind, and no visible breaks in them whatsoever. It was as if everything he passed was one continuous piece of carved stone. Yet, while they were obviously made of stone, they radiated warmth as though heated from within.

Despite the curiosity of the stonework, the halls themselves were unadorned and poorly maintained. It was as if the absence of cleanliness was excused by the darkness that was expected to hide dust and grime. And the darkness itself was strange because it was not completely dark, more akin to a hallway filled with candlelight. Yet, no candles were to be seen. In fact, Will realized that he had not seen a single candle or other light source at any place on their path. *It's just like it was before, down in the Ways.* He waited a few moments after the realization, being more attentive to the strange glow and waiting for the source to reveal itself, but his search was in vain.

"Ynarra," he said, "do you have candles?"

Without breaking stride, she nodded politely. "Yes."

Madigan chuckled slightly as Will groaned. *Oh this is going to be excruciating.*

"Do you use them?" Will said, trying to keep his voice light to hide the frustration.

"Yes," Ynarra said again.

Madigan laughed out loud at that as Will bit his tongue. *Alright, no more questions for the girl or I may end up screaming at her.*

They turned again, passing through three more corridors and a room filled with large tables and tapestries. Will could make out raised shapes upon one of the tables—*a 3D map perhaps?* He made a mental note of the room, a place that definitely demanded a second look. *Assuming we're able to sneak away long enough to look around.* Despite the harsh tones of the Crow, Will had no intention of adhering to his pseudo-imprisonment.

They climbed two sets of stairs, both spiraling in their ascent. There were no windows anywhere to be seen, no decor—the Nordoth was altogether spartan. Ynarra was silent and light upon her feet as she walked, her steps sending dust swirling in her wake. It seemed to Will that they had been walking for nearly an hour before she stopped quite suddenly in front of a door. Withdrawing a key, she opened it swiftly and without ceremony. She stepped inside and gestured.

"Please, be welcome."

Will did as he was bid and Madigan entered beside him, whistling as he did so. The Crow certainly hadn't been lying when he said the quarters would not be luxurious. They were simple and wooden and smelled of aged leaves. The room was, however, immense. It was split-level with a wooden rail separating the two, and each extended for at least twenty yards. Walls stretched high toward the ceiling, the stone jagged and jutting periodically as it reached for the domed ceiling above, at least three stories up. Drapes hung from the exposed rafters that crossed at various levels throughout the rising room. Alongside the drapery were ropes that both connected the beams and hung from them nearly to the floor. Set against the walls was grated wrought iron woven intricately, the filigree seemingly dancing against the stone. Ynarra stepped into the center and spun to face the brothers and spread her arms.

"Your belongings were brought here straightaway upon your arrival," she said. With each word she nodded, as if rehearsing a script and committing each word to memory. "They have been placed upon the beds, located on the second loft."

Madigan followed Ynarra's directing finger to a distant corner of the room where a series of wooden platforms jutted out from the stone. Reflecting over the past few hours, he chuckled.

"Oh yes," he said. "I'm certain the room was being prepared while we were being threatened with death."

Ynarra stared at him, an innocent, quizzical expression upon her face. "Threatened with death?" she said, cocking her head to the side.

Mad chuckled and gestured toward Will. "You must have missed our grand entrance."

Ynarra glanced back and forth between the two of them

before giving a polite smile and a small shake of her head. "Oh no," she said. "I saw everything!"

Madigan's grin dropped and he looked at her through the corner of his eye. "Then why . . . ?"

Ynarra smiled again and gestured to three large curtains on the opposite wall. "The windows will allow fresh air and light, if you wish it, along with a view of Undermyre, if you wish it," she said. Her tone suggested that she herself would not wish it. "Meals will be supplied at regular intervals. A washroom is in the alcove behind the third and fifth curtains on the left for all your personal needs. Clothes have been prepared and placed on your beds when you are ready for them. The fourth curtained alcove contains fresh linens."

Will glanced about, noticing chairs and benches and tables scattered throughout without any semblance of order. Mad ran his hand along one of the tables and turned to his brother. "Not bad as far as prisons go, eh, Will?"

Will snickered and crossed to the large, heavy curtains that covered the windows and drew one back with a sharp tug. Ynarra inhaled suddenly and turned away as orange light flooded into the room. Eyes widening in amazement, Will got his first view of Undermyre.

The city sprawled far beneath, set upon a hilltop at the base of the huge mountain. Studying it, Will realized that the Nordoth was part of the mountain, carved from it. Towers and spires stretched like talons clawing at the sky below him. Grand statues as tall as the tallest trees shone orange, illuminated by the evening sky. The city was surrounded by a double set of walls extending from the mountainside with a latticework of bridges stretching between them. Even at the height of this tower, Will could smell the salt air of the sea mixing with the acrid smells of smoke and city living and realized that Undermyre sat on a peninsula, the water hidden from sight by the surrounding cliffs.

It was beautiful, unlike any city he had ever seen. And yet something lingered over the city, something that turned his shock at the grandeur sour. He squinted and could see it upon the statues, cracked and worn. The buildings were tired and sagging, the air too acrid, as if the sea breeze was not capable of cleansing the scent of stale smoke from it. From above, the city looked worn and tired and neglected. He stepped back from the window ledge and turned to Ynarra.

"Lovely," Will said.

Mad was looking in a mirror, touching his bruised face and split lip with tender probes. "Not much like home, is it?"

"The windows let the warmth escape quickly," Ynarra said, not meeting either of the young men's gazes. "It is recommended that you do not leave them open for long periods of time or the chill becomes uncomfortable." She still had not looked out the window and was edging her way toward the door, eyes on the floor. "Extra blankets can be found amongst the linens in the fourth alcove. I will return shortly with food."

"So, that's it then?" Mad said. His voice was harder than it needed to be, but Will shared his frustration.

"Sir?" Ynarra said as she glanced up, momentarily swooning as she saw the open window.

"Stick us in a tower," Madigan said. "Lock the door. Keep us fed and forgotten."

Ynarra smiled again. "Exactly!" she said, the word filled with delight. "The Crow wished you to be forgotten, as you recall, and here it will be impossible for anyone to ever find you!" She curtsied and spun out of the room without another word.

"Hmm, strange girl," Mad said.

"Yeah, well, it's been a strange day," Will replied.

Madigan looked at his brother quizzically for a moment and then burst into laughter. "Yes, Will," he said as he collapsed onto a seat. "Yes, it has been a strange day."

Will grinned and looked back out the window toward Undermyre and the dark lands beyond. *We really have found ourselves in one of Grandda's stories. A strange day indeed.*

WILL EXITED FROM THE WASHROOM FEELING CLEANER THAN HE had in weeks. The shower was made from more of the warm stone only the stone was white and had multiple spouts that poured water from three sides when a lever was pulled. The water itself had been steaming and skin-reddening and Will felt invigorated.

To his surprise, the wound on his leg had completely healed itself. *Atlantean wine, for all your restorative needs,* he mused absently. As strange a thought as magical wines and the like was, he had to admit it did not sound as outrageous as it once would have. *Perhaps Grandda prepared us for this better than I'd thought, just in different ways.*

The drying cloths were woven linen and delightfully soft. For a time, Will simply stood leaning against the stone walls, wrapping himself tight, appreciating the feeling of being warm and clean and, strangely, comforted. While on the surface it didn't seem like things were going according to plan, he acknowledged that they hadn't really had a true plan in the first place.

But there they were, apparently safe, with a host who seemed set on helping them and accommodations that seemed to provide them all that they could need. Everything seemed to be progressing better than they could have hoped, in truth.

Too much seeming, he mused as he dried his hair. *Nothing is certain, yet.*

Despite not having any certainties other than that they were in an oversized locked chamber, Will allowed himself a brief moment of relaxation and appreciation. He couldn't explain why, maybe it was just the shower or the warm stone paired with the linen cloth's touch, but he needed that comforting embrace.

Finally moving away, he climbed up the steps to the second loft and tossed the remnants of his old clothes on the ground next to the bed. After Ynarra's earlier departure, he had rushed up and found his charred pack half slid underneath it. He had pulled it out and quickly upturned the contents before being flooded with relief when he saw his belt and the second fang had not been disturbed. Returning to them now, he lifted both knives from their sheaths and hefted them in his hands. They felt good. Better, even, than before, as if they were more real, somehow. He couldn't explain it. *Maybe it's just everything that's happened since we wandered into the Shanghai Tunnels yesterday.*

Will was suddenly floored by the rapidity of events. Had it really only been twenty-four hours? *Perhaps not even that much.* Could it be that he and Madigan had been in the streets of Portland that very morning?

A mild headache came on at the thought of everything that had occurred since. Doing his best to ignore the pinching between his eyes, he made his way to the shelf where Ynarra had laid out three piles of clothing for him. They were dark, lightweight, and surprisingly tough. Next to them were sets of hardened leather arm and leg guards and an unadorned, single-shouldered pauldron. There was also a dark cloak that sported a large, wide hood and, when draped about his body, sat just above his knees.

He slid on the pants then, finally, collapsed onto the bed. His stomach growled. He raised his head to see if Ynarra had brought food while he was in the washroom. She hadn't.

His hand drifted to the key where it lay against his chest. It felt warmer to the touch than before and it was still tingling. *Perhaps it always does?* He supposed that would make sense; there was no reason for it to stop now if it hadn't yet.

Will's mind wandered as he strummed the key mindlessly. Something about the keys was significant, more than Grandda let on. His gut had told him not to tell the Crow about them. The Keeper, Grandda had called himself when he gave the keys away. Senraks had called him by that name, and the Crow had said something about him being the Keeper as well. There was something important about them, something he needed to understand first. Deciding it best that the key, like his Shade, remain tucked away, he slid it from his neck and placed it in one of the pouches on the belt for safety.

"Nice pants."

Startled, Will sat up and stared at Madigan, whose wet hair dripped on the wood floor. Like Will's leg, his face had nearly healed and the bruises that covered his body had faded away almost completely.

"They're pretty damn cozy, actually," Will said, rubbing the knees of the pants.

Madigan poked through the clothes Ynarra had prepared for him and muttered something unintelligible before changing into them. His were a few shades lighter than Will's, more dark brown than charcoal in color. He sat on his bed and slid his noctori gear onto his hands.

"I've gotta say, Will, you were pretty badass today," Mad said, flexing his fingers in the glove of the noctori.

"I know," Will said with a grin. "Which part do you mean?"

"Shut up, I'm trying here," Madigan said. He was quiet for a moment although Will could tell he wasn't done. He waited. Soon enough, Mad continued. "Grandda didn't really give us much to go on and, despite the Crow's vow, I really don't know how safe we actually are here."

"Yeah but when you think about it—"

"What I'm saying is" —Mad held up a hand to quiet Will —"I know the Crow told you not to use your abilities. I know Grandda trained you for years not to use your abilities. We've been really lucky up to now that everything you've done has come via instinct. But Will, much as I love you, man, I don't want to trust in your instincts alone. We both need you to practice."

Will nodded. "No, I know," he said. Madigan raised an eyebrow and Will sat up and met his gaze. "Seriously, I know. I just have no idea where to begin or how to do any of it. Grandda never knew how to train me so I could trigger things on my own. He could do it for me, but he didn't know how to get me to do it myself."

"Well," Mad said with a shrug, "then figure it out."

"Oh, come on, Mad," Will said. *He never gets it.* "It's not that easy! Every time has been because of—"

"I don't want to hear it, Will. Grandda wouldn't want us flying blind and right now, you're a wild card. I'd rather know that you were our ace in the hole. I'm not saying don't be cautious, I'm saying we need to know what you can do."

They were both quiet for a minute before Will nodded in agreement. "I know. I'll try."

"I'm not going to make you do this alone, buddy. I'll help," Mad said. "Just try not to kill me in the process."

Will shrugged and smiled. "Like I said, I'll try."

Madigan shook his head and chuckled before running his hands through his hair. "Gods, Will, what the hell are we even doing? I've been so caught up since . . . since Grandda, that I just, I've just been going by belief, you know? Sheer will and determination. But today, the Crow, when he pointed everything out? I felt like everything was this foolish pipe dream, you know? Like, who the hell am I to do this? And just . . . this whole thing. I haven't figured it out yet."

"I know," Will said, "but you should have seen yourself out there today, Mad. You kicked ass." Madigan gave a weak smile but Will went on. "I mean it, man. You've got this. You'll figure it out and get us all squared away. It's what you do."

"Yeah, well," Madigan said. "I'll try."

"I'll help," Will said. "Just try not to kill me in the process."

"Like I said"—Madigan grinned—"I'll try."

Will threw a pillow at his brother and they both burst out laughing, each relaxing a bit. For the first time in days, they were able to be just two brothers making jokes at each other's expense. Neither imagined that they could ever lose that, that things could ever truly change. That first night in the Nordoth, before everything else that was to come, they remembered how to be a family.

❧ 15 ❧

REFRESHING REFRESHMENTS

A knock echoed through the room. Will, who had been lying on the bed dozing, rolled to his feet and looked over the railing to the door. Ynarra poked her head in and gave a timid glance around before she stepped through lightly, carrying a tray.

Will descended the stairs and made his way over to her, suddenly even more aware that he was starving. She set the tray down on the table closest to the door and, seeing Will moving toward her, curtsied quickly and then turned, scurrying from the room. Apparently, Will had already tapped out her daily allotment of words for conversation.

"So, what's on the menu at this fine establishment?" Mad called down from above.

Set upon the wooden tray were two covered plates sitting next to steaming cups of tea. Will lifted the cover and was pleasantly surprised. "A veritable feast, looks like," he called back to his brother. "Sausage, veggies, a bit of bread, nothing terribly foreign at first glance."

"Sounds like familiar fare, want to bring it up here?"

"Sure." Will hefted the tray and returned to the loft. The pair sat on their beds and ate quietly, appreciating the warmth of the food as it filled their bellies. The tea was herbal and spicy, flavors Will couldn't quite recognize but ones that certainly woke him up. After they had both finished, Madigan snatched up the dishes and the tray and returned the ensemble to the table where Ynarra had left them before collapsing back onto his bed.

"Do you have any idea what time it is?" he asked.

Will shook his head. "None," he said. "Besides that thing in the Crow's office, I haven't seen a clock anywhere."

"Me neither," Madigan said. "And the sky hasn't changed color at all. I expected it to be darker by now."

"Well, maybe their days are longer than ours?"

Mad shrugged. "Gotta be something like that," he said. "Unless, of course, they've just mastered their street lighting so nothing ever changes."

They both chuckled at that, but it was strange to think about. Their grandfather had said that time worked differently there but he hadn't said quite how. And the way that both he and the Crow talked about years and age and general time was so far beyond familiar discussion that Will couldn't help the words that fell from his mouth.

"Maybe it's magic?" he said.

Mad stared at him a moment and then started laughing. Will flushed and stammered something unintelligible but his brother cut him off.

"No, no, Will," Mad said between peals of laughter. "I'm sure you're absolutely right!"

"Man, shut up," Will muttered under his breath as his brother continued.

"No, I'm serious," Mad said. "It's just, the look on your face when you said it! Like a kid asking if Santa Claus was on the roof!"

He quieted a moment later while Will scowled back at him till Mad held up a hand to placate him. Will rolled back onto his bed and stared at the rafters high above, the day's events racing through his mind.

"Hey, Mad?"

"Yeah?"

"Why do you think they went from trying to kill us to bringing us up here?"

Madigan scoffed. "Well," he said, "if we were to listen to Ynarra, then apparently they weren't trying to kill us." He paused a moment before continuing. "But truth be told? I don't know. This place doesn't make any sense to me yet and I feel in way over my head. Maybe it has something to do with us fighting back. Maybe it has something to do with Grandda. Or maybe they just change their minds on a dime around here. All I know is I don't really trust it, any of it. Not yet, at least."

"Yeah." Will nodded. "Can I ask you something? When you were fighting those guys, what was going through your mind?"

There was silence for a moment before Mad responded. "Honestly? I don't remember. Win, I guess? Keep your guard up? Don't die?" He shook his head. "I don't know. It's just a part of things for me, just to go off instinct, I suppose. Don't get me wrong, it was scary as hell, but I couldn't tell you what I was actually thinking during it."

"Yeah, that makes sense, I guess," Will said. He was picturing Shifter, the way the commander had been toying with him at first. The way his languid, condescending smile had dropped when Will started to fight back in earnest. The fear in his eyes when he called him Shadowborne. And when Will had his knife to the man's throat, his fear had felt so . . . empowering.

Will hadn't wanted to kill the commander, but he had wanted him to be afraid. He had enjoyed it.

Realizing that made him more fearful than all the rest combined. He felt sick. He held a power within him, yes, but he couldn't blame that for the sense of anger and cruelty. He could only blame himself.

"We should get some sleep, Will, regardless of time," said Madigan, interrupting Will's depressing thoughts. "I don't know what the Crow has in store, but I don't want us to be caught unawares."

Will shifted over onto his side. "Should we, I don't know, should we alternate?" he said. "Keep watch or something?"

Mad scanned the room. "The Crow said we were safe here," he said. "But, truthfully? Yeah, that's a good idea. I don't trust it here, any of it."

"Yeah. Something feels off, right?" Will said. "It's not just me?"

"Not just you at all." As Madigan spoke, Will thought he sounded remarkably like their grandfather. "You get some rest, kid, I'll go run through some drills downstairs for a while."

Will thanked him while Mad climbed off the bed and walked down to the large open floor. Will could hear him moving chairs, clearing a space, and then rhythmic steps as his forms moved him through the room.

Will didn't climb under the blankets. He didn't want to risk anything tripping him up if something happened. Before getting too comfortable, he fastened his belt and blades around his waist to ensure they were close. He kept reassuring himself that they would be alright, but the doubt in his stomach was an iron knot. But gradually, listening to Madigan's movements below, he finally drifted into a dreamless sleep.

After a few hours, Madigan woke his brother and the two

switched. Mad collapsed onto the bed and was out before Will had even made it to the lower loft, his even breathing and occasional snore echoing in the quiet space. Will paused and surveyed his surroundings. The ground level was another ten feet down and he debated about just jumping the distance before deciding against it. There would be time for acrobatics later if he wanted. For the time being, he simply made his way down to the room and opened the window.

The view was fantastic, the orange sky just stretching out into the horizon without break. The view itself was unchanged, picturesque, but Will had already seen it. Feeling a sudden impulse, he grasped one of the nearby ropes that held the drapes and gave it a sharp tug. It was long and secured to a beam high above but, just in case, he made a small jump and hoisted himself on it to test it further. Still strong and secure. He smiled a bit and wrapped it around his arm. Then, just because he could, he leaned fully out of the window and stared straight down.

The breeze was warm and rustled through his hair with a gentle caress. It was difficult to make out anything in the courtyard far below, but at least he was able to get a better idea of how high they had actually climbed when they entered the Nordoth. Even with the rope secured around his arm, he still swooned a bit as the vertigo hit. Closing his eyes and inhaling deeply, he let himself sway in the window, the warm air a delicate kiss upon his cheeks.

Once his feet felt firm and steady once more, he opened his eyes and smiled, still swaying with the rope and scanning the surrounding area. They were in a fortress, immense and towering, that really was carved from the mountainside. The seamless stonework, the jutting passages and turning ascents of the stair, the way the stone seemed to drip and flow into itself—all of it was reminiscent of a piece of art, molded from volcanic glass.

His imagination danced to the idea of thousands of stoneworkers carving each and every hall, every alcove and room, the sheer immensity of the undertaking.

The mountain itself was the fortress, the Nordoth. What could be more impenetrable than that? He smiled as he swayed, visualizing the impregnability of such a structure. He could see the battle lines drawn, see the siege weapons in his mind's eye, see the futility for any who tried to breach the walls. No, whoever controlled this fortress held a position of great power, and to maintain control they must certainly be a force to be reckoned with.

And he and Madigan were his 'guests.'

Will hoisted himself back into the room and thought about the Crow, how easily he had commanded the people around him. How the gleam in his eye betrayed a mind that was dismantling every argument as it occurred. Despite the outwardly frail appearance, he undoubtedly held more power than he let show. How else could he have obtained such great control, maintained whatever position he held? Here in the Nordoth, high above the city of Undermyre, the Crow held sway.

Abandoning the window, Will made his way to the space that Madigan had cleared and lifted the fangs from his belt. He had barely had a chance to get familiar with the weapons and yet they were as comfortable as any he had ever held. Glancing around, he pushed a thick wooden table on its side then walked back a few paces. Hefting the smaller of the blades, Will flipped it in his hand and threw it at the table. Spiraling silently through the air, it pierced the wood easily and stuck fast.

Will smiled. The balance was amazing, far better than he had expected. He thumbed the larger blade and, after a moment's consideration, let it fly as well. To his surprise, he was rewarded with the satisfying sound of the blade biting into wood. He closed the distance and removed the knives, returning the larger to its sheath while he flipped the other in his palm. Easy. He flicked it into the air above and spun, reaching out from behind and catching it quickly. The moves were basic, but he knew that one slip would send him to the floor writhing in agony, or worse.

Despite himself, Will quickened his pace. The fangs truly were magnificent. He spent the next fifteen minutes moving with them, feeling the way the belt reacted to his body, testing the weight of the blades in a variety of actions. He ducked and twisted, sweeping across the floor while the room cooled from the open window. It felt good to move. A glistening of sweat began to wet his palms yet still the knives felt secure in his grasp. Basking in the orange glow, the gems in their pommel caught the light and shone blood red.

He paused then and admired the gems, thinking them a strange addition to the weapons. The blades themselves needed no adornment; their beauty and intrigue were sufficiently engaging due to the simple magnificence of the fangs. The gems seemed nearly identical, something darker than a ruby and heavily clouded with twisting minerals throughout. Something about them was familiar, reminding him of his key and its own swirling patterns of metal.

Will couldn't help but smile—dragon fangs, actual dragon fangs. While Madigan's noctori was magic made solid, what Will held was a remnant of magic made flesh. He wondered about dragons with all the curiosity of a child, picturing them flying through the air and men on their backs doing battle. He imagined himself amongst them, clothed in the leather armor upstairs, battling Senraks from the back of a dragon and conquering the mighty creature. Childish fancies, he knew, but still his imagination raced.

After a time, he set the blades aside and spent the next two hours exploring the room. He discovered that he could use the ropes to pull himself up to the rafters and balance along the beams. He found a small cross section where seven beams met to create a small platform, hidden from sight of the rest of the room. A small private space, tucked away, was something that Will had some ideas on how to use.

But by far his most interesting find was the alcove that contained the library. The space was not large, by any means, but it was bright and stocked with an abundance of books. There was everything from maps to histories to biographies and educational texts. Depending on how much time he and Madigan were going to be trapped in the tower, Will figured it was possible that perhaps they could make up for the lack of education the Crow had used to undermine their confidence.

He ran his hands along the books and withdrew one at random: *Cthoneric Principles of Daedlic Economics*. Hardly a riveting start. He replaced it and reached for another with more success: *Shattered Rays: The Twilight of Radiance and the Fall of Light*. He thumbed through it quickly and set it on the nearby table before reaching for another book. This one was a biography of Eriq Semnerq, a merchant who had made a fortune from his trade of metals and something called 'bindings' a thousand years before. Three centuries later, he lost everything after engaging in illegal slave trades. Will struggled to wrap his head around a world where a biography could focus on the financial leanings of a single man over a period of centuries.

He set the biography back on the shelf. A sudden excitement came over him and he scanned the shelves. His face split into a wide grin when he saw it sitting on the far end of the third shelf from the top: *The Veleriat*. His spine tingled as he traced the etched lettering on the leather binding. He pulled it down and thumbed the cover, outlining the designs. He flushed as he remembered his pretend adventures as the heroic rogue, Velier, in the battles he and Mad would imagine themselves part of. He could almost hear the timbre of his grandfather's voice reciting the stories Will had imagined as myth. His eyes stung. He set the book down on the table and looked back at the shelves.

His next find was invaluable: *Topographical Analysis of Aerillian Geography*. It was a huge tome filled with maps and legends, detailing Undermyre as well as many other locales whose names he didn't recognize. He was thumbing through it at the table when he heard the quiet knock of Ynarra at the door again. Poking his head from the curtained alcove, he watched her step into the room carrying a tray with a bottle and two glasses upon it. She set everything down and removed the remnants of their earlier meal before scurrying out of the room, eyes on the floor.

Leaving the book of maps on the table, Will made his way over to the bottle, hoping for more of the Atlantean wine. There was a note upon the tray that read, *Fita'Verxae, for a taste of home*. The bottle was warm to the touch and smelled of spice. He poured a small dram and watched the glass fog from the steam. As soon as the liquid met his lips he was transported back to nights around the campfire with his brother and Grandda, surrounded by the crackling and popping of pine and cedar. It tasted of home and health and hearth and happiness. Smiling, Will grabbed the bottle and made his way back to the library.

The next few hours passed in a strange, prolonged blink. Will was absolutely intrigued and immersed in the lands of Aeril. It was large and sprawling and each book contained maps with varying borders for the territories. He continued to pull books off the shelf and began to organize them into stacks on the desk, trying to create some sense of order. The lands seemed to be arranged in a series of cities and surrounding territories rather than any overall, larger country-based system, as if each city was its own autonomous polis. The records detailed that they all gave allegiance to Undermyre in the form of tributes and military support.

The land of Aeril itself was vast and filled with rocky mountains and peninsulas. Yet certain cities that were separated by large expanses of water shared allegiances, while neighboring cities generally had histories of uneasy truces or all-out war. Some cities changed allegiances almost every year, and the history books Will had access to went back only a few hundred years.

Despite the frequent back and forth, and the seemingly perpetual conflicts, at the heart of everything was Undermyre. Like a sleeping giant, it remained neutral, a parent watching children squabble amongst themselves, and any time things escalated too much, Undermyre swept in and restored order. Ever since the Wars of Dawning, Undermyre had maintained control. It reminded him, very much, of his studies of the ancient Athenian Empire. The biggest difference, however, was that this empire had found a way to withstand the tests of time.

Will had a stack of books devoted to the Wars of Dawning as well, the epic struggle between Radiance and Shadow that spanned nearly two hundred years. His grandfather had told of it before, but the bits of information Will gathered as he sorted the books showed that the man had barely scratched the surface. As the piles grew larger, Will began to realize how accurate the Crow had been when he chastised them for their lack of knowledge. Aeril was a world entirely beyond anything he had expected, with records extending back further than the earliest written histories of his own home.

He had no idea how long he stayed there drinking the warm wine and organizing the books. He had not even ventured into the details of the tomes yet; he simply was trying to get some perspective and determine where to start. Eventually, he heard an appreciative whistle and turned to find his brother standing in the doorway.

"Mad! Perfect, just who I needed," Will said with a start, slamming his hands down on the table in his excitement. "I'm trying to work out how best to analyze the stacks because the dates don't make sense and then all the records of battles don't follow any particular reasoning and then even if I did it would all be from Undermyre's perspective because they seem to have controlled the overall narrative of this library, which of course makes sense, but then there's all of the—"

"Have you been drinking?" Madigan said. The quizzical look on his face was hard for Will to read.

"What?" Will stared at his brother agape. "Mad, we need to focus! That doesn't even—"

Madigan burst out laughing. "Gods, Will, how much have you had?"

"And the Necrothanians," Will went on as he talked over his brother's laughter, "that thing the seneschal called us? Gods, that group was vicious! When Valmont came back, all insane and evil, they were this cult army obsessed with undeath and immortality and, Mad, they ate people. Or at least, that's what this one source says," he said as he reached for a book. It tumbled to the ground just as his fingertips closed upon it. "Oh, whoops. Regardless, they're still a problem."

"Will, seriously, how much did you drink?"

Will stared at him and then reached for his wine cup and the wonderful warmth of the bottle. "I've only had a glass or two. Maybe three. I think." As he lifted the bottle, Will realized that it was empty and the cup itself was bone dry. "Oh. Well. Still, it doesn't matter. We've got so much work to do! Do you see this? Look at all of this. It's fascinating!"

Madigan just kept laughing as his brother gestured at his discoveries. "Oh, this is perfect," he said through peals of laughter. "You should see yourself, Will. You're filthy and you're slurring and your expression is just like it always is on Christmas morning."

"Madigan," Will said, growing serious as he gave his brother a level gaze. "Christmas is far off and I don't think they even have it here. You're not getting the point here."

"Do you know how long you let me sleep?" his brother asked, raising an eyebrow.

Looking around the library and seeing how large the mess was and how many books had been strewn about, Will realized he had no clue. "Two hours, maybe? Three?"

"I'd guess closer to six or seven." Mad beckoned Will out of the room. "Come on, go sleep it off. I'll admire your handiwork while you get some actual rest."

Will stepped forward to protest and quickly realized how wobbly his legs were as the room started to spin around him. After a few jumbled mutterings, he made his way past his brother and staggered his way back up the stairs, which seemed far higher than last time, before collapsing onto the bed.

16
FINDING THE BALANCE

For a week, the brothers followed much of the same routine. While accepting the confinement was grating to both, it did allow them plenty of time to study the books in the library. Together, they began to put together a piecemeal history of Aeril and attempted to comprehend the scope of the world. When breaking their studies, they sparred in the expanse of the room, sharpening their skills and using the sturdy ropes that hung from the rafters to climb and swing as they challenged each other's awareness and responses.

There was no word at all from the Crow. Ynarra appeared frequently, supplying wine and food at regular intervals and periodically changing out the linens, but any time they tried to engage her and ask for updates or progress, she would just smile and pass over the queries entirely. Information about the food she was bringing them was rare enough; anything more important or pressing was unheard of. Despite their best efforts, they were unable to make anything of the Crow's plans for them or what he might have initiated.

Will had never really been good at waiting, particularly during periods of transition. As time passed, he continuously had to remind himself that it was best to stay within the guidelines set by the Crow, but without a flow of communication he soon grew impatient.

"Just something would be nice," he said to his brother during one training session. "I mean, aren't we guests? Aren't we supposed to get to know our host? It's just common courtesy."

"Well, are you going to do something about it or just keep waiting?"

His brother was baiting him, he knew. And Mad was right. So, determined to make good on his promise to figure out his Shade, Will began a different course of study.

After a few days of being attentive to the comings and goings of Ynarra, he soon found that her check-ins followed a relatively regular routine. Remembering the cross section of the rafters atop the room, he decided he would wait until Ynarra had come and gone. When he was certain that it would be hours before she returned, he would climb the ropes and settle in to discover what he was capable of. He told Mad his intentions and, when the moment was right, had him keep an eye on the door while Will scrambled up to the top.

He had no idea what to expect or how best to go about testing his control. Barring his grandfather's tricks, the appearance of his Shade was purely instinctual, something fueled by adrenaline and panic. Without his grandfather to guide him, he had no clue where to begin. He sat on the beams and used one of the nearby ropes to tie himself off, just in case. He closed his eyes and began to meditate, focusing inward and trying to picture the swirl of darkness around his body.

After thirty minutes, Will felt something building within him. Unfortunately, it definitely wasn't the cool energy of his Shade coursing through him. No, instead it was pure, boiling frustration.

He stood and began pacing along the beams, trying to walk off the negativity but only succeeding in berating himself and thus increasing it. He knew that dwelling on failure wasn't productive in any way but he just couldn't help it. A week of being cooped up in a single room, no matter how big, was eating away at him, and not being able to tap into the one thing that made him unique was infuriating.

Lost in his head, he misstepped on the beam, rolled his ankle, and gasped as his leg slid right off the edge. The rope wrapped around his waist was slack and, as he toppled off the edge, he shot his hand out to grasp the rafter. He missed, instead catching only the edge of one of the long draping curtains. It tore as his fingers scrambled.

Will fell.

He wheezed as the wind was squeezed from his body, the rope suddenly taut around his midsection. He swung backward and crashed into the wall. Struggling to inhale, he hung limp for a moment, all of his focus on the simple act of breathing. Slowly, he regained control of his lungs and inhaled quick and deep, his back against the warm stone as the rope dug into his torso. Realizing how bad things could have been, a glimmer of hope sprang up in his mind. He glanced around, taking stock of his surroundings, scanning for any sign that his instincts had unleashed his Shade.

Nothing.

Embarrassment crept into his disappointment and frustration. Not only was he hanging like a limp rag doll after failing to find his Shade, now his hypothesis of adrenaline and instinct had been shot down entirely. He twisted and used the wall to ease his climb back up to the beams, assessing the damage done by the rope when he fell. He had a few bruises and some definite rope burn but nothing too bad. For that, at least, he was grateful, but the injury to his pride was far more severe.

He decided not to tell Madigan about the blunder. The last thing he wanted was jokes from his big brother. He sat on the beams resting for a few more minutes before climbing his way down, chalking up the experience to nerves.

All in all, it was not a good first day.

Unfortunately, the next few days were much the same. By the end of the second week of their stay in the Nordoth, Will was getting nervous. Madigan wasn't asking any questions, trusting Will to find his own path, but Will had no clues, no insight, and no progress. Was there something he was missing? Was there something within the mountain itself that might be contributing to his inability? It was as if he was blocked in some way, like something was interfering with his ability to draw power from himself.

Or I'm just terrible at this and have no idea what I'm doing.

He didn't know what he was expecting to happen. He was untrained, a novice in every way to his abilities. He chided himself for thinking that he could just call upon them at will without work. *Naivety at its best.* He was just being impatient. His grandfather had acted as a crutch for him for so long when it came to his Shade, without him he felt lost. How had his grandfather managed to do what he had done, to call it forth? If he couldn't find it on his own, he needed something else—a different crutch to make up for the one he had lost.

ON THE THIRTEENTH DAY OF THEIR STAY WILL WAS, YET AGAIN, at the top of the rafters in the place he had claimed as his own. He was frustrated. Again. He had been for days, but it was building more than he wanted to admit. No progress had been made, nothing had changed except for sore ribs and self-doubt.

Madigan had barely left the library since they first discovered it. In that time, he had done little more than pore over the books and train his body whenever his mind needed a break. Somehow, he was managing to overcome the cabin fever that was driving Will mad, and Will was beginning to resent him for it. He resented Ynarra for her silence and polite demeanor. He resented the Crow for tucking them away in some tower and forgetting them. He resented himself for his continued failure to master his Shade.

Groaning, he gave up on trying to meditate and sprawled out on the beams and stared at the stone ceiling, brooding. He thought back once again, searching for any commonalities from the recent appearances of his Shade. When they had been climbing the cliffside, it was fatigue and frustration. Battling against the blood beast, Senraks, it had been fear. And within the Shanghai Tunnels, fighting that monster in its depths? He couldn't even remember seeing his Shade then but he had been furious and detached in his focus. Then, in the Crow's chamber, it was rage. Yet he had proven that the surge of adrenaline that stemmed from all of those wasn't the connection, so what was? What had changed?

Then it clicked. Will bolted upright. He jumped to his feet and scrambled over to the ropes, quickly descending to the main floor. Turning, he raced up to the loft and leapt onto his bed, scrambling under the huge pillow for where he had stashed the belt that held the fangs. Pulling it out, he unsnapped the pouch and withdrew his grandfather's key. It wouldn't explain the cliffside, but every other time he had been able to control his Shade had been when the key was around his neck.

He raised it over his head and tightened the cord so the key hung just below his neckline. As before, it was cool and electric and set the hairs on the back of his neck on end. It was the chill wind on a summer night. It was sipping the *Fita'Verxae*. It was coming home.

Immediately, as he felt its tingling energy coursing through him, he was invigorated—all the frustration and anger of the past two weeks were lost in the tantalizing electricity of the small key. Smiling, he made his way back up to the rafters with new determination.

He sat with his back up against the warmth of the wall and crossed his legs, closing his eyes and focusing on the key itself. He focused on the way it danced across his field of vision when he gazed at it, focused on how the lightest brush against its surface sent delightful energy coursing through his limbs. His mind wandered in exploration and sensation, lost in a state of wonder at the small, seemingly innocuous object.

Time quickly became irrelevant as his fingers brushed the key at his neck, feeling his skin burn and cool in rhythmic patterns where it lay against his skin. It was trying to recall a dream upon waking as it sifts away, returning to the scattered reaches of your mind. Whatever that something was, it was hidden in the depths of the key, shrouded in its mystery.

After focusing for so long on exploring the key itself, he remembered his original purpose. Will turned his focus to searching inside himself for what he sought and, almost like an afterthought, quickly found it, as though it had been waiting there for him all along. He opened his eyes and brought it out into the warm light of the day.

It was strange, then, seeing the Shade silhouetting about his body. For the first time, Will really focused on feeling it rather than seeing it. It was not separate from him, not a foreign entity joined in symbiotic harmony. No, rather the Shade was Will, a part of him no different than his limbs or hands or feet.

The key bounced against his collarbone as he stood. He chose to stretch his arm in front of him. Of course, his arm moved. He chose to take a step forward and his leg moved forward, coming down firmly supported by his foot. He chose to reach out and touch the nearest rafter with his Shade and, easy as that, the Shade stretched out to the beam, cloudy and swirling in the light.

Excitement bubbled in his stomach. His grandfather's warning, "Don't overextend," firmly set in his mind, he pushed outward, grinning as the Shade narrowed into a tentacle-like stream as it moved. Before going too far, he stopped and imagined the Shade dispersing like a cloud in the air. As he did, a fog covered the ground and the air became hazy and dark.

Backing against the wall, the stone's warmth touched his body. He willed it to be cool and it was cool. The brightness of the room was too much and Will sought darkness. Darkness came and the light was pushed far away. With every act, the key at his neck sang.

He moved around the space, drawing his Shade close and practicing quick movements and bursts of energy forward. Caught up in the moment, he overextended and gasped. He collapsed to the rafters, curling into a ball and gasping for air. After what seemed like an eternity, the pain subsided and he rose to unsteady feet. Choosing a more concentrated path, he focused on slow, controlled movements and controlling his breath. His Shade as a cloud, with each motion he moved it through the space, the cool darkness of it flowing naturally with the forms.

After an hour or so, Will descended to the main level. Madigan had left the library and was practicing with his noctori in the common area. Breakfast had been cleared from the table and replaced with lunch, meaning that Ynarra had come at some point while Will was high above. He whispered a silent thanks that his space was hidden away from sight, lest he risk discovery on his first successful day.

"Learn anything useful up there today?" Madigan said as the blade swept through the air. His movements were strong and controlled, the noctori a natural extension of his body.

Will grinned. "There was a bit of progress."

His brother stopped and turned to him. "A bit? That's a good sign. You'll get there, I know it."

Still smiling, Will winked. The room faded into darkness. His brother's eyes grew wide as around him swirled a dark cloud. The air cooled and he could see Mad's skin, slick with perspiration, rise in goosebumps. Madigan spun in a circle and stared at Will slack-jawed. "Will, is this . . . ? Did you . . . ?

"Alright," Will said with a casual shrug. "Maybe there was more than just a bit of progress."

He released the darkness and light again flooded into the room, which suddenly seemed overly harsh and blinding. Mad squinted and crossed the distance between them and grabbed his brother in an embrace.

"That was incredible! I've never seen you do that before— how long have you been able to do that? The room, how did it get so dark? How did you manage to . . . just . . . Will! What changed?"

Will couldn't help but feel proud of himself. It was rare to see Madigan so excited. "I can't really explain why, but once I put on Grandda's key, things just clicked. I don't what this thing is or why it helps me do what I can do but I'm never taking it off again."

"The key?" Madigan raised an eyebrow. "Really? Wow. But, the darkness? The cold? That was all you too?"

Will nodded and relayed to him what he had tried and where

he had both succeeded and failed. Madigan's excitement visibly dimmed and Will saw the face of a tactician overcome the brotherly glee. By the time he ended his recount, Mad was nodding, already back in his own mind.

"This is great, Will, we can use this. I don't know how yet but this is a game changer."

"Hey, man, you said you wanted an ace in the hole, so here I am!"

Mad nodded again. "Definitely. This is just today, however. Your control has come and gone in the past. We need to make sure this isn't a fluke. We need you to train harder."

Will's smile fell away. "I know, Mad."

Madigan went on as if not even hearing him. "I've been going over the histories and it's going to be harder than we expected. Grandda wanted us to get involved but it seems the only way to make a name for yourself here is by being some kind of warlord. Whether we want to or not, we either need to build an army or end up in someone else's. There's no way to do this without fighting. Plus, everything I've found says we'd have better luck going back home and convincing everyone there to come fight rather than help this place unify. Every city here seems to be warring with each other."

"I know, Mad."

"I have no idea how to unify anyone or even get us to a position where we could be heard by anyone who might take us seriously. The Crow's been a great start but he definitely has his own agenda. I know Grandda talked about getting you to the Halls of Shadow to train and I still think that's a good idea. But, unfortunately, it looks like if we tell anyone you're Shadowborne, well, it could go badly for us."

"I know, Mad."

"So that's why we need to keep you secret, to keep you safe.

But at the same time we need you to train harder, to be more prepared. I need you to be at the top of your game, Will."

"Dammit, Mad, I said I know!" Will couldn't understand why Madigan was patronizing him. Figuring this out had been such a massive step forward, and Mad was acting like it wasn't enough.

Why is it never enough?

Madigan crossed his arms at Will's outburst and was silent, waiting. Will, temper still flaring, finally spoke, forcing himself to keep his voice level.

"I understand the stakes as well as you do," he said. "I don't need a lecture on how I'm letting you down by not being capable of more yet."

"Seriously?" Madigan said in a flat voice. "You're going to go there with this? I'm not lecturing. I am legitimately trying to keep us alive. Do you get that? Do you even know what they do to Shadowborne who can't protect themselves?"

Will groaned and rolled his eyes. "I can protect myself."

"They flay them alive. Do you get that, Will? They skin them while they scream. They try to cut out whatever it is that makes you you and then they sew it into their clothes."

Whatever Will had been about to say, he lost. Something lurched inside him. "They . . . What?"

"Oh, I'm sorry, did you not get to that book yet?" Madigan said. His tone was flippant and he gestured to the surrounding room. "We're not home, Will. Our rules don't work here. This is a world of superstition and fear and the people who claim to protect us could very well be the same who will turn on you the first chance they get."

"They want to turn me into a coat?" Will said, a slight tremor in his voice.

Madigan stared at his brother flatly. "It'd be a pretty ugly coat."

"I didn't know, Mad."

Madigan broke his stare and ran his hands through his hair. "I'm not trying to be an ass here, Will. Really, I'm not. But this place is even more different than either of us were expecting, I think. I'm trying to find out what I can to keep us alive. To keep you alive." An awkward pause ensued. Madigan crossed the room and picked up a piece of bread from the platter of food and mindlessly took a bite out of it.

"I don't know, Mad. I disagree."

Madigan looked up as Will took a deep breath and met his brother's eye.

"I think I'd be a pretty good-looking coat."

He ducked just in time to avoid the bread.

17

UNPLANNED PLANS

With the aid of the key, Will continued to work on mastering control of his Shade. He discovered that he could fade into darkness where there was none, expanding the Shade to the edges of his surrounding space and plunging it into darkness. He could shut out the light completely while still somehow maintaining his own ability to see with ease. It even seemed like he could pull light toward him and absorb it into the Shade.

He learned that he could control and condense the Shade into tendrils that, with difficulty, could move small objects short distances or completely enwrap someone, rendering them immobile for a brief time, like he had done to the commander. He could disperse the Shade in the air to a point where it was nearly invisible, spreading it so he could control the visibility in a room without anyone knowing the source. At first, every manipulation took his full concentration to maintain, but with each passing day he became more capable.

Madigan, too, benefited from Will's progress. The pair would wait until Ynarra had come and gone and, knowing they were safe, would train together with the Shade. It started simple enough, like playing hide and seek, only Will had a remarkably unfair advantage. Soon, though, they began to incorporate Will's ability into their sparring. During an engagement, whenever Will thought that his brother would be least expecting it, he would vanish from sight or flood the room in utter darkness, attempting to catch Madigan off guard.

At first it was easy and Will's success rate was so great he grew overconfident. Before long, however, Madigan began to notice nigh-imperceptible changes in the air and the darkness. As Will faded, slinking into the black and moving as silently as he could manage, Madigan would tense and drop into a low stance, his head cocked to the side.

Will learned quickly that his grandfather had been correct; what he had mistaken for invisibility in his youth was actually something completely different—it was as if the Shade caused one's eyes to just overlook the darkness. This meant that, with enough concentration, a determined mind could pierce through his illusion. Madigan told him of this as he helped Will rise from the ground after being re-engaged so quickly following a disappearance that he had been sent tumbling.

Will was thrilled at finally, after so many years, learning to control his Shade. But by the end of the third week of their stay at the Nordoth, he had had enough of the tower. The Crow had been entirely absent, no word sent, no communication of any sort. The only person he had spoken to other than Madigan was Ynarra, and she quite apparently had no skill in the art of conversation. While he learned much from the library and learning to control his Shade had proven invaluable, he was going stir crazy.

"I just don't understand," he groaned to his brother. Ynarra had just departed and the pair had not yet begun to spar. "What are they playing at? And how are you not going insane right now? I am. Gods, I am."

Madigan sat for a moment and gave his brother an odd look. He closed the book he had been reading and leaned forward in his seat. "So, why don't you get out for a bit?"

"Because it's pretty damn apparent the Crow wants us stuck up here."

"I seem to remember a young kid who had no problem sneaking out at night when he thought Grandda was asleep."

Will flopped back in his chair and shook his head in exasperation. "That was totally different. That was home. I knew what I was doing and where I was and where I was going!"

Madigan cocked his head to the side. "And you don't think that could be valuable information to gather here?" He gestured at the table of books before him. "We've at least got some semblance of an idea of what the world is like outside this fortress. But when it comes to these walls themselves? We've got nothing."

"Exactly!" Will threw up his hands. "It would be great information to have but we've got nothing to go off of."

Madigan sighed and put his head in his hands. "So, go get the information, Will."

Will blinked. "What?"

"Go. Get. Information. You've figured out the Shade well enough to do some recon. Use it to hide and go gather intel, collect data, spy, whatever you want to call it. But get the hell out of here and go learn something we can use."

"Yeah," Will said as he furrowed his brow. "I mean, I could but . . . " He poked idly at the book on the table before him. "But what if I get caught? I mean, you've figured out how to find me when I'm hiding, what if everyone else can do that as well?"

"Do you have any idea how hard it is for me to do that, even with your predictable behavior?" Madigan said as he ran his hands through his hair. Will started and began to protest but Mad held up a hand. "You're my brother, Will. I know you. Your patterns don't change too often. They don't have that. Plus, if I'm being honest, half the time I find you it's just luck."

Will was starting to feel a bit more confident. *I could finally feel useful.* But at the same time, there were so many unknowns that he didn't feel as confident as he'd like. "And if I'm seen . . . ?"

"Don't be," Madigan said with a shrug and leaned back in his seat, resuming his book.

Will thought for a moment. Technically, they weren't prisoners; the Crow had made that clear by calling them his guests. Even if he did get caught, he supposed he could just plead ignorance, as awkward as that thought was. Then again, the last time they had been caught somewhere they weren't supposed to be, ignorance hadn't worked out for them too well.

Still, his Shade gave him an advantage. When Ynarra led them to their quarters there had not been another living soul in sight, only her and she was . . .

"What about Ynarra? She'll notice if we're gone."

Madigan shook his head from behind his book. "We? We won't be gone. You'll be gone. I'll be right here."

"What? Why?" Will felt like he knew the answer before his brother said anything but the idea of venturing around the Nordoth alone gave him the creeps. "You know I can keep both of us from being seen. You should come."

"She's never suspicious anymore if she comes around and you're not here," Madigan said. Will raised his eyebrows in surprise. Madigan waved a hand dismissively. "Oh yes, she used to be, but I explained your preference for the rafters and she accepted it quickly. But if she arrives without being able to find either one of us? That'd create some problems, I imagine."

"Yeah," Will said as he looked to the floor. "I suppose."

Mad eyed him quizzically. "Why the sudden hesitation? Five minutes ago you were bursting at the seams to get out of here."

Will shrugged. "I dunno. I just don't like the idea of separating is all."

His brother's face softened. "Getting all sappy, kid?" Will flushed at Mad's words. "We're fine. You're gonna be fine. Just go check the place out a bit. Go stretch your legs for both of us. See if you can manage to map this place out a bit without getting lost."

After a moment, Will nodded.

A few hours later, after Ynarra had come and gone once more, Will stood by the door and did a few quick stretches. At a thumbs-up from Madigan, he unlocked the door and slipped out into the hall without a sound. With the key vibrating against his chest, he cloaked himself in darkness and quietly shut the door behind him. Taking a deep breath, he hugged the walls and set off down the corridors.

In his mind, he returned to the nighttime dreams of his childhood, escaping into the depths of his imagination. Each step was precarious with traps and pitfalls as the mighty William Davis snuck his way through the fortress of the enemy. Barely avoiding detection, he was living a story fraught with danger and suspense as he narrowly avoided patrol after patrol of guards and servants and whomever else he came upon, his Shade acting as his magical shield against evil.

In truth, however, Will was disappointed. The novelty of the venture wore off as he explored the dusty corridors one by one, circling back constantly to make sure he knew the way. For the two hours that he risked mapping out the Nordoth, he never saw another soul. He tried a few of the massive doors he passed but most either led to vacant rooms or were locked. He kicked himself for not bringing along his picking supplies. Once, he heard footsteps in the distance and his heart leapt—but no one appeared and the sounds soon faded. Against his better judgment, he attempted to follow but, by the time he rounded the corner, they were long gone.

All in all, it was a dull excursion.

When he returned to the room and told Madigan, his brother grabbed a nearby ream of blank paper and something to write with.

"Go over it again," Mad said. "Tell me everything you remember."

Will did. As he spoke, his brother began to sketch out a map of the area. Periodically, he stopped Will and had him backtrack, jotting notes in the margins. Whenever Will mentioned going up or down a staircase, Madigan made a notation and then moved to a new sheet of paper. When they had finished, Will was surprised to see that his brother had drawn a relatively intricate map.

"Actually, yeah," he said as he looked at it. "That all looks about right. Since when did you have any cartography skills?"

Madigan shrugged. "You had your dorky pirate hobby, I had my own."

Will laughed. "You should've told me," he said as he looked over his brother's drawings. "I would've bugged you to make me all kinds of elaborate treasure maps."

"I'm definitely sure that's exactly why I never told you," Madigan said, maintaining an air of severity that sent them both into peals of laughter. He made a few more notations on each of the sheets and then climbed to their loft and hid the map within his pack.

"Tomorrow," he called down to Will, "do you think you'll be able to go farther?"

Will grinned. He had cut his exploration short because of jitters and uncertainty about exactly how long Ynarra would spend away—and boredom, if he was being honest with himself—but she had yet to return. She was prone to being gone for upwards of five hours at a stretch. Could he do more?

"Absolutely," he hollered up to his brother.

Madigan trotted down the stairs and jumped onto the chair next to his brother. "Good," he said. "I've got a goal for you."

"Yeah?" Will said, suddenly feeling remarkably important. "What's that?"

"Find that room with the large 3D map in it," he said. "Do you remember it?" Will nodded. "Good. If you can get there and give me as accurate a description of that as you just gave me about the halls and stairs, I think I'll be able to piece together some more about both Aeril and the Nordoth."

"You think it's a war room, don't you?"

Madigan nodded. "I do. And if it contains the surrounding territories, it'll have troop estimates on it as well as points of power. Fortresses. Populated towns. Unpopulated towns." He spoke the last with emphasis and Will picked up on it immediately.

"In other words, places to avoid and others where we can lie low," Will said. "If the Crow doesn't live up to his end of the bargain."

"I'm still trying to give him the benefit of the doubt," Madigan said, "but I refuse to let us be played for fools. Like Grandda said, always have an exit strategy."

Their conversation was cut short by the timid knock of Ynarra. Madigan's face lit up at the sound, which surprised Will. They were hardly starving.

Mad hopped up from his seat and grabbed their empty lunch tray from the table and held it up as Ynarra entered. She met his eye, flushed, then bowed her head quickly and shuffled forward, placing the fresh tray on the cleared table.

"Thank you, sir," she said quietly. "But, as always, that isn't necessary."

"And, as always, it is my pleasure to help," Madigan said with a smile.

Will's eyes grew wide and a far-from-subtle grin broke out on his face. Ynarra flushed an even deeper shade before gently taking the tray from Madigan. She turned and darted from the room. As Madigan turned back to him, Will burst out laughing.

"What?" Madigan asked, mustering up as much innocence as possible.

"Oh, nothing at all, Mad, nothing at all."

"I like to be helpful." He shrugged as he picked up a roll from the tray. Then speaking with a feigned flourish, he said, "Good sir, you know that I love to be of service, when able."

"Yeah, you'd like to be servicing something, alright," Will said with a grin. The shock on Madigan's face made Will laugh even harder and, after a moment, his brother joined in. For the remainder of the evening the pair joked and egged one another on.

They had a plan. They were regaining control of their situation.

And they'll never see us coming, Will thought with a smile.

THE NEXT MORNING, AFTER CONSULTING WITH MADIGAN, WILL prepared to set out for the map room. With both of them wracking their brains, they had been able to piece together the likeliest path that would lead him straight to it. Barring any unforeseen circumstances, he should be able to spend enough time inside that he could even bring paper with him and make his own notes while he was there.

Before long, Ynarra arrived with breakfast. She flushed bright red when she saw Madigan and Will forced himself to suppress a chuckle. *I don't think she gets too much attention, given the way she flits about when Mad smiles at her—I should go easy on them.*

After she departed, Will ate a quick breakfast while Madigan began to pore over another tome from the library. Once Will judged that enough time had passed, he made his way to the entryway, grabbing his lock-picking kit along the way. *No locked doors to keep me out this time.*

As he opened the door to leave the room, something gave him pause. He halted, door ajar, and looked around. He couldn't place it, a feeling of . . . *what?* He didn't know. But he knew he wasn't mistaken, there was definitely something awry.

He glanced around. There was something different about the halls outside. There was no one in sight, no one to see him, so he wrapped himself in his Shade. Immediately, the feeling intensified. His key was active, yes, but in a different way. The vibrations made him feel uncomfortable, sick, *wrong*. The walls were the same. The sourceless light still shone dully. There was no one else around and the dust beneath his feet showed only traces of Ynarra's footprints coming and going.

That was it: The footprints, there was something strange about the footprints.

Will crouched. *Why am I wasting my time staring at Ynarra's tracks?* Still, he couldn't deny that there was something off about them. They were outlined in the dust, but the lines seemed almost impossibly precise. He ducked down for a closer inspection and saw that it was as if every single step Ynarra took had moved precisely the correct amount of dust. There was no dragging of feet, no shuffling, not even a gust of air to mar the print. It was the most perfectly proportioned footprint imaginable.

Scanning outward, he saw that the dust itself appeared somewhat different than the previous afternoon. *There's more of it, isn't there? It looks . . . deeper.* Sure enough, to the naked eye it appeared as if it had been months since his last outing. In fact, no trace remained on the ground of his own prints from yesterday or any of Ynarra's prints from previous visits. All that remained were those left by Ynarra on her most recent visit.

Will paled. How many times had he heard that time worked differently here? Had something happened? How much time had passed? His heart suddenly seemed to be in his throat. *Something's wrong.*

He felt a strange sense of vertigo, even within the Shade. He stepped back into the room and gently shut the door behind him. "Hey, Mad?"

"Library," he called from the alcove. Will made his way there, tracing one hand against the wall for support. Madigan glanced up from his book. "Did you forget something? What did —" He stopped when he actually looked at Will. Rising to his feet, he clasped his hands together, his noctori at the ready. "What's wrong?"

"This is going to sound crazy," Will said, his voice shaky. "But, do you know how long we've been here?"

"Exactly?" Madigan cocked his head to the side and kept glancing behind Will, looking for any unwelcome guests. "No, I don't know. I'm guessing it's been about twenty-three days or so. Based on our sleep cycles and food schedules and the like, it seems the most accurate."

Will did a quick mental count and then nodded. "Yeah, that's what I thought too."

The tension hadn't left Madigan's body and Will's twitchy fidgeting didn't seem to be going away. Will stayed quiet, obviously lost in thought, until Madigan finally dropped his hands in exasperation. "Are you going to elaborate or am I just supposed to stand here and stare at your furrowed brow and be lost in eternal curiosity?"

"Oh, yeah," Will said. "Sorry." He glanced behind him, making sure he had closed the door to the room securely. "It's just weird. There's something different out there. It's going to sound crazy but . . . I mean, I couldn't place it initially, but the dust on the ground and everything seems . . . more settled. Almost too settled, if that makes any sense."

Madigan's stance relaxed and he raised an eyebrow at his brother. "Dust is making you nervous?"

"Shut up," Will said, embarrassment creeping into his already confused thoughts. "Yes, something about the dust. Something is just off. The hallway looks like no one other than Ynarra has used it at all."

"Other than you, no one has, Will."

Will fidgeted and glanced back at the door. "No, I know. This is different," he said. "There's nothing else, literally nothing. There's no sign of movement from earlier, nothing from yesterday or last night or anything."

"So what?" Madigan said and, resuming his seat, picked up his book. "You think they somehow got us to go all Rip Van Winkle or something?"

"I don't know," Will said, feeling even more insecure now he had vocalized his thoughts. "But something isn't right. I don't think it's a good idea to go out there."

Madigan set his book down on the table again and rose, passing his brother and heading to the door, muttering something uncharitable about younger siblings. Will followed, trying and failing to come up with an appropriately badgering response. Opening the door, Mad peered outside and glanced around for a moment, scanning the area before dropping to a crouch. After nearly a minute he stood and quickly closed the door and reopened it before returning to a crouch. He gave a slight "hmph" before he stood and turned back toward Will.

"Something isn't right," he said, his face set in its stubborn mask of concentration.

"That's what I've been telling you for the past five minutes," Will said as he pointed to the door. "Something isn't right!"

"That dust isn't moving."

"Thank you, Captain Obvious," Will said as he rolled his eyes. "Like I said, there is way more than there should be!"

"No, Will." Madigan fixed his brother with a level stare. "I mean it isn't moving at all."

Now it was Will's turn to get impatient. "Seriously, Mad. Did you listen to anything I said in the other room?"

"Did you blow on it?"

"What?"

"Did you blow on the dust?"

Will stared at him in incredulity. "Why the hell would I blow on it?"

"Because blowing on dust sucks," Madigan said. "It swirls around and gets stuck in the air forever. They always do it in movies and it's fine, but in real life it just makes you sneeze a bunch." He bent his head down to the dust and blew hard.

Nothing happened. The trace of Ynarra's prints were still crisp and clear. Madigan's gust had not changed a thing. He took a step back and closed the door before turning back to Will, his eyes darting back and forth in thought.

"I don't suppose you have the ability to control dust?" he said.

"No," Will said, shaking his head and rolling his eyes. Then, at a look from his brother, he thought about it for a moment. He had never tried to before. "I mean, I could probably make the air look dusty. But to actually create dust? No"—he shook his head —"not at all. All my stuff is just like an illusion. One that can also do some physical stuff, I guess."

Madigan's eyes narrowed a moment, then he nodded and began to move back to the library. "I think our little excursion plan is going to need to be put on pause."

Will followed him. "You think they know I went out yesterday?"

"I'd hazard a guess that they've got a pretty good idea of it."

Will cursed. *How did they manage that?* "So, they set out some kind of tracing element to be sure, to determine if I went out again."

Mad sat down to his books. "I don't think that they know for sure. If they did, I doubt that they would have done whatever they did. Apparently, they need to get proof for whatever reason."

"But we're probably being watched more than they've let on."

He nodded. "That's my guess. If it were me and I had two strangers in a tower, one with crazy abilities, I'd be watching them for sure."

Will flopped into a chair, thankful at least that the paranoia he'd experienced wasn't completely unfounded. The key was still making his stomach twist and he realized that he was still keeping a mist of the Shade about him. Releasing it, the sensation in his stomach lessened. Absentmindedly, he reached for the nearest book—*Lightfall: A Stratagem*—before idly opening it and haphazardly flipping through the pages. "So, lie low then? Back to the books and all that?"

"For now," Madigan said. He was glancing between the door and the window and the rafters. *He's working through something, that's for sure.* "But, truth be told, I'm about ready to get out of here." Will lowered the book and met his brother's gaze. "Dangers or no, you and I need to get moving and the Crow, well, he hasn't been the most forthcoming host."

Will set the book back down on the table and leaned forward, suddenly very interested in his brother's schemes. "What are you saying?"

Madigan ran his fingers through his hair and leaned forward, speaking quietly enough that even Will could barely hear him. "I'm saying that it's time to start packing."

❧ 18 ❧

CEPHORA

The brothers agreed to wait three more days before making any moves in order to hopefully allay any suspicions. During that time, both did their best to lie low, although Will was uncertain how that was any different than what they had been doing previously. With each meal, they began to ration and save the food Ynarra brought, gauging as best they could how to manage on so little for an indeterminate amount of time. Will, who always had a tendency to squirrel away snacks for later consumption, was perfectly suited to it, but Madigan was soon grumbling when he thought Will wasn't watching.

Ynarra showed no sign as to whether she was aware of their violation of the Crow's orders. She continued every visit as she ever had, the only noticeable difference, as far as Will could see, being that she seemed to stay a few moments longer than she had when they first arrived. That, and she smiled at Madigan more and more. Even engrossed as he was in their plans for departure,

Will felt good when he thought of his brother falling for the serving girl.

He had taken to dressing in the full garb that had been provided—hardened leather armaments and all—each day when he and Madigan trained. The threat of detection served one bene-fit: he stopped using his Shade when they sparred and realized just how much he had come to rely on it recently. As Madigan put it after one particularly painful bout, "You've gotten lazy, kid."

He was right, Will knew, but Madigan did not show any restraint in reminding him of it. Will ended each session far more bruised than he ought to be, and he couldn't help but berate himself for it. *All those years of training without, undone in a matter of days? No, that can't be it. I'm just too distracted.*

When the third day arrived, Will awoke with a fierce anxiety gripping his insides. He made his way down from the loft and, with no guarantee of the next time he would have the luxury of running hot water, enjoyed a long shower. As he dried himself, he saw that Ynarra had been by and that Madigan was already turning his attention to the food.

Will dressed and met him in the library and the pair ate in silence, tucking the greater portion of the food away for later. They borrowed some of the more useful looking maps that wouldn't weigh them down too much—Will reluctantly left *The Veleriat*—then set about checking their final preparations.

The plan was to wait until Ynarra's second visit and store everything she brought. Hidden within Will's Shade, they would descend through the halls soon after she left and make their way to the lower levels, using any shadows they could. Once low enough within the Nordoth, they would exit through a window and then skirt the edges of the courtyard closest to the mountain-side. The walls would prove a challenge, but once they passed them it would be easy enough to disappear into Undermyre. "Or, at least," Madigan said as he snuck another handful of nuts into his mouth, "I hope it should be."

Will spent the next few hours double checking his supplies and attempting to stretch, to meditate, and focus. He was not so immediately concerned with what was about to happen but rather the part that came after. Their departure from the castle was going to be tricky enough, yes, but once they made it out into the city and the surrounding territories, that's when the real challenge would begin. Two foreigners, alone on unknown roads and unknown lands with unknown dangers? Everything they had ever learned about survival would be put to the test.

Finally, he heard the entry door click. He made his way over just as Ynarra set down a fresh tray of food. She paused, looking around until she saw Will then raising her hand into a small wave. It was the most human, social interaction he had ever seen from her. He raised his own hand in return and she smiled and curtsied, glancing around the room once more with a brief look of disappointment on her face. As she collected the tray, Madigan stepped out from the library.

"Thank you, Ynarra."

She nearly dropped the tray before breaking into a huge, beaming smile. "Oh! Sir, yes, of course, sir. It, um, it is my pleasure, sir." She curtsied repeatedly as she spoke. "I mean, it is my duty, but, yes, thank you." She curtsied again and set the tray down, rearranging the empty contents. "It has been a great honor. I mean, it has been very pleasant and, what I mean is, yes." She curtsied again and picked up the tray once more before locking eyes with Madigan, her eyes brimming with tears. "Yes. Thank you. Yes." She nodded quickly before turning and rushing from the room, locking the door behind her.

Madigan and Will stood together in a shocked silence.

"Did . . . did you tell her anything?" Will asked.

His brother shook his head. "Not a word. I have no idea what that was about."

"So it's not just me, then? That was bizarre to you too, right?"

He nodded. "She knows."

Will cursed. "How the hell does she know?"

"I've got no idea. But we need to go. Now."

They didn't hesitate. Will ran upstairs and grabbed their packs from the loft while Madigan raced to the tray of food. Unceremoniously, he dumped the dry contents of the plates into the smaller pouches and fastened them on their backs. Nodding to each other, they made their way toward the door. Will was just reaching out to grasp the latch when he heard someone try the door from the other side.

Will jerked his hand away and stepped back, looking to Madigan for guidance. At a sharp, heavy pounding on the door he snapped his head back around. A voice, the first he had heard that was not his brother's or Ynarra's in some time, called out from the other side.

"Open up, by order of the Crow!"

"That's not good . . . " Will heard Mad whisper behind him.

More pounding. "I said, open up in there!"

"Not good at all," Will's voice was hoarse and his throat felt uncomfortably dry.

"Someone go get that blasted girl with the keys," the harsh voice shouted from the other side of the door. Will heard footsteps hurrying away as the pounding on the door grew in intensity.

"They don't sound too terribly patient, Mad. Thoughts?"

His brother shifted his pack and stepped backward into the room, turning and looking up to the rafters above. "Well, I don't know how cordial behavior works around here, but to me that seems like a pretty rude entry request."

"Well, obviously!" Will followed his brother as Madigan glanced back at the door. "So, I'm guessing our plans are changing on the fly?"

"Like the wind, kid."

Will cursed again and loosened his knives while Madigan raced to the wall and leapt up to one of the ropes hanging from the rafters. Following him, Will grabbed the rope and muttered under his breath. The pair began to climb.

The pounding on the door stopped. Despite the distance, Will heard a sharp cry from the outside and the sudden turning of metal in the lock. He beckoned to Madigan and began to climb higher, moving amongst the rafters with ease. Mad followed, each step slow and steady, securing himself on each beam and entwining his arms in the ropes and draperies that led upward.

The door burst open and troops flooded into the room just as the brothers reached Will's hidden place in the cross section of the beams. Will braced himself against the wall and then crawled along on his belly until his eyes were just over the edge, staring down the three stories to the men below.

They were equipped with clubs and armored in metal and leather, far better armor than the men who guarded them when they first arrived. There were fourteen in all, each peering intently around the room. One was distracted by the rough-handled bundle in his arm: Ynarra. Her eyes were tear stained and she was holding a hand to her cheek. The nerves in Will's stomach turned to pure anger.

"Spread out and find them!" one of them barked. The leader, Will assumed.

The men dispersed in groups of three except for the one holding Ynarra and one who closed and locked the door before standing imposingly in front of it. Mad was silent, his hands clenched into white-knuckled fists. They waited impatiently as the men scoured the room, shoving aside furniture and flipping their beds over. The contents of the room were scattered and thrown haphazardly. After a few minutes, they reconvened in the center of the room after calling out their lack of findings.

The leader turned to Ynarra and began to speak too quietly for Will to hear. Ynarra was shaking her head frantically and pleading with him.

"Madigan, they think she's hiding us."

"If they touch her . . . " The steel in his voice was full of anger and indignation as he shifted into a crouch.

And, as if Mad's words had been an invitation, the leader backhanded Ynarra across the face. She collapsed to the floor and curled into a sobbing ball.

The roar that erupted from Madigan was all rage and fury and spite. With the rope twisted around his arm, he raced along the beams and began to climb down faster than Will had imagined possible.

"They're in the rafters!" The shout from one of the men proved to be a futile warning as Madigan swung down and barreled into the troops. The noctori blazed to life in his hands.

As soon as Madigan had their attention, Will withdrew a fang into his left hand and grabbed a rope before propelling himself forward off the ledge. He braced himself as the rope went rigid with tension and arced him toward the wall. Catching the wall at a run, he raced along the side as more shouts rang from the troops. Gauging the final distance, Will pushed off and leapt, swinging down to kick one of the soldiers with the full force of his weight. As the man went flying, Will released the rope, withdrew his other blade, and set himself against the men.

It was the first time in his life he had engaged in any combat where he was so well and truly outnumbered. Growing up, Jervin and Madigan would team up against him at times, but Will had never before faced more than two opponents. Will finally understood what it meant to have been personally trained by the Master of Blades.

As he and Madigan spun and wove between the men, time seemed to slow down. Every move Will made was calculated and precise, whereas the troops moved as though they were battling underwater. Will flowed amongst them with ease, his fear and trepidation suddenly replaced by total confidence, amazed by his own speed.

When they had first arrived at the Nordoth and been set upon, both he and Madigan had been injured, unprepared, and utterly exhausted. Now they had had weeks of rest and recuperation. The difference showed.

The strapped leather armor that Will wore was flexible yet strong and allowed him to use his limbs to deflect the clubs with greater ease. While Madigan tore through his opponents, Will's own fell to the ground screaming as the dragon fangs pierced their armor as if it were paper, delicately caressing flesh with their anguishing kiss. Within no time at all, over a dozen groaning men were strewn throughout the room. The last had forced Ynarra to her feet and was gripping her tightly.

Madigan was in a low stance, the noctori held above his head in preparation to strike as Will stepped next to his brother. The man yanked Ynarra's head back by the hair and sank his fingers into her throat as she gave a choked cry.

"Drop your weapons!" he sneered over Ynarra's struggle for breath.

Will stared from Ynarra to the cruel man whose fingers were digging into her throat. Madigan released a feral snarl next to him and when the man turned his focus toward his brother, Will shot his hand out, the fang leaving his grasp and spiraling through the air. The butt of the hilt struck like a battering ram against the man's throat. He gasped and fell to the ground, twitching and writhing as his hands shot to his neck. A moment later, he faded from consciousness.

Ynarra, released, inhaled deeply and stepped away from the fallen man. She looked to Madigan, her bruised face lighting up with happiness.

"Are you alright?" Madigan's voice was strained with concern and the exultation of battle.

"Yes," Ynarra said. She smiled and curtsied, then quickly turned and opened the door, darting from the room before Madigan could say another word.

"Impressive," said a gravelly voice from behind them. Shocked, Will and Madigan spun. A dark-skinned woman clad in mottled black and green stood before them, a dark cloak upon her shoulders. Her arms were crossed but she had a long staff strapped to her back. In the bright room, her emerald eyes glowed unnaturally. "The Crow certainly doesn't disappoint."

Madigan raced forward brandishing his noctori. He was struck by an unseen force and flew backward to the ground. He cried out as he tried to struggle to his feet, unable to do so. Will raised his remaining blade and risked a glance at his brother. He was lying rigid and immobilized in an unnatural position on the ground.

Will turned back to the woman and made to rush forward to engage the stranger, only to discover that his legs seemed fastened to the ground. A sudden panic gripped him and he struggled to keep himself from surrounding the area in his Shade. Instead, he tightened his grip on his remaining blade and raised it protectively.

"That won't be necessary," the woman said, raising her hand

and motioning for Will to stop. The room became shrouded in a pale haze of dust. "Friends shouldn't fight."

Friends? Will had never seen this lady in his life and, after her men ambushed them, she had the audacity to call them friends? Through the haze, he could see that she was smiling.

"Who the hell are you?" Will's voice was ice, even to his own ears.

She spread her hands. "I am Cephora, young William Davis. I come at your request to aid you in your journey."

🕉 19 🕉

THE STREET OF ASH

Madigan gave a sudden, sharp inhale and sprawled to the ground as whatever had been gripping his body released. Immediately, the force that had been pinning Will's feet to the ground also dissipated and the air around them cleared. Able to move freely, Will gave the stranger a wary eye but did not lower his guard. "Cephora?"

The woman nodded. "Prime of the Seekers."

Madigan jumped to his feet and brandished his noctori, glaring at the woman harshly. "What the hell was that?" He looked ready to spring at her again.

Cephora spread her hands and smiled before clasping them behind her. "You are not the only ones with talents, gentlemen."

"I did not request your aid," Will said, his voice sharp as he spat the words. While he was trying to give Cephora his full attention, some of the men on the ground began to stir and he side-stepped so none were at his back.

"No?" Cephora said. "I received word from the Crow that the descendants of Jervin Thorne were intent on a risky venture that would most likely end in their demise, were they not guided properly. I stand before you as your guide. Was I mistaken?"

"Davis," said Madigan. "Jervin Davis."

Cephora gestured that the matter was inconsequential. "Thorne, Davis, separate names, same person. I'll not be amending my own understanding of the man this late in the game."

Madigan and Will locked eyes and Will shook his head. They did not know this woman. Was it some ploy by the Crow? If they opened up to her there was no telling how she might behave. But if she truly was here to help, he didn't want to risk turning away an ally. He and Madigan would be back on their own. They couldn't afford to throw an opportunity away. "These men, they're yours?" Madigan said.

She laughed and shook her head. "These men are barely even men. Prisoners awaiting the execution block who offered to sacrifice the remainder of their lives to serve Undermyre by engaging the pair of you. A last glimmer of honor for an otherwise miserable existence." She shook her head and stepped forward, glancing down at the bodies littering the room. "And yet, somehow you managed not to strike down a single one. Very interesting."

Will spun and looked at the men on the ground, groaning and rolling as they began to regain consciousness. "They offered themselves?"

Cephora nodded. "You could say they viewed it as their penance."

"To what end?" Madigan said. His eyes had not left Cephora. He was still tense and ready to strike, like a cat waiting for the opportune moment to pounce on its prey.

"To aid me in determining what you were capable of."

"And to do that, you wanted us to slaughter them?" Mad said

as his temper flared white hot. "You put Ynarra, an innocent, in danger just to test us?"

Cephora waved her hand again and shook her head. "The method is not my own but rather our mutual host's. While I do not necessarily approve of his methods, they served their purpose. Such is the way of things."

Will muttered under his breath at her words. *So, the Crow hasn't forgotten us.* But it was worse than that. He had brought in a stranger and found ill-trained men to send to their deaths. And after abandoning the brothers for a month, he had caused pain to the one person who had been kind to them since their arrival.

Will's lips curled in distaste. "And what is to come of them now?"

Cephora stared at Will as the young man stood bristling. "That is not for me to decide. As I said, I was merely summoned to help you. The happenings of the Nordoth are outside my control."

A knock at the door caught Will so off guard that he flinched and spun, blade at the ready. But rather than another angry force or surprising stranger, Ynarra entered carrying a tray with a bottle and three glasses. There was a bright red welt upon her cheek. She smiled and set the tray down on the table before curtsying and turning to leave.

"Ynarra," Madigan began, "are you alright?"

"Oh," she said with a quick smile at him, "quite alright, thank you!" And then she spun and walked quickly out of the room.

Cephora chuckled and crossed to the tray, lifting it and gesturing toward the library. "Come. Let's go chat and see if we can't start anew. There is much to be done."

Will didn't move. From the corner of his eye, he could see that Mad didn't either. Instead, Mad extinguished his noctori and turned his back to the retreating figure. "We'll pass."

Cephora stopped in her tracks and cocked her head back to them. "Oh?" she said. "Come, one drink."

"We were actually just leaving," Madigan said. He walked back and retrieved Will's fang from the still-unconscious man.

Cephora sighed and looked at the bottle, whispering to herself, "And not even a brief moment's respite." She turned back to face the brothers. Setting the tray of glasses aside but grabbing the bottle by the neck, she walked toward the room's entrance. "Very well, then. Let's be off."

Will glanced to his brother as Cephora closed the distance. "What?"

Cephora smiled at him. "I said I was here to help you on your journey. If you'd prefer to leave now, then we leave now. But a bit of refreshment before the road never hurt."

"We'll be fine on our own," Mad said.

There was a sharp, single knock at the entrance to the room before the doorway opened quickly. Four new strangers entered with crude clubs. They began making their way around to each of the injured men on the floor and Will felt something tighten in his throat.

Cephora sighed and gestured to the door. "Come, if you wish to leave the Nordoth, we shall leave the Nordoth. There is an inn on the edge of town that will serve far better for conversation than this secluded tower." And she stepped from the room, bottle clutched firmly in hand.

"Mad?"

"I don't trust her," he said, watching the club-bearing men as they began dragging the injured toward the center of the room.

"But if she really is here to help . . . ?"

Mad shook his head and retrieved his pack from beneath the stairs. "One drink. One."

Will nodded. Together, weaving amongst the remaining men

on the floor, the pair followed in Cephora's tracks. To Will's surprise, the hall was far cleaner than it had been the last time they peered outside of the room. There was still a covering of dust and a sense of decay, but the contradictory pristine filth of the floor was gone.

Cephora smirked as they joined her. "Good choice. The inn serves the best spirits in the city. You won't be disappointed."

In silence, the three descended through the long, spiraling halls and stairs of the Nordoth. Cephora took them a different path than the one they had taken when they first arrived with Ynarra, a far narrower path that wound with incredibly steep stairs. To Will's surprise, they reached the bottom level of the fortress in a fraction of the time and made their way outside into the hazy daylight of the courtyard. *How did I not find that stair-case before? That would have made planning an exit infinitely more feasible.*

"Is our ever-gracious host going to be wishing us well as we depart?" Madigan said as he surveyed the courtyard, his voice thick with sarcasm.

"The Crow?" replied Cephora. "He moved on to other considerations as soon as he sent a dispatch for me. I doubt he even knew you were still present in the Nordoth."

"Of course," Will said under his breath. Despite his frustration with the Crow, he couldn't help but smile as they crossed the courtyard. It felt amazing to have open sky above him, even if that sky had the strange purple-orange hue of Undermyre's.

They crossed the empty courtyard and exited the gates on foot. They made their way down a stone staircase that had been cut from the mountainside, following the winding cart path by which they must have entered the fortress. As they descended, the city sprawled before them and Will marveled at how truly large the Nordoth was to tower over the decayed grandeur of Undermyre.

The buildings began to rise around them, stretching taller than he had imagined possible when he gazed from their room in the heights of the fortress. The strange light from the foreign sky was augmented by glowing lanterns that floated along the streets, emitting their own pale light and bathing the streets in their shine. Each building was tall and narrow, as were the streets they navigated. Towering statues were everywhere, some broken, some whole, but all of them constructed with a meticulous attention to detail. There were carvings of creatures from the very depths of Will's mind, fantastical creatures that beguiled his imagination. It was splendid and beautiful and sad beyond measure as every single structure seemed to be on the brink of ruin.

The people of Undermyre were not at all as Will had expected. They were dressed in every manner of clothing, elements of every bygone era of his home springing to his mind. Everyone he passed was so terribly focused on whatever task they were undertaking that it was as if they were truly and utterly oblivious to the world around them. Such was the studious intensity that, on more than one occasion, he had to dart out of the way of someone so completely engaged in whatever they were doing that they nearly barreled into him.

"Time is a different commodity here than you are accustomed to." Cephora's voice broke the long silence. Apparently, the look on Will's face had given away his thoughts.

"So we've heard," Madigan said. His tone was still flat but Will could see that his eyes were as wide as his own.

"Here, people do as they deem worthwhile," Cephora continued as if not having heard Madigan's comment. "Petty judgments around such trivialities as clothing are almost nonexistent."

"So I see," Will said as he passed a man in splendid Victorian formal attire conversing very loudly with a brick wall.

"Things are not always as they seem, William," Cephora said as they rounded a bend. "Ah, here we are, the Street of Ash."

She gestured wide to large double doors wedged between two gargantuan, strangely contorted buildings. The moniker was plastered just above the doors in a rigid script. Cephora pushed through the doors, Will just a few steps behind and Madigan taking up the rear.

Loud music greeted him the moment Will crossed the threshold, so loud that he was momentarily taken aback. It was an electric vibration that set his body swaying lightly before he could respond. He found himself attempting to hum along to the song in real time, despite having no idea what it was.

The room itself was wide and red and curtained, the floating lanterns swaying and dancing in time with the music. Madigan's face, too, was alight, his head nodding and bobbing in a mirror of Will's own as they continued inside. In front of them were small tables of people drinking and moving, the edges of the room littered with intimate hideaways and curtained alcoves. The walls were covered in balconies and bridges that stretched upward, the lanterns spinning and weaving amongst them all. In the center of the room was a dance floor, empty save for a single dark-haired girl moving in time with the music.

A hearty laugh from Cephora broke their reverie. She beckoned them forward and they followed as she crossed the room, deftly maneuvering between the oblivious patrons, lost in the music and their own minds. Will's eyes were drawn to the dancing girl the entire time. They stepped up to the bar and

Cephora nodded with a smile toward the bartender. She waved in return and after a moment made her way over.

"Welcome, welcome!" she said with a wide smile. "What'll it be, friends?"

Cephora leaned back and gestured to the brothers with a smile. "Go ahead."

"What?" Madigan blurted out.

"Surely you're comfortable navigating the common folk of our small city," Cephora grinned as the bartender giggled. "Come now."

"Oh, right," Madigan said, attempting to bluster his way back to some sort of composure. "Yes. Whiskey, please."

The bartender's smile remained but her eyes gave Mad a pitying look. "What's that, now?"

"Oh, right, sorry," Madigan said with a flush made only deeper by the red accents of the room. "I meant, um, Will?"

Mad's nudge snapped his brother's attention back from the dancing girl to the bartender.

"We'll do a bottle of *Fita'Verxae*, thanks," Will said with as much confidence as he could muster under the watchful eyes of Cephora and the bartender.

Cephora whistled and eyed him appraisingly as the bartender beamed.

"*Fita'Verxae*?" She laughed. "Not quite. I'm afraid we're not that kind of establishment. Try again."

"Three Bottled Embers, if you would," Cephora said, tossing a few coins onto the bar. The bartender swept a hand over them and they disappeared somewhere Will couldn't see.

"Now that I can do. Have a seat, boys, it'll be by soon."

Cephora guided them to a table in the back corner of the room opposite the entrance. She sat with her back to the wall as Mad slid into a seat that gave him full view of the room. Will's own seat, he discovered, was fortunately placed to face almost directly toward the middle of the dance floor where the raven-haired girl continued to move in time with the hypnotic music. Distracted as he was watching her, it took him a moment to realize that Cephora had spoken.

"Sorry," Will said, snapping his attention back to the table. "What was that?"

"I asked if you need us to move elsewhere," she replied, raising an eyebrow. "Somewhere you won't be so taken by other interests?"

Mad snickered and Will shook his head quickly. "No, I'm here. I'm fine."

"Good," said Madigan. "Alright, Cephora. One drink, you said. Well, here we are."

"Straight to business, then? Fair enough." Cephora shook her head. "Tell me, then, how do you plan on retaining me for this venture?"

"Excuse me?" Madigan snapped. Will was just as caught off guard as his brother. *Retain her?* What the hell did she mean by that? She had traveled there to help them, not the other way around.

"I don't believe I misspoke," Cephora said. "What? Did you think my arrival was enough to ensure my aid?" She barked a laugh.

"This damn place . . . " Mad muttered.

"I came, as requested, but so far I have not yet—ah! Thank you, Clarice!" The bartender arrived bearing three glasses of a liquid that was dark as smoke yet held a wavering orange center that seemed to be continuously flickering, like the flame of a candle. Cephora smiled and flipped a coin to her which she caught with a wink before turning and departing. "As I was saying, I came at a request for help and now I need to know why you think it is worthwhile for me."

"Why it's worthwhile to you?" Mad said flatly. "Perhaps you should tell us why we need you, then we'll decide if you're needed."

Cephora chuckled. "I'm not trying to start a fight here, Madigan. The Crow said you needed me and that is reason enough for you to believe it. He told me your destination and for that alone I need to know what I'm getting myself into."

"Our destination?" Will asked. "He knows where to find the blood beast?"

"He knows a path." Cephora sipped her drink.

"So, what then?" Madigan said. "You're supposed to just waltz us over to it?"

Cephora smiled at Madigan from behind her glowing drink. "Something like that."

Will stared at her. Her position was backwards, her logic spinning and spinning just like the girl on the dance floor. He shook his head and focused on the beverage. He tasted it and was stunned, almost the same as he had been when he first tasted the *Fita'Verxae* or the Atlantean wine. *Is everything in this place filled with such complexities?* He sipped again as Madigan and Cephora bantered back and forth, his brother obviously growing more hot tempered by the minute.

Will tried his best to keep up, but the first few sips of the drink sent his head spinning pleasantly and he found himself watching the dancing girl again. Since their arrival she had not stopped dancing for a moment, her body lithe and controlled, each motion fluid with the music. The conversation at his table seemed to fade into the background as he watched her glide, arms in the air, the strange electric music drawing him in. The entire tavern faded away until it was only the girl, Will, the music, and the fiery drink in his hand.

Will was entranced. Her skin was pale. Her hair was black and short and untamed. Even from where he sat, when she raised her arms into the air, he could see intricate tattoos winding along her hands and forearms. The world disappeared when she moved, and Will found himself suddenly moved by the rhythm in the room, as if it was baring his soul to the world. He knew then that an introduction was needed, never imagining that anything else would ever come of it.

As he stood, Madigan reached out and stopped him. "Will, what are you doing?"

Will snapped back to reality, the music again just background noise. "What? Oh. I was just going to see if I could find some water."

As if she had heard the words before they left his mouth, Clarice appeared carrying a trio of glasses filled to the brim with water. She placed them on the table without spilling a drop, smiled that knowing smile at Cephora again, and departed.

"Take a seat, Will," Cephora said. "We're not done here, yet. Perhaps you can lend more insight here than your brother who isn't exactly being forthcoming."

"Oh, and you are?" Mad glared at the woman.

"Justice . . . " Will said, the words slipping from him as he watched the pixie-like girl twirling to the music.

"What's that?" Cephora asked.

He turned his focus back to her. "Justice, that's what you believe in."

Madigan stared at his brother as Cephora raised an eyebrow. "Is it, now?"

He nodded. "Those men, back in our room, they were criminals, sentenced to death, right? And yet, when you spoke of them, you saw their attempts at atonement as something admirable, something that was balancing their own scales."

Cephora cocked her head. "I suppose so."

"If you believe in justice, then you'll come with us. If even a few of the stories we've heard of Valmont are true, then his scales were far from balanced and this world suffered for it. Even with his death, the effects of his terror have lingered and grown. We need to balance the scales back in our favor."

She smiled. "A pretty idea. But are you after justice, Will? Or is it only vengeance you seek?"

The image of his dying grandfather appeared before Will's eyes, the smokiness of the drink reminiscent of the smoke in the air from his burning home as Senraks destroyed everything he'd ever known. "It's both."

Cephora nodded appreciatively. "Honesty is good. Vengeance for what, then?"

"One of Valmont's assassins, a blood beast, murdered our grandfather," Madigan said, his voice raw and jagged. "He destroyed our home."

Cephora closed her eyes. "Jervin Thorne is dead?"

Will nodded.

Cephora drained her cup and signaled Clarice to bring more. "The Crow failed to mention that."

"You knew him?" Mad asked.

"Everyone knew of Jervin Thorne."

There was a moment of silence as Madigan and Will both finished their drinks and Clarice brought another round. As she left, Cephora raised her glass. "To the Master of Blades."

The three drank and set their cups down. It was another moment before Cephora spoke again. "This blood beast, how did you know what it was?"

"We didn't," Madigan said. "Our grandfather did. He called it Senraks. The Crow offered some clarification."

"Senraks." Cephora closed her eyes and was silent for a moment. Will saw her shake her head slightly, almost involuntarily, before she looked up. "The road we are going will take some time but the journey ought to be safe enough."

"So, you're coming along then?" Will asked.

Cephora smiled. "I always was. I just wanted to know your intentions."

Madigan groaned and threw his hands in the air before taking a deep draught of his drink. "And what are yours, then?" he asked. "Why grace us with your presence?"

"And what exactly is a Seeker?" Will followed, almost overlapping his brother's words.

Cephora smiled. "All in good time."

The conversation continued with the pair probing at Cephora and her masterfully avoiding specifics. Eventually, Madigan grew frustrated enough to drop it and Will followed his lead. Cephora excused herself to go get food, leaving Mad and Will alone at the table with their third round of drinks.

"What are you thinking?" Madigan asked.

Will shrugged. "Honestly? I have no idea. She hasn't said much of anything yet. But regardless, she knows this place and we don't."

Mad nodded. "My thoughts exactly. I don't think we have much of a choice. We need her."

Will's eyes fell to the raven-haired girl again. She had left the dance floor and made her way to a tall table not far from them.

"Dammit, Will, just go."

Will snapped his attention back to his brother. "What?"

"Go already," he said, waving his brother away. "You've been distracted by her since we got here. Go introduce yourself."

"I don't really think that this is necessarily the best time to be—"

"Oh, just go already. You only live once."

Exhaling deeply, Will stood and turned to where the girl was leaning against the wall, sipping a clear drink with a greenish tint. Will glanced back at his brother who made a shooing motion and, after one last sip of his drink, Will made his way over to her. His heartbeat was loud in his ears as he walked, the intensity of the music growing volumes. The key around his throat started to hum, as if in tune with the music, and he felt his head spinning from the alcohol. As he approached, the bright-eyed girl turned toward him. She set her drink on the table, a sharp intensity in her eyes and a slightly crooked smile on her face.

"Excuse me, miss?" Will did his best to smile and quiet the nerves in his stomach. "Hello."

She laughed an infectious, boisterous laugh and held out her hand.

"Dance with me."

Taking his hand, she led Will to the middle of the dance floor. The key was throbbing now, sending charges through his skin as his head swam from the drinks. The girl's body pressed close against his own. Somehow, despite being the only two people moving to the music, he wasn't self-conscious. The room seemed to disappear. His senses dulled as the world became the music, the charges racing through his skin, and the body dancing next to him. As they spun, the night was wild with sensations he couldn't place.

Morella, she said. Her name was Morella.

Will didn't know how long they held each other, dancing. For the first time, he truly believed it when everyone said that time worked differently in Aeril. Hours passed, perhaps even a lifetime could have, and Will wouldn't have had the slightest idea, so intoxicated was he by the music and Morella. The key was fire in his chest, scorching, threatening to turn his body to ashes, yet still he was lost in time with her. Her lips grazed his own, a delicate passion lasting only a moment. She winked at him. He closed his eyes, spinning.

And then she was gone.

He scanned the room and saw no sign of her. His eyes fell to his brother at the table, still smiling widely and sipping his drink. Will shook his head, blinking hard and forcing himself from the dance floor. He stumbled back to his seat and collapsed, a cool sheen of sweat upon his brow. His throat still burning in that strange way, he reached for his drink and took a long draft, draining the cup.

"Well, well," Mad grinned, "look at my little brother go."

"I'm exhausted." Will smiled wearily. "Did you see her leave? Where did she go?"

"Exhausted?" he said with a laugh. "We need to work on your stamina, kid."

Will stared at him, the confusion plain upon his face.

"Will, you were only gone for five minutes."

"What?" Will sat straight up and started glancing around the room, as if seeing it in a completely different light. Cephora was making her way back to them. Morella's drink still sat on the table where she had been leaning, undisturbed. The bartender was laughing and smiling, serving her patrons. The music had faded slightly but all around him the room seemed exactly as it had been. "Only five minutes?"

"If that," Mad said, sipping his drink and side-eyeing his brother. "Why?"

"It . . . it felt like longer."

He smiled. "Did you get her name, at least?"

Will nodded and reached for his empty cup. "Morella."

Madigan clapped him on the back. "Nicely done."

Will smiled and searched the room again but she was gone. Somehow, she had disappeared without either of them seeing which way she had left, without a single word other than her name. Her name, a wink, and a kiss. Will was absolutely delighted.

The remainder of the evening was spent in small pleasantries with Cephora as they attempted to break the ice and discover what they could about one another. Will had to admit that he was more than a little distracted from his all-too-brief encounter with the mysterious Morella, but he still tried to remain focused on this newcomer.

Cephora was pleasant enough and had apparently known their grandfather for a brief time, long ago. Of her profession as a Seeker, all they were able to garner was that she was a skilled tracker and, seeing as they were in the process of attempting to track something down, that was good enough.

As the hours passed and the night threatened to pass to morning, Cephora called to Clarice and, after a brief exchange, secured them rooms for the night. After they made their unsteady way to the upper levels of the Street of Ash and toward their respective doors, Cephora pulled the brothers aside.

"Listen. The journey we are about to embark on will be taxing, and there is no guarantee what will be at the end of it," she said, not unkindly. "This is the last time you'll be in an actual bed for some time. Enjoy it. Appreciate it."

Will, drunk and dizzy from the drinks, started to make an offhand remark but Madigan gripped his wrist and stopped him. There was an intensity in Cephora's eyes that had not been there minutes ago. He and his brother nodded.

"Whatever you need to say to one another in private, say it before morning. When this door opens and you join me on the road there must be no secrets between us. None. What I do not know about you and what you do not know about this realm may get us all killed."

"We understand," Mad said.

Cephora nodded and turned. "Get some rest."

Madigan and Will entered their room and closed the door behind them before falling onto their respective beds.

"What have we gotten ourselves into, Will?" Mad said absentmindedly.

Will smiled from where he lay, reflecting on the evening. "I don't know, brother of mine. But at least I got a kiss from a beautiful lady along the way!"

Madigan glanced at Will for a moment before bursting into laughter. As they waited for sleep to take them, they laughed and joked like children again, ignorant of the troubles of growing up, ignorant of how much their lives were about to change.

20

ANSWERS UPON THE ROAD

The road they traveled upon was broad and wide and obviously quite old, an amalgamation of cut stone and sand. Per Cephora's instructions, all three traveled with the hoods of their cloaks raised. According to her, the Crow had made good on his promise, ensuring that no one knew about the two brothers or could possibly recognize them, but it was still better to stay anonymous. Passing a group of strange zealots near the gate, Will remembered what Madigan had said regarding superstitions around the Shadowborne and drew his hood forward further.

After a few miles, the abundance of travelers along the road lessened and trees began to appear. They reminded Will of the evergreens from home except they bore the color of autumn, browns and golds and reds. The sky brightened visibly as Under-myre fell farther behind them, the orange glowing and mirroring the flame of a candle. In the distance, snow-tipped mountains soared above the trees, a stark contrast against the strange sky.

There was little conversation that first day, whatever casual joviality they had managed to gain with Cephora the previous night obviously a fluke. They stuck to the main road as it narrowed and wound through farmland and small thickets of trees. The few passersby that they saw kept mainly to themselves and skirted off to the side when the three cloaked figures passed. One or two glanced their way, their eyes darting to Cephora before quickly hurrying themselves along. The majority of those they passed were in much more traditional clothing for rural life, rough spun and practical. Three people in dark garb, clad in leather armor and carrying visible weapons, was probably an unfamiliar sight.

The hours rolled by. Despite the comfort of the boots he wore, Will could feel hotspots beginning on his feet and the threat of oncoming blisters. Occasionally he paused and readjusted the lacings or tried to change his gait so his weight fell differently but it didn't help. Only the distraction of hunger drew his attention from it.

They ate a brief, unfulfilling lunch of nuts and dried fruit while they walked, not stopping, and the few sips of water Will drank did little to quell the growing rumble in his stomach. But despite the hunger pangs, he had to admit that he was in good spirits. After everything that had happened, he and Madigan were finally in Aeril, finally seeing the world their grandfather had told them about.

Finally on the trail of the monster that murdered him.

The scenery of the new world was beautiful, the very air seemingly teeming with the possibility of magic. Periodically, the constant hum of the key would build and crescendo against Will's chest before returning to its dull vibration. He was now aware that it seemed to coincide with strange happenings, yet he could never place exactly what. At first, he thought little of it but soon noticed that every time he searched the surrounding area, alerted by the key, Cephora also seemed to be extra watchful. Regardless, nothing ever materialized, nothing to justify such strange feelings.

The color of the sky began to darken when Cephora finally turned them off the main road. The shift to uneven ground and frequent stones made each footfall more precarious and took Will out of the pacing trance he had adopted over the past few hours. The underbrush grew progressively taller until soon it was almost at waist height. The going was slower and slower as he and Mad struggled to keep up with Cephora, while her every step seemed as sure and confident as it had been on the main road.

After walking for some time, they approached a large tree whose branches dipped all the way to the ground. Cephora brushed them aside and passed beneath the limbs, beckoning for Madigan and Will to follow. It was surprisingly cool and comfortable inside, the dry ground matted with dead needles that bounced with each step.

"We'll rest here for the night," Cephora said as she set her pack down at the large base of the tree trunk.

"Sounds lovely," Will said with a smile. He unslung his pack and let it fall to the ground as Mad dropped his and stretched his arms wide.

"I take it you've stayed here before?" Mad asked as Cephora began to skirt the base of the tree, skillfully maneuvering the debris into a pile long enough for a human to rest on.

Cephora nodded. "Many times, though rarely in the company of others. Still, there's plenty of room for the three of us."

Madigan and Will set about clearing space and building their own sleeping areas while Cephora removed her cloak and draped it over a low-hanging branch. The cleared ground was compact and smooth, the dirt undisturbed by rainfall for years. It didn't take long to build up a good supply of needles that was surprisingly soft to sit upon.

Mad removed his cloak and excused himself outside with a book. Sitting, Will removed his boots and flexed his feet, wincing a bit. Cephora chuckled as he surveyed the fresh blisters.

"Something funny?" he asked, frowning.

Cephora shook her head and smiled. "Funny? No. Surprising? Yes."

Will stretched his legs out and rolled his ankles then met her gaze. "Well, I suppose not all of us are as used to this much foot travel as some others."

She held up her hands in a placating gesture. "You misunderstand, William. Your fatigue is completely understandable. Even if I thought otherwise, I would not do you the disservice of letting you know that."

Will's brow furrowed as he tried to determine whether or not he'd been insulted. "Alright, then," he said. "What's surprising? If you don't mind my asking?"

"Only that you are a blood relative of Jervin Thorne, the Master of Blades, the Keeper," Cephora said, cocking her head to the side. "And yet, there you sit with aching feet. Years you spent under his tutelage, and yet you allow blisters to give you pause."

Will decided that he was, indeed, being insulted. "Listen, Cephora, I don't know what the hell you're getting at but you're not exactly—"

"Your knives, I mean."

"How are my knives related to my blisters?" he asked with considerable bite.

She sighed. "I mean only that after studying so long with your grandfather, I am surprised at the things you still do not know."

Will waited a moment for her to continue but she just smiled. Finally, he took the bait. "Such as . . . ?"

"Tell me, William Davis, what do you know of dragons?"

The question brought to mind a conversation with his grandfather from long ago. *William, what do you recall of Dorian Valmont?*

That had been the start of all of this. He shook the thought out of his head. "Only that they're dead, that Valmont killed the last of them."

Cephora pursed her lips. "That very well may be. Anything else?"

May be?

"I only just found out that they ever truly existed. All Grandda said was that weapons like these were feared," he said. He strained to recall anything else from their final conversation. There was something more there, he knew it. After a moment, he lit up as he remembered. "Life and death, he said. Something about the dragon's ability and wielding the power of life and death."

Cephora's white teeth flashed in a grin and she clapped her hands together. "Precisely! Their energy flows with life, restoring health."

"But he said that the ability was lost long ago . . . ?"

"Did he?" Cephora cocked her head. "Strange. It should not have been so, the gems are intact."

"The rubies?" Will said, strumming his thumb along the gem.

Cephora gestured toward the blades. "Not rubies, William. Blood. Blood and magic and something far more ancient."

Will's hand froze. He knew he should have felt revulsion at the revelation but instead his fascination only grew. "Blood?"

"Suddenly so full of questions, aren't you?" Cephora said and laughed.

"What?" Will said, suddenly self-conscious. "Oh, no, it's just that Grandda, he never said anything about them and, well, I just . . . what do they do?"

She held out her hand and gestured toward the shorter of his blades. "May I?"

Will removed the knife and handed it to Cephora. She raised it and gave it an appraising look. She turned the blade over in her hands and lifted the gem to her eyes. She closed them and muttered something Will could not quite hear. Suddenly, his key shot to life, sending its currents coursing through his chest as the embedded gem began glowing brilliantly, casting a red glow over the entire area. Cephora opened her eyes and moved her hand over the shining light, which faded to its dull, simple elegance.

"The binding is intact, but only just," she said. Smiling, she held out the blade for Will to take back. "You should have more success now."

"Success with what?" he asked almost before she had finished speaking.

"Truly?" Her gaze was different now as she looked at him. "Jervin did not teach you the manipulations when he awarded you these?"

"No, he . . . " Will hesitated. "There wasn't time."

Cephora sighed in understanding and crossed her hands behind her back. "I'm sorry."

"It's fine," Will said, looking back at the gemmed blade. "We haven't exactly filled you in all the way. You don't know the full circumstances of what happened."

Cephora nodded. "This is true. But still, perhaps I can be some help in picking up where he left off."

Will perked up a bit at that. "Extra instruction is always appreciated."

Cephora smiled. "It's settled then," she said. "We'll begin first thing in the morning."

Madigan returned to their little hideaway just then. "Begin what, now?"

His reappearance caught Will off guard. "That was fast. Usually you're off reading for hours at a time."

He shrugged. "My mind wouldn't settle enough. Why? Am I interrupting something?"

"Not at all," Cephora said. "Your brother and I were just discussing the nuances of missed opportunities and how best to re-approach them."

"Like that girl at the tavern last night?" Mad said and grinned wide.

"Hey, that wasn't a missed opportunity!"

"Easy, Will, I'm just giving you a hard time," he said as he made his way over to the makeshift bed and sat upon it. "What did I miss, then?"

"Cephora is going to work with me. Apparently, there's a lot I still don't know about what my blades are capable of."

"Just like I've been telling you for years, kid. There's a lot about a lot that you don't know."

Will snickered as Cephora laughed out loud before interjecting. "Actually, William, I'll be working with each of you. Both of you could stand to benefit."

Madigan shifted in his seat. "What do you have in mind?"

"As things currently stand? Sleep." She smiled as she lay down. "But in the morning? Well, I need to know what I'm working with. I suggest you rest up."

THEY AWOKE EARLY THE NEXT MORNING JUST AS THE SKY BEGAN to glow. Cephora guided them to a nearby patch of rocky ground with little ground cover, then directed Will and Madigan to spar with one another. She was silent as the pair skirmished bare-handed, circling them in silence. Periodically she ordered them to separate, inspecting them by having them stretch or crouch or jump. Satisfied by whatever she was looking for, she would order them to continue to spar and the cycle began anew.

Before long, both brothers were sweating and breathing hard. Each bore an assortment of new cuts and bruises when Cephora halted the bout and they ate a light breakfast of nuts and seeds with a few dried berries. Afterward, they returned to their path through the wilderness, the fatigue from the morning adding to their discomfort from the previous day's trek. Cephora didn't make her thoughts known regarding their sparring session nor offer any suggestions of how to improve.

For the next ten days, the routine continued in much the same fashion. Conversation came easier over time. Madigan seemed to warm up to their new companion and probed Cephora for personal information, who she was and who the Seekers were. She skillfully deflected each question and instead turned his inquiries in on themselves, gathering information about the brothers and their upbringing. Madigan kept things brief, glossing over specifics rather than going into much detail on most events. He seemed determined to have their story remain as secret as Cephora's.

In the spirit of encouraging open dialogue, however, Will held little back when it came to his own side of the story. In fact, with Madigan being so tight-lipped, he was able to spin himself as something of a heroic figure at times. The night that his Shade had stopped the truck? There was no thievery involved; he risked everything to save a man's life. The battle in the tunnels? No mysterious lightning at all, only skill and guile. Madigan never contradicted his brother, letting Will have his moments to shine as Cephora nodded and whistled, making all of the appropriately appreciative affirmations.

Will basked in the attention. Everything seemed to be going well until he was elaborating on saving a fearful and near-unconscious Madigan for the third time when Cephora started laughing. Will halted his tale, confused.

"Please, Madigan," Cephora forced through peals of laughter, "please tell me if he's always like this!"

"What?" Will said, caught completely unawares. "Always like what?"

Will's brother just snickered.

"Always so, so," Cephora struggled to speak through her laughter, "so absolutely full of it!"

Madigan burst out in howling amusement as Will stood there sputtering. After a moment, Madigan composed himself and gave a quick nod. "Yeah," he said. "Pretty much all the time."

Will shrank into himself. After a moment, Cephora controlled her laughter and smiled. "I'll say this, you're certainly more entertaining companions than your grandfather ever was."

Will's injured pride gave way for a moment as Madigan seized on the opportunity. "You traveled with our grandfather?" he asked.

"On occasion," Cephora said as if the information was commonplace. "He was always quite serious when we would."

"Grandda?" Will asked. Memories of hikes with his grandfather laughing and telling stories came flooding back to him. "That doesn't sound like him."

"Hunting men for execution is rarely a jovial experience, William."

Will paused, simultaneously chastised and intrigued. "Criminals?"

"More often than not." Cephora smiled as she turned back to him. "But always people who had done wrong."

"I wonder what could have been so wrong as to warrant both a Seeker and a Blademaster," Madigan said, his voice barely audible.

Cephora glanced at Madigan and her eyes narrowed. "This isn't the first venture I've embarked upon to stop agents of Valmont."

"So, you were there when Valmont was brought in the last time?" Madigan asked.

Cephora shook her head. "No. I had been tasked with a different objective then."

"What objective?"

Cephora didn't respond. Instead, she turned and moved on again. They kept walking in silence for almost a minute before Will tried to recover the conversation. "Other than going after Valmont's assassins, who did you go after?"

"Many people," she said without pausing. "His acolytes, suicidal pawns chasing eternal life. Zealots of Radiance. Sometimes the more common criminal who happened to have crossed the wrong person of influence." She smiled. "We took down more than a few."

"So, Seekers then, what, you're trackers? Bounty hunters?" Madigan asked.

"Something like that." Cephora shrugged.

"But, whenever the two of you were together, other people died?" Will knew the answer already but he couldn't help the question, no matter how much he didn't want to hear.

"You don't become known as the Master of Blades without using your blade, William." Cephora's voice was level and matter-of-fact but he could sense something else behind it.

"You were friends?" Mad asked it before he could.

Cephora paused a moment before responding. "Comrades in war is more like it," she said, glancing back. Something about the look on Will's face must have betrayed his thoughts. "You don't believe me?"

"It's just," Will chose his words carefully, "he never mentioned you."

Cephora chuckled. "Told you everything, did he? All about his life here? Everything he left behind? Everything he wished he could forget?"

"No. I suppose not. I just didn't know he was such a . . . "

"Such a what?"

"Killer."

Cephora gave a quiet "humph" before falling back into silence. Madigan, who had remained quiet, finally spoke to his brother softly, his eyes downcast. "I've killed, Will."

Will flushed, thinking back to their childhood, to the night their mother died, to the bloody baseball bat in his brother's hands. "That's different, Mad. You were defending us."

"I'm not now, though," Madigan said. "Now we're hunting, not defending. More than likely, I'll have to kill again."

Suddenly, the weight of their undertaking seemed heavier to Will than it had previously. He realized that at no point when they told anyone of their quest had Madigan spoken of capturing Senraks. No, that wasn't his way. He was taking the matter upon himself. This creature, this speaking, sentient being, would die at the hands of his brother.

"Listen, Mad, I didn't mean it that way."

Madigan didn't meet his eye and kept walking. Cephora spoke up. "Jervin Thorne was a man who sought justice, Will, a good man. Killer or no, he was good and kind."

"I know." Will nodded as he pictured his grandfather's smile, his laughing face. For once, they were not marred by the horrific image of his death. At least, not for a moment.

"And sometimes the people who are the kindest are the ones with the darkest secrets, the most skeletons in their closet," she said. "They balance their scales by being good and just."

Will didn't know how to reply. No one else spoke for a time.

"Perhaps," Madigan said in the uncomfortable silence, "we're not quite as entertaining as you thought we were."

Cephora continued at the same pace as before, seemingly unperturbed. Will pushed away a multitude of follow-up questions, fearing the course of the conversation. Everything he had expected about Aeril was in flux. He always thought that there were certain inescapable truths about the world, but they had been constantly challenged since the death of his grandfather. *Perhaps that's it,* he realized, *the truths I knew were from a different world. Everything here is different.*

The thought didn't comfort him.

Gradually, conversation resumed. Madigan and Cephora talked about the land and the surrounding areas while Will kept mainly to himself, lost in his own thoughts. After a time, he joined in but everything he said felt forced and half-hearted at best.

The remainder of the day was spent traveling cross-country and climbing low, rolling hills. The landscape grew even more beautiful as they moved farther inland. Away from the water surrounding Undermyre, the autumnal colors and hazy sky created an eternal dawn. The mountains on the horizon began to multiply as, off in the reaches of Will's sight, the outline of more snowy peaks appeared. One, far, far in the distance, towered above the rest. It appeared black, somehow completely absent of snow, and had a mist of smoke that circled the sky above.

"Is that an active volcano?" Will asked.

"The dark mountain?" said Cephora, following his gaze. "No. That is Umbriferum."

Realization dawned on Will and he nearly stopped in his tracks—Umbriferum, home to the Halls of Shadow. *Where I'm supposed to go.* Madigan shot him a knowing look and shook his head slightly. Cephora did not notice the exchange.

"Umbriferum?" Will asked with as much nonchalance as he could muster. "What's that?"

"It was once the base of the Blades of Shadow, warriors who wielded the power of darkness," she said.

"More of the evil men that you and Jervin hunted down?" Madigan asked. His tactics were far from elegant, but Will couldn't deny their effectiveness at gathering information.

Cephora chuckled. "Quite the opposite. Darkness doesn't mean evil. The Blades of Shadow were some of our staunchest allies before they were wiped out."

"What happened to them?" Will asked. His grandfather hadn't said anything about them being wiped out.

"Valmont," Cephora said as if reading from a textbook. "Or, at least, the remnants of his following. After his disappearance, there was a brief rising by them. In the aftermath of the destruction wrought by Valmont's escape, the few surviving Blades perished saving Undermyre and the Nordoth. The Halls fell into disarray soon after. Umbriferum became a monument to a dead age."

Madigan stopped walking. "By disappearance, you meant death, right?"

"Valmont is dead," Cephora said. After a moment, however, she snickered. "At least, he is as far as the world knows. I never saw a body."

Will's mind was racing. *Valmont may be alive?* And Umbriferum had fallen. So much had changed since his grandfather left Aeril. "So, all the Blades are dead? The power of darkness, you said, it no longer exists?"

Cephora did not look at him when she answered. "No one has seen Shadow magic used in a hundred years. It's safe to say that, yes, it no longer exists."

Will risked another knowing glance at his brother. The Crow's interest in keeping their arrival a secret suddenly became far more understandable. *But if Grandda hadn't known about the fall of Umbriferum, what else had he missed?* The realization that he would never be trained in whatever manner his grandfather had planned was disconcerting. He knew so little about what he was capable of, and now it looked as though it would remain that way. *Unless I keep figuring it out on my own.*

"Grandda always said that the Blades were the greatest warriors that ever walked," Madigan said. "How is it that cronies of a single, absent man were able to wipe them out?"

"It was not only men who followed Valmont," Cephora replied. "He had discovered new forms of manipulating magic, creating abominations from the dead. He forced together flesh and bone in unnatural ways before somehow imbuing them with life." She shook her head. "They were nightmares, something born from deep within his twisted imagination."

"Blood beasts . . . " Will said, his voice almost a whisper.

Cephora nodded. "Blood beasts were just some of the horrors that Aeril witnessed thanks to Valmont's insanity."

"How?" asked Madigan. "You said he found new magic. What was it?"

Approaching a large boulder, Cephora finally stopped walking and turned to face them as she leaned against it. "Various rumors exist, nothing is certain. But in my travels I heard of similar amalgamations of evil created once. Blood magic."

"Well, that doesn't sound forbidding in the least bit," Will said.

Cephora chuckled and shrugged. "Everything I know about Valmont points to that as the most likely conclusion. Your grandfather told you of his disappearance long ago, yes?" Madigan and Will nodded. "I believe he went in search of the Codex of Ahn'Quor."

"Care to elaborate on what that is?" Mad asked after a moment.

"The texts of a madman. Most believed it to be a scary story for children, like the bogeyman your world is so fond of remembering. But like him, the stories of the Codex were all grounded in truth, once."

"Wait, the bogeyman is real?" Will blurted out.

Cephora laughed. "Once upon a time, yes. But he was stopped long ago. I think, William, you'll find that many of your Casc legends are not quite as fantastical as you would prefer to believe."

"Comforting," he muttered. How many other bedtime stories weren't what they seemed?

"As I was saying," she continued, "the stories say that Ahn'Quor was an ancient, a being of pure malice and spite. Somehow, he manipulated blood magic, corrupted it. He was able to twist the primordial flows of energy that course through all things. He wrote his knowledge into the Codex of Ahn'Quor before his defeat, all his hatred and cruelty leached onto the pages. It is described as an ancient tool of evil, a book bound in the flesh of gods. Within were the secrets of life and death itself and the cruelest uses of blood magic."

"Sounds lovely," said Madigan. "And you think Valmont found this Codex?"

"I do." Cephora nodded.

"But, blood magic?" Will asked. "What do you mean? I thought there was only Shadow and Light? Er, Radiance, I mean?"

Cephora's smile made Will feel like a child. He shifted beneath it, his discomfort plain. "Once there were many things that no longer are. The magics of the universe have faded and died with time, as Shadow and Radiance now have."

"And what is it that you manipulate, then?" Mad said. His tone was almost confrontational.

"What's that?" Cephora said in a noncommittal tone.

Madigan stood square and tall and secure and met her gaze. "The day we met, you knocked me off my feet and bound me on the ground without hardly moving yourself."

"That's right," Will picked up. "Then the room turned to a cloud of dust."

Cephora said nothing for a moment and then nodded. "That it did."

Madigan didn't move. "Magic isn't dead." It wasn't a question.

There was a pause. Then, not breaking the look she and Madigan shared, Cephora shook her head. "No, it isn't."

Silence. Will stood waiting, not daring to say a word lest he stifle the answers that were teetering on the tip of her tongue. Willing her to answer, he felt his key suddenly spring to life as the ground beneath him started to almost imperceptibly quiver. It was just a slight tremor, but it was enough. Startled, he caught Cephora's eye and she smiled. "Very well. I said there must be honesty, and I honor that now. I am the last of the Earth Warders."

"Oh, this sounds mighty interesting." Madigan chuckled, relaxing, and following Cephora's example, leaned against another rock and let his pack drop to the ground.

Will grinned. *Time for answers.*

Cephora remained silent, as though her explanation had been enough. She leaned away from the rock, turned, and set off down the road again. Will paused a moment before realizing that she truly was perfectly content to leave it at that.

"And the Earth Warders were what exactly?" he asked as he rushed to catch up. He heard his brother curse under his breath as he scrambled to get moving. "People who could manipulate the ground? Dirt and dust and the like? Is that how you took Mad down?"

"Something like that." She smiled.

"Is that all it was?"

Cephora shook her head and Madigan cut in as he caught up to them. "Cephora, we're not native here, you know that. And you also know that what we don't know seems incredibly likely to get us killed. So, a little explanation would be nice."

"Very well," she said without slowing. "The basics at least. Earth Warders were the most ancient of those touched by the higher forces, predating Radiance and Shadow both. Creatures from all species and planes of existence were of the Earthen: human, centaur, minotaur, although few of the Avian races ever held the capabilities."

"Did you say centaur?" Madigan asked.

Cephora nodded. "Things change. The worlds are not as they once were. Now they are . . . diminished."

"What happened?" Will asked. First dragons, then the bogey-man, and now the creatures from myths he had heard as a kid. *Are all the myths and legends of our world true?*

"War. Genocide. All the worst things you can imagine." Cephora was shaking her head as she spoke. "Most of the stories have been lost to time. The Hesperawn were the ones who struck back and restored balance."

Madigan cocked an eyebrow. "So, it was Valmont who wiped them out?"

Cephora's brow furrowed and she shook her head. "No. This was long before Dorian Valmont. Before any of the recent horrors."

Recent? Valmont's terrors had been going on for hundreds of years, how could that still have been recent? Will looked at Cephora and asked the question that danced across his mind. "Cephora, just how old are you?"

The corners of her mouth turned up into a smile as her eyes adopted a strange, distant quality. "Old enough."

He was about to ask another question when something lying in the road off in the distance caught his eye. Mad and Cephora saw it too. Their pace quickened and as they moved closer Will could see a cart, upturned and broken with debris scattered along the road. Lying next to the cart was the body of a man, pale and lifeless in a pool of dark blood.

Madigan frowned. "This isn't good."

The body was battered and covered in stab wounds. The upturned cart had crushed his legs, trapping him underneath, unable to escape whoever had brutalized him so.

Cephora shook her head and crouched next to the dead man. "No," she said. "No, this is not good."

A woman's scream pierced the evening sky, splitting the air from a distance. All three of them shot up, their heads snapping in the direction of the scream. Will itched to move, to race in the direction of the scream, but he paused, "Cephora . . . ?"

Another scream tore through the air.

"Go!" Cephora shouted.

21

A CHANCE ENCOUNTER

T hey took off running, Cephora in the lead. Rounding a
bend in the road, they passed two more bodies that had
been cut down in their flight. Not even pausing at
them, Cephora turned and made for the woods as the brothers
followed. Another scream, filled more with anger than fear,
ripped across the air. It was closer to them this time—they were
moving in the right direction.

The ground sloped upward, the treacherous underbrush
threatening to wrench their feet from beneath them as they raced
up. They passed a torn, bloody cloak. As they neared the top of
the slope, Cephora dropped her pack and unslung her staff
without breaking stride. Flinging his own pack to the ground,
Will drew his blades and followed close on her heels as Madigan's noctori sprang to life.

Another scream. It took every part of Will to suppress his
Shade, particularly after the revelations Cephora had made, but
he was still clinging to his brother's plan of secrecy. *An ace in
the hole.*

They broke through the tree line atop the ledge of a small rock face. Below them, a drop of no more than fifteen feet, a woman was surrounded by a group of armed bandits. One of the assailants lay bleeding close by and another was dead at her feet. The bandits, though severely outnumbering her, had paused momentarily in their assault. In her left hand she was clutching a savage-looking knife while her other gripped a wound on her side. Blood seeped through her fingers.

Cephora and Madigan did not hesitate. They leapt from their perch and landed in a roll before hurling themselves among the attackers. The men, momentarily stunned by the newcomers, recovered quickly and lashed out with brandished weapons. Will followed his brother from the ledge and tucked into a hard somersault as he struck the ground. He leapt to his feet and took a wide stance, weapons at the ready. The knives in his hand seemed uncomfortably short compared to the weapons wielded by the surrounding bandits.

"Look out!" the woman shouted from behind him. Whirling, he just managed to dodge a notched and rusty sword that careened through the air where his head had been just a moment before. Will dropped low and spun, sweeping the man's legs out from under him. He hit the ground and Will kicked the sword from his hand as he struggled to recover. The woman raced over and plunged her knife into her assailant's chest. He gave a startled cry. Blood sputtered from the mortal wound.

Will's jaw dropped and he pushed himself backward, away from the corpse. He shook his head against the sight, suppressing the memories of blood and death that the spectacle brought to the surface.

"Thanks," he managed to say. He risked a glance at his savior. Her skin was pale and wet with perspiration. Her hair was dark and cut short to frame her face. Beautiful, intricate tattoos danced along her wrists. Will's jaw dropped in realization.

"Morella?" Will said.

She stared at him, no look of recognition on her face.

"Get down!" he shouted as another bandit appeared behind her. She ducked as Will flung himself forward, tackling the man to the ground and slamming the top of his skull into the assailant's face. The man didn't move, unconscious as blood poured from his shattered nose. Morella scrambled past Will with the knife and, before he could stop her, sank it into the man to the hilt.

"What are you doing?" Will cried, recoiling.

"Surviving!" she shouted back angrily and leapt to her feet.

A roaring scream of pain behind them sent Will spinning. He saw Madigan stumble, a knife buried in his leg and Will's entire body felt like fire. He raced toward his brother, seeing that he and Cephora were still fully engaged in fighting. Many of the men had fallen but the remainder pressed the attack.

Blood poured from Madigan's leg. Nevertheless, his focus was entirely on one backpedaling man who kept glancing at his companions. With Mad approaching, the man suddenly seemed to realize that the odds weren't in his favor, despite his wounded opponent. Turning, he raced toward the tree line. Without hesitating, Madigan set off after him, limping in his pursuit.

Cephora's staff spun through the air and made a sickening crack against the skull of one attacker before she quickly parried another and whirled to face a third. Their number had dwindled drastically and the fallen lay unmoving. The staff connected and Cephora's opponent fell to the ground with a thud. A single man remained, staring wide-eyed at Cephora, Morella, and Will.

He took a few steps backward before turning and fleeing in the opposite direction that Madigan had taken in pursuit of the other. Wordlessly, Cephora dropped to a knee. She took a bow from one of the fallen men and an arrow from his quiver. She nocked, drew, and before the man had reached the trees he fell, the arrow lodged between his shoulder blades.

Will closed his eyes, head spinning as he heard the man gasping out his last breaths, and turned back in the direction of his brother. He had not reappeared from the trees yet and a sudden panic gripped Will.

"Mad?" he called. There was no response. Will took off running toward where he had disappeared. He broke into the woods and, after a moment, saw Madigan in the distance, turned away and standing motionless. Will called his name again with no response. Nervous, Will made his way over toward him. As he approached, he saw his brother standing over something, his eyes fixed downward at it.

Madigan was breathing hard. The noctori hung limply in his hand. The dead man at his feet had been cut wide open. White hints of bone stood out against the red blood that was spreading along the rocky ground, pooling gently around Mad's boots. His brow furrowed, his mouth tight, he looked up and met Will's horrified stare.

"Looks like I was right," he said in a hushed tone. "I would end up killing again."

"Mad—" Will began to say but his brother shook his head.

"I'm fine, Will. That's what's scaring me."

"Jervin prepared you well," Cephora said. She had approached silently and laid a hand on Madigan's shoulder. His face was vacant. The noctori vanished from sight and he turned, wincing as he put his weight on his injured leg.

"Is the girl alright?" Madigan asked.

Will nodded as he searched his brother's face for any sign of what was going on in his mind. "I think so. We haven't really had a chance to check on her, though. You're not going to believe this, Mad, it's that girl from the inn. The one I danced with."

"Of course it is," Mad said through clenched teeth. He stepped forward and draped his arm around Will's shoulder and the three of them made their way back to where the girl, Morella, had remained. She glanced up as they emerged from the trees and withdrew into a defensive posture. She was sitting on a large stone with her back to the rock face, her eyes sunken and her face pale as her hand clutched her bleeding side. Cephora approached her gingerly.

"Please, may I help?"

Morella nodded her assent after a moment's consideration and Cephora crouched next to her. Will eased Madigan down onto another stone and glanced at Morella briefly, only to find that she was staring at him, her eyes hard.

"Who are you?" she asked. Will was taken aback; her tone was far from appreciative.

"We found your cart on the road," Cephora said while she worked on Morella's side. "Then we heard a scream. We came to help."

She jerked her head toward Will. "And that one? How did he know my name?"

Will didn't know how best to answer. He went to speak but drew up a blank. Before he could come up with an answer, Madigan cut him off.

"Like I said, Will, a missed opportunity."

Morella gave the boys an amused stare as Madigan chuckled. Will sighed and looked at her. "We met, briefly, not long ago. In Undermyre? We danced together at the Street of Ash."

"The Street of Ash . . . ?" She gave Will an appraising look. Then her face lit up as the memory came back. "Two span ago!

Yes!" She laughed before cutting it off with a wince. "You were sweet. You kissed me."

"I kissed you?" Will sputtered as Cephora snickered. "I mean, we kissed, yes. But I thought that, I mean if anything, didn't you—"

Madigan elbowed his brother hard and cut him off. "That's right. Glad you remember. Are you okay?"

"I'm fine," she replied. "But my question still stands, who are you? And why have you been following me?"

"Following you?" The surprise in Will's voice was plain. "We haven't been following you. We were going cross-country and just happened to end up here. It's pure coincidence."

She clearly didn't believe him. "I'm sure."

"Not exactly grateful, is she?" Mad muttered under his breath. The aside was said just slightly too loud to be taken as anything other than deliberate. Cephora chuckled again and Morella's gaze darkened a moment before softening.

"I'm sorry. Thank you," she said before sighing and looking at the ground. "While I don't know where you came from, I can see that you don't mean me harm the way these bastards did." She gestured toward the bodies on the ground and winced with the motion.

"I'm just glad we were able to help." Madigan's voice was thick. Will could see that despite his previous statement, the life he had taken was at the forefront of his mind. Morella smiled up at his brother with a soft sweetness in her eyes that sent a strange pang through Will's midsection.

"You'll be alright," Cephora said as she rose to her feet. "Despite the blood, the wound seems to be rather superficial. I closed it up. Just go easy on it."

Morella glanced down at her side and tested it with a few tentative movements as she thanked Cephora before turning her focus back to Will. "So, a coincidence then? Fine, I'll take that. Do you have names or should I just make some up for you?"

"Well, that depends on whether I like the one you come up with," Will said with a smile.

"Madigan Davis," his brother said as he eyed Will. "This is my brother, Will."

"Morella Darklore." Her face broke into a crooked smile as she turned her eyes to Cephora. "And you, my wonderful physician?"

Cephora eyed her warily a moment. "Oh no, I'm too intrigued, now. I'll let you choose one for me."

Morella laughed, sudden and lighthearted, and Will was transported back to dancing with her in Undermyre. Enraptured by the laughter, he smiled as Morella gazed at Cephora appraisingly.

"I'll just have to call you Medic then."

Cephora gave a bit of a pout, the most playful expression Will had ever seen from her. "That's not nearly as exciting as I thought it would be. Call me Cephora."

Will turned his attention back to Madigan's leg and saw that, somehow, it had already stopped bleeding. If anything, in fact, he could almost swear that the wound looked smaller, as though it was rapidly healing already. He stared at it dumbfounded. *Just like at the Nordoth.* His brother met his eyes and glanced at his leg before flexing it and shrugging with a wry smile. "Damned if I know, Will."

"So, what are three dark and mysterious travelers doing crossing the borderlands?" Morella asked. "Aside from rushing to the rescue of the likes of me, of course."

"Traveling," Cephora spoke quickly.

Will nodded in agreement. "Taking in the sights is all."

"I'm sure," Morella said. She glanced at Will and he flushed.

His head rushed with the silent rhythms of the music from their dance together. He found himself staring at her lips, pursed now, no longer smiling, and quickly averted his eyes before she noticed.

"And you?" Mad quipped. "Pretty damn funny that you also happen to be crossing the borderlands."

She eyed him levelly and spoke in a taunting, mocking tone. "Traveling. Taking in the sights."

Cephora looked at Madigan's leg. "Can you walk?" He nodded and she went on. "I know this area. There is an old watchtower here, a surviving remnant from the Wars of Dawning. We should move this conversation there."

Morella nodded and pushed herself to her feet, wincing as she did so. Madigan looked around at the bodies strewn around them.

"We should bury them," he said.

Will nodded in agreement at the same time that Morella protested. After a moment of awkwardness, Cephora interjected. "Why don't you two lead Morella back to her cart and gather anything she needs and I'll take care of them. I'll meet you there shortly."

Morella sneered but gave in. After a moment, she, Will, and Madigan made their way back to the main road, circumventing the rock face before venturing back the way they came. When they passed the bodies of Morella's companions, she paused momentarily at each, giving them a cursory glance and kneeling briefly, before rising and moving on without a word. As the trio approached the overturned cart she all but ignored the body closest to it before turning her full attention to the cart itself. Will was surprised by her seeming lack of compassion for the dead.

"Are you holding up alright?" Will asked as she rummaged

about, cursing occasionally but regularly pulling out various bags from which protruded rolled scrolls and maps.

"I'm fine," she replied absently. Her focus was on taking stock of the scrolls with an intensity that Will found off-putting. It was as if she had already forgotten the attack from moments before and the carnage that surrounded her.

Madigan approached, his lips twisted down into a hard frown. "Not a lot of remorse for the fallen, it seems," he said.

Morella rolled her eyes, then paused and looked up to meet his judgmental stare. "Should there be?" Her tone was flippant. "I barely knew them. I met them on the road yesterday and they were the ones who suggested we travel together for safety." She cocked her head to the side and glanced around her at the strewn contents of the cart. "It would appear that their suggestion was a bad one."

Mad stayed silent but his face, usually so composed, betrayed his thoughts. *He doesn't know what to make of her yet.* Then again, Will wasn't quite sure what his own thoughts were on the matter. She seemed so calm, so collected, as if the spectacle surrounding her was an everyday occurrence. *She just killed three men. Does that even faze her?*

He looked at Madigan and could see the conflict in his brother. After a moment, though, all the tension seemed to slip away from Mad's body. He met Will's questioning look and gave an almost defeated shrug.

Morella stood finally, her belongings gathered, and slung her bags over her shoulder. "And now?" she said.

"Let's save Cephora some time," Mad said. He presented himself as calm and controlled but Will could hear the strain in his voice. "I'm going to start digging a grave."

Without waiting for a response, he turned away from the wreckage and walked off the road. Morella, double checking her supplies, winked at Will and then set off after his brother. He let her get a few steps ahead, shaking his head as he considered the newcomer.

Oh yes, this one is tricky.

WHEN CEPHORA RETURNED A SHORT WHILE LATER, THE THREE had successfully moved the body into a shallow grave and covered it. After a quick scan of the broken cart for supplies, Cephora led them farther cross-country. Thirty minutes or so later, they approached the watchtower that she previously spoke of. Seeing the pain that plagued Morella's steps, Will offered to carry her supplies for her. She laughed politely and denied him with a quiet ferocity. Whatever it was she carried, she was passionate about protecting it. He did notice that after the offer had been made, however, her expression softened and she walked a bit closer to him.

The watchtower itself was nestled upon a hilltop and over-grown with roots and trees from years of neglect. The interior was spacious, and in a short time the group was able to clear much of the debris away from one of the larger rooms on the ground floor. Cephora set about making a fire in an ancient stone fireplace while the rest shrugged off their packs and collapsed to the ground for a time. A flat stone, nearly waist height, stood in the center of the space and they ultimately moved to surround it, using old stumps and logs as seats.

Despite her casual friendliness toward Will on the walk to the tower, Morella sat a short distance away from the rest of them. She kept herself between the group and her belongings, her eyes constantly darting to any flicker of movement. Will thought she seemed nervous, but then again, she was in the presence of strangers. *Given what she just went through, who wouldn't be cautious?*

Before long Cephora had a pleasant fire going and the room began to gain some warmth, the fire's comforting presence seeming to ease the strain of the day. She stood and brushed her hands on her long coat before making her way over to the table and seating herself opposite Morella. Taking a swig from her canteen, she looked up and smiled in a way that did not completely reach her eyes as she looked at the newest addition to the group.

"So," she began, "I would absolutely be delighted to hear a bit more about you, Morella Darklore."

Morella met the steady gaze and returned with an unwavering, unnerving smile. "Is that a fact?" she said.

Cephora nodded. "That it is."

Morella sat back and extended her legs forward, arching her back in a deep stretch for a moment before returning her focus to the group. "Well, you certainly helped me out back there and you seem safe enough. Very well then, where shall I begin?"

The warmth of the fire had done wonders for Madigan's mood and he gave her a quick wink. "Wherever seems most likely to get you to the end."

"Finishing would take far too long to get into the first time around," Morella said, giving a coy grin. "But really, I'm afraid I'm not nearly as intriguing as you'd like me to be. I'm a historian."

"A historian?" Will asked. "Wow, what do you do?"

"Well, Will, I imagine that she is someone who chronicles the history of a particular subject," Mad said with a grin. Both Cephora and Morella laughed at that.

Will felt his face flush. "I know that," he said. "I just meant that I wouldn't have pegged her for a historian is all."

Madigan chuckled. "Oh yeah? Known many historians, have you?"

"Well, no but what I meant was—"

"Oh, yes," Madigan spoke over his brother, "do tell us what you meant."

"Perhaps we should let the lady continue?" Cephora said, chiding him.

Morella laughed again while Madigan grinned. Will clamped his mouth shut. *I think I enjoyed it more when he was quiet and introspective.*

"Yes, Will, a historian," Morella said. Her face glowed with her wide, crooked smile. "Well, a historian of sorts." She paused and took a deep breath. "I study the ancient mysteries and legends of Aeril." She stopped speaking and looked at the brothers. She seemed to be waiting for something, as if she expected some kind of rebuke. When none came, her expression brightened and she sat just a little bit taller. "Usually when I say that aloud there is a bit more ridicule than that."

"Why would people ridicule you for educating yourself?" Mad asked.

Morella looked at him for a moment and then turned to Will, eyeing him up and down as though seeing him for the first time. Her eyes grew wide as they darted to Cephora, taking her in, and then back to the brothers. She turned her focus back to Cephora. "They're not . . ."

Cephora shook her head. "No, they are not."

"But from where, then?" Morella asked, her excitement bubbling.

Cephora sipped water from her canteen. "They are Casc."

Morella clapped her hands together and nearly cheered in excitement. "Fascinating! Oh, that explains so much." Her eyes, suddenly filled with a hunger, a need, flitted between Madigan and Will in quick succession. She studied the brothers as if unable to focus on either of them for fear of missing something from the other. "I have so many questions for you."

Cephora raised a hand. "Perhaps you could finish your own story first?"

Morella's eyes darkened momentarily, but then the shadow was gone as quickly as it had appeared. She bit her lip, nodded, and began a hurried speech. "Oh, yes of course. To answer your question, Madigan, it is not the education that is frowned upon. It is the subject. In this world, secrets are kept secret for a reason. I've spent years studying the secrets of Aeril, chronicling everything I discovered and"—she gestured to the scrolls in her bag—"my primary focus has been on one of the ancient stories, a work known in Aeril as *The Veleriat*."

"*The Veleriat*?" Will said in excitement. "We know that one!"

"Do you now?" Morella said, a gleam in her eye. "That's wonderful." Will beamed at his brother and Madigan rolled his eyes. Morella continued. "You see, many Aerillians view the myth as just that, a myth, a foundation for the belief system that arose in Aeril longer ago than anyone can remember. But I think there is something more to it. I think it is a true story, or at least elements of it are true."

Will's jaw dropped as he stared wide-eyed. "You think Velier was real? That the *Crimson Twilight* and Thorns of the Rose actually existed?"

"I'd stake everything on it." Morella beamed.

Cephora took another sip of water but didn't let her eyes fall from Morella. "Is that so?" she asked.

Morella nodded, obviously pleased to have found such a receptive audience. "You see, there are elements of the tale that coincide perfectly with actual surviving historical records. From my findings, I think there's more to Aeril than the world we know. Locations of great power, conduits for amplification, artifacts and the like . . . there are vast relics of untapped power."

Morella fell silent and furrowed her brow. Cephora closed the canteen and wiped her mouth with the back of her hand. "What was that last bit?"

A twitch danced along the corner of Morella's lips and she shook her head. "Just aspects of my research that are pointing me in various directions, nothing more."

"You're lying," Cephora said. Morella's happy face fell to a frown and before she was able to respond, Cephora continued. "You're searching for the Relics of Antiquity, aren't you?"

Morella clamped her mouth shut and shrank back within herself as if chastised. Will glanced at his brother, the sudden silence in the room harsh and abrasive. "What are the Relics of Antiquity?" he asked.

Morella didn't say a word. It was Cephora who finally answered. "Legends, Will. Artifacts of such power that whoever controls them could control the world. They were scattered to the winds, long ago."

Morella bit her lip and shook her head. "They're not what everyone thinks. They're not. *The Veleriat* proves that there is so much more to them than the capacity for destruction."

"I don't understand," Madigan said. "I've heard the story and I heard no mention of any relics like that."

"They aren't explicitly mentioned," Morella said, appearing to shrink back even farther as though trying to sink into the ground. "But how else could Velier have overcome all that he did? The Relics were the key."

Cephora glared at her. "I've seen their power firsthand," she said, spite dripping in each word. "And I've seen what madmen in pursuit of their power are capable of." She shook her head. "The Relics invite death to the world."

Warmth flooded Morella's pale cheeks, though from frustration or incredulity, Will could not say. "You've seen them?" She shook her head. "They've been lost for ages! How have you . . . ?" She closed her mouth and eyed the group's guide carefully. "Your name is Cephora."

Cephora flicked a twig into the fire and nodded.

"I am a historian, Cephora," Morella said in hushed tones. "What are you?"

There was the briefest pause before she answered. "I am a Seeker."

Realization that Will couldn't place poured over Morella's face. Her mouth formed into a tight line and she nodded brusquely before glancing at Madigan and Will. "And they are who, precisely?" Gone was the soft smile and easy laughter; her whole countenance had gone hard as steel.

"No one."

Morella barked a laugh and her gaze sharpened. "I highly doubt that."

"Not to interrupt," Will said, "but what, exactly, am I missing?"

Morella shifted uncomfortably as she glanced in Will's direction but did not speak. Cephora clasped her hands behind her head and leaned back, eyes never leaving Morella. "Nothing, Will," she said. "Morella was just about to continue her story."

"She's said enough," Mad interjected. "If she doesn't want to say more, that's okay."

"It's fine." The edge had left Morella and she gave Madigan a long, lingering look of appreciation. Still, she lacked her prior enthusiasm as she spoke. "The majority of my life has been quiet and bookish, most of my time spent in libraries. Legends"—she emphasized the word and glanced at Cephora—"put me on a path toward finding the Relics. I figured that if I could finally

267

find them, consolidate them even, then perhaps . . . " She sighed. "Perhaps peace would finally again come to Aeril. I've spent years following the rumors. One sent me on a path that led me through Undermyre and here I am."

"So," Will quipped after a moment, "you're just trying save the world is all."

Her eyes met his own and butterflies raced in his stomach. Morella's face, so serious only moments before, erupted into a huge grin and she let loose a boisterous laugh. "I suppose so," she said.

Will met her eyes, dark and enticing, and he felt the butterflies again. He gave a mock bow. "Well, how fortuitous for you! We have precisely the same goal."

"Will!" Madigan snapped. Will clamped his mouth shut and sent a hurt glance toward his brother. Cephora sighed audibly and put her face in the palm of her hand.

"You three are off to save the world?" Morella snickered.

"So it would seem," Cephora muttered as Will shrank beneath Madigan's glare.

She laughed with delight and seemed to relax again. "Madigan and William Davis, two Cascs, joining forces with Cephora, Prime of the Seekers, to save the world? Now there is a story I would love to hear."

"Oh no, it isn't really that at all," Will said quickly, trying to undo whatever damage he had done. "Plus, I'm afraid none of us are particularly eloquent when it comes to telling stories." Cephora stood and turned to tend the fire as Madigan just shook his head at his younger brother.

"I'm sure," Morella smiled.

"Really," Will said with as much casualness as he could muster. "Our story is quite similar to your own. We heard stories and went searching for our own adventure." *Gods, I don't sound the least bit convincing.* "We just happened to meet a guide who offered to show us the world a bit and here we are."

"Oh, well that explains everything then," Morella said, laughing again. "And you just happened to arrive here from Cascania? And happened to know how to fight? And you just happened to have weapons from the Halls of Shadow?" She stared at Will flatly. "I'm a historian, Will. I've studied weaponry. I know the arms you carry."

He shifted uncomfortably under her gaze.

"Anyone can fight, if the situation calls for it," Madigan said. "For a historian you seemed to handle yourself pretty well out there earlier."

Morella turned her gaze to Madigan and gave a cool smile. "Oh, you boys really are new here, aren't you? No one survives long in this realm without knowing how to hold their own." Her appearance softened a bit as she looked from Mad and back to Will. "Then again, I'd be lying if I said I wasn't grateful. Things got out of hand there. I just got lucky."

"Does that happen often?" Will asked. As soon as the words left his mouth, he wished that he could take them back.

"Fighting off bandits or getting lucky?" She shot him a wink. Will flushed. "Bandits have become more common the past few years. As for the latter, well, I'd say that's a private matter."

Will couldn't help but chuckle at that while Madigan roared with laughter. Even Cephora snickered, cracking her stoic demeanor for a moment before turning her back to the group and placing another log into the fireplace. The wood smoke filled the room lazily and Will realized that Cephora had placed a small pot over the fire. Whatever was inside smelled delicious.

Despite his embarrassment, he began to relax a bit. The time on the road from Undermyre had taken its toll, he could feel it, but Morella's presence was a welcome respite from the dust and grime of travel. A very attractive, intoxicating respite. *Definitely tricky, though. There's something about her that has an edge.* He shook the thought away. *Maybe I can get her to open up a bit, tell me her thoughts on* The Veleriat.

More boisterous laughter from Morella distracted him from his thoughts. She was engaged with his brother across the makeshift table, making idle, if entertaining, conversation. Her dark eyes caught the glint of the firelight and shone in the smoky room as the pair of them bantered playfully. Will felt uncomfortable, frustrated by the ease of their conversation. She placed a hand on Madigan's forearm and Will stiffened. No, not frustrated. Jealous.

Dammit.

After a few minutes Cephora brought the pot over to the table. Conversation opened up and came easy as Morella inquired about Mad and Will's home. Each of them did their best to explain their upbringing without divulging too much information and Will noted that Madigan was especially careful about any mention of their grandfather. Ignoring his pangs of jealousy, he followed Mad's lead and kept it ambiguous, although he couldn't understand why there was a need for such circumvention. Morella was a delight.

Will was already more than a bit smitten. She had woven a tantalizing spell on him the night he first met her, and each time she laughed that raucous, barking laugh he lost a bit more of himself in her. She was rough around the edges, no doubt, but it didn't faze him. Any sort of true caution was forgotten as soon as he saw her laughing flirtatiously with Madigan. Will was captivated. Something about her seemed so easy, so familiar, that he never gave it a second thought.

22

FANGS OF BLOOD

They decided to spend the following day in the ruined tower, resting and recovering. To Will's surprise, Madigan's leg continued its strange, rapid healing. The wound on Morella's side, however, was a bit more problematic. Cephora's skillful stitching and treatment had prevented it from festering but, once the initial adrenaline of the afternoon had dissipated, it became apparent how painful it was for her to move. Will admitted to himself that he wasn't entirely upset at the notion of some rest. Especially given the newcomer to their little band and the close quarters of the tower.

Early in the morning, Cephora woke Will and beckoned him to follow her outside. He rose, stumbling slightly as he got to his feet, and followed. Walking a short distance from the tower, Cephora made her way to a downed tree trunk and leaned against it, crossing her arms. Suddenly uncertain, Will fidgeted under her gaze. *Who is this woman, really? What does Morella know that we don't?*

"I thought this might be a good opportunity to continue an earlier conversation of ours," Cephora said. Will's nervousness increased and he shifted uncomfortably. "A chance to discuss in earnest the intricacies of the more magical properties of your fangs."

"Oh," Will said, the nervous tension suddenly replaced with excitement. "That would be brilliant, yes!" She motioned for him to sit on the log.

"I do not know what you know of dragons or what your world has made them out to be," she said as she took a seat next to him, "but dragons were guardians, great, powerful beings who wielded the powers of life and death."

"Yes," Will nodded. "I'm familiar with that, just not much more than that."

She smiled at him. "Ignorance is dangerous, even innocent ignorance. You must think of these blades as one would think of a surgeon's toolkit," she told him. "Such a kit, to the uneducated, could appear to be the instruments of a man who disposed death upon others, no? Something far more barbaric than their actual purpose?"

Will was quiet for a moment, considering the notion. It had never occurred to him before but, once put in such a light, it was unmistakable. "I could see that, yes. Sharp edges and metal and clamps and wrappings and the like."

Cephora glanced back at the tower as a faint noise trickled through the empty area. Madigan appeared from the tower and began to train with his noctori.

"And yet," she continued as she watched Madigan progress through his forms, "in the hands of one skilled in their use, such seeming barbarity is the most noble of trades, the most valuable of assets in any circumstance—someone who is able to restore health and vitality."

Will nodded his agreement and she held out a hand. Will unclasped his belt and removed it, handing it over to the Seeker. She gazed at it a moment, rubbing her thumb along the leather, then spoke again. "One of the dragons' many powers was their unnaturally long life, nearly immortal. Some believe that the ancient dragonkind granted this gift upon this realm at the forming of the worlds, hence why time has little effect on Aeril."

"I thought that was Velier's doing?" Will interrupted. "In *The Veleriat*, that was his gift to the world."

Cephora's eyes hardened at the interruption but she did not chide him. "There are many stories for the unknown. Returning to dragons, however, these fangs"—she plucked one from its sheath and gave it a measured look—"still bear the ability to bestow such gifts as they gave."

Will's eyes grew wide and he glanced at them warily. "Are you saying I can make people immortal?"

Cephora gave a hearty laugh. "No, no, although that would be impressive. But you are capable of restoring health and vigor to those who need it."

A spark of excitement gripped Will. "How?"

"The same way a surgeon works. Training. By understanding your tools and how to use them. By recognizing and accepting the cost of such endeavors."

Cost. Of course, Will should have known there would have to be a catch somewhere. "And that is . . . ?"

"It is straightforward enough," she said. "The cost is simple. Life for life. In order to give life, you must first bring death."

Will felt his stomach twist into a knot as Cephora gestured to the gem-like stones in the pommel of his blades. "You see, these bloodstones are connected directly to the properties of the knives themselves. They are a fount of power, the connection that binds the two blades. Through them the conduit of life from death may flow."

The twist in Will's stomach moved up, turning into a knot in his throat. "I have to kill?" he managed to say.

She laid a hand on his arm. "Blood for blood, Will."

He stared at the blades. He suddenly realized that he had no idea of their history, where they had come from before his grandfather gave them to him. How many lives they had taken. *And saved,* he reminded himself. But still, in a world of pseudo-immortals vying for power, who had wielded them before Will? How many people had died screaming by their edge? He recoiled, shaking his head. "I can't."

Cephora placed her free hand on his other arm and gave him a level look. "Not everything is so black and white as you seem to see it, Will. The world is filled with grey."

Will met her eyes and saw that they were kind, but stern. *So very much like Grandda's.* "What do you mean?"

"Have you ever been hunting?" she asked. Will nodded. "These bloodstones store life force within them, the power of vitality. Things are not always an equal scale. You do not need to kill a man to heal a broken bone. Small creatures, be it fish or birds, or even larger animals like deer and the like, anything with a beating heart and flowing blood will power the stones. The stones are a well that you both fill and tap as needed."

Well that changes things considerably. The key tingled against his chest. "Alright," he said, "you've piqued my interest."

"The art of the blood fang requires more than just two dragon fangs. They must be two very specific fangs, opposite ends of the spectrum of life. Once they have been obtained, they must be paired through the use of blood magic." She sighed, looking somehow disappointed. "As I said before, most of the art behind that has been lost or bastardized. However, once they have been paired, the bloodstones are capable of containing life-force and acting as a conduit between the two fangs. One fang absorbs life force while dispensing death. The other directs the accumulated flows."

As soon as she finished speaking, there was a soft snap in the distance. Cephora leapt to her feet and darted into the trees. After a moment, she called and Will followed after her. Only a short distance away, he found her standing over a snare that contained the limp body of a dead rabbit. "Perfect timing," she said. "What do you know of death, Will?"

"The same as anyone, I suppose. Death is death, the end of this life."

"Generally, yes. However, death is not a spontaneous occurrence. As everything in existence is the sum of many parts, death happens in stages." She crouched down to the rabbit. "Once the heart stops, brain activity may continue for up to six minutes in a human being. Skin cells can survive for days after death. Both the parasitic and symbiotic bacteria in your body continue to act independently of the brain. When a creature dies, it is still filled with life."

Removing the rabbit from the snare, she used the tip of the fang to pierce the hide at the base of the skull. Will watched as Cephora remained still for a moment, then withdrew the blade and rose. She turned back to him.

"Life is energy," she said. "And energy, in all things, is conserved. There is no true give or take, only a transference. From the life of this rabbit, not only are we able to obtain nourishment but we are also able to restore health to those who may need it. Someone like our new friend, Morella."

Will couldn't stop the grin that spread across his face. "Well, I think that could be absolutely delightful, Madame Cephora."

She let out a laugh at his sudden enthusiasm and handed the

blade back to him, carrying the rabbit in her other hand. "Let's go get this processed and have some breakfast first. Then we'll buckle down and get to work."

Will cleaned the spot of blood from the blade and followed her back to the tower. Madigan was still training while Morella remained inside, resting. As he and Cephora worked to prepare food, Will allowed his gaze to drift to Morella. Lounging on her side, she was poring over her notes and writing in a small, leather-wrapped notebook. Every once in a while, she would shift and a look of discomfort would cloud her pale features. Will grinned as he imagined her expression when he healed the pain away but then chided himself for using her pain as a method of gaining her favor.

Breakfast was simple, a quick stew of dried meats, vegetables, and the fresh, lean meat from the rabbit. Madigan offered to clean up, much to Will's delight, allowing him to return to his training with Cephora. Mad had no qualms about staying behind with Morella, and as Will returned to the small clearing by the woods he could hear them chatting easily.

The key tingled against his skin as he thumbed his blades in anticipation. Visually, the bloodstones appeared no different than before but, to Will, there was a marked change. He couldn't explain it, but it was as though he could sense that their power had increased, albeit only fractionally. He knew that the life-force contained within a single, mostly dead rabbit couldn't have amounted to much—but the sheer possibility of fluctuating power was tantalizing.

"Now," Cephora said, "what are your dominances?"

Will stared at her blankly. "What?"

"Hand, eye, what do you use most?"

"Oh, got it. I'm right-handed mostly. I'm left-eye dominant though."

She raised an eyebrow. "Right hand and left eye, really?"

Will nodded. "It always made archery lessons a bit of a struggle."

She chuckled. "But your swordplay felt more natural, didn't it?" Will nodded again and she held out her hand. "Good. Let me make a few adjustments to your belt."

Will removed the leather belt, handing it over to her. She crouched and set to work on the straps, adjusting the sheaths into a new configuration and wrapping the straps in on themselves. When she stood and handed it back to him, Will admired her handiwork. The left blade now sat upon his hip, angled slightly in front of his body, while the right had been shifted to his back, sitting horizontal in a scout-carry.

"This will allow for quicker access to the blade with your nondominant hand. Your right blade is now concealed far better by both your cloak and your jerkin. Give them a few practice draws."

She was right. Will found the drawing motion was much more fluid on the left. He was able to unsheathe the blade and raise his arm in a deflective blow in a single motion, saving precious moments that could potentially be crucial. The right blade was more difficult to adjust to as it forced him to flick his arm in a semi-circle as he brought it forward. After a few tries, he got the motion down and linked the two actions together.

Cephora nodded her approval. "Much better," she said. "This will allow you to deflect an incoming blow quickly while following up and eviscerating your opponent at the same time. You will block and counterattack at the same time, if need be."

Will imagined the razor edge of the fang slicing across the fleshy stomach of an opponent and shuddered. "That sounds lovely."

Cephora continued as if his sarcasm had gone unheard. "Your

use of the fangs should be your secondary combative option. Given the training from your grandfather and your stature, we need to get you outfitted with a sword as your primary. A saber will probably prove best, given what I've seen of your movements. That will leave your off-hand free to access the fang should it become necessary."

At the thought of training with a saber against Madigan's bastard sword, Will groaned. Cephora rolled her eyes and gave Will a level look. "Will, you are young and may still have some growing to do but it will not be as much as you might hope. You will not fill out the way that your brother has. It is simply not going to happen." He glowered as she spoke, the words stinging, but still she continued. "Your assets are your speed and mobility. That is what you need to hone. You must outthink your opponent. You must be ten steps ahead of them and plan for their mistakes rather than attempt to overcome them with brute strength. Your grandfather knew this, else he would not have given you the weapons he did."

Deep down, Will knew that her words were true but that did not make hearing them any easier. Madigan had always surpassed him in size and strength, but Will always dreamed that it was only temporary, that the years would equalize them. Not knowing how to respond, he furrowed his brow in frustration. "All of this is necessary for me to heal a pretty lady's cut, is it?"

"Yes, it is." Cephora's voice was cold and sharp. "If you want to rise to your full potential you need to know both what you are, and are not, capable of. You must be honest with yourself."

After a moment under the scrutiny of those hard eyes, Will apologized. He reminded himself that Cephora was there solely because she truly did want to help. She accepted the apology without further comment and immediately went back to her lesson as though the interruption had never even occurred.

Dropping to a crouch, she began to draw in the dirt as she spoke.

"Your right fang, the slightly larger, consumes life," she said, sketching a rough outline of the blades. "Your left grants it. The powers of the right are inherent within the fang itself, which automatically transfers the life-force of whatever it touches into its bloodstone. The left fang is not so simple."

"I would hope so," Will interjected. "It doesn't seem like stabbing someone would be the most effective way of making them feel better."

She cracked a smile and tipped her head to him. "No," she said, "it would not be. The method initially involves a far greater amount of focus, but the quicker you master it, the quicker and easier it will be for you. Eventually, it may even become a passive part of your consciousness, allowing you to act without hesitation."

"Well, let's get to it then, right?" Will quipped, trying to restore the excited, light-hearted nature of moments before. "What do I need to do?"

Cephora gestured to the belt and signaled for Will to withdraw a blade. "You strike me as a rather intuitive individual, Will. How would you go about it?"

Will thought a moment and considered the weapon before responding. Turning it in his hands, he eyed the edge of the blade. He examined the leather wrapping and the bloodstone. As he traced his fingers along the stone, he felt the excited vibration of the key as it began to tingle against his chest. Remembering his first experience with the key, he focused on the stone itself and stared into it. Like the key before, something about the stone, too, was hypnotic. Yet, while it was beautiful to gaze at, Will would be lying if he said he had any actual idea of what to do.

Finally, he broke his concentration and looked to Cephora.

"You said the flows need to be directed." She nodded. "So, I have to access them then, right?" She nodded a second time and Will brightened. *I can do this.* Thinking back to the Nordoth and how he managed to access his Shade through meditation, he tried to find connections between the two. "I would need to know the nature of the fang. I would need to will it to follow my direction."

Cephora nodded her approval. "Not bad. Not entirely correct but surprisingly close. The fang is the fang, as inanimate as your own teeth are. Its capabilities are accessed through connecting the fang to you. Binding yourself to it, as it were."

"So you're saying I get to become part dragon?" Will said, a wide grin stretching across his face. Cephora looked at him, obviously trying to determine whether or not he was joking. Will didn't move but finally laughed and winked at her.

Cephora sighed and shook her head, muttering under her breath, "This is going to take longer than I thought."

In truth, it took less time than Cephora had made it seem. For Will, however, it felt like an eternity. For the remainder of the day Cephora taught him how to focus his mind with an intensity he had never before imagined possible. Every single aspect of the blade was drilled into his brain until he felt that he knew it better than he knew his own hands. The amount of time he spent focusing on the depths of the bloodstone itself felt like days, although he knew it couldn't have been more than a handful of hours.

After the whole process, he had a splitting headache and had gotten two nosebleeds. But finally, just as daylight started to dim and the first hints of dusk stretched across the sky, Will found something new, a connection that he couldn't place—an imperfection that would drive him insane were it not remedied.

Scrambling to his feet, he began turning the blade over and

over in his hands as Cephora looked on, her face impassive. The bloodstone, there was something about it that wasn't quite right, something missing from it. Its connection to the knife itself wasn't complete, it needed something more. It needed . . .

"Blood," he whispered.

From the corner of his eye he saw the hint of a smile on Cephora's face. He was about to make his way back to his supplies to retrieve a knife but hesitated after a step. Why go back? He already had a sharp edge at hand. The memory of his first contact with the fiery fury that coursed through his body after being on the receiving end of the blade brought him up short. But the more he danced around the thought, the more it seemed appropriate: If he desired the blade to do as he wished, should he not also do as it wished? Steeling himself, he ran the sharp edge of the blade along his left palm.

The pain was even worse than he remembered. The agonizing sensation of burning coals and licking flames drove him to his knees. Distantly, in the back of his mind, some rational part reminded him that it wasn't real, that it was all in his head. Will struggled to focus on the task at hand and remembered the dragon fang. It had fallen. He must have dropped it after marring his palm.

He stretched his left hand down to it. Grasping the hilt in his blood-drenched fingers, he held it and squeezed with all the strength he could muster. His blood seeped through his fingers and ran down along the leather to the bloodstone. The key at his neck sent a lightning jolt through his body and he cried out as the pain blazed with renewed intensity. Will's eyes rolled back into his head and he blacked out.

When he came to, Cephora was standing over him and giving him a look of satisfied approval. The pain was gone. His hand, still clutching the fang, was covered in cracked, dried blood. He opened his fingers and looked down. His palm was perfectly fine, all traces of the cut gone. He stretched and flexed his fingers, wiggling them. No hint of any injury. Smiling, he looked up to Cephora. "Easy as pie."

She barked out a laugh and helped him to his feet. "Not bad, kid. Not bad at all."

In that moment, she sounded just like his grandfather and Will's heart seized with wishful desire to hear his laugh again. Shaking the thought from his head, he made his way to his feet and held up the blade for inspection. Visually, nothing had changed but Will could feel the energy coursing through it more than ever before. It was almost as if he could see the dancing patterns of power that permeated the blade. He withdrew the other and felt the same sense of connection. "Now what?" he asked.

Cephora shrugged. "Now we head back and see what you can do." Sheathing the blades, Will followed her.

As they walked, Will could feel the power of the weapons coursing around his body, not unlike the key upon his chest, although to a far lesser extent. *So, that sensation must mean magic is near?* If that was indeed the case, then the key must be extra strong to be so forceful and so constant. His mind raced. If the dragon fangs were capable of so much, then what was the purpose of the keys? What secrets did they hold?

His thoughts were interrupted as they entered the broken watchtower, replaced instead by a rush of hot anger. Madigan was lying head to head with Morella, the book of maps they had brought open in front of them. They were laughing and Morella was making quick marks in the book while Madigan goaded her for sloppy penmanship. The sound of her laugh coupled with the smile in his brother's eye reignited Will's spark of jealousy and frustration.

"Will!" Mad called when he noticed Cephora and his brother approach. "We were just talking about you!"

"Oh yeah?" Will said. His attempt at a lighthearted reply failed miserably.

Morella's grin nearly broke through his anger as her eyes met his own. "Yes! Your brother was just telling me about your abilities as a pickpocket, once upon a time. Very impressive, I must say!"

Mad said that? Will had only ever successfully practiced on his family after his first attempt had gone so awry. He softened a bit, realizing there was an opportunity to seize upon. "Well, despite it not being the noblest of pursuits, I was rather good at it." *Not really, but she doesn't need to know that.*

Morella pushed herself up to sitting and bent forward with a poorly concealed wince. Leaning toward Will, she narrowed her eyes and gave him a soft, crooked smile that set his heart racing. "How good were you?"

Smiling back at her, Will felt no need to make any attempt at humility. "I'm done in a heartbeat and they never feel it."

"See, Morella? By his own mouth he admits that he has a touch so soft you'd miss it . . . " Madigan said, barely containing his laughter.

"Wait, what?" Will asked, suddenly uncertain.

". . . and he can finish quicker than you'd imagine possible!"

Madigan and Morella burst out laughing again. Even Cephora joined in. Will's face flushed as he realized the implication. He stammered something forgettable that only caused them to laugh more. Flustered, he turned around and left the tower, returning to the small clearing where he and Cephora had spent the day in training. He collapsed onto the aged log, so bristling and brooding with embarrassment that he nearly missed the tentative footsteps that approached.

Will looked up, an insult on the tip of his tongue to unleash upon Madigan, only to stop short. It was Morella, not Madigan. As she stepped toward him, he saw that her eyes were concerned, her brow pinched above a tight-lipped frown.

"Not much of a joker, are you?" Her words were gentle and contained a hint of confusion.

Will sighed and looked back to the ground, shaking his head. "Actually, I usually pride myself on my sense of humor. I suppose this time was just a bit different."

Morella cocked her head to the side. "Why's that?"

The words eluded Will for a brief moment. Then he looked up and met her eye. "In Undermyre," he said, "at the Street of Ash, that was really nice, you know? For me, I mean. Things had been, have been, rough for a while. And dancing with you, it was good." He paused again, embarrassed by his halted speech. *Gods, I sound like a child.*

"Dancing is always good." She smiled.

"Right," he said. "Then you kissed me and disappeared and it was just this brilliant moment in the midst of so much darkness. I thought that's all it was. Running into you again and everything in the past day and a half? I don't know. It seemed, and this is going to sound absurd, but it seemed so perfect. So fated. But that's more than a bit of unfair expectation on my part, I suppose. Especially given the circumstances." A chuckle slipped from him before he could stop it. "I just got a bit jealous of Madigan is the truth of it. I didn't mean to put you in the middle."

"Fated?" Will glanced up to see Morella's grin spreading and he could hear the amusement in her voice.

"Fated." He smiled back. "Although maybe it could just be good luck." It struck him, then, how since the death of his grandfather, he had been a subdued version of himself. Elements of the him that he knew broke through to the surface on occasion, but when it was only he and Mad for so long, he had become passive and withdrawn. As he saw Morella's smile and the humor in her eyes, he realized a change was needed. "How's your side?"

Her eyes flickered in doubt for a moment. "It hurts but it'll be fine."

Will's left hand thumbed the bloodstone at his side. He could feel the energy coursing through the blades, pumping like a heartbeat. Glancing down, he could swear he could actually see the flows of power coursing through them. In that moment, he reached forward and felt the flows follow, stretching and narrowing as his hand extended. As if responding to a call, the power coursed forward beyond his hand and onto the wound at Morella's side for the briefest of moments. She gasped.

Will let his hand fall, the power of the bloodstone seemingly spent as the key at his neck was the only remaining sensation. She turned away from him and lifted her shirt before staring back at him in disbelief. "It's gone, completely gone. What did you . . . how did you do that?"

Will smiled and winked at her, feeling more sure of himself than he had in weeks. "Definitely just good luck."

Her disbelief changed to delight and she stepped forward and brushed his lips with her own in a quick kiss. "Thank you."

"You're welcome," Will said, smiling as tingles shot through his body and this time not from the key. "It ought to make your travel plans less unpleasant at the very least." Her eyes fell as he spoke and her smile became pained. Will realized that he had no idea what her travel plans actually were, now, only that she would be alone. "Them being whatever they may be, of course."

"About that," she began. "I know we've only just met and I know our paths may not align for long but I've been thinking"— she held Will's eyes with her own and reached out, intertwining her hand in his —"could I join you?"

Adding another member to their party was definitely something that should be discussed with Cephora and Madigan, he knew, but this woman with that smile and those eyes had him enraptured.

"I thought you'd never ask."

❧ 23 ❧

THE RELICS OF ANTIQUITY

Will had a surprisingly easy time convincing Madigan. Cephora, however, was warier about accepting a new member into the group, particularly one they knew so little about.

"We cannot," Cephora told him after pulling him and Madigan aside. "Our path is too dangerous to allow any unknown agents to interfere."

"But she won't be interfering," Will said as he ducked farther out of Morella's hearing. "With all her knowledge, she'll be an asset."

Cephora gave a disdainful sniff. "I have my doubts about her 'knowledge,' as you call it."

"Then think of it this way. She'll be all alone out here if she doesn't join us," Madigan said. "Whatever is out here had no compunction about attacking her group even though there were many of them. Imagine what could happen to her on her own? Do you really want that on your conscience?"

Cephora eventually relented but only on probationary terms.

"And," she said, lowering her voice even further, "say nothing of our mission, nothing of our overall goals. The stories you gave were ambiguous and left much to be desired. As a historian, she'll be skilled in connecting dots and digging up information."

"That could be useful though," Will said.

Cephora quieted him with a sharp look. "Unless it is information we would rather leave buried. Until we are able to trust her completely, secrecy is needed. Tell her nothing."

The brothers agreed but something about it seemed unfair to Will. *Morella told us who she was and what she's about.* It felt strange bringing someone who had been so straightforward with them into the fold and giving her nothing in return. Still, when the offer to join them was made, Morella quickly accepted and asked no further questions.

The next morning, they set out just as the sun broke over the distant hills. The days that followed were largely uneventful. The scenery didn't change much as they were walking parallel to the mountains at either side. The trees all began to look the same, and Will soon was surprised to realize that he had grown rather bored.

To save himself, he took to walking next to Morella and trying to learn more about her. She remained guarded about much of her past, but who was Will to judge? She was a delight to have as a companion on the road, laughing and storytelling regularly and making lewd remarks that shocked even his brother. Morella made him feel warm, excited in a way he hadn't felt before.

She was a stark contrast to Cephora. As the days passed, the guide became increasingly stoic and withdrawn. When periodic silence fell over the group, she seemed to relax and find her normal stride again. But once conversation started up again she would furrow her brow, set her jaw, and trudge along.

For a time Madigan was as enamored with their new companion as Will. The earlier jealousy Will had experienced was not, it seemed, a fleeting thing. Mad was older, strong and handsome and every bit the dark-haired hero of his own story. But Morella shied away from Mad's advances in favor of spending time with his little brother. Finally, Morella moved to Will and took his arm, claiming that she needed assistance over a rock or tree root that Will never saw. When Madigan backed away, saying nothing about it and making no further advances, Will finally felt the jealousy give way to confidence. *Well, he always was a quick learner.* Will smiled as Morella's warmth gripped his arm.

As for Will himself, he was too lost in the prospect of an adventurous history and amorous attentions to recognize the quickly souring mood of half the party. The day after Morella spurned Madigan, he began spending more time with Cephora, which was just fine with Will. His own morning training with Cephora decreased as she and Madigan spent more time together, speaking quietly and strategizing. Will didn't mind; it gave him far more time to spend with Morella, getting lost in conversation and laughter and stories. She was loud and exuberant and full of fire and, as they grew closer, her flames consumed him.

The days and miles rolled by. One morning, soon after breaking camp, Cephora took them on a short detour.

"There is a town nearby," she said as they trekked. "It is small but it houses one of the finest blacksmiths alive. It is time to get you a blade more suited for combat, Will."

"Perfect," Morella said, her voice growing in excitement. "I've been wanting a new dagger, perhaps they'll have one suitable."

Cephora's mouth became a thin line. "Perhaps," she said.

"Granted, it's a shame that no matter how fine his work is,

it will be of inferior quality," Morella continued as if not having heard Cephora. There was a hint of snark in her voice. She looked at Will and dropped her chin in a look that he had come to associate with her preparing to tell a story. "You see, before the Wars of Dawning, the finest weapons were produced by Gren'al. He discovered a method to fold all his weapons with Aerilite. Whatever was produced was"—she paused and looked to the sky, sighing—"immaculate. Pristine. Perfect. But after the Wars, the technique for working with Aerilite was lost. No one knows how or why. But the weapons would have made any produced in this age look like flimsy toys."

"If the technique was so strong," Madigan said, his tone nearly matching Cephora's, "how come it hasn't survived?"

"Gren'al never took an apprentice," she replied, stressing the words as if she had already made the point quite clear. "And the works themselves have been lost to time, either hoarded away or lost."

"How convenient," Madigan said quietly.

Will shot him a dirty look. *What's gotten into him?*

They made their way into town and found the blacksmith. His shop was small and quaint from the outside, but Will was stunned by the quality of the work within. He had never seen blades of such fine craftsmanship, had not even known something so fine could exist.

"And yet it's a poor imitation of what greatness truly was," Morella said as the blacksmith was outfitting Will with a saber. The smith ignored the comment, but Will saw Cephora stepping out of the room, shaking her head.

Once they had completed the transaction, the smith disappeared back to his forge and Will fit the blade over his shoulder with a baldric. He was ecstatic about the craftsmanship, uncertain but eager to test it against Madigan's noctori during their sparring sessions.

Wait, when was the last time we sparred?

As he thought about it, he realized it had been more than a while. *Before Morella came. Did we stop because Madigan had . . .* Had what? Become jealous? That didn't sound like him. But what else could it be? A change had come over his brother, that much was obvious. Madigan, and Cephora too, had been acting strange. Something about Morella, perhaps?

For reasons Will couldn't fathom, both Madigan and Cephora seemed totally uninterested by her stories, but he was fascinated. She knew about everywhere they ventured and every place they visited. She told them everything, held nothing back. Will could understand their frustration at the lack of peace and quiet, maybe, but he found the information she provided invaluable. He couldn't understand why they didn't seem to agree.

Perhaps they're feeling marginalized? He could see that. Morella knew the area, had dozens of maps, so Cephora's usefulness as a guide was lessened. And Will had grown close to her, finding a kindred spirit. It was as if the gods had plucked out exactly what Will had always longed for and presented it right in front of him. On some level, that new companionship had interrupted his and Madigan's. No wonder Madigan and Cephora were frustrated by Morella's presence: They were feeling replaced. *They're just still adjusting to the change.* It all clicked.

Two weeks after Morella joined the party, any remaining walls of secrecy between her and Will started to crumble in earnest. The landscape had been leveling out and losing its green in lieu of craggy rocks and red clay. They had made their camp for the night under a barren tree, and while Madigan and

Cephora talked between themselves by the campfire, Morella and Will walked together, deep in conversation.

The power of his blades had been exhausted after healing her wound, but he had spent the weeks since gradually replenishing their power with whatever game they managed to take. Will had been using small amounts of the power to restore himself after a day's long journey and found his need for sleep greatly lessened. Morella operated on very little rest herself and so their nightly walks had become a pleasant regularity. On this particular night, they found an embankment of rock with an uprooted tree at its base to sit upon. Will gazed at the unfamiliar stars and they lapsed into an easy silence.

Morella's fingers interlocked with Will's and he broke his gaze from the stars to meet her own. Later, he couldn't remember who kissed who first. He couldn't remember moving to the hard ground at the base of the embankment. But he did remember that there was nothing gentle in the act that followed, nothing sweet. There was only a sense of urgency and, strangely, competition. Her skin against his was as electrifying as the key at his chest, and that was active with an intensity he had never imagined. The electricity met the blood coursing through his body and Will's entire being became fire. Distantly, he heard her scream as her fingers tore into his back.

The darkness became still once more. They watched nighttime clouds move in to cover the stars. Morella's sudden laugh broke the quiet.

"Something amusing?" Will quipped, feeling all too pleased with himself.

"Not at all." She smiled and nuzzled in closer to him. "Just something that was very needed."

"You'll hear no disagreement from me on that point."

She rolled over to look at him and rested her head in the

crook of her elbow. She had a look on her face that was new to Will, one he couldn't read. "Where did you come from, William Davis? Why is this so easy? Why do you seem so familiar?"

"Maybe you've just been dreaming about finding someone like me your whole life?" Will grinned. She laughed and nuzzled her head back onto his shoulder.

"Oh, of course, that's it," she said. Will could hear a warmth in her voice, the careful playfulness with which she spoke. "I'm serious, though. There is something inexplicable about this, about you. Who are you?"

The warmth of her filled him with pride and confidence and fearlessness. With barely a passing thought, he shrugged aside Cephora's instruction. "You know that Mad and I come from Cascania. What you don't know is that our grandfather was Jervin Davis. Or rather, you may have heard of him as Jervin Thorne."

To his surprise, she smirked and nodded. "I'd assumed as much." She must have sensed his shock and laughed. "Come now, Will. I'm a historian. Everyone knows who Jervin Thorne is. And between you and your brother, well, it wasn't hard to figure out that while you're not exactly native here, you have a strong familiarity with our world. The general assumption amongst historians was that Thorne fled to Cascania. I just put two and two together."

Will chuckled and kissed the top of her head. "That obvious is it? Fair enough. What else, then?"

"What are you doing here?" she said as she traced the edge of his face with her short, chewed fingernails.

He grinned at her. "Aside from the obvious . . . ?"

She laughed again. "Oh, it's rather apparent what you were doing here. I want to know you. What makes you tick. Your secrets. I want to know what you're doing *here*."

Will paused before answering, considering how best to respond. "My grandfather is dead. Mad and I came here to finish what he started."

She was quiet a moment. "And that is?"

Will threw all caution to the wind. "Dorian Valmont." There was a steel in his voice that he didn't recognize. "We're here to—"

She laughed again, interrupting him. "You're hunting Valmont?" Will thought he saw a flash of darkness pass over her face, but it was gone before he registered it fully. He began to shake his head to clarify, but Morella didn't notice and instead pressed herself closer to him and kept speaking. "I'm lucky I found you."

"Oh, don't worry, I know he's dead. I'm looking for—"

"Dead? Hardly."

Will clamped his mouth shut. His mind raced. *Hardly? He plunged to his death, heart pierced by a blade. There were witnesses.* But Morella had studied and learned so much; did she know something no one else did?

"You're far from the only ones who want to find Valmont." Her voice had an edge to it and she wasn't leaning into him as much as a moment before. "Perhaps that is why our paths have crossed."

"Fate again?" he said, trying to reignite her warmth. It didn't seem like the right time to correct her assumption about his purpose, especially if she had information no one else did.

"Or just luck," she said, snuggling close once more.

Taking a risk, Will laughed. "So," he said, "the historian who knows everything about every blade of grass is after Dorian Valmont, is that it?"

The edge in Morella's words returned, only this time it was far sharper. "You're not the only one whose family has suffered because of his actions." She sat up and looked at the sky. Will followed suit and she took his hand before turning to him. She looked earnest, almost pleading. "That is why I'm searching for the Relics."

Will shifted position and scooted back to lean against the downed trunk. "These Relics you keep mentioning, what are they?"

"Ancient artifacts, I told you that before."

"Yes, that much I remember." Will sighed. "I mean what do they do? What exactly are they?"

"They're all different in their own ways," she said hesitantly. "The exact number is unknown, but sources generally agree that there were thirteen. Each of them imbued the wielder with certain gifts, gifts that enhanced them and raised them above others."

"Cephora seems to think they're rather dangerous."

"A stone can be dangerous. It can also lie as the foundation of a palace."

Will thought back to his conversations with Cephora regarding a surgeon's toolkit and he cocked his head at Morella. "So you're making a palace for this world then, are you?"

"What I am trying to do is generate a means to creating a more peaceful world," she continued, the edge once again returning. "A world with justice."

Will raised his hands and shook his head. "I get that. I'm just trying to understand how these Relics will do it."

"I keep forgetting that you're Casc," she muttered and slumped back against his shoulder. "You know the legends of Valmont? The scope of his power? These artifacts can level the playing field. No one else has been able to confront him successfully because no one understood the amount of power that would be needed."

Will considered a moment. "If he's so powerful, how do you know he hasn't got the Relics already?"

She snickered and smiled a cruel smile. "Because they've been lost for longer than anyone living can remember. Plus, there is the fact that if he had managed to obtain any of them, the world as we know it would be dead."

"Fair enough," Will conceded. "And you think you know how to find them?"

"I have an idea of where to look. Each of them exuded its own power, its own level of influence. I just need to continue tracing elements of that power and follow the clues." She reached down and pulled her cloak from where it had been discarded, drawing it close around her body. "Their power comes from both Radiance and Shadow and is augmented by the carrier."

"But there are no carriers," Will said. "You said it yourself. The Relics are lost."

Her hard eyes betrayed the smile she gave. "But I now know that certain elements of the stories are true. Cephora saw to that." At a questioning look from Will, she continued. "In recorded memory, only a single person in control of a Relic was ever documented. Jero din'Dael. He was the greatest champion of Radiance, their prime Revenant. He was also Valmont's most bitter rival. It was because of him that the combined forces of Radiance and Shadow were able to overcome Valmont in the first place. He used his Relic, some kind of emerald. He also, as the stories go, was an absolute psychopath."

"He sounds lovely," Will said. "And I assume he was buried with the Relic?"

She shook her head. "There is no record of anything about him after Valmont's Sundering of the Ways."

"Except for Cephora," Will said, realization dawning on him.

Morella smiled. "Except for Cephora. They were allies, albeit strained ones, during the war. They fought alongside one another until the end and the Seekers had kept careful eyes on din'Dael throughout. If anyone knows what happened to the Relic after din'Dael's death, it would be Cephora." She tilted her head and kissed Will's neck softly, sending a pleasant chill through him. "If we can find the Relic, we would be the first in memory. It would help lead us to the others. We could change the world."

"Well, I wish you all the luck in the world asking Cephora about it," Will said, lightly caressing Morella's arm. "She seems to have grown a bit tightlipped."

Morella pursed her lips. "I've noticed. I don't think she enjoys my being here very much. Her or your brother."

"Mad's just jealous," Will scoffed. Morella didn't seem terribly reassured by his reply so he moved in closer and wrapped both arms around her. "After all, who could blame him?"

She gave a hearty laugh that ended in a snort and pressed herself against him. "Oh yes, I am ever the object of everyone's affections."

"Well you're the object of mine, at least."

Their conversation drifted into a gradual silence before they gathered themselves and made their way back to their companions. Will was distracted, but not for the reasons one would normally assume; his thoughts kept drifting back to the Relics. He remembered Senraks's attack, a mere pawn of Valmont's, and how soundly they had been driven back by it as it murdered their grandfather. How were they supposed to defeat it? And, if Valmont was truly alive and such a creature paled in comparison to him, what would happen if they had to oppose the man himself? How would they survive?

The Relics. He knew it in his bones. Then again, they also had Cephora. Could she be enough to balance the scales? *Or better yet, give us the advantage?* It didn't seem likely. He watched the Seeker as she moved about the camp, casually avoiding Morella and her belongings. She didn't strike Will as a person who could take down the most terrible man who had ever lived, far from it. And while the Crow was touted as clever, his loyalties were far from apparent and Cephora was his agent.

The Relics, then, were paramount to surviving in the long run. If Morella was right, if Valmont lived, then someday they would face him. *Without the Relics, we'll be dead.* The Relics were the key to defeating Valmont, and Morella was the key to the Relics. Regardless of Mad and Cephora's feelings about her, Will knew that they were going to need her.

And I don't want her to go. I want to help her. He knew he had complicated the situation, but his grandfather would have supported his overall plan, wouldn't he? *He would have wanted us to help too.* Will needed advice, he needed someone else's insight. He needed to talk to his brother.

Something twisted in his gut. He didn't *want* to talk to Madigan. His brother had been so quiet lately, so secretive, distant ever since Morella joined them. Whatever Will wanted to say, there was no way Madigan would be interested. Mad was cold and reserved. Both he and Cephora had completely omitted Will from any discussion of their plans and there was no part of him that imagined either would be receptive to his suggestion of changing their course. *I still have to try.* Begrudgingly, he made his way over to Mad.

"Well, hello there, stranger," Madigan said, glancing up from the map he was studying as Will approached. "Where've you been the past hour?"

"Morella and I were just off chatting," Will replied quickly.

He wasn't sure why he felt guilty. If anything, Madigan would cheer and clap him on the back.

"Of course," Madigan said. He snickered and looked back down at his map. "Chatting."

"Listen, Mad," Will said, ignoring his brother's tone. "What's our plan? We've seen how strong the thing we're going up against is. How are we going to take it down?"

Madigan put the map aside before he pulled a new one over and began scanning it. "You've got an idea, I take it?"

"I've been thinking," Will said, choosing his words carefully, "that we need to level the playing field. And I think I know how."

"Oh?" Madigan didn't look up when he spoke, tracing a line along the map and then shifting back to the previous one.

"Morella told me more about the Relics. I think we can use them to our advantage."

To Will's surprise, his brother didn't contradict him. "Haven't they been lost for generations?"

"Yes, but we could find them. That's why I think we should hold off on finding Senraks until we collect them."

Madigan snickered again and put the map aside. "And how long do you think it'll take to find these ancient artifacts? These powerful items that have been lost to time in a world we don't know?"

"I don't know," Will said. This wasn't going at all how he had expected. He glowered. Talking to Mad had been a bad idea. "But it's better than rushing in bullheaded. You're strong, Mad, but not that strong."

"I have no delusions about my capabilities, Will."

"Then we should listen to Morella! She was searching for the Relics before us and she has a plan for finding them. If we help her then that monster can be defeated that much easier!"

"So, this was her idea?" Madigan shook his head. "Of course it was her idea. Will, she's here to pursue her own agenda, not ours. She said she wanted companions on her journey and then she joined us. Remember what happened to her last group. Don't let her distract you from our mission."

"She knows more than you give her credit for," Will said, suddenly defensive. "Going after the Relics makes sense. What if people have been wrong about Valmont? What if he's still alive?"

Madigan groaned and finally met his eye. "Gods, Will, she really has you wrapped around her finger, doesn't she?"

Will's temper flared. "You're just jealous."

"You think that's what this is about?" Madigan said, frustration and exasperation plain in his voice. "Yes, she's a very interesting woman. She's also a distraction who has been doing an excellent job of manipulating you into doing whatever she wants. Don't you see that?"

"I just don't see how you plan on being successful here without help," Will said. He was doing his best to stay calm but Mad was being infuriating. *For no good reason, either.*

"I'm planning on getting help, Will. The plan takes time, not shortcuts. I'm thinking beyond the blood beast. Grandda was right, there is a world here where we could really do some good. That's exactly what I intend to do."

"So, what then? You and Cephora have this all figured out? We're going to find Senraks and your plan is what, just observation? Take a gander and then go play politics for a bit?"

Madigan stared at his brother in shock. "What are you going on about? What the hell has come over you? I trust Cephora. Yes, she's helping us gain intel and wherever she's leading us, she knows the stakes. But we're not going to just blindly rush in once we find that monster. We need a larger force. We need time and numbers."

"It'd be far easier to do as a dagger in the dark," Will said, brushing over his brother's suggestions.

"And is that what you propose?"

"I propose," Will said through clenched teeth, "that we arm ourselves with anything that could give us the advantage and then end this."

"And you think Morella will just give you the Relics if you help her find them? You think she'll just hand them over and let you do as you please? She's got her own goddam agenda, Will. She was searching for them before we came along and she's not about to turn them over to us even if she does find them."

"She's with us! She wants to help. It doesn't have to be just our responsibility anymore, Mad. We can have someone on our side who wants the same thing we want. Not someone who was hired, someone who came because they believe."

"I'll think about it." Madigan sighed and shook his head. "We'll talk it over with Cephora. In the meantime"—he ran his hands through his hair and gave Will a tentative glance—"there's something important that I really need to talk to you about."

"You know exactly how Cephora will react." Will couldn't help himself; he saw the momentary crack in his brother's resolve and pushed. "You saw her when the Relics got brought up before. There's no way she'll go for it."

"Dammit, then maybe that's something we should consider then, isn't it?" Madigan rose to his feet and towered over Will, his calm demeanor completely vanished. "She knows more about them than we do and doesn't trust them for a reason."

"And how do we know we should trust her judgment?" Will said as he glared at his brother.

"You're actually going to ask that?" Madigan stared at his

brother. "After everything she's done for us? I'd trust Cephora over Morella any day."

"You're just trying to create a rift between us, aren't you? It all comes back to your jealousy."

"Will, you're wrong." Madigan reached out to his brother and laid a hand on his shoulder, imploring him. "I don't like the effect she has on you. Ever since she came around you've been distant. You stopped training with Cephora. You've barely spoken to me. The two of you spend every night secluded. You're shutting us out."

"You don't know what you're talking about," Will said, shrugging his brother's hand away.

"You know what?" Madigan said, looking remarkably similar to their grandfather as he looked at Will with disappointment. "There's no need to discuss the Relics with Cephora. I'm saying no. Maybe when you pull your head out of your ass we can talk about it again. But right now? You're just being petulant."

Will turned and stormed away. He had finally begun to regain some sense of self-confidence and Mad was doing everything in his power to knock him back down. Boiling with frustration, he climbed into bed filled with anger and doubt. His thoughts raced between Morella and Madigan, between meeting Valmont's assassin with an army at their backs or with an ace up their sleeves.

An ace in the hole, that's what Madigan said he needed me to be.

The Relics of Antiquity would be his.

24

SHADOWBORNE

Five days later the group approached the edge of a sprawling desert. The terrain had grown steadily rockier as they traveled and the trees became sparse and barren. At the sight of the expanse of rock and sand, Madigan took a deep drink from his canteen and shook his head. "I'm guessing our path doesn't skirt along the edges of this, does it?" he said.

Cephora gave a quick "Hmph," then led them to a large, dying tree that offered what little shade was possible. "We'll camp here."

"So early?" Will asked. He and Morella had been walking a bit behind, casually brushing fingers as they talked in hushed tones. Mad was surprised that Will was even aware they were stopping; he'd missed most everything else over the past few weeks.

"Set up camp," Cephora said. Her tone brooked no argument. Madigan had watched as the guide had grown increasingly reclusive, even to him, as they traveled. From what he had been able to figure from the maps, it looked as though they were nearing their destination. And then what? *She said she would act as our guide.* Hopefully he had managed to convince her to act as more than that.

"We shall get a few extra hours of rest. We go no farther today," Cephora said, dropping to a crouch and moving a few rocks before seating herself. "The next few days will be hard enough."

Morella chewed her lip. She glanced at Cephora before looking out at the wasteland before them. "We're going into the Daurhi Wastes?"

Cephora nodded. "We are. Our goal lies in the heart of the sands."

Madigan dropped his pack near Cephora. *We are close, then.* It was a strange notion, to be so close to the blood beast's lair and yet to feel so unprepared. *Assuming it actually made its way back there.* He looked at his companions. They were ragged. They had been traveling hard for weeks and were on scarce rations. As he stared out at the Daurhi Wastes, he shook his head. From the look of things, it was only going to get harder. *And the group is fracturing.*

He watched as Morella and Will set their bedrolls down near to one another. Morella seemed fine enough, all things considered. She was knowledgeable about many things and that was valuable, although she did a poor job of keeping her thoughts to herself. Madigan tried not to fault her for it, though. From what he had seen in Undermyre and the Nordoth, social skills didn't seem to be a strength for the population of Aeril. Or, at least not social skills as he knew them.

No, Morella rubbed him the wrong way because of Will. Perhaps it wasn't her fault, perhaps it was just the nature of his brother, but Madigan saw less and less of the Will he knew and more of someone . . . *consumed.* He needed Will right now, more than he knew how to say. Cephora had been an amazing aid but Will would *understand*. The one time he'd tried to talk to him, he hadn't even been able to tell his brother what he needed to say. How was he supposed to—

"Will there be any place to resupply once we get to this destination of yours?" Will's question interrupted Mad's thoughts. He focused back on the task at hand and saw that Will was examining a chart and measuring his supplies against it. "The map says there's a spring not far from here but shows nothing out there." He gestured toward the bitter expanse of desert.

"I can't say," Cephora replied. "It has been more years than I care to admit since I last ventured into the Wastes."

"Well then, we had better drink up while we have the chance," Morella said. She sounded somehow both perky and sarcastic at the same time. It grated at Madigan. "Hey, Will. Do you want to head down and fill up some canteens with me?"

"Cephora," Will said, clearly biting down his frustration. "Please, where exactly are we going?"

"Shale." Her eyes were hard as she looked at the sands. "The Shale Prison."

"A prison?" Will said, confusion in his voice. "Why are we going to a prison?"

To Madigan's surprise, it was Morella who answered.

"Before the rumors of his death, Valmont was housed in the Shale," she said quietly. "Gods, this is a suicide mission."

Will was incredulous. "The great Dorian Valmont was imprisoned in the middle of a desert? I find that hard to believe."

"I'm inclined to agree," Madigan said. "Was it his prison? Did he use it as a base of operations?"

Cephora and Morella both nodded. "That is what my sources have said," Cephora said.

So, they were going to an abandoned prison in pursuit of a

monster. Madigan flexed his palms; he didn't care for the situation. "And you believe that Senraks would have returned there, after . . . " he trailed off.

Cephora shook her head. "I do not know. It would make sense for the assassin to return to check in, if Valmont did use it. And given that the creature does not know that Valmont is dead, it may be waiting for his return."

"Maybe we'll catch it sleeping," Will said with a smirk. "Then we can finish the job quickly"—he looked at Madigan very pointedly—"like a dagger in the dark."

"I do not know," Cephora said again. "The Crow charged me with getting you two to the prison and ensuring that no one else knew our destination." She glanced sidelong at Morella. "The information he gave me did not go beyond that."

"Lovely," Will said. "So, this place is a former haunt of his, right? Abandoned now? Or is there is a very real possibility that we may not receive a particularly warm greeting at this prison? Is that it?"

Again, it was Morella who replied. "The Shale has never been abandoned and our reception certainly won't be warm. The warden there, the guards, they kill anyone who isn't one of them. They're an elite force, a mercenary army in their own right. Valmont didn't control them, he hired them." She shook her head as her eyes fell back to the Wastes. "It doesn't matter who is in control of it, they will kill us the moment they see us."

As if the whole thing was scripted perfectly, Madigan thought, a hint of nervousness pinching at his back.

"Which is why they won't see us," Cephora said. "I am here to get you close. Someone else will get you inside."

Madigan saw Will tense and felt ashamed for a moment. *I'm sorry, kid.* Dusk fell rapidly over the camp yet the sun did not move in the sky. The air adopted the vaporous, wavering quality that rises from hot stone in the midst of a summer's morning. The haze cooled rapidly as a dusky shadow covered the area. Will looked petrified and he spun in a circle. Then, his eyes fell to his brother.

Madigan's own eyes were clouded and distant, his features grim. He had tucked his arms tight against his ribs but his fingers were splayed forward. The darkness poured from his hands. He saw the shock and confusion on his little brother's face. *I tried to tell you.*

"Shadowborne . . . " Morella's voice was quiet, filled with what Madigan could only assume to be fear. But at the same time she looked . . . *angry?* Beneath that glare he began to falter.

"Maintain focus, Madigan." Cephora was nodding in approval. The air swirled around them as Madigan stepped forward. "Be aware of your surroundings. Make sure we are all concealed as you move. Yes, very good. Be vigilant. Don't overextend."

Don't overextend. He saw the color drain from his brother as their grandfather's warning to Will rang in Madigan's ears. *Yes, Will, we are the same.*

The soothing darkness receded and the warmth of the afternoon flooded the campsite once more. Madigan felt exhaustion threaten to consume him but Cephora walked over and placed her hands on his shoulders, directing him to a place of calm. Morella looked on warily, but Will met his brother's eyes. In that look was one of the most pained, frustrated expressions Madigan had ever seen.

"Well done." Cephora smiled. "Your hard work has yielded impressive results in so short a time."

"Thank you, Cephora," Madigan said as he reached for his canteen again. "Were it not for you, well, I never could have gotten this far."

"What the hell was that?" Will's words were harsh as they bit through the still air.

"Will," Cephora said, shaking her head. "There is no need for pretense. The Crow told me of the day he met you both in chains, that his guards were overwhelmed by a Shadowborne. Madigan told me everything else."

Will stared aghast. "And when you told us that Shadow magic was dead?"

"A ruse."

"Will," Mad said as he saw the emotion raging across his brother's face. *Don't give yourself away, kid.* "It's okay. Cephora figured the rest out on her own."

Will stared at him and Madigan met his stony look. Finally, it was Will who looked away, tears brimming in his eyes. Mad knew that he must be suddenly questioning himself, suddenly doubtful of his own gifts. *It's not like that, Will, not at all.* When his brother spoke, his voice was choked with strain. "How did she figure it out?"

Madigan breathed a sigh of relief. *Good, he'll play along.*

"You're a Shadowborne." Morella's voice was flat. When Madigan turned to look at her, her darkened expression had gone completely. In its place was a quick succession of emotions, from wary to thrilled. Finally, a wide grin broke across her face. "This is amazing! I should have guessed it. But this is amazing. They'll never see us coming, both figuratively and literally!" She laughed her loud, rowdy laugh. Thinking back to the moment before when her face had seemed so strangely furious, Madigan had felt uncomfortable. Watching her now, however, he dismissed it. *I must have just imagined it.*

"Well, at least it's out in the open now," Will said, recovering some of his composure. He caught Mad's eye again and gave him a pointed look. "No need for secrets."

That stung. Madigan furrowed his brow but it was Cephora who spoke up. "Exactly," she said. "And while I know we all agreed to absolute honesty at the beginning of this venture, I understand why you kept this one from me as long as you were able to. Shadowborne are not as well received as they once were."

"So I've heard," Will muttered under his breath.

"The risk of exposure is worth the training," Madigan said. "With the lessons I've had from Cephora, it'll be far easier to train without her, as needed. As it currently stands, we've got an ace in the hole."

He saw it click on Will's face, the thinly veiled message behind his words instantly recognized. A flurry of emotions crossed his face but, nevertheless, Will couldn't help but roll his eyes.

"Right, our secret weapon," Will said. "So, now that it's out in the open, let's get back to the matter at hand. What is this Shale Prison? How far out is it?"

"Depending on the conditions, roughly five days into the desert," Cephora answered. "The prison itself is a different matter entirely. It is known to have a penchant for"—she paused a moment—"shifting."

Morella chuckled. "That's putting it lightly," she said. "And you think you can locate it, is that it?"

"Yes," Cephora said plainly before turning her focus to Mad and Will. "It phases somewhere on the edges of this plane of existence, similar to the Ways but less refined."

"So, your skills as a Seeker will help us find this place then?" Will asked.

"More or less," Madigan replied. Will glanced at him side-long and he went on. "Cephora is able to tune in to a frequency that the prison emits. As such, she can track its location easier and lock onto it."

Will seemed to be fuming even more than he was a moment ago. "Oh really? You knew this?"

"Some of us haven't had our head in the sand with certain distractions." Madigan's rebuke was cold. He knew it wouldn't do anything but escalate the situation, but Will's temper was getting out of hand. *And there I was thinking I was the hotheaded one.*

"Alright, I think that is quite enough," Morella cut in before Will could fire off a retort. Her tone was sharp but earnest. Again, though, her eyes looked dark, almost cruel. She gave Madigan a calculated smile. "Will, your brother is right. There is no harm in admitting it."

Mad stared, wide-eyed, as his brother seemed to deflate with Morella's words. *Another surprise from that one. What's her game? What's she up to?*

Morella then turned her focus toward Madigan and Cephora. "But that doesn't excuse either of you from not making more effort to bring him back on course. I'll own my part in this just so long as you both do as well."

There was a moment of silence as they eyed one another, each mouth set in a line and each jaw clamped tight. Finally, Madigan nodded, pushing aside his reservations. "She's right. I'm sorry, Will. There's been too much change lately and, while we've each handled it differently, I haven't been straightforward with you."

Will's face raced between surprise to frustration before, finally, settling to a passive calm. His shoulders dropped and when he spoke, his voice reminded Madigan of easy mornings lounging by the fireplace at home, swapping stories. "Yeah, well. I'm sorry too, about being distracted and all that. Like you said, there've been lots of changes."

Morella glanced at Cephora. Their guide held up her hands and shook her head. "I refuse to get involved in family politics." Both Mad and Will chuckled. Morella started to protest but looked at the brothers and cut it off, shrugging. Cephora went on. "What Madigan said is correct. I will get us there. Once we are there, however, the game changes completely. There is no telling what is inside. No maps have ever been made, no escapes or prison breaks. No information has ever come from within. What enters the Shale Prison never emerges again."

"Well, doesn't that just sound like a walk in the park?" Will said. "Anything else for us to go on? Any other tidbits of vital information?"

"Only a reminder of my position here," Cephora said.

What does she mean by that? Madigan wondered. He looked at Will and raised an eyebrow.

"Meaning . . . ?" Will said.

"Meaning that I am a guide," she said simply. "As such, it will only be the three of you going in."

They all looked at her in shock.

"What?" Madigan asked. *She can't be serious.*

"My mission"—Cephora gave him a pointed look—"is to get you into the prison and to ensure that, if you are successful, you manage to get out of it."

"Which will be a hell of a lot easier if you're in there with us!" Madigan burst out. Morella and Will voiced their protestations as well. Cephora said nothing, merely waiting for the clamor to die down before speaking once more.

"For one hundred lifetimes, I've walked these lands. In the entirety of that time, the Shale has never been breached." Her voice was hard, stern. It sounded to Madigan like one of his grandfather's lectures after he or Will had done something to disappoint him. "Once it is found, there is no guarantee that it will remain where it stands. From the inside, I would have no power. Only from the outside can I make your escape possible."

"Just the three of us against Senraks? In the depths of a realm-phasing prison? And you think our best bet for survival is for you to sit this one out?" Madigan blurted out. *What the hell is this? Why is she abandoning us?* "Not to mention the army of mercenaries. Gods, did the Crow put you up to this? There are far easier ways to kill someone!"

"Mad, don't," Will broke in. "It's pointless."

Mad glanced over and saw that although Will looked none too pleased with Cephora's decision, he seemed to be accepting it. *Why?* He turned to Cephora and saw the grim expression on her face. Her stance would not change, that was clear, but why hadn't she told them sooner? It wouldn't have changed anything, but they would have had more time to at least process it. *Fine. We'll just have to do it on our own.*

"If she says that she can support us only from outside then we have to believe her." Morella, who had remained silent, finally spoke up. She didn't bother to hide the mirth in her voice.

The veins in Madigan's neck were bulging as he strained against himself. Finally, he relaxed and attempted to regain his composure. The odds weren't in their favor, but then again, they never had been. Perhaps with his own newfound power coupled with Will's, though, perhaps they weren't as bad as they could have been. "Of course. My apologies, Cephora."

"None needed," the Seeker said, ending the discussion.

They all set about making camp, the atmosphere palpably tense. Madigan tried to catch his brother's eye, tried to glean some information from Will as to his thoughts, but Will kept his head down. As Will laid out his blanket, Morella brushed against him in a manner that could hardly have been accidental. Madigan barely saw her crooked smile and quick wink before she wandered off in the direction of the spring. With a grin, Will hurriedly set the last of his supplies on the ground and made to follow her.

"Not to interrupt, Will, but can we have a quick chat?" Madigan asked as he placed a hand on Will's arm, stopping him. A momentary battle played across his brother's face as Morella retreated into the distance. Will nodded with reluctance and followed Madigan in the opposite direction. After they had gone out of earshot of the camp, he turned to Will, standing tall and sure, and spoke.

"I wanted to tell you sooner."

"Tell me?" Will asked, cocking his head to the side. Realization dawned on his face and he nodded and snickered. "Ah, yeah. That wasn't quite what I was expecting."

"I know. I'm sorry I didn't tell you as soon as I figured it out." Madigan paused and held up his hands, his Shade billowing from them as smoke from a flame. "But I didn't know how you'd take it. And there was Cephora, who was already suspicious, so I had to pretend that it wasn't something new. And then we got into it about the Relics and Morella and everything and . . . " He trailed off.

Will picked up the train of thought. "And then time just kept passing."

"And the moment was never right," Madigan nodded. "Exactly."

"I get it, Mad. I do." Will glanced back, making sure that Morella and Cephora were still well out of earshot. "Do you remember how terrified I was when I first figured out about mine? I didn't know how to handle it at all." He smiled and nudged his brother. "At least now the scales will be a bit more even when we spar. I was getting tired of winning all the time."

"Ha!" Madigan laughed. "Is that the case? Perhaps it's about time to bring a bit of humility back into your world."

The shadows were tracing his palms and dancing across his fingers. Will glanced back at their camp once more, then held up his own hands. Without hesitation, his Shade appeared and mirrored Madigan's. They both smiled.

"Quite the pair we make," Madigan said. *If only Grandda could see us now.*

"Perhaps we should start calling ourselves something awesome, come up with superhero names," Will said with a wide grin. Madigan rolled his eyes and Will nudged him with his elbow. "No, I'm serious! Something epic and awesome, like the Brothers of Darkness."

"That is neither epic nor awesome, kid." Madigan shook his head and smiled. "You're absurd."

"Always have been, always will be." Will returned his smile and the darkness vanished. His eyes trailed after Morella. Madigan watched and immediately knew his thoughts. He snickered a bit and Will snapped his attention back.

"Somehow, in all of this, you managed to find a little happiness, eh?" he said.

"More like it found me." Will shrugged and grinned wide. "And hey, I'm not the only one."

Madigan raised an eyebrow. "Meaning . . . ?"

"Ynarra. Didn't you two kinda—"

"That's different," Mad said quickly. "Plus, I'll probably never see her again."

"I hope you do. Morella and I, well, she's good. I feel like a spectator half the time wondering 'how did I get here?' But I'm definitely not complaining."

"As long as you're good, Will."

Will looked at him, tilting his head and frowning a little. After a moment he said, "I'm good."

Madigan opened his mouth to say something further but paused. Instead, he clapped his brother on the shoulder and gestured after Morella. "Then go get her, Brother of Darkness." Grinning, Will winked and sped off. Madigan watched, torn, and called out after him. "You're my brother, Will. Always."

Will turned back and gave the smallest hint of bowing his head. "Always, Mad. You're stuck with me."

As his brother disappeared after Morella, Madigan returned to his bedroll and closed his eyes. *The Brothers of Darkness.* He smiled and allowed himself a moment of wishful thinking filled with thoughts of the adventures he and Will could get into, thoughts of all the good they could do with their abilities.

THE DAURHI WASTES

The journey into the vast expanse of the desert was not an easy one. There were no trees, no cacti, nothing that could provide any kind of shade. The land was sprawling and sloped, never level, with as many sharp rocks underfoot as sand. The shifting nature of the terrain made every step treacherous, and casual walking was an impossibility, being on high alert as they were. To Will, it always seemed that there were cliffs far in the distance that could offer them respite. But whether they were a mirage or just that far away, they never grew any closer.

The group took to traveling only in the early mornings and the evenings, splitting the day in two and taking their rest during the hottest parts of the day while they braced themselves against one another during the coldest parts of the night. The dark nights were awash with countless stars that littered the sky. The moon remained full and vibrant, never waxing or waning, and would have allowed enough light to travel by had the cold not been so overwhelming. How a place that was so scorching during the day could accumulate such a level of frost at night boggled Will's mind.

Cephora had estimated five days' travel through the Wastes to find Shale, but it was not until the ninth evening that they discovered it. In that time they had nearly exhausted both their water supply and rations and were forced to spend the final day filled with hunger pangs, each on the verge of utter dehydration. Morella and Cephora both somehow fared far better than Will and Madigan on that front. Finally, Will ended up using some of the power stored within the fangs to soothe their fatigue and the first hints of sickness from lack of water. But knowing of the potential dangers still to come, he refrained from using too much.

They had climbed a steep mound of razored rocks when Cephora stopped them suddenly at the summit. The mound ended in a sheer drop on the opposite side, as though half of it had been cleaved away by a giant sickle. She dropped to a knee and touched the stones on the ground, closing her eyes. Her mouth moved quickly as it voiced incoherent, nearly silent words. After a moment she stood and turned to the group. "This is where it will be."

"Will be?" Will asked, his throat cracked and parched from thirst.

"It is not currently phased into our plane," Cephora said as she rose. "But when it does, this is where it will be."

Madigan stepped to the ledge and surveyed the area as Morella spoke up. "And do we have any idea of when that will be?"

Cephora wiped her dusty hands on her cloak. "Minutes. Hours. No more than a day. If the intonations of the stones are accurate then I would presume it will present before daybreak."

Will chose to ignore his urge to ask after the intonations of rocks and set about trying to turn the glasslike stone shards into some semblance of a bed. At a questioning glance from Madigan, he explained. "I'm exhausted, and if the information we have about this place is to be believed, we're about to walk into Hell. If Cephora says we have a window to rest, well, I'm going to milk it for all it's worth."

"Mmm, good idea," Morella said as she made her way over to Will. "Mind if I join you?" It was the first time she had been so blatant about them being more than travel companions. Cephora, although obviously aware of what had been going on between them, still raised an eyebrow, disapproval plain upon her face. Will didn't care for the look and bristled.

"Not at all, Morella," Will said as pleasantly as possible. "Please, make yourself as comfortable as you can."

Cephora shook her head and pulled Madigan aside as Morella unrolled her blanket and draped it around her. While Will tried to ignore the jagged rocks below him, she pulled her body close to his and draped her arm over his chest. Suddenly, he became very aware of Madigan and Cephora's presences and hushed voices in contrast to the measured, carefree breathing of the woman at his side. He didn't sleep one bit.

After lying there for almost an hour, he rolled away and rose to his feet. Madigan and Cephora paused in their conversation as he approached and crouched next to them. "Sorry to interrupt."

"You're not interrupting," Mad replied. "Your input is always welcome."

"Input on what, exactly?" Will asked.

"Where we go next," Cephora answered.

Will hadn't given it much thought but, as soon as she said it, his mind jumped to the Relics. Their rumored power was tantalizing and all too inviting. He was about to voice his suggestion but hesitated. If they managed to kill Senraks, despite Madigan's insistence that this was purely recon, what need would there be for the Relics?

Morella said Valmont may still be alive. While Senraks had been the agent of his grandfather's death, Valmont had been the hand that guided the blade. Could they find him and, if so, should they?

His thoughts drifted to Morella, sleeping soundly despite what was coming. He wondered what she would do. After spending so long in search of the Relics so she could defeat Valmont and find the justice she sought, where would she go? *And what if he really is dead?* How would she feel knowing that her quest for them was for nothing? Everything seemed to hinge on what was about to happen and what information they would get from it.

Will sighed and ran his hands through his hair. "I don't know," he said.

Cephora smiled as Madigan spoke. "Hard to imagine that we're already here, isn't it?"

Will nodded.

"We'll be okay, Will," Madigan continued, giving a small smile. "Grandda trained us well. We can do this."

When he mentioned their grandfather, it triggered something within Will. He knew exactly what he wanted to do after defeating the blood beast. Hesitation be damned. "Valmont, that's what's next. After Senraks is defeated, we take care of Valmont."

Cephora sighed and shook her head. "Valmont is dead," she said. "Why do you press this point?"

"His influence, I mean," Will said, although he didn't believe it for a moment. "If he is dead, then we track down his . . . what do they call them? His Necrothanians. We end all traces of Valmont's influence."

"There was only the one blood beast, yes? Senraks?"

Cephora asked as she looked off in the distance. "It will be difficult to track the rest of the brood but not impossible."

"There's more?" Will asked, feeling his stomach sink. Cephora nodded and he groaned. "Do we know if we're on the trail of the right one, at least?"

"I'm not the one who traced the creature to Shale. That information was gathered by an agent of the Crow," Cephora reminded him. "I was just brought as a guide to make sure his hunters reached it."

"Either way," Madigan said, taking control of the conversation in a tone that brooked its end. "We need more data. Until we get into Shale, we're only operating on open questions."

The conversation drifted. Will ran his thumbs along the bloodstones and felt the meager power coursing through them, simultaneously hoping he wouldn't need to use them while praying that they held enough energy, just in case. It had been weeks since there had been any new source of fuel for them and the drain from reinvigorating Madigan and himself had depleted the majority of their stores. He sighed. There was nothing for it now; they just had to keep pressing forward.

The coldest part of night came quickly, biting and chilling. As its frosts covered the area, Will returned to Morella and lay down next to her for warmth. Her breathing was smooth and he wrapped the blankets over them tightly. She made a small, sweet noise of appreciation.

Suddenly it didn't seem right that she was there with them, entering such a dangerous place. She was a scholar. She had no training. She said herself that her success in defending herself against the bandits had been due more to luck than to anything pertaining to skill. The more Will thought about it, the more concerned he became.

Finally, as the chill of the air started to lessen, he nudged her gently. "Morella."

She groaned in annoyance but snapped her eyes open. "I was having a good dream," she said.

"Here? I'm surprised." Will chuckled. He shifted and brought his forehead close to hers. "I've been thinking. Are you sure you want to come into the prison?"

Her eyes narrowed and she pulled away just enough for Will to notice. "Of course I'm sure."

He hesitated briefly on whether to press the issue. *She can make her own decisions. It isn't my place to boss her about.* He nodded and gave a little smile. "Alright. I just wanted to make sure that you felt comfortable with it."

She pulled away farther, shifting onto her elbow and giving him an unflinching glare. "Comfortable? What, do you think that just because I'm a woman I can't handle it?"

"A woman?" Will said, confused by the rapid change in her demeanor. "What, no, that's not it at all. It's just that you're a historian and none of us know what we're getting into in there." She raised an eyebrow at him. "You said yourself it was only a matter of luck that you held off those bandits as long as you did! I just didn't want you to be dragged into something this dangerous because . . . " He trailed off as her face softened and broke into a smirk.

"You're sweet, Will, really. I can handle myself better than I let on. I wasn't always a historian and I have a few tricks up my sleeve. Those bandits caught me unawares but this time?" She dropped her elbow and nuzzled her head into his chest. "This time I'm ready for blood."

"Well, with any luck it won't be any of ours," Will said with an edge of severity. "In and out. We do what we need to do and then we get out without them knowing a thing until we're gone and they find Senraks dead."

She smiled. "Sounds like you've got it all worked out then."

Will chuckled but there was no humor in it. "Oh yes. Everything will go according to plan. It always does."

As if acting on some unknown cue, Will's key started humming against his chest. Although he knew that no one could sense the sensation but himself, he still became suddenly self-conscious. The humming grew to a near audible level and his entire chest started tingling. From the corner of his eye he saw Cephora stand and race over to the ledge. She cursed suddenly and dropped to the ground, signaling for the rest of them to do so as well. Already prone on the ground, Will pushed himself up enough that he could scramble across the jagged stones and join her at the edge. The electric activity at his chest was forgotten as soon as his eyes crested the top.

Where before there had been only the Wastes, now immense walls stretched thirty feet tall and ranged at least three hundred yards across. Their surface was covered in the same jagged stones that made up the landscape, making the barrier as solid as rock but as dangerous to the touch as shattered glass. There were no watchtowers like those Will would have expected to see on a prison, but rather there were jagged spires that curved this way and that into the night sky. And wherever he looked, lightning rippled across every surface. There was no sign of any gate, no breaks in the stone of any kind. It was a mass of razor-sharp, electric death.

A soft curse from behind him signaled Madigan's arrival. "We're going into that?" he said. Cephora smirked and nodded. Madigan cursed again. "Do we have any idea where to go once we're inside?"

"The creature would have returned to its master's lair, probably the most secure part of the prison. The high-priority cells, most likely. I suggest you make your way to the center of the lowest subterranean level."

"Subterranean?" Will blinked.

Cephora eyed him. "It means underground."

"He knows what it means," Mad snapped. "We just weren't expecting it. How far down does it go?"

Cephora turned her stare to Madigan. "Do you not recall our previous conversation where I informed you that no one knows the layout of the prison? That no one has ever escaped or given up its secrets?"

"I remember it," he said.

"Then why would you ask a question when you're already aware that I do not know the answer?" Cephora said flatly. Her demeanor had changed with the appearance of the prison. She seemed ill-at-ease, less certain.

"Just testing your own recollective abilities, Cephora," Will interjected in an effort to keep the conversation light. "Keeping you on your toes is all."

Madigan snickered briefly as the hot tension eased out of him. Cephora shook her head and went back to studying the terrain leading down toward the walls. Will turned his head back toward Morella. She hadn't moved but merely continued to lie there with her eyes closed and a small smile on her face as she hummed quietly.

"This is gonna be hellish, isn't it?" Mad said quietly. He smiled and gave Will a light nudge with his elbow. "Thanks for diffusing that, by the way."

"Not a problem at all," Will replied. "The diffusing, I mean. This prison looks like it will be quite the problem."

"Does she know?" Madigan jerked his head toward the still form of Morella.

"Morella? About the prison?" Will said. "Only as much as the rest of us."

"Not the prison, Will, about you," Madigan said quietly. "What you are."

Will stared at him blankly for a moment before he realized what his brother meant. He shook his head. "Of course not."

Madigan nodded. "That may change soon. Once we get in there . . . " He broke off and sighed, running his hands through his hair. "I don't know what we're going to find. We need to be on our guard and at our best."

Will grinned. "So, my leash gets to come off, finally?"

"You haven't been on a . . . " Madigan's mouth tightened. "What I'm saying, Will, is that I'd rather you risk exposing your secret than have us spend eternity in a place like that."

"Relax, Mad." Will held up a hand to placate his brother before turning his eyes back toward the prison. "I have no intention of letting anything happen to any of us if I can help it."

Mad nodded and glanced back at Morella. "Is she going to be alright in there?"

Will smiled. "She may end up surprising both of us."

"I'll take that as a yes, then," Madigan said. "Grab whatever gear you need and let's do this."

Thumbing his blades, Will surveyed his belongings and, frankly, could not come up with a single item that seemed worth bringing. His cloak, his weapons, and his key were all that would matter once they got inside.

Turning, he saw that Madigan had adopted much the same strategy. Morella, recently arisen and silently bustling about, had laden herself with nearly everything she carried. When Will caught her eye and raised an eyebrow in question, she hugged her satchel of scrolls closer. "This is my life's work and I'll be damned if I let it out of my sight."

Will smiled and winked at her to which she bit back a laugh. The nerves were starting to crawl in his stomach, worming their way through his insides. He refused to acknowledge them, to give in to their power and despair at the monumental task before him. No, while Mad might force them away with his own silent determination and brooding quiet, Will's own methods involved a foolhardy invitation for them to do their worst so he could smile and grin, maniacally telling himself that he was unaffected. Laughter and wide-mouthed grins had once been his approach to apprehension and, in the face of imprisonment and certain death, it appeared that that side of his brain was reigniting.

He crawled to the ledge once more and stared down at the jagged, cruel behemoth that was the Shale Prison. His eye twitched as he saw the lightning crackle over its surface, mirroring the patterns of his key. The lightning came from nowhere he could determine and danced mesmerizingly across the jagged stone. It began to call to him, inviting, as though it was the visual representation of the key itself. It was hailing back to the crackling power that obliterated the creature that blocked their way in the Shanghai Tunnels. That lightning held answers. It was taking every ounce of restraint not to throw himself from the ledge and discover what mysteries were locked behind the nonexistent gates of Shale.

Face stretched into a nervous grin, he turned back toward his brother and Morella who had finished their preparations. He glanced at Cephora, whose onyx eyes were hard and distant. His heart racing, his fingers twitching to be on and active, he mustered up as much nonchalance as he could.

"Well, shall we begin?"

❧ 26 ❧

WITHIN THE SHALE

At a signal from Madigan, the four of them crept down the jagged embankment and turned toward the prison. The cover of the cool night aided them some, but as soon as they came around into full view of the prison, Madigan surrounded them in his Shade. His face strained with the effort of maintaining it in so controlled a fashion as they moved across the sands. On more than one occasion Will nearly added his own power to his brother's, thinking it would go unnoticed in the circumstances. With an effort, he showed restraint and trusted his brother to see it done.

Will couldn't see any kind of opening in the prison, nor were there any guards. The structure itself was massive, continuing to grow in scope and magnitude as they drew closer.

"Cephora," Will whispered as they crept along, "how many people are inside?"

"Prisoners? Unknown," she said in a voice that was barely audible. "As far as guards? The entirety of the Shale army is housed in the prison."

Will fought back the urge to curse. "Do we have any record of the size of the army?"

Cephora shook her head but Morella responded. "Nothing accurate," she said. "When they last marched in force, just after the Sundering, it was estimated to be nearly ten thousand strong."

This time the curse flowed freely from Will's lips. "So, there could very well be the population of an entire city housed within these seemingly impenetrable lightning walls, is that it?"

"So it would seem," Mad said through gritted teeth. Will frowned, suddenly very concerned about the odds. *We'll just have to stay out of sight.*

As they neared the base of the wall, Cephora held up a hand to signal them to stop. She knelt and placed her palm to the earth, closing her eyes as her mouth moved in silent words once more. After a moment, she stood and turned to the others. "There is no breach nearby. We'll have to keep circling at this distance or else . . . " She trailed off and gestured at the lightning before setting off again.

Will dropped back a few paces to come alongside his brother. "Are you holding up okay?"

"Nothing to it." Madigan forced a casual smile but the tension in his neck and sweat on his brow betrayed the lie.

"Can I help?"

He shook his head. "Nothing you can do, Will. I'm fine."

Will wracked his brain briefly and then it came to him. Stepping closer to Madigan to ensure no one else would hear his words, he spoke. "Mad, remember what I told you in the Nordoth about Grandda's key. Focus on it." Madigan gave him an impatient glare but Will persisted. "I know you're at your limits but please, just try it."

The Shade's cover of darkness lessened a bit and Cephora

shot a sharp glance backward. Will made a placating gesture and she shook her head before continuing on. Will watched Madigan. Nothing changed. He waited and doubt crept in. *Maybe it's something unique about my key?*

Then, suddenly, Madigan's eyes softened and the tension seemed to ease out of his neck. The Shade darkened and grew, extending until there was room for each of them to move easily within it. Morella turned and raised an inquisitive eyebrow at Will. He grinned and shrugged.

"It's like a soothing balm of cool on a summer's day." Madigan's voice was filled with a deep sense of calm awe and had taken on the cadence of a poet. "Will, yours, does it do that too?"

"Uh, something like that," Will whispered as his attention turned to the jolting shocks that were regularly emitting from his own key. There was no soothing balm associated with that power, not unless he counted the brief respites of inactivity from it.

"How did you . . . ?"

"It worked for me at the Nordoth," Will said. "I figured it may be the same for you."

"These keys . . . " Madigan nodded and smiled, a new gleam of determination in his eye. "This is a game changer."

"Well, if we get in there and find ten thousand troops waiting for us, I hope you're right," Will snickered. There was no humor in it.

"There's no way there are that many soldiers in there," Madigan replied, giving his brother a level stare. "They would have run out of food long ago and it would be way too cramped in there for good morale. Therefore, they've probably all killed each other by now anyway."

His facade cracked on this last bit of speech and they both chuckled. Their lapse was cut short as Cephora spun abruptly and quieted them with a gesture. The brothers each gave her an appropriately chastised look. Cephora muttered under her breath before pressing forward while Morella smiled. The smile hinted at something that Will couldn't determine, as if she was in on a joke that only she knew. *Just more of her delightful mystery,* he mused.

The walls loomed overhead as they drew closer to the prison and the brief levity soon faded. From a distance they were imposing. Up close, they were impossible. The stone was jagged and sharp and the bolts of lightning that scoured the walls whipped across them constantly. The ground near the walls was hot to the touch even through their shoes.

Morella's eyes were on the sky as it crackled and split with lightning. Madigan's brow pinched as if the strain had returned, but when Will gave him an inquiring glance he brushed him away. The sky began to brighten as day stretched forward and Will wondered what would happen if the prison phased away before they gained access. *Or after we're inside.* He felt raw and blistered and he soon began shifting his blades from frustration and nerves.

Cephora, though, was all business. Periodically she would stop and reach a hand to the ground before shaking her head and ordering them forward. The farther they moved along the prison wall, the more often she checked the ground and the more her pace quickened between stops. Finally, after another ten minutes of starting and stopping in silence, she drew her hand upward sharply. The group stopped. She dropped to a knee and, without hesitating, thrust her hands into the broken, scorching sand.

"Here," she said, her voice tight. "Quickly."

As they closed the distance to the wall, a gaping hole suddenly began to tear along its surface. A fissure grew, roughly torn along the wall, yet as the stone broke, it did so in silence.

The tear was black and impossible to see through. Will stared at Cephora with questioning eyes.

"This will get you in. I don't know how long I can hold the rift, so you need to hurry," she said in hushed tones.

"A rift?" Madigan raised an eyebrow. "You mean to tell us that this hole isn't a hole?"

Cephora nodded. "And if you don't go now, there is no telling how long it may take me to find another breach."

"Then let's go," Morella said. Without pausing she stepped forward and into the gaping blackness. Madigan, eyes growing wide as he saw her disappear, gestured to Will.

"You next, I want to give Cephora cover as long as possible."

Eyes darting between Madigan and Cephora, Will nodded and stepped forward. Just before he stepped through the darkness he turned back and leveled his gaze at the Seeker. "You'll get us out, right?"

"I'll do everything I can."

He took no comfort in her tone and everything behind it left unsaid. As Madigan gave one final urge, Will turned and stepped into the crack of darkness.

When Will was nine, his grandfather took both boys to the state fair. There was a ride called The Twisting Terror that Will begged to go on. As the ride spun and lifted and dropped, Madigan was laughing like a madman all the while. Will, however, did not find the same pleasure in the experience. His own knuckles were white as he gripped the safety bar and felt the hot dog and soda from lunch lurching dangerously in his stomach. The entire experience had been reminiscent of leaning too far back on a chair that tipped onto one leg—that momentary balance of the impossible and the knowledge that it is all about to come crashing down.

The Twisting Terror was the only thing in life that prepared

Will in any way for the sensation of entering the rift. The biggest difference was the roar of icy, deafening winds and the overwhelming scent of earth, and that the rift was about a thousand times more forceful than The Twisting Terror had ever been.

He collapsed onto smooth, stony ground as the blackness of the rift disappeared. Pushing to his feet, he stumbled and fell against a wall. Fighting the wave of vertigo that needled at his brain, Will scanned his surroundings. There was no one in sight other than Morella, and she had inched her way into a darkened corner not far from him. She gave him a feeble smile that Will returned with a thumbs-up before making his way toward her. No sooner had he cleared the exit point of the rift than Madigan came barreling through with the quick sound of air being sucked through a pinhole. He stood tall and erect and drew the noctori. He scanned the area, looked up, and saw his brother.

"That was awesome!" His face split into a wide grin and he released the shadowblade.

Will shook his head. "Yeah, Mad, really awesome."

The rift had deposited them on the inside of a small storeroom. All the shelves were empty, all the racks bare, and the air held the dusty scent of disuse and abandonment. Morella pushed forward to the door and tried the handle but it was locked. Madigan nodded to Will who reached for his lock-picking kit. He made his way forward but Morella waved him away and withdrew her own. Quickly, Will heard the click of tumblers and the door cracked open. Madigan swept the room in the darkness of his Shade and stepped forward.

"We stick to the shadows as much as possible," he said as Morella slid the door open. "Cephora is probably right about Senraks being somewhere in the lower levels."

"And the Shale army?" Will asked.

"Hopefully we can avoid them."

"And if not?" Morella quipped.

"Then we do what we have to," Madigan said. The look on his face told Will exactly what his brother meant.

Without another word, Madigan swept forward through the doorway and into the corridor beyond. Will and Morella followed, glancing down the corridors as they did so.

Everything looked identical. There were hallways and doors and passages but no signage to mark what was where. There were no windows. There were no carpets or tapestries or any detail to offer any differentiation. *How do people find their way around in here?*

"Well, this looks promising," Morella whispered, her thoughts mirroring Will's own.

"Any suggestions?" he asked her.

She looked up at him and then turned her head askew as if he had said the dumbest thing she had ever heard. "Why would I have any suggestions?"

"You're a historian," Will shrugged. "Perhaps something turned up that could be useful."

She shook her head, still giving him that tilted glance. "No, Will. I would have told you before."

"Come on, let's get moving," Madigan cut in.

He picked a path, seemingly at random, and began to walk. Will couldn't place it but something about Morella seemed harsher than before. *Nerves, that's all.* Gods knew his own stomach was trembling. But still, be it an extra flick of her fingers or the way her eyes narrowed, there was an edge about her that he couldn't place.

Keeping the storeroom at their backs, they pressed forward through the corridors. Silence surrounded them and there was no trace of any other living creatures. They made their way inward, Madigan taking point and guiding them along the impossibly long hallways. They found their first junction after five minutes. Will's key suddenly began humming more than usual, sending quick shocks to his body.

"There's something nearby," he whispered as they peered down the halls.

Morella cocked her head to the side. "How do you know that?"

Will hesitated. "Just a feeling in my gut," he said.

Madigan nodded and backed him up. "That's good enough for me," he said. "Your instincts are usually right. Which way?"

Will nodded to the left passage and Madigan gestured for him to take the lead. Morella muttered under her breath and shook her head. Her mood had definitely soured but Will couldn't figure out why. *Reeling from the rift, maybe?* He brushed his hand along hers but she pulled away and shot him a contemptuous look. Disconcerted, he began to move again.

As they progressed farther in, the corridors began to shorten and they found themselves turning and winding, sometimes seeming to backtrack. With every path looking identical to the last, it was not long before Will realized that there was no way he would be able to find their original entrance. Morella's muttering increased and whenever he glanced at her, her eyes were set square on him and filled with something he couldn't place. What was going on? *Does she suspect something more as to why Mad let me lead?*

Sounds from the corridor ahead of them broke his train of thought. He glanced at Mad who jerked his head to the side, gesturing toward a nearby alcove. It was small and cramped, barely more than an entryway to a cell, but the three of them crowded in. Madigan drew his Shade close and masked them in darkness. Morella flicked her wrist. A blade appeared between her fingers and she braced it at the ready. Each of them held their breath and waited.

Slow, heavy footfalls echoed through the hallway. A mass of darkened shadows appeared, stretching out toward them, their forms an uncertain conglomerate of spikes and tall plumes. The clang of metal against stone and the swishing sounds of leather followed as the scent of horse filled the air.

"Are they mounted?" Will risked a whisper, incredulous at the notion but unable to escape it.

Morella shook her head and pushed into the wall at their backs, as though the stone might give way to her flesh and allow her to sink fully from view. As the warriors of Shale entered his field of vision, Will soon understood.

The Shale Prison was a seemingly impenetrable, inescapable fortress, and the army who shared its name was ancient. They had survived countless wars, countless centuries of battle and blood, by adapting. What passed before Will that day looked human, yes, but barely. Three soldiers marched, each as indistinguishable from one another as the halls of the prison, but they looked as hard as the Shale itself. Their bodies were covered in leather and mail armor, but coarse hair protruded from the breaks in the armor. Their helms were not adorned in plumes, in fact they were wearing no helms at all, but their hair was shaved close along the sides while remaining long and flowing about the top.

But the faces of the Shale, their exposed skin, were a horror beyond Will's understanding. The shadowed spikes he had seen were just that, spikes, only these had been impaled—*No, embedded*—into their faces. Their skin was coarse like scales and pierced with spikes as well as, upon closer examination, what appeared to be razor blades and jagged strips of metal. The barnyard smell was coupled with something sour, something vile—a battlefield hospital before the discovery of penicillin and sterile conditions. Though coarse, their skin looked wet and Will realized that fresh blood covered their faces, though whether from the cruelties carved into their flesh or those wrought on an unfortunate prisoner, he did not know.

Will grit his teeth and held his breath. The figures neared the hidden trio and time seemed to slow down. Will felt his heart threatening to rip itself from his chest. But as it pounded and stuttered, the Shale warriors passed, never glancing in their direction.

Their footsteps drifted away and the group stayed frozen in place in their alcove, wrapped in Madigan's Shade. No one moved a muscle. They waited until finally there was no echo of footsteps, no lingering smell in the air. A small laugh escaped Will's lips, breaking the silence.

"Light's fall, Will, what?" Morella snapped. "What could possibly be amusing at a moment like this?"

Will stared back at her, incredulous. Her face seemed somehow transformed, as though a mask had been removed and the laughing, whimsical Morella had gone. This anger and rage, these contorted features, this was the real Morella. He stood speechless, not by her outburst but by the transformation. "Nothing," he said finally, stepping away from her and into the corridor. "Just releasing some tension is all."

Morella scowled and stormed past him into the passage and out of sight.

Mad's brow furrowed. "Lover's quarrel?"

"I have no idea." Will shook his head as he stared in the direction Morella had gone.

Madigan's mouth was a thin line. "Best not let her get too far ahead," he said. "Let's go."

Morella didn't acknowledge either of them when they caught

up with her. She walked at the edge of Madigan's Shade, taking it upon herself to lead. Will's key continued its hum as they moved but she walked with such determination that he was not about to question or contradict her. The key soon began to pop with electricity again, small sparks that sent his heart racing, but he kept his mouth closed.

As the passages twisted and wound, the ground began to slope downward. They passed through a large stairwell in the middle of a huge, darkened room lined with columns. Down and down their path took them and slowly, ever so slowly, signs of recent inhabitation began to appear. A trace of smoke on the air. A door left ajar which, when Madigan risked opening it fully, led to a storeroom. But they neither heard nor saw any other soldiers. It had been more than an hour since their arrival and they had nothing to show for it.

Suddenly, Morella cursed and backed up against the wall. Ahead of them in the long hall, walking away from the party, was one of the Shale. She whirled on Will and Madigan. "This is ridiculous," she spat, and Will was again taken aback. "We wander and hope to find him? This is your brilliant plan to save the world?"

"Do you have a better one?" Madigan said coolly as he met her glare with one of his own.

"We ask someone," she said venomously.

Madigan snickered. "You want to politely ask one of those, those things if they wouldn't mind terribly giving us directions to something they wish to keep secret?" He rolled his eyes. "Oh yes, sounds brilliant."

"Mad." Will raised a hand to placate him. "Maybe she's right, we can't just wander forever."

"And how, pray tell, do you suggest we go about such a thing, Morella?"

She glared at Madigan and Will caught the hint of a smile in her expression. "We carve it out of them."

"Whoa, what?" Will turned his attention back to Morella. "We what?"

"We can't leave them alive afterwards, regardless." Her expression was hard and she gave a noncommittal shrug. Her knife appeared rapidly, twirling between her fingers. "First we ensure our information is correct and then we dispose of them."

"You can't be serious," Madigan said with a disgusted sneer. "That's not—no, that isn't how it's done. Will, back me up here."

Will was about to agree with his brother when Morella's face changed for a brief moment. She looked at him with such earnest hope and fire that, for a moment, she was once again the laughing, dancing girl in the bar. She was the girl who breathed life and passion. Who pulled him close to her, regardless of the world around her. She looked at Will and something inside his throat seemed to drop and fall into his gut.

"Maybe she's right, Mad," Will said. The words were strained. He wasn't sure if he believed them, but he said them.

Madigan stared incredulously at Will before turning back to Morella. The shock faded. His face grew passive, disappointed. He shook his head and stepped back. "This one's on you."

Will felt sick. Morella slipped out from the shadows and moved forward with her blade poised to strike. She stalked the Shale in silence. The way she moved was completely foreign to Will, as if a veil of cruelty covered her entire form. The woman before him was a killer; there was no joy in her heart, no love in her soul. She was a bringer of death and ruin. He gave his brother a pleading glance and then set off after her. Madigan cursed and followed.

Morella was outside the reach of Madigan's Shade but it didn't matter, the Shale was unaware. It descended another long flight of stairs and Will quickened his pace when Morella disappeared from his sight. He reached the stair and started down just as she set off through a low-ceilinged passage. At the end of the passage was a large double door with light peering through from the other side.

Will's key began to pop and crackle, hot against his skin. A wave of sudden dread swelled up over him and he sprinted down the stairs, taking them two, three at a time. At the landing he saw Morella right behind the Shale, blade in hand, preparing to strike. The warrior shoved open the door and light flooded into the corridor.

Will ran for Morella.

Behind the double door was a grand hall, impossibly large for being far underground. Within the hall sat what seemed to be the entirety of the Shale army. When the doors swung open and the lone soldier stepped through, Morella was completely and utterly exposed in front of all of them, frozen. For the space of a blink she was laid bare, plain for all to see, weapon in hand.

Then Will was upon her, shielding her in the soothing darkness of his Shade and ripping her back from the light.

The two of them crashed to the ground as the door eased itself shut. Morella's eyes were wide and white. No sound came from the army, no footfalls on ground or cries to arms. They had escaped unseen.

27

THE PRISONER OF SHALE

T he hazy fog of darkness around them dissipated. Will removed his hand from where he had inadvertently cupped it over Morella's mouth. "Are you okay?"

"How did you do that?" Morella stared wide-eyed, her skin nearly ghost white.

"I . . . I . . . " Will stammered.

"He didn't do anything," a groaning voice at their back said. Will turned and saw Madigan, doubled over and leaning against the wall with his noctori in hand. "I, apparently, overextended."

Trepidation gave way to relief as Will listened. It was a farce, of course. Madigan had seen what Will had done and was covering for him. *My brother, ever the hero.* He gave Mad a quick, appreciative nod and rose to his feet. Morella, shaking, did the same.

"Are you two okay?" Madigan asked. They both nodded. Morella looked stricken.

"There were so many of them," she said in disbelief. "An impossible number."

"I've changed my mind." Will's voice was shaky. His brother and Morella both gave him furtive glances. "I think I'd prefer to wander aimlessly over dealing with any of them."

Morella wrapped her arms around herself and nodded, eyes downcast.

Madigan pushed himself away from the wall, apparently recovered from his charade. But Will could see that there was, in fact, something off about his coloring. Something sickly. "There was a door back there at the bottom of the stairs," Madigan said, slightly out of breath. "Let's try that and see where we get."

They doubled back then and moved with even greater caution. The close encounter had shown Will just how many warriors of Shale there were, and he had no intention of allowing them to become aware of their presence. *Nothing could stand against so many.*

Madigan moved with his noctori drawn. He encircled them tightly with his Shade, bathing them in darkness. Still, Will felt exposed. Naked. Before long it became apparent that perhaps the Shade alone wouldn't be enough to keep them concealed. He wanted nothing more than to help, to wrap them in his own Shade for protection. But it would have revealed everything to Morella. She believed Madigan about the rescue and Will thought it best to follow his brother's lead.

The maze of corridors continued deeper underground. The air grew thin, electric, sending the hairs on the back of his neck standing. Far from normal static though, there was something different about the energy. It was power, raw and primal. The lower they went, the more Will felt it bite at his skin. Like the key at his chest, the air itself was vibrant and alive with magic.

He glanced at Madigan. A thin sheen of sweat was on his brother's forehead and he periodically rolled his shoulder back and forth. Morella, too, had adopted a strange twitch at the corner of her eye. She glanced around constantly, scanning the low roof above them and every curve of the wall with a harsh intensity.

"I need to stop," Madigan said finally, slouching against the wall. "I can't . . . whatever this energy is, it's too much."

"Something's wrong," Morella agreed. "This isn't right."

Will glanced around. The light of hall made the darkness of the Shade stand out. "Mad, release your Shade. It's a strain and it isn't helping right now."

Madigan glanced at Morella. She nodded quickly and the hint of darkness around the trio vanished. Now, they truly were exposed. Madigan collapsed breathless against the wall and slid down to a crouch, placing his head between his knees and allowing the noctori to fizzle out. Morella fidgeted back and forth, flicking her fingers open and closed and shaking her head.

"This is wrong," she said again.

"What do you mean?" Will asked as he stepped over to check on Madigan. His brother waved him away and pushed himself back to his feet.

"Valmont was Shadowborne," she continued. "Practically his whole army was made up of Shadowborne. If his forces were in control of the Shale there wouldn't be the slightest hint of Radiance here, his minions wouldn't be able to stomach it. But somehow it's as if this entire place is flooded in it."

"What are you saying?" Madigan still sounded breathless.

"You should be feeling empowered," she said. "Instead, you're faltering."

Will snapped his attention away from his brother and back to Morella. "Mind elaborating?" he said as he glanced past her and back down the corridor.

"That's why the air is affecting Madigan so much. This whole place is fighting against everything he is." She gestured to the area and shifted uncomfortably. "The static. The stifling heat. Radiant energy is coursing through the entire prison and it's only getting stronger the farther down we go. Shadow and Radiance don't coexist well."

"That's not a bad thing," Madigan said through clenched teeth. He strained to push forward again. "It just means Valmont's forces aren't in control."

Will's mind suddenly raced. "But if it was to control a prisoner, if a Shadowborne could be subdued by this much Radiant energy . . ."

"Then the Shale could be guarding a Shadowborne." Madigan picked up his brother's train of thought. "Putting them into a weakened state."

"Morella," Will said, thrilled and terrified simultaneously, "what were you saying about Valmont being alive?"

Morella's face dropped as realization dawned on her. "Gods above and below," she cursed, shaking her head. "This just got even more dangerous than I imagined."

"And if it is him," Madigan said with a hint of strength returning to his voice, "then he'll be weakened just like me."

Wait, no, Will suddenly realized. *That can't be right.*

The truth was, he would have loved to believe it. But if Radiance affected Shadowborne the way Morella said, Will would have been just as incapacitated as his brother. But he wasn't. He was fine. Plus, it wouldn't explain why Morella was exhibiting signs of discomfort. *Something's wrong here, something we're not seeing.*

Morella shook her head and straightened up a bit. "No, I don't think it works like that. Nothing I've read suggests that is a possibility."

Will shook his head. *We need to move. Whatever's wrong, we won't find out what it is by sitting here.* "Well, there's only one way to figure it out. We press on and do what we came here to do."

"Valmont or no," Madigan said, "Will's right, we need to figure out what the hell is going on."

They set off. The air pulsed and more than once Madigan had to pause for a break. Progress slowed even more the farther they descended. Will cast anxious glances at his brother, who was looking worse and worse. After Madigan stumbled three times in a short number of steps, Will had had enough. They approached a fork in the corridors and Madigan slumped against one of the walls for support before lurching toward the left passage. Without waiting, Will gripped the hilt of his fang and guided the restorative power toward his brother. Color flooded back into his brother's cheeks in a sudden rush.

Then, the power was gone. The weapon's stores had run dry.

"Will," he gasped as Morella groaned. "What have you done?"

"You're our muscle in here, Mad," Will responded sharper than intended. "You're the Shadowborne trained in weaponry by Jervin Thorne himself. We need you primed for whatever may come."

"And if what comes involves the need of your fangs, we're just out of luck now?" Morella said, her snark laid bare as she glared.

"Yes," Will said. *Back and forth and back and forth with that one, ever since we got in here.* "Up until recently we did just fine without their power. If we play it smart, we'll keep being just fine."

Madigan's face bristled with frustration but he threw up his hands and pushed past his brother. "There's nothing for it now. Let's move."

"At least you seem to be feeling better," Will quipped after him. Madigan turned and glared. Will smiled back at him, trying desperately to come off with more nonchalance than he actually felt. *We'll be fine,* he tried to say through the look, *I'm still your ace in the hole.* His brother growled and spun away, somehow managing to move silently as he went storming down the halls.

The air began to change again. The thickness disappeared and instead the atmosphere grew impossibly dry. Disconcerted, Will scanned the area. There was no dust floating in the air, as though the air itself was oppressively preventing it. *Always something with the damn dust.*

They each threw off the hoods of their cloaks but before long they were all sweating. *This just keeps getting better and better.* It was not until he removed his hood that Will realized he couldn't recall how long it had been since they had passed a door. Thinking back, there hadn't been any junctions since Madigan stumbled. Wherever the path was taking them, it was isolated from the majority of the prison and kept deep underground. *The perfect location for containing a murderous psychopath.*

Morella suddenly reached out and grabbed Madigan's shoulder and stopped him. All three of them froze as, voice barely audible, she spoke. "Movement at the end of the corridor. There, up ahead of us."

How she had managed to see it was beyond Will. Far ahead of them the corridor curved slightly and came to an end at a large, arched doorway. Within whatever lay beyond were the faintest flickers of motion, hardly distinguishable from half the distance.

"Well." Madigan rolled his shoulders and drew his noctori. "Looks like we've arrived."

Morella withdrew her own dagger and a wicked-looking stiletto Will hadn't seen before. It reminded him of the one used by Commander Shifter, but this blade was a strange blend of red and purple, like the skin of a plum. "Let's end this," she said, a dark smile spreading across her fair features.

Will suddenly realized how dry his mouth had become. He flicked his fingers and shook his wrists before drawing his saber. It was still pristine, untested. He was so nervous that he stifled a laugh. Mad and Morella both glanced back at him and he put on what he hoped was a dashing smile.

"Let's go say hello, shall we?"

The group closed the distance to the end of the path quickly. A hum filled the air. The room before them was an entryway to a larger chamber spread over three levels connected by ancient rafters and scaffolding. The motion they had seen was the distant flickering of the shadows of four Shale. They were on the plat-form below them and they maneuvered around a collection of bizarre machines unlike any Will had ever seen.

In the center of the bottommost level was a clear box with a rack inside it. A piece of a man was strapped to it. *No, multiple pieces of a man.* An arm and the upper part of a chest appeared to be there but then, a moment later, it looked to be his other arm or perhaps a leg. The more Will stared, the more the pieces seemed to fade in and out of existence, fluctuating before his eyes.

"Valmont." Madigan's whisper was filled with a cruel hunger. "It's really him."

"It's him," Morella said through gritted teeth, her voice filled with a growling rage.

Will couldn't take his eyes off the body. "Why does he seem to be . . . "

"Gods, he's phased," Morella whispered. Will glanced at her and raised an eyebrow. "Just like the Shale prison phases between worlds. Somehow they've managed to do it to a prisoner."

"You're saying that he's here but not here?" Mad asked, unable to take his eyes off the distorted mass of flickering human flesh.

"That's what I'm saying," Morella said. "They must have managed to suppress his powers by splicing him between worlds."

"That's horrifying." Will shook his head as the pieces of the man twitched and strained against their bonds.

"No less than what he deserves," Madigan said.

Morella shot him a harsh look and then crept forward, risking a glance. "We should take out the controllers first. Get him solid and whole back in this plane."

"Wait, won't that make him stronger?" Will asked. *I can't believe we're actually doing this.* "And whatever happened to gathering intel?"

"Damn intel," Madigan growled.

Morella nodded back to Will. "Yes, ultimately it will make him stronger. But I can only imagine the strain and torture his mind is under now, being ripped apart like that. He'll be weak."

"And we don't know if we could do anything to him with him phased like that," Madigan agreed. "She's right, we can't leave any room for doubt." His voice had hardened, adopting an impassive timbre that Will didn't recognize. He didn't like it.

"Four Shale and Dorian Valmont," Will said. He felt like he was on the deck of a sailboat that suddenly lurched. His head swam, but he drew his face into a mask of a smirk that was filled with far more confidence than he felt. "Right. This should be easy."

Without another word, Madigan shrouded them in darkness. In silence, they crept forward to the stone ladder carved from the wall and considered. Will risked a glance over the ledge. The drop to the lower level was not much more than eight feet, easily made, but could they make it in silence? There was only one way to find out. Replacing his weapon, Will crouched and gripped his hands on the ledge before him as Morella followed suit. Madigan remained by the ladder, noctori gripped firmly in one hand, the other clasping the rail embedded in the wall. They watched the Shale below for a moment—none had the slightest idea of what was about to befall them.

In unison, Madigan, Will, and Morella attacked. Will propelled himself forward and somersaulted over the ledge, tumbling to the ground and landing solid as he withdrew his unblooded saber. Morella was at his side, her weapons at the ready, as Madigan quickly slid down the rail and came rushing toward the Shale from their flank.

They descended upon the stunned force with a fury, immediately incapacitating three of them in a blink. The fourth, spinning rapidly, let loose a flurry of hidden weapons at his unseen assailants but it was to no avail. With a single strike from the guard of Will's sword, the final Shale dropped motionless to the ground in a heap.

They paused and listened. Silence. The attack had taken only a matter of seconds and, thankfully, no alarms had been triggered. The protective darkness around them disappeared. Madigan stepped forward to stare at the prisoner below, twitching and writhing.

"Now we end this," was all he said as he approached the control console. Morella stepped to his side and placed her hands on the railing beyond the console, a hunger in her eyes. Madigan gripped the large lever and with a smile, shoved it forward.

The room flashed in a sudden storm of lightning. An ear-shattering scream echoed through the room as the imprisoned man flickered in and out of existence. Finally, his form became solid and whole. There was no sound.

The man's brown hair was cut short on the sides and had designs carved into it, reminding Will of pictures of Vikings he had seen growing up. The figure was quite tall and, being stripped to the waist as he was, Will could see that his muscular body was covered with countless scars. His eyes were wild and he ripped at his bonds frantically but uselessly. After a moment, his eyes rolled up and he collapsed, motionless. Morella had been right; he was weak.

"No, Gods, no." A faint, terrified voice broke the silence.

Will's eyes were drawn from the unconscious form on the table to Morella. The pale skin of her face was well and truly white. Her eyes were stretched wide and her body was trembling. She was gripping the railing so tight that the color of her knuckles matched that of her face. Her mouth was agape and she seemed unsteady on her feet.

"Morella, what?" Mad asked, his noctori ready to strike.

"Valmont," she whispered as she shook her head. "That's . . . that's . . . "

"Morella." Will placed his hand on her shoulder and spun her to face him. "What? What's happened?"

"That's not Dorian Valmont." Her voice was barely more than a breath. Her eyes were glistening and filled with terror as she kept shaking her head. "That's Jero din'Dael."

28

AN AWAKENING

"Jero din'Dael?" Mad stared at the prisoner and shook his head. "No, that has to be Dorian Valmont."

"Morella, are you certain?" Will was staring into her fluttering eyes, holding her shoulders with both hands. "Morella, I need you to talk to me. What do you mean, that's Jero din'Dael? I thought he was supposed to be dead."

"He's supposed to be." Her eyes came back into focus and hardened rapidly. "That's him."

Mad cursed. "You're sure?" he said.

"The air, the electricity surrounding the prison, everything suddenly makes sense," Morella stepped back from the rail. "Oh Gods, his power is permeating this entire prison. That's what was slowing you down, Madigan! He is too powerful to be contained, even in this state."

"You're certain that that's Jero din'Dael?" Will said, trying to meet her eye.

"How many different ways do I need to tell you?" she snapped. "Yes, that's him!"

"Dammit," Madigan groaned. "Dammit, dammit, dammit. Why the hell did the Crow send us here? What the hell was he thinking?"

While Madigan raged, Will quickly scanned his memory for anything and everything Morella and Cephora had ever mentioned about din'Dael. There wasn't much, but he remembered two key things: He was Valmont's greatest adversary and he was in control of one of the Relics of Antiquity.

"If we rescue him then perhaps he would be useful," Will said, the calm in his voice surprising himself. "He could join us in our fight, level the playing field." Both Morella and Madigan turned to stare at him. "Think about it. The Crow probably knew it was din'Dael here. He wants us to break him out."

"Or we took a wrong turn and we need to go find Senraks instead," Madigan said. "This place is huge."

Morella hadn't heard Madigan; she simply stared, looking aghast at Will. "There is no way I'm helping that monster. You've got to be insane."

"Mad," Will said quietly. "We've gotta make a decision quick. There's no telling how much time we've got. He could help us defeat Senraks."

"Absolutely not." Morella grit her teeth as her anger flared. "Jero din'Dael was almost as dangerous as Valmont! Releasing him is the worst thing we could do."

Madigan shook his head after a moment. "No. Will's right. Alone, without Cephora, stopping Senraks was going to be next to impossible. With Jero din'Dael fighting alongside us we've got a chance."

"Right." Will nodded. "We share a common enemy of the worst kind. He'll help us."

Morella glared back and forth between the two brothers. "You foolish outlanders." Her lips curled into a snarl and her words were filled with venom. "Unleashing the force of Radiance again to battle Shadow is to invite destruction upon everything you have seen. You know nothing of the horrors that man has wrought, the insanity that grips his brain. I will have no part of this."

She spun and moved to the ladder despite Will's protestations and attempts to calm her fears. Her body trembled, gripped by fury. Will's key was screaming on his skin as she passed him.

He turned to Madigan, imploring, as she climbed the stairs, but his eyes were hard and he shook his head. "No, Will, we're committed." Will's chest tightened and he fought the urge to run after her as her footsteps quickly faded away. And just like that, Morella Darklore left them.

Will shook his head in frustration. "What if she's right?"

"She may be. But at this point?" Madigan snorted and ran his free hand through his messy hair. "At this point I'm just going by instinct and I can't help but feel we're going to need him."

No sooner had he spoken than a loud horn sounded somewhere far off in the distance. The brothers froze, holding each other's eyes, waiting. After a moment, the slow pounding of a drum echoed through the prison. Will's heart dropped. He looked at Madigan in terror as his brother's face paled in the stagnant air. Sweat appeared on his brow. The pounding drums picked up speed. Will felt faint.

"They know we're here." Madigan's voice sounded as far away as the drums. "We've got to move."

He flung himself over the railing and down to the lower level that housed din'Dael's cell. He rushed forward and scanned the clear box for a seam, any kind of opening they could use to break out the unconscious man within.

Will turned in the direction that Morella had gone—had they found her? Was her capture what had raised the alarm? No, there was no way she had made it so far in such a short time. Like her, their only way out was the tunnel through which the drums were echoing. Then, as if in imitation of the drums, he heard a distant rumble—the stomping of footsteps racing down the corridor. For a brief moment he hoped it was Morella returning, but there were far too many for it to be so. Madigan was right: they were discovered.

"Mad, they're coming!"

Madigan cursed as he set to work attacking din'Dael's enclosure with the noctori. Will ran to the stone ladder and raced upward toward the room's entrance. If the Shale got in, they would surround them easily, overpower them, but if he could trap them in the passage their numbers would be meaningless. The choke point would be his and Madigan's only hope.

The rushing footsteps were growing louder. As Will stepped through the passage he saw the shadows of the soldiers approaching. He drew his saber and gripped his key with his left hand. He closed his eyes and looked inward.

Time to play the ace.

The hallway was enveloped in blue-purple darkness as Will's Shade poured from him into the corridor. He could see soldiers approaching, not more than twenty yards away. He braced himself, whispered a silent prayer to whatever gods were listening, and ran forward to meet them head on.

The force of their collision sent him flying backward. Their formation, however, was broken as well, the middle Shale flung aside and crashing into its allies. Recovering quickly, Will set about them, pressing with his Shade, refusing to allow them to close the gap. Within the cramped space the soldiers could not turn to fight him properly and wield their weapons; they were only able to press forward with their shields. Will managed to disable another Shale with his saber and sent two more flying backward with his Shade. Still, their numbers were too great and he was beginning to lose ground.

An arrow whizzed through the air above the heads of the Shale. Instinctively, Will batted it away with his Shade. In doing so, however, he had withdrawn it enough to allow the center of the shield wall to recover. This time there was no breaking it. These warriors were from a different age, an age where they had been trained in battling Shadowborne. Every attempt of Will's to press them back failed. Another arrow screamed through the air and Will dove to the ground to avoid it. The battle cries of the Shale pierced his ears. He somersaulted backward and rolled to his feet as they charged.

There was nothing for it. Will turned and ran, shouting to his brother as he burst through the doorway into the cell. Madigan had managed to crack din'Dael's prison, attacking it with both his noctori and his Shade. Realizing that Mad needed more time, Will spun back to the doorway and braced himself to meet the Shale.

The entrance, curved as it was, exposed the warriors' flank as they tried to enter the room and forced them to come two abreast. Their shields were useless to them as Will set about them with his saber and his Shade, trying to hold them in position. He knew that if any managed to pass by there was little chance of holding the rest back.

His Shade smashed into helms and shields, his saber slashed their limbs, piercing the soft places of their armor and biting into the flesh beneath, but still they came. One of the Shale broke through the rest and into the room. Will sent it careening into the stone wall with his Shade and it collapsed in a heap. Two more burst through and he struck at their legs and forced them backward briefly. A sword came down and Will brought up his saber to block it as he shoved them back with his Shade. Another blow rained down and he caught it on his hand guard. Then, as he kept the blade locked, a strike came from the side. Will ducked and a huge axe struck the flat of his stuck saber and snapped the blade clean.

Dropping the broken weapon from his hand, Will staggered backward and drew his dragon fangs as the forces of the Shale raced into the room. Fully able to use their weapons, they set upon him from all sides. His back to the railing, Will defended himself with every ounce of his being. His fangs parried blow after blow and ripped through armor and flesh, sending the Shale screaming. His Shade was obscuring visibility and knocking soldiers backward—but it was not enough. On the warriors of Shale came.

Will's right arm suddenly screamed in fire and he saw one of the Shale withdrawing its pike. It had slashed clean through his tricep and blood cascaded from the grievous wound. His arm fell limp at his side. Will slashed wildly with his left as another weapon bit into his hip. He collapsed to the ground, Shale warriors swarming over him.

Time crawled. Somewhere far away, Madigan was shouting. The Shale were plunging their weapons downward impossibly slowly. The world seemed to be frozen in death, only Will's key was alive and vibrant in the haze of muddled time.

Fire erupted within his chest. The dark fog of the Shade around Will vanished. Electricity crackled in the room and a shiver went down his spine. Will saw the Shale around him and felt the power of rage build within his bones—a rage that he unleashed upon them.

Lightning ripped through the room in a thousand bolts as the Shale screamed in agony. With his good arm, he lashed out and drove his dragon fang into the chest of the nearest warrior. A sweet scent, like roasting pork over an open flame, overtook the air before it was overshadowed by that of burnt hair. Lightning tore through the Shale leaving cracked and blackened corpses in its wake. More than a score of Shale lay dead.

Will gasped and coughed up blood. His right arm hung useless. He felt faint. The hilt of the dragon fang was slick in his hand, but he felt the freshly accumulated flows of energy course through it. He blinked and tried to focus on the flows, to staunch the blood flowing from him and bind what had been broken. Like falling into a freezing pool, shock swept over his body. Feeling returned to his dead arm and the sensation of his lifeblood pouring from his side ceased. He reached out and gripped the fang's twin from where it had fallen and pushed himself to his feet, gazing in horror at the scene surrounding him.

"Mad?" Will's voice was a hoarse croak as he called out to his brother.

"Jesus, Will," Madigan responded. He raised his head above the ledge and pulled himself up from the stone ladder. He rushed over and threw his arms around his brother. "I couldn't get here in time." His voice cracked as he spoke and there were tears in his eyes. "I'm so sorry. I'm so sorry. I thought I'd lost you. I couldn't get through and then the lightning came and, Will, I'm so, so sorry."

"I'm alive, Mad," Will said, trying to sound reassuring. "It's okay. I'm okay."

Tears streaked Madigan's dirt-stained cheeks as he looked his brother over, refusing to let him go. "I saw you go down. I saw them swarm you. I heard your screams."

Will tried to stand up and felt the strain of the movement. "I know. I'm okay." He held up the fangs and nodded to them in explanation. Madigan looked at them and then pulled his brother close again.

"And the lightning again?" he asked.

Will nodded again and risked another glance around the room at the charred bodies of the Shale. His stomach lurched and he turned, hurling the remnants of his last meal over the railing before he collapsed to the ground, shaking. His head spun and he struggled to take a deep breath, but with every attempt to inhale he could smell the smoky death in the air, he could taste the charred ash on his tongue. *Looks like we're both killers.*

Will began to sob.

For a moment, they both sat there, Madigan's hand on his shoulder as Will buried his face in his hands at the horror he had wrought.

Drums.

Will glanced up at Madigan. "Mad . . . "

"We don't have much time," his brother said. He took a deep breath, wiped a tear from his eye, and raised them both to their feet. He approached the doorway with his noctori drawn and Will stared at the bodies around him, realizing what he needed to do and dreading it. He gripped the dragon fangs tightly as Cephora's words echoed in his mind. *Life is energy,* she had said. *And energy, in all things, is conserved. There is no true give or take, only a transference.* Will's eyes lolled as he momentarily swooned.

He set to work filling the bloodstones.

"Not quite the in and out we thought this would be," Madigan said quietly. "Maybe Morella had the right idea."

Will's focus was elsewhere as his blades slid into the bodies of the Shale he had killed, sapping the final vestiges of life from them.

"Maybe she had the right idea," Mad continued as he shook his head. "I managed to get a small breach in the casing to din'-Dael but nothing else. He's alive but he's completely unresponsive. The whole venture is for naught."

Will nodded absently and moved to another of the Shale. He struggled to justify his actions, that perhaps whatever they had done to din'Dael made this fate of theirs deserved. Years or decades or centuries, even, of torture, who knew what that could do to a man? Enough, apparently, to break his mind completely. Even if they somehow managed to survive and get extracted by Cephora, there was nothing for the broken body of the once Champion of Radiance. Nothing to restore him to being the worthy adversary of Valmont that could even the score against Senraks.

Realization poured over him. "Mad!" Will shouted. "A breach? You say you made a breach?"

He nodded. "Not much of one, but yes."

Will threw himself over the railing and plummeted to the lowest level of the room. He braced himself in his Shade as he landed, rolling and running toward the casing.

Madigan's work was evident from the cracks that spidered along the casing from a central impact point. Will stared at the cracks, searching for the breach Madigan had mentioned as the drums grew louder and more incessant. Finally, after a moment's searching, he found it, small as a grain of rice.

"I couldn't get beyond there," Mad shouted down. "What are you planning?"

"To get us an extra set of hands," Will said under his breath. He drew forth his left dragon fang, its bloodstone filled from the deaths of so many Shale, and guided the power it contained through the tiny opening. Focusing on din'Dael, praying for Morella's fears of him to be wrong, Will swept the energy to the inert man strapped to the rack.

For a moment there was no change. Then din'Dael's eyes shot open. He roared. From above, Madigan whipped around and stared as the muscular man tried to rise, struggling against his bonds once more. Anger clouded his face and he grit his teeth. Then, with a deafening crack of thunder, the entire cell burst into white lightning, so vast and terrible that Will was forced to recoil from the wall. The chamber exploded and he barely managed to take cover as flying shrapnel shot outward, twisted metal and shattered wood and whatever glass-like substance had made up the cage.

Amidst the wreckage stood din'Dael. He stepped forward toward Will and stared down. Motionless, Will stared back. The corner of one of the prisoner's eyes twitched. The drums grew louder and shouts began to echo down through the corridor above. Din'Dael glanced up toward the sound and leveled his gaze at Madigan, eyes narrowing at the sight of the noctori. Madigan weathered the glare and returned it in kind. After a moment, din'Dael turned back to Will and his mouth spread into a wide grin as he extended a hand down.

"What say we slaughter some Shale?" din'Dael addressed Will.

Will took his hand and was pulled to his feet so forcefully he nearly stumbled. He went to respond but the man turned and raced up the ladder before he was able. Quicker than Will thought possible, din'Dael reached the top level and squared off against Madigan. Will watched as the Lightborne took in his brother and the noctori. Jero din'Dael snickered.

"Shadowborne." Din'Dael gave an impassive nod. He glanced about at the charred corpses strewn about the room, then back to Madigan, then back to Will and smiled again.

Will made to move to the ladder but din'Dael held up a hand and shook his head. He whirled and stepped into the entryway as the clamor of troops grew ever closer and held up both his hands. Bright as the sun, they glowed as he unleashed a wall of pure white fire in a wave and sent it flying up the corridor in a roar.

The war cries of the Shale turned to shrieks of pain and misery that overshadowed the cacophony of the flames. Amongst it all stood din'Dael, howling in laughter.

The screams were over a short moment later. The drums were silent. The scars covering din'Dael's bare arms danced and crackled with streaks of white lightning as he reentered the room. He strode forward to Madigan and cocked his head to the side, the hint of a smile twitching upon his mouth. A hesitant silence stretched between them.

"Shadowborne," din'Dael said again.

"Jero din'Dael," Madigan responded.

"You knew me?" Din'Dael cocked his head to the side as Madigan nodded. "Interesting."

"My name is Madigan Davis. This is my brother, William. We've come for your aid."

Din'Dael burst into laughter again and turned from Madigan, kicking the charred corpse of a Shale from his path as he strode forward and leapt over the railing to the ground below where Will stood. He laid a hand on his shoulder.

"It appears I am indebted to you, William Davis."

"Well." Will swallowed. "Very good. I always prefer to have debts owed to me rather than be the one doing the owing."

Din'Dael chuckled and gestured toward Will's belt. "The blood fangs, you wield them?"

Will nodded.

"That's very interesting. And you destroyed all those Shale up there?"

Will's eyes flickered with pain as he nodded again.

Din'Dael grinned again, wider than Will imagined possible. Slowly, he raised his palm to Will's face. Crackling with energy, the man cupped Will's forehead with the heel of his hand and gripped his fingers into his hair. The Lightborne's eyes rolled back into his skull and Will felt a wave of power surge through his own body. His limbs splayed as electricity coursed through him like he had been struck by a bolt of thunder. Madigan shouted for his brother and threw himself over the railing, rapidly closing the distance to din'Dael, but was swatted away by a blast of fire to his chest that sent him careening into a wall.

"There we are, William Davis." Din'Dael grinned as he removed his hand and Will slumped to the ground, gasping for air. "Consider my debt repaid."

Will's entire body ached. He curled into the fetal position and gave a violent cough. His insides felt like ash. He pushed himself to all fours and looked up at din'Dael. He tried to speak and broke into a fit of coughing. He heard his brother groan and managed to regain control of his lungs. He glared up at din'Dael.

"What did you do to me?" Will said.

"Think of it as 'accelerated training.'" Din'Dael grinned again. "A century's worth of daily practice may be comparable, but only just." He shrugged. "You'll be the judge, ultimately, Lightborne."

William froze, tendrils of fear snaking through his body. "What?"

"A rarity for siblings to align differently and not have killed one another yet," din'Dael continued as if not hearing him. "Still, who knows what the future may bring? Now, where is Dahla?"

Madigan stirred against the wall and let out a low moan, but Will was in too much shock to take notice. *Lightborne,* din'Dael had said—an impossibility. Will looked inward and sought the soothing darkness of his Shade. He could not feel anything. Fear overtook him and he grasped his key in futility.

His Shade was gone.

29

JAILBREAK

"What," Will gasped, "what have you done?" He stared at din'Dael, fear and outrage pouring over him. He felt empty, hollowed out, burnt from the inside. Violated. He was incomplete.

Jero din'Dael gave him a look that was a blend of disappointment and disgust. "I've elevated you, fool. You've ascended to the level of a true Burner and hardly lifted a finger to do so. Your fire is beyond your wildest dreams." He sneered and turned from Will, crossing the room and placing his hands on the wall there. Madigan had recovered enough to stand and crossed to his brother quickly.

"Will," he said, coughing and staggering a bit. "Are you alright?"

Will knew that the only thing sparing him from welling up with tears once more was the complete absence of any spare moisture in his body. His lips felt chapped and cracked and his eyes were dry and scratchy. There was a thirst in him, far greater than any he had ever known. He turned to his brother, stricken.

When he spoke, his voice sounded empty and dry. "Mad, my Shade, it's gone."

Madigan's brow raised in horror before turning downward in rage. He spun toward din'Dael and raced for him, both Shade and noctori ablaze. Before he could close the distance, however, din'Dael raised his hands from the wall and the stones exploded before him.

Madigan and Will threw themselves to the ground and covered their heads as sheets of rock and dirt flew through the room. When Will raised his head, din'Dael was marching through the chasm he had created into a growing tunnel of scorched and blackened earth.

"Come!" the man barked over his shoulder. Madigan and Will rose to their feet and steadied themselves, watching the retreating figure disappear from eyesight.

"We owe him nothing." Madigan leveled his gaze at his brother. "We leave him. We get out and start over."

"No." Will shook his head and tried to swallow but his throat didn't seem to work. *So thirsty* . . . "Not until I know what he did to me." Giving a tense nod, Madigan beckoned him forward and the pair chased after din'Dael.

The tunnel reminded Will of volcanic caverns that had long since been absent of lava. The floor slanted upward and twisted periodically, showing a gradual rise from the entrance. Jero din'-Dael was far enough ahead that they could hear the echoes of his roaring fury but see nothing of the man himself. The force of his blasts had left the walls smooth, the molten rock rapidly cooled and stabilized. Occasional flashes of light ahead of them showed that he was still at work, carving his own path from the prison as he made his escape.

The hollowness in Will's chest began to subside and he felt something flutter within. Stifling a cry of joy, he gripped his key and felt its electricity burning and firing as never before. Yet, the moment of hope diminished in a moment as, despite every effort, his Shade was utterly gone. He clutched the key as it decreased its wild vibrations until only a simple hum remained. Attempting to use it as a conduit was fruitless. Like the failed attempts to recall a dream, the paths in his brain through which he knew how to access his Shade began to crumble and fade.

A boom sounded and the tunnel became flooded in natural light. Will and Madigan raced forward, believing that din'Dael had breached the exterior of the prison, but what they saw was not even remotely that. The tunnel opened wide into the large hall where they had seen the massed Shale.

Din'Dael was unleashing havoc on his jailers. Lightning whipped through the air. Horrific sounds of death filled the room. Bodies were flying from din'Dael as he forced a path forward. The one man was cutting through hundreds like they were butter. Will had never seen a battlefield, never seen so much death in one place. *Slaughter.*

With weapons drawn, Madigan and Will followed in din'-Dael's wake. The cries and moans of the brutalized Shale sent Will's head swimming. Din'Dael was at the end of the room, climbing a ladder to the dais that overlooked the area. The Shale had fled from him, pulling back to regroup, it seemed, and the brothers had a clear path to him. Rapidly scaling the ladder, they found din'Dael casually flipping switches and twisting levers on the console in the center of the dais. He whirled to face them, an immense claymore raised high. When he saw who it was, however, he chuckled and dropped the weapon before turning back to the controls.

"What are you doing?" Madigan's voice was hoarfrost on steel.

"Enacting justice, of course."

"And you're doing that how . . . ?" Will's voice sounded tired, even to his own ears. Tired and parched. *Gods, so thirsty.*

Din'Dael's hand settled on the largest lever on the panel and he met Will's gaze with his twisted, twitching smile.

"Why, by bringing freedom, of course!"

He flipped the switch and the entirety of the prison shook and groaned. There was a brief silence, then a roar of drums and a hum of arrows as the Shale, fully regrouped, attacked. Din'Dael calmly held up a hand and the arrows were incinerated midflight. The Shale, racing toward the dais, halted. Off in the distance, more drums sounded but this time with no steady rhythm, no cool battle song; rather the air was filled with a frantic percussion.

Suddenly breaking off from the three men, the Shale began racing for the entrances to the hall and arraying themselves into battle formation. As Will stared in horror, a horde began pouring into the room. Men and women, bone thin and ragged, seemingly appeared from nowhere and began pressing themselves upon the Shale violently.

"Glorious," din'Dael said, his face brightening with a jubilant smile.

"What have you done?" Madigan roared as the room began filling with more and more people who appeared as likely to tear one another apart as they were the Shale.

"I've brought freedom to every soul in this forsaken prison." Din'Dael grinned. "And after centuries of imprisonment, they appear to have some issue with their jailers."

Will gripped the metal rails of the dais as he watched the chaos unfolding before him. He pictured it happening throughout the entirety of the massive prison and knew for certain that any dream of safe passage had just been dashed. His thoughts lurched to Morella, alone and wandering the prison's winding maze of passages. He prayed that somehow she was safe. Perhaps Cephora had managed to get her out, or maybe she'd found an exit on her own. Maybe she had fought her way out. But as the mass of people clawed and hacked and tore one another into gory shreds before him, his thoughts turned toward finding an exit of their own.

"Mad!" he shouted over the roar of the crowd. "We have to get out of here!"

"Come on!" his brother yelled back as he raced down the ladder.

Will followed and started down before realizing that din'Dael had not moved. His arms were spread wide as he stood tall and erect, eyes to the cracking ceiling, drinking in the chaos. Will shook his head. Perhaps Morella had been right. Perhaps it would have been best to leave him locked up. Perhaps it would be best to leave him down here in the chaos that he wrought under the pretense of freedom. But after seeing what he was capable of, and aware that even this man, despite his power, hadn't been able to defeat Valmont, they couldn't leave him behind.

"Din'Dael!" Will shouted. "We've got to get to our extraction!"

The Lightborne cocked his head to the side, as if trying to remember who Will was and why he was addressing him, before he grinned and ran forward.

"Lead on, young Burner," he whooped as he leapt from the dais. "Lead on!"

Madigan was pressing through the crowds, noctori bared and spinning in controlled brutality as he cleared a path. Will was right behind his brother with din'Dael hot on his heels. For his part, din'Dael had stopped fighting entirely and seemed perfectly content to follow. Will's blood fangs were out and working their way through anyone who happened to get close enough. Every time they connected with flesh, every time the screams began, Will felt more and more apart from himself, as if he was watching the entire event unfold from far above the throng of berserk combatants.

They finally managed to reach an exit that wasn't crowded with prisoners or Shale and raced through. The corridors spun this way and that but gradually began to climb higher. They encountered more Shale and more prisoners battling as they went —there seemed to be an endless supply of both—but after a few minor skirmishes the three emerged from a passage into an open courtyard under the cover of night.

The entire courtyard was filled with a rampaging battle. The three ducked into a passage between towers and ran toward the outer wall, some distance away. As they drew closer, they encountered a platoon of fresh Shale. Madigan rapidly sought to cloud the three of them within his Shade but it was too late, they had been seen. At an unintelligible order, the entire contingent turned and began running toward them.

Madigan darted down a side passage at a sprint and cursed as the Shale pursued. Cutting left and right and left again, the three raced to distance themselves from their pursuers, but to no avail. They emerged back into the courtyard to find that the main gate of the fortress was swarmed with prisoners attempting to scale the walls as Shale unleashed volley after volley of arrows against them. It seemed to be slaughter without end.

Madigan halted suddenly as a new stream of prisoners poured from the facility. In their maddening haste, they crashed into Will and Madigan and knocked them backward. Din'Dael kept at a distance, watching.

Madigan, deflecting their every blow, was forced backward toward a tower. With a battle cry he forced the assault back, but only just. Will raced to his side as din'Dael skirted into the tower.

Unable to stem the flow of the horde, they were pressed backward into the tower as the mass of people proved too much for even the combined forces of Madigan's Shade and noctori. Will struggled against the heavy stone door, inching it closed as Madigan fought off the throng. He risked a glance behind him and saw din'Dael sitting calmly on the floor in the center of the tower, watching the brothers fight them off.

"Din'Dael!" Will shouted. "Help us!"

The silent, seated form stared back at him blankly.

"Breach the walls, push them back, something!" Will cried as he struggled against the door.

Din'Dael, covered in blood and soot and sweat, simply stared back. "I'm cold," was his only response as he shrugged.

They were losing ground. Despite Will's bracing of the door, it continued to get pushed open bit by bit. The first hints of panic started to rumble in Will's breast as he saw din'Dael lie back and sprawl onto the ground, seemingly unaware of the press of people clamoring for blood.

Anger replaced panic as Will stared at him, lying there and humming tunelessly to himself. Were it not for him, he and his brother would never have been in this situation. The anger burned, a roaring blaze, and he could feel it coursing through every inch of his body. In that moment, Will knew exactly what needed to be done.

Without warning, he sprang away from the door and watched it crash open under the force from those screaming outside. Roughly, he shoved his brother out of the way and sent him sprawling into the nearby wall.

A Burner, that's what din'Dael had called him. Lightborne. Will's Shade had been the evidence that proved otherwise, but now that power was gone. In its place was a white-hot fury, a fount of roaring fire. Will *burned.*

He surged forward into the throng, the power rippling through him. As the prisoners closed in and blows rained down on him, he released his fury. It manifested in a ball of fiery lightning that spiraled out in countless bolts of white-hot death.

In an instant, the bodies of the dead and the dying surrounded him. There was a momentary quiet. He was bleeding from dozens of cuts and scratches, and black bruises were already beginning to swell his left eye shut, but he had earned a moment's respite. He stumbled back into the tower and collapsed to the ground.

"Again, you bloody idiot?" Madigan raced forward, crying insults and berating him. He knelt and helped Will roll over to lie on his back, nearly mirroring din'Dael behind them. "You're going to get yourself killed!"

"You can shut the door now." Will coughed. *My life for a drink of water.* Sitting up was out of the question, let alone standing. He fumbled for the power within the blood fang but the motion made his head spin. He forced himself to abandon the task.

Madigan cursed again and ran to the door. He began to shove the bodies that now blocked it out of the path, covering his nose and mouth with his arm. He paused in the gruesome task, glancing outside the tower, and cursed a third time.

"Shale," he said.

"I'm coming." Will struggled to lift himself. He nearly made it to his knees before he lost his balance and fell to the side. Violent coughs wracked his body. *So damn thirsty,* he thought sluggishly.

"No, Will," Mad said. Will looked up and saw his brother shaking his head at him. Madigan didn't meet his eye, instead surveying the corpses on the ground before drawing his noctori. "You've done enough. This one is on me, kid."

"Wait," Will croaked. "Mad!"

His words were lost as his brother stepped out from the tower and slammed the door behind him. The ground shook as the Shale swarmed over Madigan out of Will's sight.

Will groaned and rolled over. He forced himself to focus through the pounding spins of his mind as he reached for his knives. Fumbling momentarily, he managed to draw the correct one from its sheath and felt the hum of its power. *I should name them,* he thought drunkenly, unable to keep track of his thoughts. *All good weapons in stories have names.*

He shook himself out of the stupor and forced himself to focus. It took every ounce of concentration to guide the powerful flows over his body and work to remake the battered flesh.

"You're going to overdo it if you're not careful," a thin, tremulous voice said from nearby.

Weary but whole once more, Will turned to din'Dael and pushed himself onto unsteady feet. "Your concern for my well-being is overwhelming," he said.

The Lightborne snickered and sat up. "Keep your temper."

Wobbling slightly, Will made his way to the door. Just as he was about to open it, a sudden rumbling from the rear of the room caught his attention. Whirling, he saw a dark crack appear in the stone wall, as though the stone itself was bending. Din'-Dael spun on his seat and cocked his head to the side, eyes narrowing as from the strange crack emerged a dark figure wielding a long staff.

"Cephora!" din'Dael said and barked a laugh. "How are you not dead?"

Cephora's eyes momentarily widened but there was nothing else about her that showed any hint of shock. "Jero din'Dael," she said, "it has been some time." The warrior leapt to his feet with a laugh as Cephora rushed toward Will. "William, you're alright? Where is your brother?"

"The Shale." Will swallowed. "He's out—"

Something slammed against the door so hard that it shook roughly on its ancient hinges. Understanding dawned on Cephora's face. She grabbed the door handle and yanked it open. Will ducked under her arm and darted out from the tower.

Madigan was leaning heavily against the wall opposite them with his weight borne by his noctori. Lacerations covered his face and torso and one of his legs didn't seem to support him. Around him, his Shade hung in the air like a dense, rolling fog. Hanging within the fog were the mangled bodies of dozens of Shale, limbs snapped and twisted. They fell to the ground with a sickening thud as he looked over at the open door.

"You're a sight for sore eyes." He smiled a blood-filled grin at Cephora. "How did you find us?"

"Morella," she replied. "Will, can you help him?"

Will was already on it. There seemed to be a brief lull in the seemingly unending flow of prisoners and Shale and he used the window to tend to Madigan. The power remaining within the bloodstones was enough to heal the majority of the cuts that poured blood, but his leg was truly broken. With the stores tapped and knowing that more energy was needed, Will withdrew his blood fangs and began to work amongst the bodies on the ground to refuel them. He could feel Cephora's eyes on his back. He glanced up and met them.

"It appears that much has changed since this morning," was all she said.

Having refilled the stones and repaired Madigan's leg, wearily they made their way back into the tower. Will began to close the door behind them but hesitated. "Mad." He took one last glance at the bodies on the ground, robbed of life by both his brother's and his own hands. "Are you alright?"

"We do what we must to survive." Mad's voice was hollow with frustration. *No, he isn't alright at all.*

Another storm of shouts split the air as the battling forces moved back within sight. Will closed the door as quietly as possible and leaned against it.

"It's a good thing you showed up when you did, Cephora," Madigan said. "I don't know how much longer we could have held out."

"Especially without any help from him." Will jerked his head toward din'Dael.

"You never asked," din'Dael said matter-of-factly, giving him the same blank stare.

"What? Yes he did, you bloody, blundering oaf!" Madigan shouted. Din'Dael glared a moment, then shrugged and turned toward the crack Cephora had made and stepped forward, strolling through it nonchalantly.

"We need to move." The urgency in Cephora's voice was plain. "I don't like him being out of sight."

"Not to mention the madness of this place," Madigan muttered.

At a gesture from Cephora, Madigan and Will both rushed into the blackness. Again came the sense of falling, the roar of deafening gales. Cold wind and the scent of earth overwhelmed him as Will's body was caught in the throes of Cephora's magic.

The spinning sensation lasted only a moment before he emerged outside the prison walls. Lightning no longer crackled along their surface and they seemed somehow diminished. Something terrible had broken within the Shale prison.

Madigan had set off running in the direction of din'Dael who was racing toward a distant hill. Faintly, Will saw a human form atop it, waving. He followed on unsteady legs after his brother while Cephora closed the rift behind them. The roar of battle from the prison trailed after him as he pushed himself to a sprint —he needed to be away from the horror of so much death.

When he grew closer, he made out the figure on the hill and his heart leapt into his throat—Morella. When din'Dael reached the summit of the hill, Will saw her falter and step back, retreating from him. The man dropped to his knees and shoved his hands into the earth while raising his face to the sky. As Will climbed, he heard him speaking unknown words in a long-forgotten tongue.

Storm clouds gathered above as lightning streaked across the sky, bathing the hilltop in its brilliant light. Will reached the top and threw himself into Morella's waiting arms. They held each other and stared at din'Dael. His skin glowed like burning embers as electricity danced across its surface. Madigan was shouting to him, his words unintelligible over the roar of the thunder that cascaded across the darkened sky. Cephora stood silent and solemn, clutching her staff.

The burning scent of electricity entered Will's nostrils and the key around his neck sprang to life in response. He pulled away from Morella and stepped toward din'Dael. The Lightborne ripped his hands from the earth, clutching sand and stone in both. He raised one hand to the sky as the other stretched toward the prison. A bird shrieked in the distance. For the briefest moment, din'Dael's eyes flicked away from the sky above and met Will's. His mouth spread wide into a grin.

"First, freedom," he said. "Now, justice."

A hundred massive bolts of lightning shot down from the clouds in a monstrous clap of thunder and collided into din'Dael. The whole party was thrown backward, somehow unharmed by the strikes but sent tumbling down the hillside. Will struggled to his feet and watched as Jero din'Dael, alternating between screams and laughter, channeled the lightning toward the Shale prison.

It was like staring at the sun. Power surged from the Light-borne and smashed into the walls. The earth shook as the ancient fortress crumbled. Fires erupted as far as the eye could see and everywhere, the prison seemed to implode upon itself. The energy surging from din'Dael was incessant. He stood, both arms spread wide and the stones and sand in his hands suddenly glowed hot and burst into dust.

Will watched in horror as the prison did the same. He fell to his knees from the force of the shaking, then the entire facility caved and exploded. Lightning and fire overran the land like floodwaters and surged deep into the chasm that opened and sucked the structure into the ground.

A wave of ashen dust raced out from the fallen prison toward the hill. Covering his face in the tattered remnants of his torn cloak, Will hid from the stinging, scorching, shattered stones. The dust storm began to cover them as they fought against the shaking earth and pummeling debris to climb back to the hilltop. Again and again, Will felt the emptiness inside as he longed for the protective embrace of his Shade but felt only the destructive fire that had replaced it. Hands bloody and torn and burnt, he clawed at the ground and struggled to reach the summit.

The wind died. The clouds faded. The night air grew still. Will shook himself and turned to search for Mad, for his friends. Madigan clapped him on the shoulder, coughing, looking stricken and disheveled. Morella, too, was coughing and glaring hard at din'Dael. The man himself sat on scorched earth, humming tunelessly once more. Cephora stood not far from them, staring.

Will turned and followed her gaze. Nothing remained of the

Shale Prison. Where it once stood, a canyon now ripped through the ground. The black chasm shot straight down, empty but for the cloud of dust that rose into the sky like a fading mushroom cloud. Behind the cloud, a crack like frozen lightning was ripped across the night sky, pulsing with white light. Not a soul was in sight other than the five of them.

❧ 30 ❧

THE WINDS CHANGE

"**W**hat have you done?" Morella's eyes were fixed on the fractured sky. It was the first that any of them had spoken in the moments since the tide of destruction waned. Her whispered voice sounded as terrified as Madigan felt—he too could not take his eyes off the strange, terrible mar in the night, somehow more horrific than the destruction of the prison.

Jero din'Dael rolled his head from side to side and his neck cracked. He looked awake, alert, and did not speak as he followed Morella's gaze toward the crack.

"Everyone is dead," Will said to din'Dael. It wasn't a question. "Why?"

"Justice," the Lightborne replied. "The Shale army was corrupt, evil. They needed to be purged."

"And the rest?" Madigan said. He glared at din'Dael. *This man is an abomination. What have we done?* "The prisoners? Everyone else?"

Din'Dael turned and stared at Madigan as if he had asked the most absurd question he had ever heard. "The prisoners?" he said with a laugh. "Each of them was in there for horrible offenses, guilty of unspeakable things. They died exactly as they deserved."

"If they deserved to be killed, then why were they kept alive and imprisoned?" Morella said, turning her glare from the sky to the seated man.

He waved a hand dismissively and Cephora spoke up for the first time. "The majority of them were cultists of Valmont or worse. Their sentences bound them to the Shale until their death. With the destruction of the prison"—Cephora faltered slightly as she spoke, something Madigan had rarely seen from her—"well, justice wouldn't have been met if they spread back into the lands."

"Exactly!" din'Dael said with a clap. "It is good to see that one of you, at least, understands the way the world works."

"No," Cephora said. "I only remember the way you think. Too well." She frowned and turned, shaking her head as din'Dael scoffed in response and rose to his feet.

"Justice." Madigan's voice sounded hollow, broken. He shook his head and faced Will. "Justice we said."

"What?" Will asked, drawing his eyes from din'Dael.

"With the Crow," Madigan said. "You told him we wanted justice. He agreed to justice. We assumed he meant he would help us deliver Grandda's killer to justice."

Will paled. "You mean you think . . . you think the Crow knew this would happen? That he planned for us to be his, what, his agents in this?"

Madigan nodded, his body trembling with fury. "Morella." He turned to face her. "Perhaps we should have listened to your advice. I apologize for not listening."

"There's nothing for it now." Her voice was flat, but he could hear the scorn hidden beneath it. "We must move forward with the plan."

"The plan?" Din'Dael raised an eyebrow. "And what, pray tell, is your delightful little quartet planning?"

"The remainder of the cult of Dorian Valmont," Will said. The Lightborne's eyes flared as he directed his gaze at Mad's brother. *Careful, Will, careful now.* "We're here to destroy them." Will stood a little taller and stared at din'Dael square on, his eyes defiant. "More than that, we are here to destroy Valmont, if he yet lives. And you, Jero din'Dael, are going to help us."

Jero din'Dael stared at Will for a moment as if he had uttered words of complete nonsense. Then, as the smoke from the crater of the prison wafted through the air, he lifted his head to the sky in peals of uncontrolled laughter. Morella muttered under her breath as din'Dael doubled over. Madigan felt himself glare again and turned away from the man before he let his emotions control him. *I don't know how much of this I'm going to be able to take.*

"He's serious," Cephora said.

Din'Dael stopped laughing suddenly and stared back, glancing between Will, Madigan, and Morella. "These ragtag whelps are hunting Valmont? A useless Shadowborne, a fledgling Burner, and"—he gestured carelessly toward Morella—"whatever *that* is?"

"Says the madman to his rescuers." Morella's temper flared. "Says the inept warrior who stumbled and failed at every opportunity to stop Valmont. Your own vanity caused the deaths of countless innocents in your self-righteous quest to stop him. You're no better than he is."

Static crackled in the air as din'Dael turned his cruel gaze to Morella. Madigan inhaled deeply and breathed out his Shade in the way Cephora had taught him. Yet, in the face of din'Dael's power, he felt his own wane. Nevertheless, in an instant, he and Will were poised to strike should the man lash out at their companion. Still, he noticed, Morella did not falter under din'-Dael's glare.

Breaking his gaze from Morella and eying Will and Madigan, din'Dael spoke. "You know nothing, girl. You do not know the man Valmont nor my reason for hunting him. From what I can discern, you, better than anyone, should know that the ends justify the means."

Madigan glanced quickly at Morella. "What does that mean?"

"You hunt him to satisfy your own goals." Morella glared at din'Dael, ignoring Mad.

"No," din'Dael replied as his eyes grew dark. "I hunt him because he brought about the end to thousands of years of peace. I hunt him because his own selfish ambition led to the destruction of ancient temples and brought devastation to the lives of millions across the realms. I hunt him because he is evil and speaks poison. And I will kill him because I am the only one who can."

As he spoke, the air around him started to crackle. Small wisps of pure white lightning, darting with each venomously articulate and enunciated syllable, swirled through the air. His eyes, brightening as he spoke, became white-hot fire, flames that seemed to penetrate Madigan's mind as din'Dael's gaze moved across each of them before falling to rest on Will. His very skin seemed to radiate white light and the air became dry and hot. Madigan coughed, feeling his own throat parching and eyes drying and scratching.

"I will destroy him utterly." His whispered voice reverberated harshly. "And when his body lies cold I will burn it in the radiant fires of Light while I laugh at his damned soul. He will die for his crimes and he will die by my hand alone, for I alone hold the power to end him."

Madigan could not help but notice that Morella perked up at this. She quickly looked at Will and Madigan caught her mouth the word 'relic.' Will nodded in understanding. *So, they're still at their foolish game, are they?* Madigan shook his head.

The crackling air stopped and Jero's eyes returned to their normal green. With a maniacal grin he threw his head to the sky and howled with laughter again, sending shivers down Madigan's spine. *What is up with him and the constant laughter?*

"With your eyes watching of course, my friends." Din'Dael chuckled, wiping tears from his eyes. "I will bathe in his blood and laugh with you all at my side!" He slipped back into uncontrollable laughter. All else was silent as each of them eyed him warily.

"Friends, is it?" Madigan asked. *Not bloody likely.*

"Of course!" din'Dael replied casually. "I am not ignorant of the service you have done me this day. And as the first followers of my camp, you will do well in joining my quest."

Madigan and Will glanced at one another. "Your quest?" Will said.

"This day I set out to bring an end to the plague of this land, Dorian Valmont, and the lingering cancer of his cultists. Together we shall raise an army and purge the land of every trace of Dorian Bloodbane!"

Madigan's focus on his words waned as din'Dael's rhetoric became more elaborate, speaking of how he would cull Valmont from memory. On the surface it was in line with everything that Grandda had set he and Will out to accomplish and he knew that he should feel some sense of relief, but he didn't. As the man spoke, Madigan could only see the madness in his mind and the fervor that burned in his breast.

He feared for the future as he looked at where his brother sat, holding Morella's hand and watching din'Dael warily. Their grandfather had said that those touched by Radiance ended up consumed by insanity. The fear grew in his heart when he realized that Will was now counted among that select group. Whatever din'Dael had done to him had erased the touch of Shadow and replaced it with fire and ash. He could lose Will forever, his last and only family. When he listened to din'Dael again, he realized that there was nothing he could do to stop his brother following the madman down a destructive path.

". . . and with the combination of our forces, and the strength of the Relics of Antiquity to empower us, we shall strike Valmont down!"

There was no roar of applause. None stepped forward to proclaim him the future savior of Aeril. But he had Will, Madigan could see it. Until he learned how to undo what had been done to him and found the treasures he sought, Will would follow Jero din'Dael. And judging from the way her eyes had sparkled as he mentioned the Relics, so would Morella. *She'll follow din'Dael whether Will does or not, regardless of what she said about din'Dael before. She's up to something.*

"You assume much," Cephora said, breaking the silence. "And offer little."

Jero din'Dael turned and met the Earth Warder's gaze. "War is coming. Undermyre will fall, Cephora. Do not pretend like you do not recognize your need for me."

"Undermyre has already chosen its champion," Cephora said with a gesture to Madigan, catching him by surprise. *What?* He and Will shared an uneasy glance. "The machinations of the Crow have already set about laying the foundation for his coming."

Din'Dael glanced at Madigan and snickered. "Again your

foolish Crow places his faith in darkness?" He spat. "The old man's mind is feeble."

"Your imprisonment has done wonders for your own," Cephora replied.

The air crackled with sparks as the two squared off. After a moment, din'Dael laughed and his face changed completely to a soft, handsome smile. "You're as pleasant as ever, Cephora. Very well, in the morning I shall leave you and this rabble to fend for yourselves, barking at the Crow's commands as you have done for so long. But"—he turned his attention to the remainder of the group—"should any of you wish to join me, you would be most welcome."

"First, the death of Senraks, the blood beast," Will said immediately.

Jero din'Dael raised an eyebrow. "One of those pesky little things? Consider it done."

And with that, he collapsed to the ground right where he stood, crossed his hands behind his head, and was immediately asleep. The other four stood staring at the madman in their midst, the smoldering wreckage behind them and the horrific crack in the sky a constant reminder of his capabilities. Madigan shuddered. *No one should wield so much power.*

Morella broke away from the group and set about scribbling in her journal. Cephora strode down the hill toward the wreckage of the prison without a word. Mad and Will were left alone with the sleeping figure. He beckoned his brother forward and the pair stepped away, out of earshot of Morella or din'Dael, should he awaken.

"What do you think?" Madigan asked once they had settled a short distance away.

"I think I'm tired and sore," Will said. "And far too thirsty."

"About din'Dael, Will."

"I know," Will sighed. "I think he's insane—"

"That much seems apparent."

"But I need him, Mad."

Madigan closed his eyes. The way that Will said it, he *needed* him, he knew what that meant. He composed himself and raised an eyebrow to Will. "Go on."

"Whatever he did to me." It was apparent that Will was struggling for words. "I feel different, Mad. I feel hollow. But at the same time I feel lighter, like I could fly if I wanted to. But it isn't a good feeling, it's . . . angry."

Madigan nodded. "When din'Dael was speaking, it was like I'd been holding my breath. The air was searing and dry again, like it was in the prison." He paused and looked up at the crack in the sky. "We should never have come here, never gone near him."

"I need to undo whatever he did to me," Will said, pleading.

"Will." Madigan paused. *How the hell do I say it?* "Whatever din'Dael did may have increased your power, but it was already there."

Will gave him a wary eye and shifted uncomfortably, glancing around. "What are you saying?"

"Whatever happened to your ability to control your Shade, I don't know." Madigan ran his hands through his hair and rubbed his temples. "But he didn't make you into something you weren't already. I've seen you wield lightning before, Will. I've seen you do things I can't explain. Maybe Grandda was wrong, maybe you're not Shadowborne . . . "

"What, you think I'm actually Lightborne?" Will said, his voice pitched with incredulity. "Mad, we both know that my Shade awakened years ago! Only Shadowborne have Shades!"

"But they don't control fire and lightning! They don't burn people to a crisp!"

Mad knew he had said too much, too harshly. Will tensed up and he saw the fear on his brother's face—the fear and the weight of the dead, slaughtered by his hand.

"Look, I don't know," he said, backpedaling. "Maybe you're something different. Maybe you could have gone either way and din'Dael pushed you over the edge. All I know is that our plan has gone off the rails and—"

"And din'Dael seems to be at the heart of whatever is coming next," Will said flatly.

Madigan paused, looking at his brother. *No, that's not where I was going, actually, but . . .* But he was right, of course. Senraks and the Necrothanians, the Relics of Antiquity, Jero din'Dael, all seemed to be spiraling around him however he looked to the future. *And yet . . .*

He was silent then, the plan forming in his head as he tried to reconcile the new factors with what he already knew. He sighed. *I'm sorry, kid.*

"What are your thoughts?" Will asked. Without even having to say the words, his brother's voice told him that Will would go with whatever Mad said.

"You're not going to like them."

Will scoffed and shook his head, glancing back toward Morella and idly fingering the hidden key around his neck. "Since when has that ever stopped you from seeing them through? Spit it out, Mad."

"We split up."

"What?" It was clearly not what Will had been expecting.

Madigan gave him a level look. "Something big is about to start, Will," he said, shaking his head in thought. "Or maybe it's already started and everything is only now just coming together. But regardless, Jero din'Dael is going to raise an army to find Valmont. I know you and I disagree about him being alive, but either way, there's going to be a madman at the head of a large force. Plus, he said that along the way he intends to turn up some of those Relics you and Morella seem so interested in. You stay with him. You learn what he's planning, fix whatever he did to you. You fight from the inside."

"And what are you going to be doing?" Will said softly.

Madigan snickered. "Something neither Grandda nor I ever planned. I'm going to go with Cephora and find the Halls of Shadow and learn everything I can. Even if it's fallen into ruin, there's got to be something there that can help us. But no matter what, I have to try to find a way to check din'Dael's power, if I can."

Will was quiet for some time. "You're serious?" he said finally.

"Stay with him, Will. Ask Morella to join you."

"Morella hates him. She'll never stay."

"Don't make her decisions for her," Madigan said, thinking back to the way Morella had looked when din'Dael spoke. "Talk to her."

He watched Will take it all in. Mad hated the idea of splitting up, but it made sense for Will to keep tabs on din'Dael. And, despite his excitement at discovering his Shade, it stung that somehow their roles had been reversed. Now, he was the one going to attempt becoming a Blade of Shadow while Will would be the one building an army.

As if his thoughts mirrored his brother's exactly, realization dawned on Will's face. "But Mad, Grandda said that the Halls takes years! We'll be separated that entire time. Anything could happen and—"

"I know," Mad said. "But like Cephora said, Umbriferum fell. There may be nothing there anymore and it may take no time at all."

"Or it'll take even more. You're the only family I've got left," Will said, refusing to look away from his brother. "I don't want to lose you."

Madigan chuckled and laid his hand on his brother's shoulder. "That goes for the both of us, kid. I don't like it any more than you do. But we knew when we started that at some point we would split up. It just isn't quite the way we imagined it."

"None of this has been," Will said as he stared at his hands, flexing his fingers.

"No, it hasn't." Madigan shook his head. "Watch din'Dael, Will. Learn his strengths and his weaknesses just in case. If something happens, I know you, you'll find a way to stop him. You're still my ace."

It took him a moment but eventually Will nodded. "As you say, Mad. I'll watch him."

"Good."

The conversation lapsed for a time. When it resumed, neither talked about the day's events, the horrors of the prison. Instead they focused on brotherly banter, casual connection and easy conversation underlined with the knowledge that it was soon to come to an end. After a little while, the pair fell into silence. Night was waning, and the stars littered the strangely broken sky above, a beautiful, terrible mirror to the desolate destruction that surrounded them on the ground.

They broke from each other and moved back toward their strange party and laid out their bedrolls, understandably desperate for sleep. But once sleep finally came, for each of them their dreams held only the sight of twisted dead and the smell of their broken, burning flesh.

✹ 31 ❧

MANIFEST DESTINY

A deafening clap of nearby thunder jarred Will from his restless sleep. He shot to his feet, kicking off his blankets. The air was heavy and cold and smelled of damp earth, a strange contrast to the dry burning of the previous day. His ears were ringing. *Still so thirsty,* he thought. Mad and Cephora were shifting in their groggy, unexpected waking. Jero din'Dael had not stirred. Morella was nowhere to be seen.

"So, you're the ones who have been seeking me out."

Will's hackles rose and he spun around to face the source of the cruel, lilting voice. The man's features were high and angular. His hair was long, a strange mixture of blond and brown that hung down his face. He was adorned simply in black trousers and a long, black coat. A scarf was wrapped around his neck. A sword was strapped to his hip. Shadows spun around him, twisting and dancing against the starry night.

Dorian Valmont.

Will's voice caught in his throat as he struggled to shout. The terrible man gestured toward him and shadowy tendrils lashed out, striking Will in the chest and sending him flying backward. He tripped over an immobile figure and fell, crashing to the ground. The figure, din'Dael, murmured in the throes of sleep but did not awaken.

By then, Madigan had fully woken at the sound of his brother's body hitting the ground. He leapt to his feet, the noctori blazing alive in his hands, his Shade sweeping the area. Cephora was kneeling, her palm against the ground, eyes closed as her lips moved in silence.

Valmont snickered at the noctori and the swirling tendrils of his body shot forward again, this time toward the blade. Will watched as Madigan side-stepped out of the way and carved the blade in an upward arc. The blade should have caught Valmont and passed clean through, but as the dark man's shadows careened with the blade, the noctori winked from existence. Madigan rapidly made to form another but nothing sprung from his hands. He looked on in shock.

Valmont's head cocked to the side. "You play at dangerous games with dangerous people, brothers Thorne."

Madigan's Shade surrounded him and Will scrambled to his feet, the air surrounding him alive with electricity. White lightning danced along the surface of his skin. Cephora's eyes opened and stared at him in shock, her mouth twisting downward in horror. His secret was out.

"How quaint," Valmont said with a sneer as the two brothers stepped forward to face him. As lightning cracked around Will's body, he drew the blood fangs and leveled one at the dark figure.

Cephora reached forward and grasped the back of Madigan's belt and shouted, "Din'Dael!"

Will briefly turned his eyes to her only to see the ground suddenly open up beneath her and Madigan. Before he could move, they disappeared, swallowed by the earth—the startled expression of confusion the last thing Will saw upon his brother's face before he vanished completely.

Valmont stared at the spot they had been and pursed his lips in annoyance.

Shock swept over Will. Fear cut through his rage. Din'Dael had not moved and Morella, thankfully, was gone. Still, he was alone with Valmont.

"Will?" The cry came from a short distance away. Morella. Valmont's position blocked her from Will's sight. "Will!"

There was another crack of thunder and a bolt of white lightning shot past Will's ear as a rough, dirty arm encircled his waist. Valmont stepped aside, easily avoiding the bolt and, in the brilliant flare, Will saw that the land stretching behind the dark man was alive with the movement of a shadowy horde of men.

No, not men, not anymore, Will realized in horror. They were too ragged, too steeped in decay, too dead. An army of the dead.

"Ah, Jero din'Dael." Valmont smiled. "It has been too long."

Lightning split the sky. Valmont's brow furrowed and Will could barely breathe within din'Dael's strong grasp. Jero din'-Dael's voice was level and low as he spoke. "You will die soon, Dorian. But not this day."

The sky shattered into brilliant, terrifying fire. The scattered white pieces of the rent heavens cascaded down, engulfing din'-Dael and Will in their raging fury. Before his world filled with fire, the last thing Will saw was Valmont's smile as he turned toward the horde. The last thing he heard was Morella screaming his name in the night.

WILL OPENED HIS EYES, HIS MIND A GROGGY MESS. HIS MOUTH seemed to be filled with cobwebs. He coughed. He was lying on a blanket, the distant sun barely peering over the horizon. *A dream, nothing more.*

He rolled over to his side, eyes fluttering closed again with the intent of returning to slumber, when the scuff of feet along sand caught his attention. Blinking against the brightening sky, he opened his eyes again and stared directly into the face of din'-Dael. He was crouched, his head dipped low to bring him nearly at eye level, watching Will intently. The prison rags were gone, though where he had found the clothes he now wore Will could not say. A sword, larger than the claymore he had wielded at the Shale Prison was strapped to his back. His face broke into a wide grin beneath his scraggly beard and he rose to his feet.

"Good, very good. You're still alive."

Alive? Startled, Will shot to his feet and scanned his surroundings. The hilltop seemed somehow different, taller. The wreckage of the prison had disappeared, somehow, and the desert floor was smooth again as though the land itself had consumed the remnants. An eagle screeched off in the distance and Will looked at the sky. The crack seemed larger.

Will spun around completely. They were alone. Wherever he looked, there was no sign of the others, no supplies whatsoever, only Jero and himself. "Gods, it wasn't a dream?"

Din'Dael's head cocked to the side. "You play at dangerous games with dangerous people, William Davis," he said in an eerily accurate imitation of Valmont. "Every day that you wake up alive is a surprise."

Will's voice caught in his throat. "What the hell happened, din'Dael?"

"Please, call me Jero."

"Jero." Will pushed, fighting back waves of panic. "Where is everyone?"

"Gone."

Will froze. "What?"

"They say the end is coming soon." Din'Dael's grin was manic as he looked at the sky. The eagle screeched again, growing closer. "They don't realize it is already here."

"What the hell are you talking about?" Will said, pleading with the strange man. He looked around again. The desert was different. The prison hadn't been swallowed by the earth, it had never been there. They were in an entirely different place. And he was right, they were entirely alone. "Where are they?"

"Probably in the same place we left them," Jero said as though the answer were as obvious as asking whether water was wet.

"No." Will's heart was racing. "No, no."

"You seem troubled." Jero stared at the young man, his mouth twisted in confusion.

Will turned on him. "What have you done?"

He held up a gloved hand to the sky. "I've set things in motion."

A sudden movement from above caught Will's eye. A dark shape soared through the sky, swooping in low and fast. It whirled and plummeted straight toward them before coming to a sudden stop upon din'Dael's outstretched hand. The eagle gave a deafening scream and spread its wings, its astonishing wingspan stretching almost ten feet. Jero threw back his head and roared with glee in a strange unison with the bird's cries.

"Dahla . . . " His voice was reverent. "This is the Dahla, William Davis. This is the bird of peace. We are ready to begin."

"Jero, what is going on?" Will shouted.

"Peace over the corpses of my fallen enemies," he continued, ignoring Will's outburst. "Death and destruction to all. Valmont will die. The bastard Necrothanians will die. Radiance will once again rise as Shadow falls. There is no time to waste."

Jero din'Dael's left glove began to glow an emerald green. The surrounding air seemed to become dull and hazy as din'Dael raised his hand to eye level, forming a crescent between his thumb and index finger. Jero's eyes narrowed as he twisted the crescent shape and spun in a slow circle. He stopped halfway as the dim air suddenly grew clear and vivid, a vast array of colors suddenly shooting past his outstretched fingers. As his hand formed into a brilliant green fist, a wild grin spread across his features.

Some kind of emerald, Morella said, Will realized, *din'Dael's relic . . .*

The huge bird shrieked again and shot into the air. Jero lowered his hand and took off running in the direction the creature flew, feet racing along the sand and jagged stone faster than Will's eyes could follow. He hesitated and scanned his surroundings one last time, faint hope flickering into despair even as he wished it to brighten.

There was nothing, no one he knew. Madigan was gone. Morella was gone. Cephora was gone. All that remained was the madman, Jero din'Dael, running through the desert with a great eagle soaring nearby.

Will was alone.

He checked his meager supplies and made sure his blood fangs were secure. He checked his canteen and found that it was empty. With a pained sigh, he turned his attention toward the retreating figure of din'Dael.

A beautiful voice filled his mind, echoing as it had all that time ago.

Come, it said.

Heart heavy, chest heaving, William Davis set off in pursuit.

THANK YOU

Thank you for reading *Shadowborne Book One of the Relics of Antiquity*.

Please consider leaving a review—any and all feedback is greatly appreciated.

Honest reviews of my books helps to bring them to the attention of other readers. Reviews are the most powerful tool that an author has for getting attention for their work, particularly for independent authors.

The adventure continues in *Borne Rising: Beyond the Shadows* book two of The Relics of Antiquity!

GET A FREE COPY OF VALMONT'S DESCENT

Building a lasting relationship with my readers is one of the very best parts about writing.If you want to connect, jump on my mailing list over at my website. I occasionally send out a newsletter with information about news, upcoming releases, and special offers related to my work. In addition, for signing up you will get a FREE copy of my short, *Valmont's Descent: A Tale of the Relics of Antiquity*.

Get your FREE copy of *Valmont's Descent: A Tale of the Relics of Antiquity*.

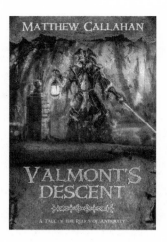

Pre-dating the events of Shadowborne by over five-hundred years, this tale is a look at Dorian Valmont through the eyes of Fen Kuang, a warlord from beyond the Daurhi Wastes. Filled with magic, suspense, and history, follow this powerful pair as they enter a realm of death and decay in search of an artifact that can turn the tide in Valmont's battle against the Hesperawn - the Codex of Ahn'Quor.

Claim your FREE book now!

Get a FREE copy by signing up to be the first to hear about new releases and special offers!

Bottled Embers: A Tale of the Relics of Antiquity

A hidden past.

A murder unavenged.

A mysterious stranger.

Clarice, proprietor of the finest drinking house in Undermyre, has a secret. To protect it, she abandoned her home, her life, her very name, in order to start over in a new city. But when a mysterious, charming stranger enters her establishment, Clarice's meticulously crafted world begins to tremble and crack. Will she be able to keep the ghosts of her past hidden? Or will this newcomer's charm tear down all the walls she has built to hide behind?

Order your copy of *Bottled Embers* now!

More titles coming soon!

ABOUT THE AUTHOR

Matthew Callahan is the author of the ongoing saga, *The Relics of Antiquity*. In the real world, he can be found in Portland, Oregon with his wonderful wife. In the virtual world, he can always be reached online at roguishmanner.com.

You can connect with Matthew on Instagram and Twitter at @RoguishManner, on Facebook at Facebook.com/roguish-manner, on Goodreads, and you can always send him an email at matt@roguishmanner.com

facebook.com/RoguishManner
twitter.com/RoguishManner
instagram.com/RoguishManner

For my moon, who illuminated the sky when the night was darkest.

Made in the USA
Monee, IL
17 May 2020